Mrs. Darcy was a reasonably young female–perhaps four-and-twenty–neatly but not fashionably dressed. He could not help but notice that she was undeniably a Beauty. Face and figure were absolute perfection, with rich dark curls peeping from beneath her bonnet, and large, flashing eyes which were surveying him with no corresponding admiration. Indeed, the lady was alarmingly rigid. Whatever the purpose of this strange visit, it did not seem to be of a pleasant nature.

"You, I presume, are Lord Denham?"

"If my parents are to be believed," he replied, at his most laconic. Her voice, he noted, was low-pitched and her speech that of a gentlewoman. "And have I the pleasure of addressing Mrs. Fitzwilliam Darcy?"

Unexpectedly, she grinned. "Impressive is it not? Like *Mrs. Drummond Burrell*. I borro from a novel which I read recently."

From "A Ch
by

A Regency Sampler

To Kathy Z —
A favorite critique
partner + true pal —
All the best —
Victoria Hinshaw

Edited by Kelly Ferjutz

Regency Press
Cleveland Heights, Ohio

This is a work of fiction. Other than clearly historical personages, all the characters and events portrayed in these stories are fictitious, and any resemblance to real people or events is purely coincidental.

A REGENCY SAMPLER

Copyright © 1999 by Kelly Ferjutz

All rights reserved, including the right to reproduce this book, or portions thereof, in any form.

Regency Press is a division of
Crack of Noon Enterprises, Incorporated.
The name Regency Press and the Crowned R are registered trademarks of Crack of Noon Enterprises, Incorporated.

ISBN: 1-929085-00-1

First Edition: August, 1999

Printed in the United States of America

0   9   8   7   6   5   4   3   2   1

These stories are all original, and have not appeared
elsewhere prior to this publication.

/=/

The 19th-century sampler pictured on the cover is
from the collection of the Milan Historical Museum, 10 Edison Drive, Milan, Ohio, and is used
here through the kindness of curator Ellen Maurer.

Gentle reader –

What you are holding in your hand may resemble a book in every regard. What it is, however, is a dream. A dream come true. For the editor/publisher and the writers, only one of whom is currently a well-known name in the field of Regency novels. Sandra Heath entered her story *Neptune's Quizzing Glass* in our contest, and was judged, just as were the other writers.

As founder and editor-in-chief of Regency Press, I have long believed that a market exists for the more traditional type of Regency novel–one with the humor and elegance that marked the many delightful books of Georgette Heyer.

This is not to say that all of these stories are pseudo-Heyer in type. Not at all. There are mysteries and fantasies and adventure in addition to those where the element of romance assumes a more important role, but is yet not the entire plot.

We hope that you will enjoy the stories presented here, and remember Regency Press in the months to come–when we begin to publish the full-length books. Our first three 'new' authors are also represented in this anthology. Beth Andrews is first with *The Marplot Marriage* about which **Edith Layton** says: "Readers who enjoy Regencies that romp–lightly and brightly–will relish this lively tale of stuffy but virile Charles and beautiful mischievous Phoebe. Their merry mis-mating makes jolly Regency reading. (P.S. One of the best first lines I've ever encountered!)"

Following that will be *The Reluctant Guardian* by Jo Manning. Our third book will be a bit of a departure, as it is the first of the 'reprise' volumes. Reprise as in, 'bring it back' or *encore*. *Peerless Theodosia* by Rebecca Baldwin was first published by Coventry in 1981. We plan to reprise other such classics–and if you wish, please tell us your candidate.

Next April another debut will be that of Sarah Starr with *Lady-Lessons*.

Our publishing venture began with a contest: this book is the result. Everyone who entered is a winner, even if their story is not found within these pages. At least they dared to try. (For the purists among you, I must add that the time period was expanded from the normal Regency {1811-1820} to Prinny's lifetime.) Another contest is currently underway; the deadline for submission is November 30, 1999. With a winter holiday theme, the winners will be part of the next Regency Sampler in November, 2000. It is our hope to feature such a contest every year or perhaps every year-and-a-half. What better way to find new writers? Please do let us know what you think of this collection, as well as our other books. Up-to-date information is always available at our web-site: **http://www.regency-press.com** We also have an occasional newsletter. If you would like to receive this via regular mail (not e-mail) please send us your name and mailing address. We'd also like to know what you think about this book, as well as the ones to come.

Several people encouraged me in this venture above and beyond the call of duty: especially my friendly librarians who served as the judges–JoAnn Vicarel, Anne Wilson, and Becky Katzenmayer. The rest of you know who you are–you'll be singled out in future volumes, I'm quite certain.

Read! Enjoy!

Kelly Ferjutz
Editor-in-chief
Regency Press
June, 1999
(kelly@regency-press.com)

With special gratitude to

my daughter Kris,
Ken, Ty, Roger, Karla, Fred, Kathy,
Lorraine, Susan, Peggy, Donalene

and our shareholders--all of whom
believed!

A Regency Sampler

Table of Contents

There are two Christmas stories in this book. Coincidentally, The Christmas Bride *was the first received;* The Viscount's Angel *was the last, and that is how they appear here. This was also put into first place in our anthology, because* **Beth Andrews** *is the author of our first full-length novel* The Marplot Marriage, *coming this fall. You will love the spirited characters in this charming romp!*

The Christmas Bride
Beth Andrews

Lord Denham paused in his writing and looked up as his butler entered the study.

"A Mrs. Fitzwilliam Darcy has called, my lord, and requests the favor of a brief interview."

Denham frowned, eyeing Westcott with considerable surprise. The other man's face was as impassive as always, giving no hint of the unprecedented solecism he had just committed.

"I believe, Westcott," he said, exercising considerable restraint, "that your wits must have deserted you. I requested that I not be disturbed–particularly by some female of whom I have never heard!"

Westcott gave a slight, apologetic-sounding cough. "When I informed the lady that you were not receiving visitors, she–ah–refused to–ah–heed me, my lord."

Before he could comment on this pronouncement, his study door swung open and a rather tall woman entered the room. She stood just inside the

1

aperture and glanced briefly at the astonished Westcott before directing her attention toward his master, who was not entirely sure whether he was more annoyed or amused at so bold an intrusion.

Mrs. Darcy was a reasonably young female–perhaps four-and-twenty–neatly but not fashionably dressed. He could not help but notice that she was undeniably a Beauty. Face and figure were absolute perfection, with rich dark curls peeping from beneath her bonnet, and large, flashing eyes which were surveying him with no corresponding admiration. Indeed, the lady was alarmingly rigid. Whatever the purpose of this strange visit, it did not seem to be of a pleasant nature.

"You, I presume, are Lord Denham?"

"If my parents are to be believed," he replied, at his most laconic. Her voice, he noted, was low-pitched and her speech that of a gentlewoman. "And have I the pleasure of addressing Mrs. Fitz-william Darcy?"

Unexpectedly, she grinned. "Impressive, is it not? Like *Mrs. Drummond Burrell*. I borrowed the name from a novel which I read recently."

He deemed it time for privacy and nodded a curt dismissal to the curious Westcott. In spite of himself, he was intrigued. What was she about? For a moment he wondered if she might not be another of the endless supply of husband-hunting females who had tried for years to snare one of the ton's most eligible matrimonial prizes. Then he dismissed the thought. Not even the most determined spinster would enact anything so absurd.

"You may be thankful, at least, that you do not at all resemble Mrs. Drummond Burrell, who is rather long in the tooth, and can never have been more than tolerably good-looking." He smiled. "But will you now tell me your real name?"

"I am not such a simpleton, my lord."

He stared at her, more confused–and more fascinated–than ever. "Will you at least inform me why you wished to meet with me, ma'am? Strangely enough, I have not the least notion what you are doing here."

He watched her eyes narrow as she looked directly at him, with an odd expression as though she were accusing him of something. When she answered, it was with another question–and one which was completely unexpected.

"Lord Denham, do you have any idea where your niece is at this moment?"

"My niece?"

"Your niece," she repeated. "Lady Georgiana Enscombe."

"I believe," he answered slowly, "that my niece is presently residing with Lady Rudgebourgh–the sister of my late brother's wife."

"You are mistaken, sir," his visitor informed him.

"Indeed?" He was not certain that he cared for the direction this interview had taken. "And dare I inquire where she might be?"

"I have her."

"She is here with you?"

"Certainly not."

Beauty or not, the lady's cryptic utterances were becoming extremely irritating, and it was with something of a snap that he replied, "I would be exceedingly grateful if you would tell me plainly what your purpose in coming here might be, madam. If you are my niece's governess–"

"I am no such thing!" She seemed quite as affronted as he. "It is simply that I have taken your niece away from her aunt's house and wish to know what you intend to do about it."

Lord Denham had led a life that was anything but sheltered. This, however, was something quite novel. He could scarcely credit what he was hearing. Perhaps the strangest aspect of the situation in which he found himself was the fact that, for some peculiar reason, the woman before him–who was clearly out of her senses–made him feel oddly guilty, as though he was somehow in the wrong!

"How much do you want?"

"What?"

"The ransom," he elucidated. "It seems that you have abducted my niece–"

"*Abducted*?" Her eyes flashed, and she actually took a step closer to him. "No, sir. I did not *abduct* your poor niece. On the contrary, I rescued her from a woman who is unfit to have charge of a dog–never mind a child!"

"I beg your pardon?" He was even more taken aback.

"Have you any idea," she demanded, breathing heavily and controlling her voice with obvious effort, "what that little girl has endured in her aunt's household?"

"I have not," he confessed, his gaze never leaving her flushed countenance. "But I surmise that you are about to inform me."

"It is high time that someone enlightened you on the subject. Although, to be frank, I find your lack of interest in your niece's welfare perfectly appalling!"

"Yes," he mused aloud. "Frankness would seem to be your only flaw. But if you have anything of length to say, you had better sit down."

"Thank you." She perched herself on the edge of a large chair. "I wondered when you would recollect your manners, sir."

He inclined his head at this rather prim remark. "Forgive me, ma'am. But, under the circumstances, etiquette seemed rather a minor trifle."

"You are quite right."

4

"Now, kindly explain to me what this is all about."

/=/

The tale which followed had more to commend it than many a novel and was told with an intensity that certainly commanded all of Justin's attention. The woman who called herself Mrs. Darcy had met Georgiana by accident one afternoon, while walking home from a visit to a friend. Georgiana had managed to slip out of the house unnoticed, following a cat which she had spied from the window of her aunt's house in Bedford Square. She was very fond of kittens, although her aunt refused to have any animals in her immaculately kept rooms. Turning a corner of the street in pursuit of the elusive feline, she found herself lost, and, being rather timid and only eight years old, had done the most logical thing which occurred to her: she sat down by the side of the pavement and started to cry. Thus it was that "Mrs. Darcy" discovered her.

"And when I think–" the woman on the other side of his desk gave a shudder. "When I think what might have become of her had someone else found her instead…some jug-bitten lout, or an abbess with an eye to future gains–"

Justin was shocked, though whether by her language or her casual knowledge of the more sordid side of London–a world which most virtuous women had never dreamed of–he was not sure. He cleared his throat a little, interrupting her.

"Just so." Then, with a quizzing look, he added, "Instead of which, she was merely spirited away by a perfect stranger."

"If you are referring to me, I did no such thing!" She drew herself up in her seat and glared at him. "Once I was able to calm her down, I dis-

5

covered where she lived. To my surprise, she seemed just as upset at the prospect of returning there as she was at being lost. She begged me not to take her back. But it did not occur to me that there was any alternative."

In a few minutes, Georgiana, trembling and weeping once more, was standing before her aunt's front door. Her rescuer presented the girl to the astonished butler. This person wasted no time with pleasantries but drew Georgiana inside and shut the door in the face of the woman who had brought her there. The last words she heard were spoken by someone whom she assumed to be one of the housemaids, to the effect that Georgiana's aunt was "going to *wallop* her good!"

"I confess that I felt uneasy about the incident," the lady continued. "I tried to put it from my mind, but I could not. I found myself passing by the residence several times in the next few days. It is not very much out of my way, but I would not generally have walked along that particular street."

Eventually, she had determined to find out what she could, and called at the house in order to see how her little friend was getting on. The butler was ready to turn her out but was forestalled by Georgiana herself, who ran forward eagerly to greet her. They had exchanged but few words, however, when a stout, pinch-faced woman appeared in the hall. This, it turned out, was Lady Rudgebourgh, who demanded to know the stranger's business.

Lady Rudgebourgh was certainly formidable, and it was no surprise to see the child cower before her. "Mrs. Darcy" was not so easily intimidated, however. She politely informed Lady Rudgebourgh of the circumstances under which she had met Georgiana, and that she had called to inquire after her. In response, she was told that, if she had come to beg for money, she would not get a groat. Furthermore, that she had best not show her face there again.

Mrs. Darcy did not give a verbatim account of her reply to Lady Rudgebourgh, but Justin could well imagine that she had told his sister-in-law a few home truths, which would not have improved that lady's temper!

"I would have given a fairly large sum of money," he mused, smiling, "to have seen Louisa's face at that moment."

"It was not pretty," his guest said.

"Alas, it never has been."

Mrs. Darcy was apparently bored with this topic and reverted to her tale. "I could see she was a dragon, but I never really suspected much beyond that she had no heart and not much more in the way of wit." His lips twitched ever so slightly at this, but he made no comment. "Still, I continued to pass the house every day for almost a sennight."

Georgiana must have noted her vigil, because one evening she appeared from behind a pillar at the corner of the house. She was weeping once more, but this time her request was for the lady–whom she seemed to have confused with a guardian angel–to take her home with her! The child was on the verge of hysteria, and Mrs. Darcy spent a considerable amount of time trying to calm her down. But when she went to put her arm about her and the little girl winced, she realized that the tears were not merely from petulance or fear, but pain as well.

In an instant, she made a decision. Wasting no more time, she led Georgiana up the street. In less than a quarter of an hour, they had reached the rooms where she lodged with her own aunt–a woman who was very unlike Lady Rudgebourgh. Once she had explained the situation to her astonished relative, she suggested a bath. At first Georgiana refused, insisting that she did not need one. However, they gently but firmly overruled her and soon filled a large basin with warm water. Only when they had undressed the child for the bath did they realize what they had to deal with.

"She was covered in welts and bruises, from her shoulders to her buttocks," Mrs. Darcy said. Although she tried to remain composed, her voice trembled and there was a suspicious moistness about her eyes which Justin did not fail to notice. "There was a burn mark on her arm. When I questioned her, she told me that it was an accident. She was so clumsy, she said!"

"But you did not believe her?"

"I am not a fool, sir."

"And then?"

She swallowed. "I went to a neighbor, to procure some ointment, and when I returned I told Georgiana that she must return to her aunt's house. Of course she began to cry again. In the end, she confessed a great deal of what had happened to her. After that, there was no question of my taking her back."

"But what brought you here, to me?"

"In the course of my conversation with Georgie, she mentioned an uncle, of whom she seemed rather fond." Here she paused, and the look she directed toward him seemed to indicate that she had not yet discerned in him any qualities which would inspire affection. "I knew your name, of course–and your reputation."

"Ah yes." he murmured. "I wondered when you would arrive at my reputation."

"I am sure every fishmonger in Cheapside must have heard of Lord Denham, the noted Corinthian …"

"And confirmed rakehell," he added, rather enjoying the tinge of color which his remark brought to her cheeks. After all, she was not the only one entitled to be brutally frank.

"I could hardly seek assistance from Lady Rudgebourgh," Mrs. Darcy said hurriedly. "All things considered, there seemed to be no one else to turn to."

"I am, in fact, your last resort?"

She did not deign to answer this. "From what Georgiana told me, you were not entirely unapproachable."

"Beautiful females often find me *extremely* approachable."

"I am not at all interested in those other females."

"Curiously, neither am I."

For a brief instant, their glances met and held. What beautiful eyes she had, he thought. Not just the color, which was a clear dark brown, but the expression: honest, brave, passionate. They were the truest eyes he had ever seen. It was she who finally looked away, dropping her gaze to the desk, where an open book of acquatint prints lay.

"This is not very good work." She pointed to the print before her. "The foundation washes are adequate, but the detail coloring is poor. It was probably done by some poor, undernourished child from the Foundling Hospital Estate."

He was surprised. Most ladies, he wagered, would not have been well enough informed to make such a criticism. "You would probably find my copy of the *Microcosm of London* more enjoyable."

She shrugged. "Mr. Rowlandson's characters are entertaining enough, but I prefer the work of William Danniell."

"Ah yes." He nodded. "I was quite impressed with his *Oriental Scenery*."

"I have heard of it," she acknowledged. "The cost was quite high, I believe–though that would not be of importance to you. Do you also have *A Voyage Around Great Britain*?"

"Naturally. But you seem very well acquainted with the subject, including the techniques involved."

There was a very faint curl to her lip as she answered, "I am rather too well acquainted with the techniques." Then, apparently realizing that they had strayed from the point, she said, "However, that does not provide a solution to the problem at hand."

"Which is?"

"What are you going to do about your niece?"

He leaned back in his chair and raised his brows. "My dear lady, I do not see that there is anything I can do."

"You cannot be so heartless as to abandon Georgiana to such a fate!"

"It is not a question of heartlessness." He leaned forward to press his point. "Georgiana's mother died in childbirth. Three years later, my brother–Georgiana's father–passed away, leaving his daughter to the care of his late wife's sister and her husband. They are her legal guardians. There is no more to be said."

He watched the expression on the woman's face as she absorbed the full meaning of his words. There was a swift succession of emotions: disbelief and consternation, followed by pure anger.

"Lord Denham," she said, when she had gained command of herself, "I refuse to believe that a man of your wealth and influence can do nothing to help his own niece. It is merely that you are selfish, slothful, and uncaring!" At this point in her diatribe, she stood up, glaring down at him. "I should have known better than to seek assistance from someone like yourself. Good day to you, sir."

She turned on her heel. It was plain that she was about to depart.

"What do *you* intend to do about my niece, madam?" he asked.

"That is not your concern, is it?" She did not even turn, but merely cast a derisive glance over her shoulder. "You are not the girl's guardian, as you have been at pains to inform me."

He had risen to his feet. "Where do you live?" he demanded, but she had already passed through the door and was disappearing down the hall.

"Damn!" He rang the bell to summon a servant.

/=/

Exiting the house in a rush, the lady known as Mrs. Darcy turned to the left and headed down the street, her head low against the icy December wind. She reached the end of the street and, for some reason, looked back toward the entrance of the house she had just left. It was the fifth house from the end of the corner, its plain facade no indication of the opulence within.

As she looked, a man emerged from the front door. Although his features were obscured by a hat and thick woollen scarf, she could tell that it was not Lord Denham because the figure was far too short. The man looked up and down the street as he stepped onto the sidewalk, then began walking purposefully in her direction.

Lifting her skirts, she dashed into the road, straight across the path of an oncoming barouche. By some miracle, the driver avoided running her down, but she heard a fluent stream of invective

11

above the neighing of the horses as she reached the opposite pavement. With another swift look behind her, she ascertained that the man she had seen was now going at a brisk trot.

No time to waste, she thought, resuming her flight. Despite the slippery stones beneath her feet, she kept up a fast pace, darting through alleyways and around corners. She'd wager that she knew these streets as well or better than the man behind her! Only occasionally did she turn her head but never again caught a glimpse of him. At last, when she was fairly certain that he was no longer within sight, she slowed to a brisk walk and soon found herself at her destination.

Turning the key in the lock, she pushed open the door to a fair-sized chamber, sparsely furnished but clean, which served as a sitting room, work room, and dining area. A middle-aged lady with plump cheeks and small, bright eyes was seated at a work table, a paint brush in one hand and squinting down at the paper in front of her. A small golden-haired girl sat by the fire smoldering in the narrow hearth. She was stroking a large black-and-white tabby, who obviously revelled in the adulation which cats consider their just and proper reward for being cats. All three occupants of the room looked up as she entered.

Little Georgiana seemed frozen, staring at her with a heartrending mixture of anxiety and hope in her flushed countenance. The cat, Titania, merely acknowledged her presence with a brief twitch of its luxuriant whiskers before closing its eyes in complete unconcern.

"Well, Jenny?" The woman was the first to speak. "Did you—did you see the marquis?"

"That I did, Aunt Mattie," Jennifer Prentice answered. She came forward, frowning down at the unfinished picture on the table. Sighing, her aunt blinked at her. "I gather that it did not go well?"

"He's not going to send me back to Aunt Louisa, is he?" Georgiana asked anxiously.

"He cannot." Jennifer gave a sudden grin. "He does not know where you are!"

This seemed to satisfy the child, but the woman was not so easily pacified.

"I gather that he *would* send her back if he could?"

Jenny did not bother to answer this. "He is insufferable!" She clenched her hand into a fist. "A typical indolent, selfish, unfeeling, unthinking aristocrat."

"Uncle Justin is always kind to me," Georgiana spoke up, her voice wistful. "He gave me a lovely doll for my birthday."

"Of course, my dear," Aunt Mattie reassured her. "He was probably not feeling quite the thing today! Jenny shall visit him some other time, and things will be very different, I daresay." This speech was accompanied by a frown and a shake of the head directed at her niece, who correctly interpreted it as a warning to guard her tongue.

"I hope I never have to endure that man's company again!" Jennifer whispered to her aunt.

"That is all very well. But if he does not lend us his support in this matter, what are we to do?"

"I shall have to think of something else."

The older woman's eyebrows rose. "I sincerely hope so, Jenny." She glanced over at Georgiana, who had curled up with Titania and joined her in an afternoon nap. "Much as I like the child, the truth is that we can barely contrive to keep ourselves out of dun territory. And if we have an extra mouth to feed...well, we cannot do it!"

"I know." Jenny was quite as conscious of their dilemma as her aunt could be. She looked about her at the spartan furnishings, comparing them to the luxury of the house she had just left. Although the two dwellings were physically less than a mile distant, they represented two distinct worlds. The pitiful wages she and Aunt Mattie earned from coloring acquatints and taking in a little sewing were barely enough for two. Besides, it was obvious that they could not hide the child forever. Something must be done. But what?

"What did he look like?" her aunt interrupted her thoughts with typically feminine curiosity. "Is he as handsome as they say?"

"Oh yes. Reports have not exaggerated his attraction." Jenny's eyes narrowed as she remembered her recent encounter. "His appearance is all one could ask for. He lacks nothing but a heart."

"Such a shame." Aunt Mattie could not hide her disappointment.

The devil take Lord Denham! Jenny thought, pursing her lips. His image rose clearly before her mind's eye: the tall, muscled figure filling out his closely fitting jacket, the raven-dark hair and eyes, the slightly sardonic smile. Handsome, mocking, self-assured: the quintessential Corinthian.

She wondered what he was doing at this very moment.

/=/

Lord Denham was, in fact, exerting himself rather more strenuously than he was accustomed to do. When the servant returned with the news that the young lady had managed to elude him, he cogitated briefly before calling in his secretary, Mr. Geoffrey Bascot.

Mr. Bascot was a sandy-haired young man, attired with a neatness and propriety that reflected his orderly mind and unobtrusive character. His countenance was pleasant without being particularly memorable. Nothing at all dashing about him, but anyone who took him for a flat would be sadly mistaken.

"Geoffrey," Lord Denham said, absently fingering a silver-filigree inkstand, "I am canceling my visit to Wiltshire. Write a letter to the Earl and Countess, expressing my abject apologies, would you?"

"Not going to Wiltshire, my Lord?" Mr. Bascot's look and voice betrayed such astonishment that his master could not help but smile.

He was to have departed on the morrow, and Geoffrey, of all people, must be well aware that there was more behind this visit than a desire to celebrate the Yuletide season in traditional English fashion. Lord Denham's motives were seldom as pure as that! No, it had been the presence of Mrs. Caroline Cavendish which had lured him to the countryside. Mrs. Cavendish was a dashing young widow whose figure might be tightly laced, but whose morals were rather more accommodating. Their liaison was of recent vintage–barely a month, in fact. Until today, he had still been in hot pursuit of his latest partner in pleasure and eager to continue their flirtation amid the mistletoe and holly. Even Mr. Bascot, who was used to seeing his passion for a new paramour cool suddenly, must be surprised at this.

"A very short time ago, there was a young lady here," Denham began.

"Ah…" Mr. Bascot cleared his throat softly. "I see."

"I doubt it." His smile widened. Without elaboration, he related the circumstances of his recent encounter, rather enjoying the look on his secretary's face as he listened.

"She sounds a most–unusual–female," was Geoffrey's comment when at last the tale was done.

"Quite unique, in my experience."

They looked at each other.

"I gather that you wish me to find her?" Mr. Bascot said.

"You must find her."

"For the sake of your niece, of course?"

"Naturally!" He raised his brows, silently acknowledging Geoffrey's gentle sarcasm. "But it would seem that my fate as well as Georgiana's is in the hands of the lovely Mrs. Darcy."

"I hardly know where I am to begin searching for her."

"I think I may be able to assist you there." He thought back over what had passed between them in that brief interview. "From what the lady told me, it would seem that she lives but a short distance from Louisa's home in Bedford Square–but certainly not in the tonnish part of town." He eyed the younger man. "Does that suggest anything to you?"

Mr. Bascot tapped a finger against his chin for a moment. "Somewhere in Bloomsbury–possibly in the vicinity of Mecklenburgh Square."

"Very good, Geoffrey."

"It is a fairly large and populous area," Geoffrey said drily. "One cannot be certain of quick success."

"One merely has to describe the lady to the nearby inhabitants. Anyone who has seen her is not likely to forget."

"So it would seem."

He thought it best to ignore this demure comment. "I may have other pertinent information which may save you some time." He described the lady's comments on his acquatints, concluding, "Make a few inquiries, if you will."

"And what will *you* be doing, sir?"

"Mind your impudence, puppy!" Justin laid an affectionate hand on his shoulder. "Your task will be far easier–and less dangerous–than my own. I go to beard that dragon, Louisa, in her own lair."

"God have mercy on you, sir!" Geoffrey grinned.

"Amen to that."

/=/

Within half an hour, Denham's black stallion, Othello, was saddled, and he was navigating his way through streets crowded with characters of every station. From highborn ladies loitering in linen drapers to dissolute noblemen purchasing expensive Christmas gifts for their latest ladybird, and poultry sellers and pickpockets preying on unwary pedestrians, London was all bustle and business.

It did not take him many minutes to reach his sister-in-law's address in Bedford Square. The half-dozen capes on his coat fluttered in a sudden blast of cold air as he handed Othello's reins to a waiting flunkey and mounted the short flight of steps leading to the front door.

The butler informed him that both the master and mistress of the house were at home. Since he was well aware that poor old George was a person of no importance, he demanded to see Louisa, and waited in the small salon decorated in a hideous sham gothic style, which was certainly of Louisa's own fancy. His hostess trotted into the room presently. Lady Rudgebourgh, he considered, had the cunning of Cleopatra and the looks of Jim Belcher.

"Good heavens, Justin!" she said without preamble. "Whatever brings you to this house?"

"A reasonable question, Louisa." He made a slight bow. "In the spirit of this blessed season, I have come to visit my beloved niece. Where is dear Georgiana?"

A look of consternation passed over her features but was quickly suppressed. There was no removing her formidable frown, however.

"I have never known you take very much interest in Georgiana before. Is it not a little late to be developing such avuncular feelings?"

"Not too late, I trust." He smiled.

"I do not know what can have possessed you."

"You would scarcely believe me if I told you." The smile faded. "Now, may I see my niece, if you please?"

She drew her thin lips in between yellowed teeth. "I am afraid that she is not here just at the moment ..."

"And where might she be?" He was quite pleasant and polite still, but something about his look or voice must have unsettled Lady Rudgebourgh, because she dropped her gaze from his and started to finger the lace collar of her gown with nervous fingers. "Where might she be, Louisa?" he repeated, and this time she could not mistake the menace in his tone.

"I...well, really, I...just at the moment," she stammered, "I do not..."

"Enough!" he snapped, and her speech was suspended completely. "Shall I tell you what has become of her?" The woman's eyes seemed likely to desert their sockets now. "She has been stolen away by a total stranger, and neither you nor I can tell where she might be. Is that not so?"

Seeing that she could not prevaricate, Lady Rudgebourgh unwisely decided to take the offensive.

"I do not see that it is any concern of yours, Justin! *You* are not her guardian, after all."

He crossed his arms over his chest and surveyed her with some amusement. "I was telling

18

someone much the same thing barely an hour ago," he mused. "They disagreed with me; and I am sorry to confess it, but I am inclined to think that they were quite correct. It is time I took a more active role in the care of my niece."

"What do you know about raising children?" Louisa almost snorted her disdain.

"Not much, perhaps," he acknowledged with a mock bow. "But I could scarcely be a more dismal failure at it than you have proven to be. At least I would not be so careless as to misplace a child left in my charge. It seems that my informant was quite correct in her assessment of your abilities."

"Aha!" Louisa was almost purple with rage. Combined with the deep blue of her bombazine gown, she was an awful sight indeed. "It is *that woman!*" She fairly spat the words at him. "She has been to see you and filled your head with stupid tales."

"If you are referring to the young lady who rescued Georgiana from the street, she paid me a visit this morning. I found her revelations most enlightening."

"I would not be surprised to learn that she is behind this!" Lady Rudgebourgh's eyes narrowed. "She is a lying, scheming hussy!"

He took a step toward her, and the look on his face must have alarmed her, for she stepped back in turn and almost fell over a high-backed chair.

"I would advise you not to use such terms in reference to the lady. You will find that my forbearance has its limits."

"What is it you want me to do?" she demanded, recovering her self-possession. "Inform Bow Street?"

"That will not be necessary." He looked down at her, not bothering to mask the contempt he was feeling. "I have already taken certain measures and do not doubt that Georgiana will be found very shortly. I will not, of course, allow her to return to this house."

This was too much for the lady. "You forget, sir, that you have no legal claim to her! The terms of your late brother's will were quite specific: George and I are her legal guardians until such time as you shall marry!"

"Then you may be the first to congratulate me, my dear Louisa." His smile was one of pure delight. "My days of single blessedness are almost over."

Louisa's jaw dropped like a shot partridge. "You cannot be serious, Justin! Do not tell me that you mean to marry that high-flyer, Mrs. Cavendish. You could not!"

"Really, Louisa!" He drew on his gloves and moved toward the door. "You pain me by such low-bred suppositions."

"Then who...?" She followed him into the hall.

"Good day, Lady Rudgebourgh." He doffed his hat. "I trust that I need never darken these doors again."

She continued to trail him down the hall. Her brow was furrowed with the effort of concentration. Then, as she passed through the door and a stray snowflake struck her on the nose, some terrible premonition seemed to take hold of her.

"Good God!" she cried. He mounted his horse. "It could not be–you cannot mean to...for God's sake, Justin, do not–"

But he was already off at a canter, laughing aloud and certainly paying no heed to her stammering. Foolish woman! He had heard quite enough from her for one day.

/=/

That evening, as he sat daydreaming by a brightly burning fire, Mr. Bascot returned. He looked dishevelled and rather weary, but Lord Denham detected no sign of defeat about him. On the contrary, his eyes were bright and there was the merest hint of a smile about his thin lips.

"What news, Geoffrey?" his employer asked.

"I have found her, sir."

"Tell me."

Geoffrey accepted the seat which Justin indicated and proceeded with his narration. He had, as suggested, sought out several acquatint publishers. The first had been of no avail, but at R. Havell & Son, he had much better luck. They proved to be well acquainted with a certain Miss Jennifer Prentice and her aunt, Miss Matilda Prentice. These ladies were the daughter and sister of an old friend of the publisher.

Jennifer's father had been a colonel in Wellington's army. He had been killed in battle and left his family in extremely straitened circumstances. The two women had kept household together but were forced to sell the family's small house and move to London to seek employment. They managed to subsist primarily by coloring engraved prints. Miss Jennifer, indeed, was a fine draughtswoman, whose sketches of the Hampshire countryside had provided the basis for several successful acquatints.

"Their lodgings are not at all far from Lady Rudgebourgh," Mr. Bascot concluded.

"Are you quite sure that this is indeed the lady I am seeking?"

"Quite sure." Geoffrey smiled. "The description provided by several gentlemen at the establishment left no room for doubt."

"What an excellent secretary you are, Geoffrey." Justin leaned back in his chair. "But I'm afraid that your labors are not yet at an end."

"No?"

"I want you to inform Mrs. Mullens at Cottle-fold that I will be arriving with a small party of guests for the holidays." He paused. "How many days is it until Christmas, by the by?"

"Five, sir."

"Good." Justin folded his hands, well pleased with the way in which things were progressing. "That should give me ample time."

"Forgive me, sir." Mr. Bascot gave a slight, apologetic cough. "But are you quite certain that Miss Prentice will, ah, be amenable to your plans?"

"You doubt my powers of persuasion, Geof-frey?" His Lordship gave his companion a challenging glance. "I would not advise you to wager against me."

"Indeed, I would not dare!"

"Then you will not mind your other task, which is even more urgent."

"I think I can guess what it is, sir." Geoffrey leaned forward. "There is a certain item you wish me to procure?"

"How well you understand me." Justin chuckled.

"I wonder if *you* understand Miss Prentice?"

"Who can ever fathom a woman's mind?" He shook his head. "I know only that I am tail-over-top in love for the first time in my sorry life. It will not happen to me again, and I do not intend to love in vain, my friend. By no means!"

/=/

The following morning was bright, clear and cold. A thin coverlet of snow had descended on London overnight, lending a fairy-tale look to the usually gray and dreary city. The great dome of St. Paul's, rising up in the midst of it, had a curiously oriental splendor, which stirred Jenny's imagination with images of Bethlehem and the Christmas star. As a gift for Georgiana, she had extracted a sheet of drawing paper from her carefully guarded hoard and set about sketching a scene of Christ's nativity, using the remembered features of neighbors and friends as models for the characters involved.

Aunt Mattie had taken Georgiana with her to buy a few meager provisions, so she was quite alone this morning. Jenny thought of the open fields and yew-trimmed lanes of her former home and sighed. She did not care for city life, especially in winter. Well, at least Papa's old friend, Mr. Havell, had invited them to his home for Christmas dinner. For one day, at least, they could feast on a fat goose and forget the privations of the rest of the year.

She supposed that Lord Denham would enjoy a Christmas dinner of immense proportions, with enough plum pudding to feed a small village. She shook her head and realized with a start that she had sketched his exact features for the face of Joseph. Really, she had not stopped thinking about the man since their meeting yesterday! She compressed her lips as she recalled his indolent manner.

And yet...there was that moment when their eyes met, and she had felt such a strange sensation in her breast. It was merely that she had not eaten—that was all. Yet she could not forget. Such a personable man, to be so cold. To look at him, you would not believe that he could neglect such a dear child as Georgiana.

A sharp rapping at the door roused her from her reverie. It could not be Mr. Havell's messenger with more prints to color, for he was not expected until the morrow. She put down her pencil and, rising from her seat, went over to the door. A moment later it was open and she was staring in astonishment at the man who stood there.

"Lord Denham!" she gasped.

"Mrs. Darcy." He bowed. "Or are you using your own name today, Miss Prentice?"

She was unable to speak. For a wild moment, she even contemplated shutting the door in his face. But it would be quite useless, she knew. He had discovered them, and there was nothing more to be done.

"How did you find this place?" she demanded, regaining her voice at length.

"Your comments on my books yesterday led me to suspect that you were involved in the coloring of acquatint engravings." He shrugged. "That and some other matters suggested to me the likeliest places to search."

"I did not think you clever enough to guess," she mused, more to herself than to him.

"So I perceive. But you made your estimation of my character and intellect perfectly plain at our first interview."

In spite of herself, she blushed. Then, realizing that he was still standing outside, she said, "I suppose you had better come in, since you are here."

"Gracious as ever."

She chose to ignore this remark, well aware that he was deliberately quizzing her.

"You are come to fetch Georgiana, I gather."

He did not answer at once, but surveyed the cramped dimensions of the room. His face was quite inscrutable, but she surmised that he did not find it to his liking.

"I intend to take Georgiana with me," he answered her at length.

"Back to that horrible woman?"

"I am taking her to my own house in St. James's."

She stared at him, unable to disguise her surprise. "I thought you had no legal claim to her."

"Nor do I."

She sat down by her drawing and gathered her woollen shawl more closely about her, for even with the small fire the room was chilly. "If you are jesting, sir, I must tell you that I do not find it at all amusing."

"You see, my dear Miss Prentice, my sister-in-law has guardianship of Georgiana only conditionally." He pulled forward a small wooden chair and seated himself opposite her at the table, glancing down briefly at her unfinished sketch.

"Conditionally?"

He nodded. "My brother made it clear in his will that, in the event of my marriage, Georgiana would become *my* ward. He had a firm belief in the beneficial effects of matrimony."

"A belief which you do not share, apparently."

His rather attractive smile appeared, and she looked away as he responded, "I must confess that my views on the subject are not what they once were."

"Yet you remain a bachelor."

"That is a condition which I intend to change."

"Why did you not tell me this yesterday?" She turned to face him once more. "You behaved as though you did not care a fig for poor Georgie!"

"I have never been a great lover of small children," he admitted. "It is not that I am not fond of my niece, but I certainly would not contemplate marrying merely to take her into my care–although I must admit that the prospect of annoying Louisa provides a fairly strong inducement."

"No." In spite of herself, she smiled. "I can

understand your reluctance. It is a great deal to ask anyone to marry for someone else's happiness, at the expense of one's own."

"Would you be willing to do so, Miss Prentice?"

"Well, really–" He seemed so serious all at once, his quizzing tone gone. "I do not know. I have never been asked to make such a sacrifice."

"Until now."

"I beg your pardon?"

"Will you marry me, Miss Prentice?"

She stared at him, unable to accept that she could have heard him aright. Yet it was unlikely that she would imagine such words issuing from his chiselled lips. His eyes seemed to burn with some strange emotion, and she blinked at him, considering how best she might respond to something so fantastic.

"Forgive me, ma'am." He rested his elbow on the table and leaned his forehead against his hand, giving a rueful chuckle as he did so. "I am making a shocking mull of this. But it so happens that this is the first honorable proposal I have ever made to a woman!"

"That is painfully obvious."

"I may be inept," he said. "But I am sincere. In fact, I have never been so much in earnest. I have not lived the most virtuous of lives. I am not proud of my reputation–which, by the by, has been somewhat exaggerated by the London gabble-grinders! But I assure you that such exploits are now at an end."

"I think you are all about in the head!"

"Unquestionably," he agreed with perfect affability. "But, though the prospect of uniting yourself to one who is clearly deranged may be daunting, I ask you to consider carefully before you refuse me."

"Sir," she said, "if this is some foolish conceit of yours–some wild scheme to discomfit me–"

"On the contrary, my dear," he interrupted. "I desire rather your comfort and happiness. If you marry me, it will not only be of benefit to my niece. As my wife, you will be a wealthy woman with an estate in the country and a host of servants at your command. You and your aunt will never want for anything, I promise you that."

Jennifer shook her head, trying to clear it of the all too pleasant visions his words had inspired. She had never been so confused–so dumb-founded–in her life. But, however tempted she might be, she could not possibly consent to some-thing so absurd. Attempting to marshal her thoughts, she stood up and walked over to the hearth, only to find that he had followed her and was standing far too close for her to be able to think clearly.

"There are many women, far more eligible than I," she said at last, "who would be only too eager to wed someone like yourself."

"But you, Miss Prentice," he answered, his mouth slightly askew, "seem oddly loath to accept such a golden opportunity."

"My Lord–" she spoke slowly, patiently, at-tempting to be as rational as possible under the circumstances "–I can certainly perceive the ad-vantages to myself in this–arrangement. But might I ask what could possibly tempt you to marry me?"

Once again, as on the previous day in his study, their glances met and held. "In this in-stance," he said, "marriage will secure for me something that I want more than I have ever wanted anything in my life."

"What is that?"

"You."

It was impossible to doubt that he meant what he said. Her heart felt as though it would leap from her breast as she gasped out, "You are mad–quite mad!"

Whether to prove that she was correct, or merely from impatience, he seemed to abandon any further attempt at reason. With unexpected swiftness, he pulled her against him and pressed a very forceful–and, in truth, extremely pleasant–kiss upon her upturned lips. Nor was he satisfied with one only, but immediately added another and another, until she was so entirely giddy from the sensations which his kisses produced that she thought surely the whole room must be revolving about her. It was some time before he released her, grasping her shoulders in his strong hands and staring down at her rather sternly.

"Well?" he demanded.

She supposed he must be wanting an answer to something, but she could not even remember what it was he had asked. She recalled that she had at some time or another said that he was mad. Did he want to know whether she had changed her opinion?

"I–I think," she stammered, recovering her speech, "that I must be mad as well."

"Shall I kiss you again?" he inquired.

"Yes, please."

He gave a curiously boyish grin, drawing her against him once more. "I take it, then, that you intend to marry me after all?"

"Oh!" She blinked at him, some remnant of reason beginning to return. "Will you kiss me again if I refuse?"

"Certainly not! It would be most improper."

"In that case, I accept."

"Very sensible of you."

She sighed expectantly as he lowered his

head...

At that moment, the door burst open to admit her aunt and Georgiana, both of whom halted on the threshold at the sight before them.

"Bless my soul!" cried Aunt Mattie.

"Uncle Justin!" Georgiana squealed and rushed forward. Lord Denham's right arm was still occupied in embracing his bride-to-be, but he managed to catch his niece in his left arm and hoist her up that she might deposit an enthusiastic kiss upon his cheek.

"Are you going to take me home with you?" she asked.

"I am going to take all of you home with me."

"Hurrah!"

Jennifer, recollecting her manners, attempted to introduce him to her aunt, but he forestalled her.

"This can be no other than the lovely Miss Matilda Prentice. It is my pleasure to make your acquaintance, ma'am." He deposited Georgiana gently on the ground and made a very correct bow.

Aunt Mattie was so flattered and flustered that she hardly seemed to know how to respond. "So it was your carriage we saw outside," she said, looking from her niece to his lordship.

"Indeed. And now, if you will collect your belongings, I will have that same carriage convey you all to my house."

"But...we cannot...you do not..."

He smiled at her with genuine kindness, not unmixed with amusement. "Perhaps it will help if I explain that your niece and I are to be married tomorrow."

"Tomorrow!" Jennifer squealed, very much as Georgiana had done a few minutes before.

"Certainly tomorrow." He was perfectly cool. "My secretary is even now procuring a Special License."

"Is this true, Jenny?" Aunt Mattie asked.

"I suppose it must be." Her niece looked up at the man beside her. "Are you quite certain that this is what you want?"

"Are you?"

She found herself laughing suddenly. "Bird-witted though it may be, I do indeed wish to marry you, sir."

"Then let us waste no time, little bird." He raised her hand to his lips. "We have much to do, and I am eager to celebrate Christmas with my new bride!"

/=/

Beth Andrews was born in Nassau, Bahamas, and is the youngest of four children. Beth has worked in the editorial department of Nassau's oldest newspaper, The Nassau Guardian (1844) Ltd., was an accountant at a furniture store, and is now the assistant manager in a small music store.

Beth enjoys music (classical, country, and calypso are favorites), theater, dinner with friends, and the beach. Travel is another enjoyable activity, including trips to Germany, Italy, Israel, and Cuba as well as two Caribbean cruises, and a short hop to Florida, the only place visited so far in the US.

Beth loves to write … everything, from poetry and song lyrics to short stories, novellas and, at last, full-length romance novels.

(Editor's Note: Beth's full-length novel *The Marplot Marriage* will be published by Regency Press in October, 1999.)

If you've enjoyed the Sharpe's Rifles *television series, you will enjoy this adventure set during the Peninsular Wars. At what point did you, gentle reader, figure out what was happening here?*

Just Like Old Times...
Karl Richards

The sun was relentless, beating down on the solitary figure of a man as he trudged down the dusty pathway. His bare feet as well as other areas of skin exposed to the sun through the openings of the tattered shirt and ragged pants were all a naturally dusky hue. Dark and dusty curls framed a pleasant, open face with surprisingly blue eyes. A medium-sized bundle was slung over one shoulder.

Squinting against the bright sunlight, he wondered anew at the way an artist would be able to look at these million or so different shades of brown and see tan and gold and cream and deep russet. Obviously, his eyes weren't that experienced. He sighed, hugely, but continued his forward trek, stirring up little puffs of the dry dirt beneath his feet as he did so.

Far off in the distance, shimmering in the glaring light, one could make out a tree or two, if one searched diligently enough. Perhaps their presence signified also the presence of water–a most highly wished-for commodity. If he didn't allow himself to think of it, perhaps he wouldn't desire it quite so avidly.

After a few more steps, from that same opposite direction, his ears picked up the sound of the high-pitched jingle of harness, accompanied by the deeper thudding sounds of horses' hooves. Many hooves, if one's ears could be believed. Showing a deal of sense, the walker quickly moved to the side of the road and knelt down in the dried grass.

The lone man fumbled with the bundle that had fallen to the ground. He had barely time to ease himself to a sitting position and take up a sketch pad and wisp of charcoal before the approaching horses became visible.

It was a small troop of French soldiers, in uniform, chattering amongst themselves. The leader spied the would-be artist and signaled for his troops to halt. "*Chien!*" the man shouted, disparagingly, causing the artist to grin in spite of himself. It was a lopsided, loose sort of expression, one that would not have been recognized by any of his friends, had he any in this forsaken place.

"*Attendez-moi!*" the leader commanded, but the would-be artist ignored him. An angry movement of an arm caused one of the troops to hurriedly dismount and make his way to the artist. With a great flourish, the soldier withdrew his sword from the scabbard at his waist and advanced upon the hapless, dusty vagabond.

Appearances can be very deceiving, and that presented by the artist–primitive, dusty and, truth-be-told, apparently not too recently visited by cleanliness–led the troop leader to believe that this was a person of little or no consequence. The leader nodded to his subordinate, whose manners were none too nice as he then prodded the artist to his feet, helped along by the tip of his sword.

A sharp word directed at one of the other soldiers led to a piece of rope being thrown loosely over the prisoner's head, where it rested lightly on his broad shoulders. But when the leader tugged on the rope to encourage his captive into motion, a spate of rough words emerged from the hitherto silent man. He turned toward his small collection of belongings, indicating by a few sweeping motions that they must accompany him.

With a grunt, the leader loosened the rope, and motioned for his captive to gather up the measly belongings. Without another word, the little caravan headed down the roadway, stirring up more puffs of dry dirt as they did so.

/=/

At a knock on the rustic door to an even more rustic appearing office, the only occupant raised his head. "*Oui*," he called out, at the same time unfolding his tall frame from the chair behind the desk. Not by a flick of an eyelash did he indicate that he had ever before seen any of the persons who now entered his office. Those men in military uniform saluted, briskly and with many flourishes. The one who was not in uniform stood slackly, weaving slightly from side to side.

His dark face was now marked by light-colored streaks, where perspiration had made rivulets as it moved downward, contrarily leaving darker stains on his clothing. The leader of the troop who had escorted him to this place prodded him to stand still, at attention. To no avail, however. Either the prisoner did not speak the correct language or chose to ignore the instructions.

At a signal from the higher-ranking officer, a torrent of words issued forth from the leader. With a sound of disgust, that worthy demonstrated how he had gained obedience from his prisoner, clanking his sword in an effort to display his competence. He motioned to one of his men, who, without ceremony, tossed the dusty satchel containing the prisoner's belongings at his very feet.

"No, no!" the prisoner cried, cringing, falling to his knees to better protect his possessions. He turned his face upward, and with wide pleading eyes silently begged for compassion from the officer who had yet to utter a sound.

Some kindness, some inner feelings, perhaps, prompted the officer to lower himself to the prisoner's level, and he held out his hand. The prisoner studied the face of his captor, then silently handed over the satchel.

Standing, the officer carefully placed the bag on his desk and began a silent but thorough perusal of the poor contents. A battered tin cup, a piece of charcoal, a pad of paper, tattered at the edges. Something that might once have been a shirt, but was now not much more than a collection of loose threads.

Carefully watching the prisoner, the officer picked up each item in turn. It was only after observing a very slight reaction that the officer picked up the pad of paper and began to thumb through it.

"No, no!" came again from the prisoner, as he reached out one hand, tentatively, to protect his paper.

A careful perusal showed only very rudimentary sketches on several of the pages. Perhaps with instruction, the artist might have someday graduated to a ranking of tolerable. As it was, however, the sketches were hardly better than might have been made by a child of six or seven years. But still, this one was certainly a church, and, several

34

pages later, there was a bridge. Further on, a lightning-struck tree, listing badly to one side of the page. And finally, one sheet removed from the last one, a lady. Rather, it was a poor copy of a portrait of a lady, a miniature, in fact, housed in a pearl-encrusted oval-shaped frame.

The officer glanced down at the prisoner. Holding the pad of paper in one hand, the officer pointed to the kneeling man with the other and raised one eyebrow in question.

"*Si*, me," came the response, replete with bobbing head. One hand tentatively reached out for the remembered treasure.

"No, I think I'll keep this for a while," the officer stated. In an outrush of words, he issued instructions to the little troupe. Two men approached the prisoner and, each of them taking one of his arms, pulled him to his feet and then out of the room. One of the soldiers so far forgot himself as to offer the captive a drink from his own canteen.

With a show of poor grace, the troop leader flung the bundle at the man, grasped him roughly by one arm, and dragged him to a door leading outside–and to freedom. "*Allez!*" the troop leader said. "*Vamos!*" He flung one hand out to demonstrate where the prisoner should go.

It took no further encouragement for the dusty and tattered man to leave the building. Exhibiting a surprising burst of speed, he ran, heedless of the pebbles in the pathway, not stopping for breath or a furtive look, until he was a mile or more down the road. When he was sure that he was very much alone and unobserved, he allowed a small smile to creep across his face.

His shoulders seemed suddenly straighter, as was his back, and a cheerful tuneless whistle accompanied his steps as he hastened from the vicinity.

Several months later, at a posh gentlemen's club in London, two old friends ran into each other, literally, rounding the same corner at the same time, but from opposite directions. "Hastings!" cried the taller of the two and grasped eagerly to clutch the hand of the other.

"Bigelow." A wide smile creased the face under the dark curls and the startling blue eyes. "By Jove, it's about time." The two stood still, facing each other, looking for the proper words.

"Share a bottle with me?" inquired the man addressed as Bigelow. "I've never had the chance to thank you for what you did for Becky last year."

"Is she… ?"

"She's fine. Just fine, thanks to you. Entirely to you." Bigelow motioned Hastings into the cozy room, where a fire was crackling merrily in the huge fireplace. There were comfortable chairs placed, one to either side of the marble surround, perfectly positioned for easy conversation, yet with a degree of privacy.

When a waiter appeared, unobtrusively, the order was given for a bottle of the best brandy and a pair of glasses to be brought in immediately, and then for them to be left alone.

The men raised a glass each in silent toast to the other. It was a few minutes before Bigelow, otherwise known as the Earl of Poston, broke the silence. "And now, if you please, Hastings, I should like to know all."

The Viscount Richard Hastings, he of the blue eyes and dusky curls, turned toward his friend. "When Chris took that bullet, Becky insisted on staying behind to nurse him. It was just a fluke, of course. There was no reason for anyone to have been in that area, certainly no one with weapons. It can only have been a deserter. I couldn't find anyone, and I did look. I stayed with them until Chris died, and saw that he was buried properly. Becky was all a man could hope for, she even said the proper words over him and all, and then..." After a moment's silence, Hastings looked at his friend, and added, in a soft voice, "It isn't what I would have wished for a hero, but I didn't know what else to do just then."

Only one who had been through such an ordeal could understand the necessity for a moment of reflection, to regain one's composure before continuing with the sad story.

"We had decided to head for the coast and planned to leave just after sunset, traveling at night, resting up during the day. But we weren't able to get a start before there were several stragglers wandering through the area. Heaven only knows what might have happened to Becky had she left there, even with me to offer what protection I could. Gave her my provisions, including my rifle and ammunition, my sword–all my rations. Told her I'd do my best to get her out, but it might take a day or two. She'd have to stay quiet, be careful until then."

"She always was the best of good playfellows, you know," said Bigelow. "I'm sure we never considered that she'd put to use all her experience at being our prisoner." In spite of the somberness of the story, both men chuckled in remembrance of those earlier days, so long ago now–when they were all young.

Hastings said, "I had heard you were in the area, gathering intelligence, but still, you could have knocked me over with a feather when I found you, there in that hut, in a Frenchified uniform! But then, you always did speak the language like a native."

"How better to be in a position to hear things one shouldn't hear than to be in such a place? And don't forget, our mother was French, and always spoke it to Becky and me when we were children." Bigelow gave a sudden grin. "Talk about surprised! When you raised your head and I saw those blue eyes, I came close to giving it all away. But then I remembered that game we played as boys. How we spent days devising ciphers and secret codes. You were so reluctant to give up the pad of papers, I was sure there was something there for me."

Hastings laughed. "For certain it wasn't in that cup or the raggedy shirt. Becky spent an enjoyable evening taking it apart to look so tattered. Said she'd spent years as a girl putting threads in things, now she could take them out for a change." He took another sip of wine.

"Yes, I remember well how m'sister used to complain about forever running a needle into her finger, or else she was tangling her threads. Who would have thought it to come in handy so many years after?" Bigelow mused. "Clever, though, your pictures," he continued. "I'd ridden past that church just the day before. So, after you were let go," again he chuckled in remembrance, "I set out, apparently just wandering through the countryside."

"I rode a few miles in one direction, but it didn't feel right, so I turned back, and went past the church again, but going the other way this time. It wasn't long before I passed the bridge. I took the pad out to look at it more closely, and realized that there were blank pages between the drawings, and not always the same number of blank pages. I decided they must have some significance."

"You needed to be aware of the proper tree; if you'd turned too soon, you'd have missed the road to the hut where Becky was."

"I soon realized that the number of blank pages meant something, and before I knew it, I'd found the tree you drew so accurately, along with the miniature of Becky hanging from one of the branches. From that point on, it was a fairly simple rescue."

"Yes, but you had a good horse, and money. We'd had neither."

Bigelow faced his friend, surprised by the look of longing on Hastings' face. "I say. Come home with me for dinner. The Dowager is here in town, you know. And Becky. Surely you'd give them the chance to say 'thank you'. Becky has asked about you several times, you know, and I had to tell her I'd had no word."

"After you dismissed me I had to go on acting the fool, or risk being taken up again. I made my way to the coast, all right, but all the ships were going in the wrong direction. It's taken me entirely too long to get back to England, and I promise you, I don't intend to leave it again."

"Then come with me. We'll celebrate–"

"Celebrate?"

"Oh, any number of things." Bigelow stood up, encouraging his friend to do the same. "First and foremost, I think, will be a toast in appreciation at being all back together again. Just like old times."

Hastings smiled as he stood, and nodded his head. "Just like old times," he agreed.

/=/

Karl Richards lives in southern Michigan with his wife and son. This is his first published work. He conceived the story idea after seeing the movie *Sense and Sensibility*, and *Sharpe's Rifles* on PBS, then visiting historical sites from the War of 1812 in Michigan and Ohio.

39

*The shimmering haze of a sunny day, a glass of black-
berry cordial at a picnic, an unhappy spinster living off
her brother's charity, the sudden rush of memories long
suppressed, the yearning for what could have been...A
potent mix, at any time!*

Belvedere
Jo Manning

'Twas a sunny, cloudless day, a day the rhapso-
dizing Romantic poets would surely immortalize
in their lays and sonnets, odes and ballads. The
sky was a perfect blue, a blue rivaling the eggs of
robins; the sun blazed Apollo-bright. Today,
thought Juliana, today we shall have a picnic!

/=/

Marshalling the culinary forces in the Hall's
massive kitchen and flattering the cook, Mrs.
Sears, took no time at all. Juliana was a formidable
organizer; the Iron Duke could have made good
use of her skills on the Peninsula. All her energies,
the ones that might have been expended on husband and children and good works in town and
country, were now centered on her recently-
widowed older brother and his two motherless
girls. She had moved in with Thomas and his
family after the death of their father, a wealthy but

lesser aristocrat. Thomas's family had inherited Juliana as well as the estate and holdings of their departed grandfather. She, firmly set on the shelf at thirty-seven years of age, found herself with little in the ways of resources to continue to live in the style to which she'd been accustomed. No other options were open to her, so, with Thomas she remained.

A fifth wheel in the household, she occupied her time reading the classics of Greek and Latin literature and dipped into the gothic romances published by the Minerva Press. The death of Thomas's wife had changed all that. Suddenly, the two girls were her major responsibility, girls soon to become young women. Absent a mother to prepare them for their London Season, Juliana became by default their mother and guide. Juliana's own Season, so long ago, had been a notable failure. Indeed, it had almost been a minor scandal. Recalling it now, even after all those years, made her wince. She would do better by her girls, she vowed. If nothing else, she had been taught a lesson in the ways of the *ton* she'd never forgotten. All the better to pass it on. She would navigate her girls through the treacherous shoals of the Season, her hands at the helm, steadfast and focused. They would not founder on the sharp, unforgiving rocks as she had.

She had been schooling them in etiquette, dancing, needlework, water-color painting, light conversation, and the like, while impressing upon their young and impressionable minds that a good match took into consideration bloodlines, properties, titles, and status. Good looks were nice, but not necessary; mutual fondness was encouraged, but not expected. A good match had the approval of the families concerned, for the greater good of future heirs. *Tendres* were to be discouraged; rakes were to be warned against and turned away. Romances were all well and good for leisure reading, but the real world loomed ahead, and Amy and Jessica were not to repeat their aunt's errors.

But, now, now there was a picnic to prepare! There were precious few days left before the girls became women and would no longer romp amongst the wildflowers and meadow grasses with their maiden aunt. The thought saddened Juliana. It brought nagging reminders of what life would, indeed, be like when the girls married and left the Hall. 'Twould be her and Thomas, alone together...for the rest of their lives, except when the girls came to visit, or she and Thomas journeyed to visit them. If Thomas were to remarry, however... That thought had also crossed Juliana's mind. Thomas was not an old man. Barely forty years of age, he could marry again and father a whole new brood. What, then, would Juliana's role be? She and Margaret, her late sister-in-law, had rubbed along tolerably well. Margaret had been a gentle, passive soul. A new wife could introduce new complications. This line of thought was disturbing; Julianna pushed it out of her mind with alacrity.

"Come, Amy. Come, Jess. The day is waiting for us to enjoy it," she called out merrily.

Dimpled Amy and shy Jessica appeared, parasols in hand, with an embroidered cloth bag containing needlework and a slim book of verse. The parasols gave notice they were concerned for their fair complexions. Juliana considered, then eschewed, her need for a parasol. No one cared, least of all Juliana, whether or not she was browned or freckled by the sun. Her personal appearance had ceased to concern her years ago. Twenty years ago, to be exact.

Juliana shepherded her charges into the dogcart one of the grooms brought to the front door and drove into the meadows, keeping to the large rut that passed for a road leading from the Hall to the Home Farm. Bursts of yellow proclaimed the presence of meadow-rue, celandine, dandelion, Welsh poppy, and charlock. The white petals of the ubiquitous Ox-eye daisy dotted the grassy green meadow, and Juliana recollected how, as a girl the age of her nieces, she had wondered who loved her or loved her not. She still wondered. Yellow water lilies floated in the deeper water and golden iris stood tall in the shallows of the creek that meandered toward the woods. The woods... if Juliana took the larger rut that jutted to the left, just up ahead, she'd reach the ruins of Belvedere.

Belvedere...it would be lovely there today, she decided. The blue and purple of speedwell, the field, Wall, Germander, and Ivy-leaved varieties, were the only spots of color in the dark woods through which the dogcart ambled. The girls shivered at the sudden cold. "La," Juliana tsked aloud. "We should have brought our shawls." The Cashmir shawls, she remembered too late, had been folded neatly on the Chippendale settee in the hallway. Juliana shrugged off the drop in temperature, rejoicing when the presence of brambly honeysuckle proclaimed the edge of the woods and they began to climb the hill that led to the ruins of Belvedere. She heard the short series of notes culminating in a rapid trill that signaled a Blue tit in the branches of the oak trees bordering the grounds. She recognized a half-dozen Grizzled skippers fluttering by her head; they alighted on the reddish-purple honeysuckle stems, diving eagerly into the inviting orange-yellow trumpet-shaped flower heads.

Belvedere stood atop the highest hill in the district, perhaps not a very high hill, but one that commanded a view of the forest, the meadows, and, off in the near distance, the Hall. The sinuous blue of the creek glistened as it wound its way through the landscape, about to disappear into the large river that marked the county boundary. Once the largest stately mansion in the county, Belvedere had burned to the ground during the Civil War, fire encouraged by a relentless barrage of Roundhead cannon too much for its fragile timbers to withstand. Its Cavalier owners, the Beaulieus, had fled. Visitors came not to see what had once been, but to view the line of perfect Ionic columns that rose from a tangle of wild grapevines on the top of the hill. The golden stone columns had been part of an enclosure, perhaps used as a pleasure pavilion by the Beaulieu family. Only eight columns remained. Five were perfect, scroll, fluting, plinth, intact as if erected only yesterday. Three–at the end of the line–were broken midway down their shafts, at exactly the same spot.

A frieze of maidens carrying baskets of food and garlands of flowers ran the length of the entablature over the five whole columns. The smiles frozen on their beautiful young faces were as gay as the day they were sculpted. Juliana held her breath. She'd never been to the fabled Parthenon, in Greece, but Thomas had taken the Grand Tour after completing his university studies and had described that magnificent site to his enraptured little sister. The drawings he brought back from Athens had always reminded her of the columns of Belevedere. Juliana studied the flowing robes that barely covered the slender limbs of the Greek girls. Ah, what freedom! Although the dress now worn in England-following the French Empire style-was relatively loose and comfortable compared to English styles of yore. How wonderful it must be, she thought, to wear almost nothing at all. Nothing at all, she mused...Her own limbs warmed, not only because the sun was now shining, unimpeded by clouds, upon her and her little party.

It was just past noon, the air clear and still. Bees buzzed busily, darting from the woods to the wildflowers in the meadow, and back again, their black-and-yellow-barred bodies little blurs of colored motion. Amy and Jessica took their white kid slippers off their dainty feet and ran toward the still, waiting columns. Juliana called, "Girls! The baskets! I cannot carry them all!" Amy and Jessica stopped, giggled, and raced back to help their aunt. Amy carried one food basket, Jess another containing fruit and eating utensils. Juliana had charge of the picnic cloth and the beverages, apple cider and lemonade for the girls, Mrs. Sears's homemade blackberry cordial for her. She laid out the off-white linen cloth, and Jessica passed her the cutlery, china dishes, and mugs for the drinks. Amy sorted out the food: roast chicken and ham, crisp new asparagus spears, potato and cabbage salads, a fresh, yeasty brown cottage loaf, a jar of peach and ginger jelly, apples and figs. She allocated a large white cotton napkin to herself, her sister, and her aunt. Juliana filled the mugs with drink, and they helped themselves to the sliced meats and vegetables.

Juliana plopped a whole juicy purple fig into her mouth and savored the soft, textured flesh. She sipped the undiluted blackberry cordial, enjoying the mix of sharp alcoholic flavor and pure sweetness of fresh fruit. The liquor brought a warm flush to her face. She licked her parted lips delicately. From the corner of her eye, she saw Amy and Jess, having eaten their fill, fashioning wildflowers into long garlands. Juliana blinked at the garland-waving Greek girls on the frieze; they

45

seemed to be moving forward. She blinked again, and they were stationary. A trick of the light, she reasoned, that was all. She rose from the picnic cloth and stretched her arms toward the blue sky. She began to walk slowly toward the columns. A flicker of light between the tall, straight shafts caught her eye.

The light was wavering between the columns, as if the air itself was trembling. A flock of dark-winged, screaming swifts flew out from what remained of the cornice capping the columns. They rushed by, as if escaping the gates of Hades, in a stream of dark color and loud sound, and quickly disappeared from sight. Their sudden appearance unnerved Juliana, and she paused, unsteady on her feet. She took several quick breaths. Of course, she reassured herself, there must be gaps, crevices in the stonework where the birds nested.

The sun was high and bright, the sky still cloudless. The shimmering golden columns beckoned to Juliana, and she drew closer. A slight breeze rustled the deep green grapevines curling upwards from the broken columns. There was a movement... There! Yes, something was moving behind the edifice, something...

A deer, Juliana thought, a lone fallow deer that had wandered off by itself from the Hall's herd, or perhaps one of the sheep from the Home Farm flock, escaped from under the vigilant eyes of the shepherd and his dogs. Yes, of course...what else could it be, all the way up here? Then it was still, quiet, and Juliana wondered if she was losing her mind. There was nothing. *Nothing.*

She proceeded up the rise, her mind wandering as her bare feet crushed dead-nettle, white clover, and fairy flax. The tough stems bruised her soft soles, but she barely felt them. Worrying about the girls' come-outs distracted her momentarily, and she recalled her own terrible Season. Ah, but it wasn't so terrible at first. The routs, the balls, the musicales, the operas, the plays...receiving gentleman callers in the mornings, driving in Hyde Park in the afternoons. There were some special gentlemen, to be sure. George Beaulieu...how odd! She stopped. Beaulieu...How come she'd never associated that name with this deserted place? Surely Beaulieu was a name with which she had been familiar all her life? But the Beaulieus of this place had fled-to the continent, to France, someone had said. Ah, it was but a coincidence. There had been no Beaulieus hereabouts for generations. *A mere coincidence.*

George Beaulieu, one of her gentleman callers, had been a handsome man. Too handsome. The kind of handsome she would be warning her girls to avoid. It had been reckless, indeed, to walk with him during a waltz interval at the Graylings' ball, to walk with him through that large, dark garden with its hidden nooks and crannies. It had been a mistake to allow him to take liberties, to allow-welcome!-his touch upon her innocent, but eager, skin. Lucky for her that Great-Aunt Amanda, her chaperone, had gone looking for Juliana. That maiden lady had near fainted at the sight of her great niece in *deshabille*, at that handsome gentleman half out of his inexpressibles...Julianna had hurriedly been extricated from the situation, extricated back inside the great house, and then out the front door, bundled into a carriage, and taken home. And sent home. Next morning she was on her way back to her father's estate. The word given out to the curious *ton* was that she'd been taken ill. Her Season was over.

Juliana sighed, sucking on a dandelion stem, tasting the bitter, milky liquid and reflecting on her wasted youth. After that aborted Season, there were no others. She sat firmly on the shelf, rusticating in the country. She had often wondered what had become of handsome George Beaulieu. He'd been dark and tall, with a deep voice that had sent thrills up her spine. A frisson of anticipation echoed that long-remembered feeling. Ah, to feel that way once again, just one more time...She threw away the half-chewed stem, holding her skirts above her still-trim ankles as she trod through the long stalks of tough grasses underfoot. The erect columns of Belvedere beckoned.

The air before her eyes, shimmering between the golden columns, was tremulous. The susurration of trees from the woods whispered plaintively in her ears. She stopped. From between the third and fourth column a form emerged, a physical form, a human form. A man. A tall, dark man. Naked as the day he was born.

Juliana's knees buckled. *George!* 'Twas George Beaulieu!

She gasped, catching her breath. She heard the swifts return, darkening the sky above her head. They disappeared noisily into the hidden crevices of the tall stone columns. She blinked at the apparition, for surely that was what it was! But, no, the man stood there, one arm upraised, against the sharp fluting of the third shaft. He held a gnarled wooden staff in one hand, defiantly thrust out at her. Juliana took a long, hard look at the intruder. Or was *she*, she thought, the intruder here at Belvedere? The silence vibrated with mystery. Who was he? What was he? Surely he was not flesh and blood! Naked men did not freely roam the countryside. Did they?

He stared at her, his dark, insolent eyes daring her to come closer. His unashamedly naked body moved slightly forward. She hesitated, and in that hesitation, he was gone. Her hand flew to her throat. The space between the columns shimmered. From above, shredded twigs flew down from the cornice where the birds nested and broke the eerie silence. The grapevines rustled, the splintery, loud noise breaking the spell. For spell it was, surely! Spell...or too much of Mrs. Sears's blackberry cordial? Juliana's throat was dry. She suddenly needed to quench her thirst, but with lemonade this time. *No more cordial for her*.

She heard her nieces' shrill voices calling. The girls pointed to the sky, which was clouding over. Gray storm clouds threatened overhead. They would have to pack the remains of the picnic quickly and leave before they got drenched! Above, she heard the increasingly nervous screams of the swifts.

Shaken by what she tried to convince herself was a too-hot, sunny day and a blackberry-cordial-induced experience, Juliana gathered the girls and took the dogcart back down the overgrown road, back to the welcoming comfort of the Hall. She would stay there for what remained of the summer. The outside world, as she'd learned to her ever-lasting regret, was dangerous, wild, no place for her. She would take a nap with a cool, damp cloth over her eyes and try to forget what she'd seen. She must try to forget. She had always been good at forgetting.

Why, now, did she fear she'd not succeed?

/=/

Behind her, the golden Ionic columns of Belvedere, brought by ship to England from a long-deserted Greek island by a young country gentleman on his Grand Tour, shimmered their magic as the storm clouds dissipated and the clear, sharp trills of an ancient Attic tune wafted in the still, sun-drenched

air. The satyrs frolicked, once again left to them-
selves on the top of the rise. 'Twas easy, as always,
to keep unwelcome visitors at bay.

/=/

Jo Manning, born/bred/educated in New
York City, recently moved to Miami Beach with
her husband, Nick, a filmmaker. She was the
founder and director of the *Reader's Digest* General Books Library, and also worked as an information specialist at ABC News. Now an Assistant
Professor/Reference Librarian at the University of
Miami in Coral Gables, Jo reviews fiction for *Li-*
brary Journal and other magazines, writes articles
for professional journals, edits newsletters, and
was published several times in the love stories
page of the *Star*. Her short story *By The Rivers Of*
Babylon, in the *Herotica 4* anthology, was one of
only 7 selected for the audio-tape and CD-ROM
versions. An ardent Anglophile and enthusiastic
world traveler, she frequently visits her granddaughter, Zoë Violet, in England, and her grandson, Julian, in Texas.

The Reluctant Guardian, Jo's first full-length
novel, will be published by Regency Press in December, 1999.

Judged a 'perfect' little romance, this well-plotted entry received the second-highest score. What else would you expect, though, when Freddy and Amanda had help from those truly immortal lovers of old-Tristan and Isolde?

The Boxford Legacy
Victoria Hinshaw

Richard Fassett, the Earl of Boxford, tossed and writhed in his wrinkled bed. He fumed at the brightness of the day outside and fretted that his charade might truly hasten his demise.

Although just the shady side of sixty, he feared his feigned illness might never bring him what he required. He suffered the affectionate ministrations of his only daughter, the simpering solicitude of his tiresome sister, the forbearance of his valet. He digested an amazing variety of pap from his cook, distressingly cheerful reports from his bailiff, and the confounded purges of that country fool who called himself a physician, on what basis the earl had never deduced.

He desired none of these. He needed his London solicitor, a man in whose abilities the earl had ample confidence. Although his assertion of imminent expiration was a shocking fraud, Boxford craved the immediate guarantee of his succession, of the future of his lineage.

Despite his vociferous claims of dangerous deterioration and the fast-approaching end of his life, Amanda had not sent for Pinchbeck to settle his affairs. When he took to his bed, the earl had envisioned his daughter immediately summoning the solicitor. But Mandy refused to take his complaints seriously, brushing aside his allusions to the Final Judgement. Now he would have to tip his hand and make the outright request.

Amanda was too smart for her own good. Too bad, she could never inherit his estate. The fertile fields and orchards of Boxford, on the border of Kent and Sussex, were entailed to the next male in the Boxford descent, an ancestry which stretched back seven generations. He would see his daughter Amanda married to his heir and the matter resolved once and for all.

His heir, Mr. Frederick Easton, now six-and-twenty years of age, was a distant cousin and Amanda's betrothed since she was ten and Freddy was sixteen, more than ten years ago. Until Freddy reached his majority, the earl kept a close eye on him, bringing him to Boxford for frequent visits and providing him an excellent education. In those same years, the earl was satisfied that his plans would succeed and bear fruit, in the form of a male child, his grandson, who would grow up strong and healthy long before the earl himself was lowered into his grave.

Even when his plan went awry and Freddy ran off to join the army in Portugal, the earl had not despaired. Almost two years were needed to bring the battle-eager fellow back to England. Since then, the worst said about the boy involved sundry streaks of bad luck at the gambling tables of London, a predicament common to all young bucks. No, Freddy was not the current problem.

The difficulty involved Amanda. His daughter

grew much too independent and forceful in pursuing her own unconventional interests, far removed from marriage and motherhood. According to the earl's sister, Lady Clara Tarrant, the books into which Mandy constantly poked her nose were not frivolous novels but historical accounts by scholarly monks and ancient chroniclers. The compliant Lady Amanda was changing into Willful Mandy, determined to follow her own convictions.

The situation was clearly out of hand. Desperate measures were in order. The earl knew he must force the issue.

He raised an eyelid to glimpse his sister tiptoeing into the room. The witless Lady Clara's ample girth was hardly flattered by her somber dress of gray bombazine. Her white-streaked hair, pulled back into a severe bun, was topped by a lacy cap. Between her ears, he was convinced, not a particle of useful brain matter existed.

The earl let out a moaning sigh and rolled onto his side. He heard Clara sniff and visualized her touching a hankie to her tears.

"Richard, I have brought you some gruel."

He made a gagging sound.

"Now, please, brother, take just a tiny taste."

"Don't be a good-for-nothing peagoose, Clara. Can't stand the swill."

"But you must take nourishment..."

He groaned piteously. Then he saw the answer, and he silently praised heaven. "I need to change my will," the earl lied. "Make yourself useful for once, Clara. Send for Pinchbeck."

With a mournful sob, Clara backed out of the earl's room.

/=/

Mr. Jeremiah Abbott Pinchbeck, Esquire, regarded the summons by the Earl of Boxford, one of his most estimable clients, as superseding all other official affairs. He considered it his due to be called for by the earl's fine traveling coach, complete with two postilions astride. He appreciated the velvet cushions and hot bricks to fend off chilly spring drafts as amenities appropriate to his eminence. Mr. Pinchbeck assumed the earl wished an in-person report to supplement his regular written missives on the activities of that young coxcomb, Mr. Easton, and his associates, sad rattles all, on whom Mr. Pinchbeck kept a close eye.

Upon arrival at the estate, Mr. Pinchbeck's distress knew no bounds when he learned of the doleful condition of his honorable employer. Instead of refining upon the wide swath being cut by Mr. Frederick Easton through the establishments of St. James, Mr. Pinchbeck found himself turning right around to collect that young man and help him secure a special license to wed Lady Amanda in a matter of mere days. Mr. Pinchbeck was particularly disappointed to be deprived of the earl's fine brandy, the origin of which was never to be considered.

/=/

From her second-floor window, Lady Amanda noted the departure of her father's solicitor only an hour after his arrival, confirming her suspicions of her father's affliction. She had little doubt of old Pinchbeck's destination and why.

Mandy always knew this time would arrive, the time when odious Freddy Easton came to claim her in marriage, thus gaining not only Boxford's thousands of acres and ancient title but also her fortune in the bargain. She crossed her arms and glared at the carriage now disappearing into the trees at the edge of the park.

When she was a child, she adored Freddy. After her mother's death, the thought of having him forever beside her soothed and comforted. On his school holidays, they were companions in frequent adventures carried out beyond the scrutiny of assorted nursemaids and governesses.

Pushing her abundant auburn tresses out of her eyes, Mandy turned back to the table, spread with books and papers covered with her careful script. She had only a few more chapters to complete before she could send the last half of her manuscript to her London publisher. But the story of Harold's exhausted army gathering to face the Norman invaders was the most difficult part to write. Mandy wished to remain as dispassionate as any great historian, yet she wanted to reflect the real affection in which the last of the Saxon kings was held.

She perched on the edge of the table and considered her prospects. She would not escape marriage to Freddy. She had known it would be so since her mother's death when she was a child of ten. Countless times, she had pondered ways to avoid the inevitable, but her father persisted in his resolution.

And why would Freddy resist? The Easton branch of the family claimed neither land nor wealth. She felt sure her father had paid for Freddy's years at Oxford, a matter she bitterly resented.

Once she considered cutting off her hair and sneaking into Oxford lectures attired as a young man. Instead, she considered herself self-taught, the fortunate beneficiary of an excellent library rich in classical volumes and antique texts. Under the name of A. J. Cantwell, she had published several articles in historical journals and was soon to finish the first volume of a history of England written specially for children.

All in all, Mandy arranged her life as she wished it. She shared supervision of the household with her aunt Clara, rode the finest horses with her father, tended her gardens, and studied her books. Her father had been solicitous, allowing her to come home after only half a season in London two years ago. She found the parties dull, the people pretentious. With most of the bacon-brained young tulips of the ton, she found she had no conversation at all. The lisping misses just out of the schoolroom were obsessed with fashionable gossip, and they considered her a dowd, a situation she secretly found rather flattering.

She had not cared to flirt, for her future was all arranged. But now when her writing gained praise, she had a different view. She ignored her books for once and curled her tall form on her bed, wishing that, by some miracle Freddy had wandered off to Russia or left for the colonies.

She simply must postpone the inevitable marriage. Not forever, for she wanted to keep Boxford. It was so much a part of her, she could not imagine a life lived any other place. Sadly, she could have the estate only by marrying Freddy.

Besides, she loved children and sincerely wanted her own one day. For this purpose, Frederick would be useful. Otherwise, she hoped, he would spend most of his time elsewhere. In his absence, she would run the estate, particularly the stables full of her father's fine string of brood race horses. And she would continue to write.

But she wasn't ready. She didn't wish to become a wife. Not yet. His current caper notwithstanding, her father enjoyed hearty good health and would live on for many years. Furthermore, she was certain Freddy was not ready to become leg-shackled or learn estate management.

Five years would be about sufficient. By then, she would have finished more volumes in her children's history extending to the reign of Elizabeth, her favorite of all monarchs of the realm. When she was further along in her work, she would acquiesce to her father's schemes.

Mandy rose, gathered up her skirts, and hurried to his room. She swung open the door of her father's vast bedroom with no particular caution.

"Shhh," whispered Aunt Clara. "He is sleeping now."

"I know he is awake. I can see he is faking." Amanda walked to the bedside. "Father, your color is quite good, and you haven't coughed all day. If just your gout bothers you, we should raise that foot and tent the sheet above your toe."

The earl groaned, eliciting a sniff of disbelief from his daughter.

"Yes, my dear, a very good idea. But I am ill, sadly so, with aches that oppress every joint and the headache to vanquish a saint."

"You ought to get up and eat a decent meal. How can your digestion operate properly if you remain recumbent?" Amanda propped his foot on pillows, set a small tea table on the mattress, and draped the sheet over it.

"Thank you, my dear." The earl drew his words into a dismal moan.

"I'll send Williams to do a proper job as soon as you tell me why old Pinchbeck was here."

The earl sniffled again, wishing he could think of a way to turn his ruddy complexion a pasty white. Amanda's frown was skeptical rather than worried.

Amanda set her arms akimbo, fists at her narrow waist. "If you are thinking of getting Freddy down here for some new agreement or other, I must tell you that this is a most inconvenient time for me."

Lady Clara came up beside Mandy and took her hand while peering earnestly at the earl. "Mind your manners, Mandy. You must let the poor man get some rest, my dear."

"I think rest is the farthest thing from his mind. I think he wants to get my marriage over and done with before Raven's Wing is ready to foal. That is just a matter of a week or two. He wants to be on hand in the stable."

The earl waved his hand in a pathetic gesture of dismissal, but his daughter only chuckled.

Lady Clara tried to shoo her out of the room, but Mandy turned at the doorway for a few parting words. "Cook tells me she has a particularly fine turtle steak if you come downstairs for dinner. But if you are truly ill, she'll use it only for soup."

/=/

"So," drawled Anthony Meredith, "I hear we are to wish you happy." The tall young man draped himself over a chair and grinned at Mr. Frederick Easton.

"Is there a secret code by which news is spread all over town?" Swirling claret in a cut-glass goblet, Freddy stared moodily at the ruby reflections in its crimson depths.

"Good news travels with excessive speed," Tony declared. "Ain't many with prospects like yours. Fine estate, respected title, and wife with a handsome fortune. Not to be sneezed at, my dear fellow."

Freddy shrugged, not at all sure he agreed. His fate had long ago been sealed, but he was not quite ready to give up the delights of town. He did not mind living on his prospects or tolerating his tailor and bootmaker pestering him for payment.

"So," Tony said, "you don't relish being buried in the country?"

"I may even prefer the bucolic life."

Mr. Meredith motioned to the waiter for another bottle. "Everybody knows Boxford's land prospers. So what's the source of that blue-deviled look, Fred?"

Another friend, Sir Charles Liddington, punched Freddy's shoulder. "Got to be the parson's mousetrap, Tony."

"What's wrong with the gel? Got a crooked nose or crossed eyes?" Tony peered at Freddy, trying to ascertain his reaction.

"More like a sharp tongue and a taste for books," Freddy said. "Not a bad looker." His words seemed to imply a lack of beauty.

"Not bookish!" Tony's horrifying thought caused him to take a huge gulp of wine.

Charles was equally shocked. "A bluestocking! You don't say so? Drink up, old man."

Tony filled Freddy's glass and topped off his own. "Thought you knew the chit."

"Known her all my life," Freddy muttered, keeping his eyes on his sloshing wine.

Charles nodded. "Been betrothed to her for donkey's years. Everyone knows the story. She's the lucky one, I think."

Tony agreed. "Lookit him. In prime twig, nobody's fool. Bang up to the mark with the ribbons, when he has the blunt for a team. What gel wouldn't consider him prime husband material?"

Charles nodded in agreement. "I remember Lady Amanda Fassett from two seasons ago. We all did the pretty with her at Almack's."

"She did not stay long. Don't like town." With that statement, Freddy Easton drained the goblet and held it out for more.

"She a managing female?" Tony asked.

"No idea." The wine tasted more and more sour to Freddy. Tomorrow he would leave this genial circle of friends to travel to Boxford where he would stand beside Lady Amanda at the altar of the village church and pledge his troth.

Freddy had known Lady Amanda as long as he could remember, nearly always as his intended. They had got on well until just a few years ago, when she suddenly appeared as much a prim and proper lady as her title indicated. No longer the friend who hunted tadpoles in the pond or chased geese or explored the deep beech woods. No longer did she ride her pony bareback with her skirt hiked up to her knees. No longer did she swim in the river clad in a borrowed homespun shirt.

One summer when he'd visited Boxford, her manner was frosty. She ridiculed his pink satin waistcoat and proclaimed him a dandy. He, no doubt, deserved her censure, for in his early Oxford days, he temporarily acquired a host of foolish conceits. Since then, awkwardness prevailed between them. Their previous compatibility had swerved into clumsiness for the last few years. But, knowing the earl was ill, surely she would be more agreeable by now.

Freddy raised his glass and toasted his friends. "To the friends I'll miss more than you know."

Freddy had indulged in all the requisite Corinthian activities, according to whether or not he had the ready. His skill at cards was his only source of income other than a very small allowance paid quarterly. When he was sailing under full canvass, he tooled his curricle to Brighton and presented bangles to his occasional light o'love. When his pockets were to let, he worked out at Jackson's and danced with the wallflowers at Lady Jersey's balls. Most of all, he lingered at his club. Which was how he celebrated his last evening in town.

/=/

Frederick arrived at Boxford after a meandering ride through a countryside about to burst into the full flower of spring. As he passed Lewes, he sniffed the fresh breezes off the Channel. The distance from London had never seemed shorter.

The butler bowed low to him, another first, and escorted him upstairs to a suite of rooms. "Mr. Easton, Jack will serve your needs while you are here." The man bowed his way out.

Freddy thought his humble saddlebag looked ridiculous on the sumptuous carpet and beside the satin bed hangings. He had never had the use of such an elegant bed chamber. Nor a personal man servant. On previous visits, he'd stayed in a small room with a narrow couch.

When he answered a scratch on the door, Lady Clara hastened in with the news that the earl was resting and would receive him later. After she withdrew, Freddy sat gingerly on the soft feather mattress and bounced once or twice to take its measure. What fun he would have had in here years ago. He almost decided to stretch out for a nap but decided, instead, to seek out Amanda and get their first meeting over with before he saw the earl.

He found her in the morning room and had the opportunity to gaze at her for a moment before she realized his presence. Her hair was pulled back severely, and her brow wrinkled in concentration over a book.

"Good afternoon, Lady Amanda."

"Hello, Freddy." She was not surprised to see him.

"Your father sent for me. Is he well?"

She stood and walked around the table. "I think he enjoys the best of health. But he has taken to his bed. Do you know why he summoned you?"

Freddy nodded. "He wants us to marry right away." He found her willowy and graceful, though hardly fashionable.

"So he says. But it is not necessary."

"Are you suggesting we defy his wishes? You are no longer willing to marry me?"

She tossed her head, and her eyes flashed. "Our betrothal was arranged without my assent, as you well know. I was too young to know I might have a say in the matter."

"And now, when your father wants the matter, as you say, settled, you are reconsidering your position?"

"I have not noticed you seeking my company. I doubt you have much stomach for the match either, Freddy."

"I, ah, wonder what you would have done in my position?"

"If I had been fortunate enough to have been born a male, I would never have been in your position. I would have inherited both Boxford and the money. Neither of us would have been forced into a wedding."

Freddy laughed in amazement. Of all things, he had not expected her opposition.

Mandy gave a hint of a smile. "I suggest we agree to postpone our nuptials for at least five years."

/=/

Lady Clara tiptoed from the adjacent music room and hurried to her own apartment. Alarmed by the conversation she had overheard, she sank onto her tufted sofa and stared blindly out the window. What a bleak future those two children

62

faced. Not the tiniest spark of affection passed between them, nothing that might eventually be fanned into the flame of ardor. One might characterize their exchange as downright hostile.

Though she had longed to know romance, Clara had no experience with love. Her short, unhappy marriage to Sir Algernon Tarrant was arranged by her father. She considered herself fortunate that her much older husband died of a putrid throat and inflammation of the lungs in the third year of their cheerless union.

Mandy should not have to suffer Clara's gloomy fate, where every night was dreaded and prayers for frequent bouts of inebriation were not always answered. No, Lady Clara, thought, Mandy did not deserve such a destiny. Nor did Freddy, a bright and handsome young man. He always treated Clara with the greatest respect and deference. She wanted the two of them to find romantic love.

What was love all about anyway? In the novels she read, Lady Clara found unlimited examples of love conquering every sort of obstacle. But where did it come from? In some stories, love grew out of a miraculous rescue or a hair-raising escapade. But there were no dungeons or secret caverns or monstrous hermits at Boxford to threaten Amanda. And Lady Clara would not have recommended such a course, if indeed she knew how.

But there must be something she could do. Her brother's charge of her uselessness stung. And she would prove him wrong.

Clara went downstairs to the library, a room she rarely visited. Her own bookshelves were crowded with volumes, but not the sort as in this august room. She stopped for a moment, frowning at the books scattered on the large table in the center of the room. She wrinkled her nose and shivered when she saw the titles, all having to do with ancient accounts written by monks.

She squinted at the bookshelves, running her finger along the old leather bindings. None of the titles seemed to address the subject of romantic love. But she continued her search, methodically moving from one corner to another, row by row. From time to time she called upon a footman to reach the highest shelves.

Lady Clara started in surprise when she heard the clock chime, heralding the approach of nuncheon. She almost turned away, almost gave up her quest, when she noticed one title, in small gold letters: *Tristan and Isolde*. The names stirred an old memory, one she could not quite place, but, she was sure, related to lovers of some kind.

She grasped the book and without opening it, hastened upstairs to her room. An hour later, she arranged to have soup brought to her in her room. She would not have time for nuncheon.

The discovery of *Tristan and Isolde* elated Lady Clara. Now she would show the earl who was good for nothing! The story came from old legends and concerned the sudden creation of deep and abiding love between the knight assigned to bring a bride to King Mark. By mistake Isolde and Tristan drank a magic love potion and were forever bound in devotion and passion.

Lady Clara shrugged off their subsequent problems and searched the text for a receipt for the love elixir. But as her candle burned low, she found no hint of its ingredients, only evidence of its potency.

/=/

Jack, tallest of the earl's footmen, doffed his wig and scratched his head as he ambled into the servants' hall after serving nuncheon. "Doan know 'bout Lady Clara. Seems a bit tetched in the head."

"What ye mumblin' bout?" Emmy, the house-maid, asked.

"She got me pulling down old books. From the highest shelves in the ly'bury. Talkin' 'bout magic and potions."

"Trying to help the earl, bless his soul." Cook shook her head in sorrow as she beat a batter. "Something to make him feel better."

Jack set his wig on a stand near the door, yawned, then sat down beside Emmy. "Mandy don't think he's poorly. Sez he's faking."

"She is Her Ladyship to the likes of you!" Cook beat even harder. "As for potions, my soup's likely the best thing for him."

"Lookin' for some kind of Aphrodite-ack, she is."

"Get away with ye." Emmy moved her chair away as Jack tried to hunch over her sewing.

Cook learned more about the potions a half hour later when Lady Clara called her to the still-room.

"Would you have a receipt for an aphrodisiac? A love potion?" Lady Clara had set out an array of small bottles and jars. "None of these things look quite the thing."

"No, milady. These two be for back pain, and this one is fer burns. I don't know anything about love potions."

"Can we mix one? Isn't rosemary supposed to be the herb of remembrance?"

Cook began to understand what Lady Clara had in mind. Together, they tried various herbal infusions mixed with honey.

When Jack wandered in to see what they were doing, he shook his head in disgust and left. In moments, he returned with a bottle of the earl's French brandy.

"This is more to the cause," he commented.

Cook frowned. "Spirits can addle a body's brains."

"Yes," Lady Clara agreed. "But, perhaps, in a love potion that isn't entirely a bad thing. Perhaps just a few drops." She uncorked the bottle and added a small amount, then sniffed the mixture and passed it to cook.

"Very fine, milady."

"Do you think it might work?" Lady Clara's forehead crinkled in worry.

"Why, I say if Lady Mandy and Mr. Easton think it works, it surely will." Cook poured the reddish-gold solution into a glass beaker and corked it tight. "Jest let the mix sit for a night, and tomorrow I'll put it up in vials for you."

Lady Clara bit her lower lip. "I do wish we had some sort of receipt that was successful in the past."

"Now, don't you worry none." Cook patted Lady Clara's shoulder and watched as the worried lady traversed the kitchen and went upstairs.

Cook looked around to see if anyone was paying attention, but Jack was teasing Emmy again and paid Cook no heed at all. Quietly and surreptitiously, Cook uncorked both the brandy and the beaker, adding a goodly portion of the dark liquor to the potion. After again peering around the corner, she poured a bit of brandy into a glass and concealed it under her apron.

"Jack, you better get this decanter back to the sideboard." Her voice was as gruff as she could make it. She handed the brandy to the footman, untied her apron to hold it over her glass, and took herself off to her room.

Jack grinned at Emmy. "What d'ye think of love potions?"

"Peck o'nonsense, if you ask me," she replied

with a giggle.

"And I'm asking, ain't I?"

"I heard Cook tell you to get a'moving." Emmy's words belied her coquettish grin.

Jack edged back into the stillroom, and looked at the beaker. He got down two glasses and un-corked the potion, filling the beaker to the brim with brandy, then filled the glasses from the beaker. When he held it up to the light, the re-maining liquid looked much darker than before he added the brandy. He frowned, then sauntered out to the hall with one of the glasses.

"Give this a try, Emmy. See if ye fall fer Tom there." He pointed to the cat curled near the huge iron stove.

"Get on with ye," Emmy said, tossing her head like she'd seen the other girls do when the lads came to call.

Jack stepped from the hall, then bolted up the stairs to the room he shared with the other two footmen. From beneath the shirts in his wicker basket, he pulled a bottle of gin and hustled back downstairs.

He grinned as he noted the lowered level in Emmy's glass, then sidled into the stillroom with the gin behind his back. He poured gin into the beaker until the mixture looked to be about the right color, then topped off his own glass, and hid the gin bottle at the back of the shelf until he could return it to his room.

When the earl's valet walked into the servants' hall an hour later, he could have sworn the scuffle he heard was a couple of people rearranging the furniture. And why Emmy's face was bright red and Jack was panting like a hound in August, he could not imagine.

/=/

Lady Amanda came back into the house after seeking a little solitude and comfort in her herb garden. When she entered her room to prepare for dinner, she was surprised to find Mrs. Cooper, the housekeeper, hanging a dress on the corner of the wardrobe door.

"I had this pressed for you, milady, and I've got the tongs heating to do up your hair." Mrs. Cooper bustled up and started to untie the ribbon holding back Amanda's hair.

"Why, that is my best gown. I want to wear-"

"Now, Molly worked hard on it, milady, and she even went to the village for new ribbons to match."

Amanda submitted and tuned out the housekeeper's prattle. No one had to explain anything more to Amanda. She grasped the new circumstances well enough. The servants saw their future in pleasing Freddy. Silently she fumed as Mrs. Cooper, soon assisted by Molly, fussed over her hair and helped her into the pale blue gown with little cap sleeves.

"There now, milady. Don't you look a picture." Mrs. Cooper stood back and beamed when she was finished.

"Thank you for your assistance, Molly and Mrs. Cooper." Amanda glanced quickly into the looking glass, then away again before she could be too taken with her image. To her utter shock, Mrs. Cooper hugged her, then pinched both cheeks.

"Ooh, that hurts."

"A bit o' natural bloom gives yer eyes a sparkle."

Not only did the servants see their future in pleasing Freddy, they expected her to please him also. Amanda smoldered as she went downstairs. How swiftly they altered their loyalties.

Freddy awaited her in the hall. He was dressed

in formal evening clothes, complete with white silk stockings and a stylish sheen to his golden blond hair. In spite of herself, she found him manly and elegant, with no hint of the dandified trappings he once sported. She tried to stamp out the twinge of enchantment that rippled through her.

"Good evening, Freddy."

"Your servant, my Lady Amanda." He gestured to a footman. "Would you care for a sherry?"

She nodded and took a glass from the silver tray offered by Jack, then led the way into the saloon.

"What did Father say to you?" Her question was blunt.

"What you would expect. Refused to detail his health. Asked me if I had the special license and told me to arrange a wedding ceremony for the day after tomorrow. Said I should inform you this evening, and you should come to see him later. He said he is very ill, but I am not sure what is wrong."

She watched his expression carefully, but his face revealed no sentiments, either for or against the immediate marriage. "His intention is to appear near death and have us wed. I do not believe he is sickly at all."

"Then why...?" Freddy's voice trailed off.

"Certainly nothing to do with my activities. What have you been doing? Continuing to ruin your reputation?"

"As if I had any reputation. Believe me, Mandy, I am among the least of the capital's denizens."

"Such false humility is most unbecoming and smacks of protesting too much." She did her best to dredge up the sources of her disapproval, but the old stories now signified little.

"Nevertheless, it is true."

She lapsed into silence as dinner was announced, and they walked to the dining room where they sat at the ends of a table quite long enough for twenty guests. The distance precluded most conversation. They ate in near silence, but the minds of both diners were busy.

Inside her head, Mandy carried on a lively debate on the veracity of conversations overheard years ago when the maids had gossiped about Freddy's probable London *amours*. In truth, she envied him his freedom more than she condemned him. Even so, she would not trade her life here at Boxford...her writing, her care of the horses and gardens, her involvement with the village and the tenants.

From his end of the table, Freddy noted Mandy's new hair style with pleasure. She wore a pretty gown, which enhanced the blue of her eyes. Her entire countenance deserved high praise. He had never thought her an antidote; tonight, in the golden glow of the several branches of candles adorning the table, she looked particularly appealing. No, he corrected, she was a beauty.

He was similarly impressed with the attentive service and quality of the dishes set before him. If Mandy would only shed her prickly manner, life at Boxford would be quite comfortable. He set himself to considering why she might be resisting their marriage.

When the covers were removed, Mandy stood and gave a little curtsey to Freddy. "I shall be up early to ride. If you wish to accompany me, we can meet at the stables at eight. Now I must attend Father, so I wish you good night."

Nicely said, Freddy thought as he stood and bowed to her, but the wrinkles on her brow did not foretell of a change of mood. "I shall join you at eight tomorrow."

Glumly, he sat back down and filled his glass from the decanter of port placed on the table. Mandy had not given him anything like the reception he expected. Her coolness was almost enough to challenge his self-consequence. Made a fellow feel he must be lacking somewhere to see his betrothed treat him like somebody's cast-off poor relation. As a matter of fact, he thought, she would have been much more polite to such a one. He had not seen Mandy for several years, years in which she had changed. For the better in her appearance, certainly. But for the worse in her demeanor, which had become decidedly peevish.

But after all, what was it Sir Charles said a few nights ago? Any miss ought to be happy to have a betrothed with the polished grace and accomplishments of Mr. Frederick Easton. Apparently, Freddy thought, he would have to convince Lady Amanda just how lucky she was.

/=/

Having achieved nothing in the talk with the earl, Amanda returned to her room in a rare state of anger. He refused to postpone the wedding. She stripped the ribbons from her hair and threw them in a tangle on her dressing table. She wiggled around, trying to unhook her dress.

After quietly scratching, Lady Clara cracked open the door. "Amanda," she whispered, then hastened to assist.

Lady Clara noted Mandy's frown and felt the tension as she unfastened the hooks and tapes. She saved her words to soothe for later, when the young lady was calmer.

Mandy shoved the dress to the floor and

stepped out of it, leaving it in a heap. She perched on the edge of the bed and unrolled her silk stockings, muttering half under her breath. "All those candles burning when half the number would have been plenty. What a waste on that nodcock Freddy."

Mandy scowled at Lady Clara as her aunt hung the blue dress carefully away. "Where did you eat, Aunt? Why didn't you join us? Don't tell me you are also among the ranks of the indisposed?"

Lady Clara smiled and decided to tread lightly. "No, not at all. I was quite absorbed in a book and had a bit of fish and soup sent up to my room."

Mandy shrugged. "When you finish that book, perhaps I could read it. I could use something absorbing these days."

"The story is very entertaining. Drawn from ancient Celtic legends."

"Sounds exactly like the kind of book I would enjoy. As soon as I finish with Harold and William, I shall read it." Amanda pulled her nightgown over her head.

"Let me tuck you in, my dear." Clara drew back the counterpane and folded down the covers.

Mandy gave a deep sigh as she climbed in.

Now, Lady Clara thought, Mandy looked sad rather than angry. After a kiss to her niece's forehead, Clara dared to pose her question. "What have you and Freddy and your father decided?"

"I have decided nothing." Mandy's voice was tinged with irony. "Father has decided everything. Freddy is quite willing to go along with Father's plans. We are to be married the day after tomorrow."

The appearance of a tear on Mandy's cheek appalled Lady Clara.

"Oh, my dear, I so hoped there would be time for you to engage in a bit of romance before the ceremony."

"Our dinner tonight was more an ordeal than a romantic occasion." Mandy brushed away another tear. "I know I will marry Freddy, but why now? Father's illness is only an excuse."

"I do not know the earl's mind, but you must obey if he insists."

"He insisted at the top of his lungs a few moments ago. He will not listen to reason."

Lady Clara kissed Mandy again, then took her candle and left the room. As she stole back to her own apartment, she breathed a little prayer that her magic potion would effect the needed result.

/=/

Breakfast the next morning put Clara in mind of what the final meal must have been like before a French aristocrat went to the guillotine. Mandy wore her shabbiest riding skirt and jacket, hair snarled from the wind. Her complexion glowed a lovely pink from that same wind, but again her forehead was creased by a frown.

Clara couldn't have known how put out Mandy was that Freddy had outdistanced her this earlier, when they rode across the home farm. Mandy's mare was not up to her usual pace and Freddy's long-legged gelding passed her as they neared the river.

Freddy, on the other hand, felt downhearted indeed. If he had let Mandy win the little race, she might have thought him weak and unworthy. Now the defeat perturbed her. He was thoroughly baffled about what to do next.

As Mandy rose from the table, Lady Clara stopped her. "Wait, my dear. I have a little favor to ask of you two. Would you fetch me some watercress from the stream that runs by Sherald Hill?"

"Both of us?" Mandy sounded crotchety enough to spoil more of Freddy's day.

"I know you will want to show Freddy the hills and the stream, which has very fine fishing, the earl says."

"I seem to recall," Freddy said. "I would like to go there today, Lady Amanda, if you will show me the way." He smiled at her sparkling blue eyes and pursed lips. Perhaps, if he could get her alone for a while, he could pierce that fearsome armor.

"I will be ready in half an hour. I want to look in on Father and then change into walking boots."

"Capital!" He watched her flounce from the room with a swish of her long velvet skirt.

Before Freddy could leave the breakfast room, Lady Clara grasped his arm. "Mr. Easton, I need you to do me a favor. You may think I am a silly old woman, and I suppose that I am. However, I do wish you and Lady Amanda all the best. And I have something for you."

She paused for a moment, then plunged ahead before she lost her nerve. "This is a magic potion, a love potion, a secret mixture, which is guaranteed to engender affection between a man and a woman who partake of only a few drops. I want you and Mandy to try a little. Just a tiny bit," she added, remembering the extra spirits she had added only an hour ago. From a deep pocket, she handed him a large silver flask. "Promise me, Mr. Easton. Even if you think it is all a hum, you must drink some and give a few drops to Mandy."

Freddy tucked the flask into his coat pocket. "Thank you, Lady Clara. I am sure this will be exactly the thing." And whatever could it hurt, he thought to himself, not that he believed in any magic nonsense. Might as well summon up a wizard to make this marriage work.

The vicar had been only too glad to arrange the

ceremony for the next day, and the cleric's wife promised to decorate the church with wild flowers. All the Boxford servants, abuzz with excitement, were preparing a hearty dinner. Several were even now notifying all the tenants to attend. He and Mandy would be the only two who would not enjoy themselves.

Unless, he thought with a silent laugh, this potion stuff worked its magic.

As Freddy and Mandy started past the kitchen garden, the sun peeked through the clouds and the day took on a special radiance. Freddy took the empty basket from Mandy and hung it over his arm, delighted to see her dressed in fetching yellow muslin.

They cut across a pasture filled with gamboling lambs, snowy white and adorable in their youthful vigor. Even Mandy couldn't help smiling at their clumsy antics. Their path took them down a wagon lane next to fields, where several mares tended new foals.

"Some of Father's racing stock." She made a sweeping gesture. "Surely, you are well aware of their value."

Freddy ignored the implied affront. Even magic potions needed a helping hand. "Tell me about the bloodlines," he suggested, correctly presuming she would appreciate the topic.

Mandy proudly regaled him with the honors and distinctions earned by progeny of the Boxford stud. Unlike her earlier barbs, she made no snide remarks about his probable knowledge of his eventual inheritance's value.

He was heartened that she overlooked this aspect of her tale, since he, indeed, knew of the prizes she recounted, for he had won tidy sums betting on several of his prospective possessions. Wisely, he kept this information entirely to himself.

Before long, they reached the stream where willows draped their branches into the fast running water. Bright green clumps of tender cress grew in the shallows. Clusters of primrose and sweet violets garnished the banks.

"Do you remember this place, where we used to fish?" Mandy asked.

Freddy nodded. "Does your father stock trout?"

"In this and several other streams. The earl will have his fillets in lemon sauce every week."

Freddy picked a bunch of violets and presented the bouquet to Mandy.

"Thank you, Freddy. These simple little violets are as beautiful as roses, just smaller. I love wildflowers. Remember when we braided that long daisy chain?"

"Yes. And I remember when we carved our initials on a tree. Perhaps one of these willows?"

"We should look." Mandy led the way past two willows to the largest of the trio.

"Aha," Freddy said. "*F. E.* and *A. F.* How many years ago did we do that?"

"Before life became complicated, I assume." She ran her fingers over the bark. "We were mere children."

"What happened, Amanda? We used to be friends."

She sighed deeply and turned away from the tree. "When you went to university you came back an arrogant fribble, full of affectations, swaggering around and bragging about how wonderful you were."

"What a harebrained ass I must have been."

She nodded fervently. "Then you went to Portugal and tried to get yourself killed. Not the sort of endeavor that made a girl feel cherished by her

76

betrothed."

Freddy couldn't help chuckling at her candor. "I have been an utter cad, haven't I?"

"Not to mention a snob, a swine, and a sap-skull." Her eyes twinkled as she spoke, and she turned her head away to hide her smile.

"I hope you will forgive my abominable behavior. I shall attempt to atone for my transgressions."

"I accept your apologies, at least provisionally." Mandy sat down on the grass and removed her half boots and stockings.

Freddy did the same, then remembered the flask. He pulled it out and showed it to Mandy.

"Perhaps you would like a little sip of this to ward off the chill of the water."

"Oh, pooh, I've done this many times."

"Then have a sip just for fun. I have it on very good authority that this is an excellent restorative."

"I hardly need restoring, but I will have a taste." Mandy assumed the flask contained wine. She took too large a mouthful and nearly choked, covering her chagrin with a smacking of her lips. "Delicious!"

Freddy laughed and, following her example, took a healthy swig, almost gasping from the sting. Whatever was in the brew Lady Clara had given him? Something mighty strong, but not bad once his breath was restored, for it warmed his gullet. He took another sip and passed the flask back to Mandy, who tipped more into her mouth and handed it back again.

She tied a cloth around her waist and pulled up her skirt to keep the hem out of the water. From his vantage point as he sat and stripped off his own stockings, Freddy could not help stealing an admiring glimpse at her shapely ankles.

His appreciation was cut short when she gave

him a pair of scissors. Side by side, they waded into the icy water. Each trimmed off several handfuls of cress and placed the tender greens in the basket, continuing until it was full.

"My feet are freezing," Mandy said as she set down the basket and wiped her hands on the grass. "I think I need a little more from your flask. The wine made my stomach feel nice and warm." She gave a little giggle.

Freddy felt rather light-headed himself, probably from leaning over to reach the cress, he thought. He handed Mandy the flask and watched her take several sips.

When she finished, he also drank again, tipping the last drops down his throat. "Are your feet warm now?"

"Not yet." She wiggled her toes in the sun.

He sat down beside her feet and took one in his hands. Rubbing gently, he felt the skin gradually warm. When he finished with her other foot, he let his fingers dance above her ankle and back down to the sole.

"Ooh, Freddy. That tickles!" Her laugh was as airy as the chirping of the birds in the meadow.

He stretched out on the grass next to her and smiled up into her face. The sun turned her chestnut hair to red-gold fire. Tenderly, he pulled her down onto the grass, where they lay side by side.

"Freddy, what is in your flask? I'm feeling decidedly giddy."

He felt like confessing. "A magic love potion."

"Oh, you fibber, you great big nodcock."

"I speak the truth." He heard himself laughing, too, in a way that sounded very much like her silly giggle.

"Where did the potion come from, if it is supposed to be magic?"

"From wizards, centuries of Celtic wizards

hiding in the forests and underground caves. Probably a whole passel of them live right under that hill."

She laughed and flung out her arms. "I've never heard anything so ridiculous in my life. The Sherald Hill Wizards. Come out, wizards, and show yourselves!"

Freddy was entranced at the beauty of her laughing face. He rolled to his side to caress her cheek.

"Are you daring the wizards to prove their magic?"

She did not move, just opened her blue eyes wide and gazed at him, suddenly quiet. He leaned toward her and brushed his lips across hers. Once, twice, three times.

"Is that the proof you seek?"

"Perhaps," she answered, her voice tremulous. The softness of his lips set her heart pounding. "I think you might try again."

This time, he touched his mouth to hers and wrapped an arm around her back, pressing her body against him. After a few breathless moments, he drew away. "I find the wizards most convincing," he murmured against her hair.

She laid her cheek on his chest and listened to the thump of his heartbeat, almost as rapid as her own.

"I do not believe in magic or wizards," she said.

"Do you believe in kisses?"

"I can ..."

He interrupted her reply with an example, delighted to feel her melting even closer.

She caressed his chin with the ball of her thumb and snuggled into his arms. "Really, Freddy," she murmured, "kisses seem very nice. Much better than I expected."

"Oh, Mandy, I'm finding them beyond expectations myself."

/=/

On the way back to the house, they paused at the wall of the kitchen garden for one more kiss. When they heard a bray of laughter from behind a shed, they broke apart quickly. But the source of the laughter was the footman, Jack. And he was much too busy kissing a housemaid to notice anyone else.

/=/

Hovering near the back stairs, Lady Clara waited for the return of Lady Amanda. She paced nervously, pacing in and out of the kitchen, the stillroom, the servants' hall, and the pantry. Her agitation spread to Cook, whose fertile imagination pictured all sorts of dreadful possibilities as she mixed her pastry. What if the potion worked too well and Mr. Frederick had ravished Lady Mandy? What if it hadn't worked at all and they fought until they fell into the water?

At last, Lady Clara retired to the front hall to escape these harrowing narratives.

"Aunt Clara," Mandy's voice called.

To Clara, Mandy's voice sounded lively and bright, much different from her sullens of the last days.

Mandy and Freddy burst out of the back hall. "Your cress is in the pantry," Mandy said, beaming from ear to ear.

Clara felt an explosion of joy in her heart as she watched Freddy grinning and clasping his hands above his head in victory.

Mandy gave Freddy an adoring smile. "Let us go up to Father. I foresee his instantaneous recovery."

/=/

Victoria Hinshaw is a fan of Jane Austen, Fanney Burney, Georgette Heyer and a host of works by contemporary Regency authors. A lover of all travel, Vicky particularly likes visits to England to search for her roots-and cruising on the Great Lakes. She is a graduate of Northwestern University and holds an M.S. in International Relations from The American University, Washington, D.C. The Voice of America, the University of Wisconsin and the Milwaukee Art Museum are former employers, but the best is her current position as free-lancer and full-time writer. Vicky is married to a broadcast executive and has two grown sons.

Did you ever balk at a well-meaning suggestion from someone? And then discover that perhaps the suggestion had merit, after all? Our hero, Julian, <u>thought</u> he wanted to choose his own bride...

An Arranged Marriage
Alexandria Shaw

Viscount Julian Hedley looked out the window of his elegant travelling chaise. The four matched chestnuts, the envy of many an aspiring whip, were sidestepping and snorting indignantly. His postilions were hard pressed calming his cattle. Where the devil were the ostlers! He wished to be in London by nightfall. He was well known at the posting-house, being a frequent visitor on the London to Bath road, and was liked for his courtesy as well as for the largesse he generously bestowed on those fortunate enough to do him a service. He was certainly not used to waiting.

The scene was chaotic. People milled in the yard, a dog ran excitedly among the horses causing them to shy and stamp the ground. Their owners lashed at the dog with their whips and tried unsuccessfully to calm their animals. Above the angry voices of the travelers, the shouts of ostlers, and the frightened neighs of horses came the squeal of pigs.

Some mischievous urchin had let four piglets loose. in the innyard. The ensuing chase to catch them was causing panic among the high-spirited horses of the visiting gentry, much to the young scoundrel's delight.

In the confusion, the ostlers were nowhere to be seen. Julian resigned himself to an annoying wait. Nothing could be done until the animals were caught.

A quiet but angry voice near his carriage made him turn. The speaker was a tall, slim young woman, not in the first blush of youth but nonetheless quite striking. She was dressed in a drab travelling costume but sported a fashionable bonnet with an upstanding poke-front.

"I will not be bargained off like some horse at an auction! It's outrageous! The shabbiest thing! I have a mind to set up my own establishment."

"My love, don't go flying up in the boughs," said her elderly companion. "You know your family are thinking only of your welfare. They wish you to be happy. A young woman should be married and have children to care for. It's only right and proper. You don't want to dwindle into an old maid, do you?"

"If I ever marry, and it seems extremely unlikely now that I am five-and-twenty, I will decide for myself. I am not on the catch for a husband, and I will not be party to an arranged marriage."

"My dear, such an advantageous match. I am given to understand he is a well favoured gentleman and quite plump in the pocket."

"In all probability he is a fashionable fribble with little in his cockloft but thoughts of gambling and his bits of muslin."

Julian felt sympathy for the unknown woman. He understood her feelings completely. He was thoroughly blue-deviled for precisely the same reason. He had no wish to be party to an arranged marriage either and was decidedly annoyed to have his hand forced. Even the numerous glasses of claret, excellent though it had been, and which he had consumed at luncheon, had done nothing to ease his displeasure.

He sprawled against the squabs of his carriage, his high-crowned beaver tossed carelessly onto the opposite seat and his usually immaculate neckcloth slightly rumpled. He cursed the current circumstance.

"Deuce take it!" He was tired of waiting, and the pounding in his head was getting worse as the noise increased around him. Where the devil were the ostlers with his change of horses? He wanted service now.

Exasperated, he looked for the landlord and saw him talking to the young woman on whom he had inadvertently eavesdropped.

Angrily, he strode across the innyard, ignoring the confusion around him. He reached the group almost at the same time as a piglet, which was being pursued by two red-faced ostlers. The piglet raced under the young woman's skirts, knocking her feet from under her. With a cry she fell backwards. Julian deftly caught her and swept her into his arms. A startled gasp escaped her. Her arms slid around his neck.

Julian found himself looking into a pair of blue eyes, smiling shyly at him. Her bonnet had been knocked askew, allowing golden curls to escape in unruly disorder. There was a faint suggestion of freckles across her nose, not enough to mar her complexion, Julian decided, but enough to give her an elfish air. She could never have been an acknowledged beauty, but she had a great deal of countenance. Not in the least in the common style! And a deuced fine figure to match! He could feel the softness of her breasts and hear her quickened breathing as he hugged her to his chest. He watched the faint blush steal across her cheeks as their gazes met and held. His own breath quickened. Julian was loath to release her. There was a quality about her which intrigued and attracted him.

"Are you hurt, my love?" Her companion's words broke the spell.

"Thank you, Sir. I'm much obliged to you, but you can release me now. I really will not fall apart if you set me down," she said, with a hint of amusement in her voice.

"I beg your pardon," said Julian, his usual smooth address deserting him for, what must have been, the first time in his life. He put her on her feet, but before he had time to introduce himself, a postilion interrupted.

"Begging your pardon, Miss, but we're ready to go now. It might be wise, Miss, if we leave immediately while the horses are quiet. The pigs haven't all been caught yet. There's still one loose somewhere."

"Excuse me, Sir. Thank you for your help. Goodbye."

Julian watched her step into a hired chaise and bowed as her carriage bowled past him. She was obviously a lady of quality, and he wondered whether he might be fortunate enough to meet her again. If only he had managed to acquire her name and direction instead of behaving like some green youth just out of the schoolroom.

The piglets were all caught and the inn returned to its usual bustle. Julian continued his journey, his thoughts still on the lady. He ordered the postilions to spring his matched bays and soon overtook the young woman's chaise. Should he stop her chaise and ask for her name and direction? No, she would surely think him jingle-brained or a trifle bosky. He glimpsed her face at the window and acknowledged her look of recognition.

An arranged marriage! His sympathy was with the young woman.

The previous evening, his grandfather, the Earl of Buxton, had suggested a similar proposal to him. The old gentleman was concerned with his heir's bachelor state. After all, at one-and-thirty it was time for Julian to think of his responsibilities, the Earl stated. If there was not one society lady who met with Julian's approval, then he wished to recommend the granddaughter of an old friend. She was no schoolroom miss with silly romantic notions but a pretty-behaved young woman who would make him an admirable countess. Furthermore, she had a considerable fortune, left to her by a spinster aunt, not that Julian had to hang out for a rich wife, of course. The last few years she had remained in the country caring for her invalid aunt. He believed that she had had one London Season but had found town living not to her liking.

More than likely she did not take, thought Julian. With a fortune to recommend her and still no serious offers she must indeed be bracket-faced. And his grandfather was seriously proposing he marry this antidote.

Her grandfather, General Hamilton, was also in favour of the match. Julian must call when he returned to town; the General was expecting him.

In vain, Julian protested he had no wish to be leg-shackled, and certainly not to some unknown lady who was, by all accounts, on the shelf. His grandfather insisted that he meet her before passing judgment and quietly rejected all Julian's excuses with reasonable arguments. He assured his heir that no one was forcing either party into a marriage if it was not to their mutual liking. In the end, Julian, much against his will, had to acquiesce.

He was still angry with himself for allowing the old Earl to coerce him into calling on the lady. Not that the old gentleman had cut up stiff! On the contrary, what had unsettled Julian was the general air of melancholy which the Earl assumed when he spoke of his heir's bachelorhood. Somehow, he contrived to make Julian feel devilish guilty. Before he died, the Earl said, making it sound as though his demise was imminent, he wished to see Julian married and setting up his nursery. He could then die happy. There had to be an heir to carry on the family name. It was his last wish.

As a noted Corinthian and one of society's most eligible bachelors, Julian was used to the many caps cast in his direction. He had enjoyed mild flirtations with some of each season's accredited beauties, but he had not yet met a young woman whom he wished to marry. He was certainly opposed to this arranged marriage, especially as he had had no say in choosing his bride. He was annoyed that the two old gentlemen had contrived to put him and the unknown lady in a highly embarrassing position.

When he married, and he had no intention of doing so just yet, he would select some young lady who would know her duty as his countess. She need not be a beauty, but she must have countenance and be well up to snuff in order to take her place by his side. The image of blue eyes glinting with amusement rose unbidden in his mind. He brushed it aside determinedly. Added to those qualities, she must have no tiresome romantic notions. She must not expect him to be forever dangling after her. He had seen too many so-called love matches turn sour, and he had no wish to add to their number.

This young woman proposed by his grandfather sounded rather bookish and more than a trifle prosy. She was probably a bluestocking and looked down her nose at anyone with some town polish. He could imagine her prim, tight little mouth and disapproving air. Not at all the bride for him! Deuce take it! Why had he agreed to meet her? The answer was simple. He loved his grandfather and had no wish to cause him concern, but he had no intention of immediately carrying out the Earl's wishes. He would visit in his own good time.

Often during the succeeding three weeks he found himself thinking of the young woman he had met at the inn and wondering who she might be. There had been no coquetry in her manner, and her expressive face seemed to hold the promise of a lively sense of humour-someone who could see the ridiculous in a situation. He contrived to ignore the strongly worded missive from the Earl, reminding him of his promise to call on General Hamilton's granddaughter.

Would he be fortunate in meeting his young woman at Lady Thurlow's ball tonight, he wondered? It was the first large event of the Season, and everybody who was anybody had been invited. It promised to be a famous squeeze.

The press of traffic worsened as he skillfully tooled his curricle and pair down the street. At the far end of the roadway, there seemed to be some situation that was causing an obstruction. He drew level with the crowd. At first glance it appeared to be a group of storekeepers and street urchins wrangling.

Suddenly he saw a parasol brandished in the air and applied liberally to a storekeeper's body. He recognised the furious lady who seemed to be keeping several irate persons at bay while trying to shield someone behind her back. The man being hit caught her parasol and snapped it in two, while another grabbed the child who clung to the lady's dress. The mood of the small crowd was ugly. Julian tossed the reins to his groom and jumped down quickly, oblivious to the shouted curses of the other drivers as he dashed in front of their vehicles. He pushed his way through the crowd to stand beside the lady.

"What the devil do you mean by accosting this lady?" he demanded.

The lady turned and smiled in relief as she recognised him. "Oh, Sir, perhaps you can make this insolent man understand. This young boy-" she pulled the begrimed youngster from behind her skirts, "took an apple from this man here, who is now demanding that the boy be handed over the Authorities. You can see that the poor child is hungry. Look how thin his little arms are. I offered to pay for the apple, but this man is the veriest monster and will not heed me."

The greengrocer appeared disconcerted by Julian's presence, but did not back down. "I be tired of these young rascals stealing my fruit. Day after day they be at it. The only way to stop them is to hand them over to the justices. Send them to the workhouse. Now hand him over! No cause for the gentry to interfere."

"Here, here." Angry mutters came from the crowd.

Julian judged it time to take a firm line. He whispered to the lady, "Take your charge and slip through the crowd while I try to keep them occupied. My curricle is waiting a few yards from here."

She cast him a grateful look, grabbed the boy's hand and allowed the crowd to press forward as she backed away. Julian gave the shopkeeper two gold coins. "I think that should be sufficient recompense. It is more than you deserve, treating a lady in such a way."

The man glared. He appeared to be shaping up for a fight, then, after a good look at Julian's muscular frame, thought better of it and took the coins muttering angrily about interfering nobs who didn't know what it was like to earn honest money. Julian breathed a sigh of relief and chose not to hear. Disappointed that there was not to be a mill the crowd dispersed, and Julian walked back to his curricle. The young woman and the boy were nowhere to be seen.

"Where did the lady go, Jason?" he asked his groom.

"She said to thank you but judged it best to take the child away immediately. She went off in a hackney, my lord."

"Deuce take it!" He still had no idea who she was. He realised it had been important to him to find her again. There had been something in her expression when she turned to him for help that had made his heart skip a beat. He admired her courage, and she had certainly looked magnificent in her fury. He remembered the feel of her breasts against his chest when he had caught her in his arms and his overwhelming desire to kiss her. He mentally shook himself. He was behaving like a lovesick youth because of a pair of speaking blue eyes. Admiration! It was only admiration that he felt for her. He wished to see her again only to assure himself that she had suffered no ill effects from the incident.

That night Julian surprised Lady Thurlow by appearing at her ball at an unfashionably early hour. He had no expectation of enjoying himself, although the champagne was always an excellent vintage, but he hoped his young lady might attend. The crush of people made it difficult for him to move freely about the rooms, and he was frequently stopped by friends or ambitious mothers drawing simpering daughters to his notice. He was polite but distant and could not help thinking that the young women he met would never have braved an angry mob to rescue a dirty little urchin.

"Julian."

"Robert, what brings you here? You're not usually one to grace such a squeeze as this."

"I've come to try my hand with the heiress, of course. Hasn't everyone?"

"Who's that?"

"Surely, you've heard. General Hamilton's granddaughter. Now don't go cutting me out. Your pockets aren't to let."

Julian laughed. "Robert, you've been saying you're out to marry an heiress ever since I've known you. It is my belief it's all a hum. Where is she anyway? What is she like?" he asked, deciding not to tell his friend of the Earl's proposal.

"I'm not sure she and I would suit," mused Robert. "A little too forthright, I'm told. However, it's a tidy little fortune she has and one could overlook a few imperfections. She's five-and-twenty, I believe, and still on the shelf. It makes one wonder."

"Point her out to me, please."

"She was talking to that woman in puce." Robert gestured vaguely across the room. "Now, I ask you, Julian, did you ever see such a ravishing creature," he said, drawing Julian's attention to a young girl who was just being presented to the host and hostess. "I really must find someone to introduce me. She is a diamond of the first water. I wonder whether she is an heiress." Robert moved away.

Damn Robert! If his friend had clearly identified Miss Hamilton, Julian could have made it a point to steer clear of her. The more he thought of his young lady, the more he wished to avoid a meeting with the General's granddaughter.

Julian looked around the room and saw a matron in a distinctive shade of puce sitting in an alcove talking to a plump, fussily dressed young woman. That must be the person Robert meant. He wove his way through the crowded ballroom toward her. Suddenly, he stopped abruptly causing several people to mutter angrily as they bumped into one another.

Over the heads of the dancers he caught a glimpse of a familiar figure. His young lady. He was sure it was! She disappeared into one of the small saloons off the ballroom. Hurriedly he pushed his way through the crowd, but when he reached the doorway of the saloon she was nowhere to be seen. A footman told him he thought she had left the ball.

Julian, feeling rather like Prince Charming running after Cinderella, saw her enter a carriage just as he reached the top to the stairs. Dash it all! He had missed her again.

He turned his attention to the heiress. She was expensively dressed in a fashionable ball gown adorned with masses of pink ribbons and rosebuds which would have better suited a débutante. She was pretty enough, and as he looked at her critically he was conscious that she probably fitted his idea of a comfortable bride. Somehow that was not enough anymore. A trim figure, unruly golden curls, and blue eyes kept intruding into his thoughts.

The sooner he presented himself at the General's house, the sooner he could put to rest any expectations of marriage between himself and

Miss Hamilton. The next day he sought out the General at his club and made a time to call the following day.

He duly presented himself at the General's house. His coat of blue superfine fitted immaculately across his wide shoulders, his neckcloth fell in intricate folds, and his Hessians were mirror polished.

He was shown into the General's study.

"Good of you to come, my boy. Sorry it's a wasted journey. That granddaughter of mine has a maggot in her head. Refused to stay in. Said she had a pressing engagement and couldn't cry off. Don't' believe a word of it! Pitching me a Banbury tale! She's piqued because I proposed this match without consulting her. Told her she had to receive you because you had something very particular to say to her. But she wouldn't hear of it. Headstrong she is, but nonetheless a good lass. But, don't worry, she'll come about, my boy. Just give her time."

Julian was considerably startled, not to mention alarmed, by this forthright speech. It stood to reason that the lady had refused to be at home when he called. From her grandfather's words he assumed she must have been led to suppose that the match had been agreed upon, and he had called to make her an offer.

"General Hamilton, I think you are mistaken. I called this morning simply to make your grand-daughter's acquaintance."

"Taking it slowly. Fix your interest, and then pop the question. Good idea. I suppose you wish me to the very devil. I've made her run shy. Isn't that so? Females take odd notions into their heads at the strangest times. You young fellows know best how to proceed. Promise I won't meddle any more.

"Just so, Sir," Julian said faintly, completely flummoxed by the General's attitude. He would give a monkey to know just what the two old gentlemen had hatched between them. "I will take my leave, Sir."

"Call again and take her by surprise. That's the best idea."

Julian was quite out of charity with his grandfather and the General. This fool suggestion had gone too far. The lady expected a marriage proposal, by all accounts, but apparently it was as distasteful to her as it was to him. He must meet Miss Hamilton and put her mind at rest. Then he must find his young lady. He needed time to think.

"Jason, drive my curricle home. I've decided to walk," he told his groom.

As he walked, his young woman's expressive face haunted his thoughts and he was conscious of looking for her in the passersby. He had to find her.

Frightened screams broke into his reverie. He glanced around quickly. A horse with a broken tilbury in tow and no driver was bolting down the street. Pedestrians pushed and shoved one another to get to safer ground, oblivious of anyone else's danger but their own.

"Help. She'll be killed."

Horrified, he saw a young serving girl caught in the path of the bolting horse. Thrusting people aside, he dashed out into the street. The horse bore down on him. He glimpsed the flaring nostrils, the frenzied glint in the eyes of the terrified animal, before he caught the girl around the waist and half lifted, half pushed her to safety, shielding her with his own body. The wildly lurching carriage veered and struck him a glancing blow on the shoulder, sending him reeling. He fell and hit his head sharply on the roadway. A glimpse of shocked faces was all he remembered before a wave of blackness engulfed him.

Distant voices seemed to be arguing near him. He wished they would go away. He felt as queer as Dick's hatband, and his head was throbbing. The noise increased. Deuce take it! What the devil was happening!

"The young gentleman's coming round," said a motherly voice. "Mercy me! It's a wonder he weren't killed. Such a brave thing to do."

Memory flooded back. The girl, was she injured? He opened his eyes and groaned as the faces bending over him swam drunkenly before his blurred vision.

"Please step back and allow him some air."

Julian recognised the voice. His young lady. She knelt beside him and rested his head in her lap. He struggled to sit up.

"Please remain still, Sir. You have suffered a nasty accident. I have sent for my carriage. It should be here soon, and I can convey you to my home, which is only a short distance from here. But in the meantime please remain still."

Julian, feeling decidedly out of sorts, was only too ready to obey her request. He closed his eyes. He had to find the energy to move, but at the moment every movement worsened the pounding in his head.

He lay still and allowed the ache in his head to dull. It was only when this lessened in severity that he was aware of soreness in his left shoulder. The tilbury. It had hit him, of course. The girl, had she escaped? He opened his eyes.

"Is the girl safe?" he asked, annoyed by the weakness in his voice.

"Perfectly safe. That was a very courageous act. Here is my carriage, Sir. Do you think you can rise if I help you?"

The throbbing in his head had eased and Julian was able to fully appreciate his position and was rather loath to relinquish it. He struggled to his feet and was glad of the firm arm around his waist steadying him. The world had an unnerving propensity to spin, and he was considerably relieved to gain the comfort of the carriage away from the interested eyes of the spectators.

Julian looked ruefully down at his clothes. Blood stained his neckcloth, and dust covered his coat which appeared to have a large rent across his left shoulder. He closed his eyes and swallowed as nausea threatened to overtake him.

"We will be at my home soon, Sir. If you give me your direction I will alert your family. But you must rest and see a doctor."

"No," Julian protested. "I don't need a doctor. But I would be obliged if you would send for my carriage. My card."

He handed her his card. Bile rose in his throat, and he closed his eyes and leant thankfully back against the squabs of the coach.

"Viscount Hedley."

Her voice sounded strange, but he was concentrating too hard on not being sick to question her reaction. Perhaps it was surprise at his title, he though vaguely.

"We are there, my lord. Let me help you."

Again he was thankful that her strong arm was there to support him. He was disappointed when she surrendered her position to a footman.

"Help the Viscount into the Yellow Saloon, Harris, and then send someone for the doctor."

"No," protested Julian, as he sank gratefully onto the sofa. He was pushed back firmly against the cushions and looked into the concerned eyes of his young lady. He had found her, and she would not escape from him again. He clasped her hand.

She smiled and did not pull away but sat beside him on the sofa.

The door of the saloon opened and two old gentlemen entered. "Julian, my boy. You're hurt," said the Earl, bending anxiously over his heir. "Here, have some brandy."

The brandy cleared his head and settled his churning stomach. "Sir, what are you doing here?" asked Julian, considerably surprised at seeing his grandfather in his young lady's house.

"I came up to town to see you, of course, but you're a sly one, my boy. You never mentioned to the General or to me that you two had already met."

Julian closed his eyes. He was still feeling a trifle out of curl, and dull-witted as well. How did his grandfather know of their meetings?"

"I think it best, Lord Buxton, if we do not tax him with talk. He has sustained a severe knock on the head and must be confused."

What the deuce did his young lady mean? He might not be in prime twig but there was nothing wrong with his reasoning power. It was his grandfather who was not making sense.

"Very sensible, my dear," said the Earl.

Julian frowned. "What do you mean, Sir?"

"Why, my boy, I mean you should have told me you already knew Miss Hamilton."

"Miss Hamilton, but..." Suddenly, everything fell into place. "You're Miss Hamilton?" He sat up quickly and immediately regretted his action. The world spun alarmingly. He was pushed back against the cushions.

"Yes, my lord, I am Clare Hamilton," she said, amusement alive in her eyes. "I am sorry I was not at home when you called, but I was annoyed at what I considered my grandfather's high-handed actions."

"I remember your sentiments. I overheard you at the posting-house where we first met."

Neither was aware that the Earl and the General had left the room.

"I fear it was cowardly of me, but when you called today I had no wish to receive you, so I invented an urgent errand and left the house although I did not go far. That is how I was on hand so quickly after your accident."

"Do you feel differently now?" Julian sat up and took both her hands.

"My lord, I hardly know what to say." Clare tried to rise from the sofa, but Julian constrained her.

"No, listen please. I have been looking for you ever since we met and to think that you were right under my nose. I do not mean to let you disappear again."

Clare made half-hearted attempts to pull her hands away but did not protest when Julian tightened his grip.

"Please. If you find our grandfathers' suggestion distasteful I will say no more on the subject. But I wish most sincerely to call on you again." Julian gazed at her and waited anxiously for her reply.

She smiled shyly at him. "I do not find their suggestion at all distasteful, my lord. And I would wish that you would call again."

Forgetting his sore shoulder and the pounding in his head, he gathered her in his arms and kissed her soundly.

They did not see the two old gentlemen quietly close the door.

/=/

Alexandria Shaw lives in Brisbane, Australia and is a speech/language pathologist by profession. She has always been fascinated by the Regency period since first reading Georgette Heyer in high school. Her favourite Regency authors are, naturally, Georgette Heyer as well as Clare Darcy and Sheila Walsh. Alexandria has dabbled in writing since early primary school and has numerous stories in many genres taking up space in her filing cabinet. Her two loves in writing are Regency romances and science fantasy for the young adult. Currently, she is working on a Regency novel and a science fantasy for twelve to fourteen year olds. This is her first story set in the Regency period to be published.

Our judges awarded this unusual, superbly-plotted story a very nearly perfect score–the highest score, in fact, of all the entries. This light-hearted correspondence between two bosom bows unveils more than just the frivolous goings-on of the <u>ton</u>. A model piece of mystery writing.

An Unusual Correspondence
Susan McDuffie

Lady Evelina Mytton to Angela Rothley
Curzon Street, April 17, 1793

My dear, you would simply not credit what has happened! I could not wait to see you, even though I am sure we shall meet at the marchioness's *soirée* tomorrow evening–no, nothing would do but that I write you *immédiatement*!

You see, I was at my mantua maker's–you know, the little French miss who would have us all believe she has just escaped the Terror. I firmly believe she is just as French as my footman, who hales from Coventry, but a French mantua maker does have a certain *cachet* that one from Dover would not, so I let "Mme Bertrand" persist in her stories of the wonderful life she lived across the Channel before that nasty Robespierre and Marat and all the rest of them–whoever is in power this week–came upon the scene. I simply listen whilst she pricks me with those dreadful dressmaker's pins–I would not tolerate it except she <u>does</u> have a way with fashion, as I am sure you agree, as I have seen you and your mama there myself.

But I digress and am <u>quite</u> sorry for it as, no doubt, Harry will return home at any moment and look for me to smile charmingly whilst he regales me with tales of the latest stupidity at White's. Although Harry is a dear, and certainly accommodating, and I can only wish that you find someone half as pleasing when you marry. So let me get straight to the point.

I was standing in the fitting room while Mme Bertrand checked the fit on a charming creation, which I hope you shall see at Lady Waterton's–a fetching little confection of silver tulle with beading–when the shop bell rang, and kept ringing such a peal that I wondered at it. Mme Bertrand excused herself, pushing her spectacles up on her nose–she is becoming quite shortsighted, and I hope her sewing does not suffer as a result–and went out into the shop to answer. I heard a man's voice, insistent, and her voice, but I could not make out the words–I would not have concerned myself with it, except one of the pins pricked me under my right arm, and as I was trying to assume a more comfortable posture I happened to move somewhat closer to the door–it was not due to any <u>attempt</u> to eavesdrop on my part, although I <u>was</u> getting frightfully bored as Mme Bertrand was gone for quite some time. So you see, it is the woman's own fault for leaving me alone. She does not even have an assistant to answer the bell!

Well–I fear I digress again–some of what I heard was <u>quite</u> intriguing and I felt you should know of it immediately, so I came home and put pen to paper despite the most fearsome megrim, which, I am sure, will grow much worse as soon as Harry comes in. Perhaps I can cry off from listening to his stories, but I fear he will not stand for it.

The speaker demanded jewels from Mme Bertrand–as if such a person has two pennies to rub together, let alone diamonds or rubies! I could not hear her reply, but she sounded frantic although her visitor remained implacable. And then Mme Bertrand returned, even paler than before, and her hands shook so as she made the final adjustments that she pricked me quite horridly–I was forced to cry out and admonish her, which only made her tremble all the more–she is such a rabbit!

The most fascinating part of the whole *affaire* is that I could have sworn I recognized the man's voice in the shop! I am convinced it was the Earl of Denby, who has been flirting with you so dreadfully these last six weeks. You know he has such a gravelly-throated voice that it is nearly unmistakable–a true *basso profundo*. And I felt it my duty to let you know, in case he turned out to be an old *roué* or gamester or some such thing. Or imagine if Mme Bertrand–for she is not so very old–is his ladybird, despite her drab plumage! It makes me laugh to think of it, as I am sure it does you. But now, at least, my megrim does seem to be improving–it was all for concern over you, my friend.

I trust I shall see you at Lady Waterton's and do feel free to write–I can always provide an attentive ear.

Yours, Evelina

/=/

Angela Rothley to Lady Evelina Mytton
Cavendish Square, April 17

My dear Evelina,
    I received your note and can assure you that all

your worries are groundless. And I have news of my own to share! The Earl of Denby, or Kenneth, as he says I must call him now, has asked me to be his wife, and I have consented.

Or rather Papa has, with alacrity. The Earl has vast estates in Yorkshire; Papa has thoroughly looked into it, so you see, I shall be a countess! And you must also see that it could not have been Denby at the mantua maker's, as he was speaking with Papa most of the morning.

Mama is beside herself, wanting to make plans already for the wedding, but the earl told Papa he only wants a very quiet ceremony. He wants me all to himself as soon as may be–and I confess, Evelina, I do not quite know what I think about that, as his voice sends shivers down my spine and I am not quite sure of what type–but Papa will agree to whatever Denby wishes, so Mama's hopes for a splendid nuptial may be thwarted. And mine as well. He has promised to return tomorrow with a betrothal gift, and I feel confident that that will go a long way towards making it up to Mama.

I do sometimes wish, Evelina, that Papa were not so title hungry. I suppose it comes of having made his fortune in India, rather than inheriting it. He blusters and swears, dares me to defy him, and says over and over again how it is Denby who should be grateful to be getting me and my 50,000 pounds, even if he is making me a countess. I know Papa has my best interests at heart, but I must confess also to you that I wish Denby were not so old. He must be all of fifty; Mama assures me such matches are unexceptionable.

Meanwhile, I shall see you at Lady Waterton's, and you shall marvel at my newly betrothed state. Is she having musicians, do you know?

Your affectionate friend, Angela

/=/

Lady Evelina Mytton to Angela Rothley
Curzon Street, Evening, April 17

Dearest Angela–
What exciting news! But what a pity there is to
be no grand wedding, as I have just the thing to
wear. I am desolated for myself, but rapturously
happy for you.

Of course I must have been in error at Mme
Bertrand's, although the voice was very like D's.
Who would think there could be two such voices
in all of London? But, as you say he was speaking
with your Papa, it could not have been D. whom I
heard at Mme Bertrand's, and there is an end to
that.

No, I do not think Lady Waterton will be having musicians, as the Marquess is quite sadly deaf.
How are your violin lessons coming along? I quite
forgot to ask. I do hope D. will let you continue,
although it may be difficult to find a fiddle master
in Yorkshire. I hope he will not spirit you away
too quickly, as the Season is just barely underway.
How fortunate you have found a match so quickly,
even if he is a *basso profundo*!
            Yours, E.

                    /=/

Angela Rothley to Lady Evelina Mytton
Cavendish Square, April 18

Dearest Evelina,
I am to be married on Sunday! Can you credit
it? I scarcely can; indeed, I do not know my own
feelings,as everything is happening so quickly. But
I shall hope to tell you all tonight.

The earl has already brought me the most exquisite necklace of diamonds and emeralds, along
with a bracelet, although we have barely broken

our fast. Papa insists I am to wear them tonight to Lady Waterton's, so you shall see them at that time.

I must fly, Mama has called for the carriage. We are off to Mme Bertrand's to see what can be done about a wedding dress in only four days.

Your loving friend, Angela

/=/

Angela Rothley to Lady Evelina Mytton
Cavendish Square, Noon, April 18

Dearest Evelina–

I fear you may have to do without your silver tulle dress tonight, and as for myself, I may have to stand up in my walking dress! You could never guess what happened, so I shall endeavor to enlighten you, although my hand shakes so that I can barely hold the pen.

We arrived at Mme Bertrand's to find the shop closed and throngs of people milling about. In fact, the crush was such that we could barely come within a half block of the shop. The tiger jumped down to investigate, and came back with disturbing news–Robbery, and Murder done! It seems some ruffian broke into Mme Bertrand's shop last night and stole what little cash she had. Apparently the poor woman heard the noise and came downstairs–her rooms are overhead, as you know–and was found, throat horridly slashed, in her own shop!

The poor woman. To escape the guillotine in France–for I do believe she was not from Dover, no matter what you may think–and die so savagely here. I thank Providence, such has not been our fate.

It does make me wonder, though, about her

visitor yesterday. Do you think you should tell a Bow Street Runner?

Mama, of course, had hysterics and is prostrate in bed with a tisane. I have a violin lesson which I do not wish to miss, despite this horror. I hope I shall be able to hold the bow–perhaps it will improve my vibrato, which is sadly deficient, so I am assured. Of course, one should not be facetious at such a shocking time–

I do hope the earl will let me continue with my music. I cannot yet bring myself to call him Kenneth. Do such intimacies come more easily after the wedding vows are spoken, dear Evelina?

Your friend, Angela

/=/

Lady Evelina Mytton to Angela Rothley
Curzon Street, After Nuncheon, April 18

Angela–

How sadly shocking for you–how <u>overcome</u> you must be! Are you sure <u>any</u> exertion is wise this afternoon, dear Angela? Your news has made me feel quite faint, and I am quite at sixes and sevens besides, wondering what on earth I shall wear tonight to Lady Waterton's–I had my heart set on the silver, and the thought of it spattered with blood–well, it is a horrid thought and I am ashamed for even thinking it, but there it is–I have no idea what I shall be wearing tonight, perhaps an old calico–I am only joking of course, but I simply cannot think what I shall wear. The green velvet, perhaps, but it is so wintry, and then I did wear it to the marchioness's a month ago.

But poor Mme Bertrand! How sad to think she shall never prick me with another pin! And her prices were always so reasonable, but I should be praying for her soul and not thinking about fashion. Harry always accuses me of being ruthlessly selfish, and I am afraid he is right.

There is no point in going to the Runners. It might be a scandal, and at any rate, I have no doubt the voice yesterday—was it only yesterday? It seems a year—was a dunning agent. I guess they shall not get their money now!

There, I am being smart again, and it does not make me feel good, in fact I feel quite evil about these nasty things I have said and think I am getting another megrim. So I shall emulate your mama, lie down for a while, have Patty bathe my temples with lavender water, and hope to see you this evening restored to full vigor and sweetness of tongue, if such is possible for me.

Yours, Evelina

/=/

Angela Rothley to Lady Evelina Mytton
Cavendish Square, April 19, mid-morning

My dearest Evelina,

I am sure your Harry would say that you were "in looks" last night, despite the absence of the silver tulle. And perhaps he did say just that, as he certainly seemed most attentive to you at Lady Waterton's. Dare I hope for such felicity from the married state?

Were not the ices superb? And the charming conceit of the Italian Grotto? I found it lovely and thought the violin music added greatly to the effect; I am glad the marchioness paid no heed to her husband's infirmity as I felt myself spirited away to a mysterious recess, like Miranda in *The Tempest*, and the music added greatly to that fantasy.

But such girlish fancies will soon be behind me. I await my wedding day with some trepidation, but Mama tells me not to be so skittish, and Papa just blusters, saying I must not be such a fool as to contemplate turning down such a match as this. And truly, I would not wish to turn down the earl; it is too late to do so now, even if I could. I know my duty to Papa, and of course I shall be a countess, as Mama keeps reminding me. Still, I could wish Denby just a bit less imposing. (I cannot bring myself to call him by his given name.) I quite shake when I am in the room with him. He seems so <u>ancient</u>, and his *basso profundo*, as you term it, makes me start and tremble. And Evelina, I must confide further–

He has kissed me. Perhaps it is my maiden shyness, for you know the only person who had kissed me up till now was your brother last Christmas holiday–but such fumbles as George's sad attempts to romance me cannot compare with a kiss from a man so worldly as the earl. But I felt no excitement, no sensual anticipation of the delights of the married state, despite your assurances that such joys exist. Rather, the pressure of his lips upon mine filled me with an unaccountable terror, and his grip on my arms left an ugly bruise. I am glad the wedding dress is to have long sleeves! Indeed, I must be skittish, as Mama assures me, and, no doubt, all will come right in the end. And the end, my dearest friend, is fast approaching. I fear I look forward to Saturday night with all the enthusiasm of an inhabitant of Newgate for the rope! There, I am being overly dramatic, and must go now to get my dress fitted. I hope you shall find time to write to me in Yorkshire–how I will miss you, dear Evelina!

　　　　Your friend, Angela
　　　　　　/=/

Lady Evelina Mytton to Angela Rothley
Curzon Street, April 19

Dearest Angela,

You need not worry about confiding your fears
to me. I am sure every bride in the world has
shared them. Fortunately for most of us, our
imaginations are far too developed (and for that,
my dear, we have only to blame Mrs. Radcliffe). I
have seen your bookshelf, you silly goose, and I
would wager that D's house in Yorkshire is not a
gloomy castle but a gem of Palladian style. In fact,
I have heard that the gardens were designed by
Brown. Not that this will necessarily make your
husband a tender lover–I speak bluntly, dear Angela, but with your well being at heart–however, I
wager the man is not the ogre you fear. Most men
are more little boys than ogres, at least Harry certainly seems so, with his cattle, so like toys, and
his adventures at the gaming table. They–here I
mean men, not their toys–are not so bad once you
get used to them. The act itself, I blush to say, can
be <u>quite pleasant</u>, and I am sure you will find it to
be so after you become accustomed to it. At least I
hope so sincerely, for Yorkshire winters can be
quite long and cold, and a considerate husband
would go a long way toward making them a bit
warmer.

So you must not worry, you silly pea-goose. I
wish I could come to your wedding, but, as you
say it is to be just family, I must stay away. And
you shall not get a chance to see the coquelicot
silk twill pelisse and bonnet which would look so
well at such an occasion!

Yours, Evelina

/=/

Angela Rothley to Lady Evelina Mytton
Cavendish Square, Evening, April 20

Dear Evelina–
　　Just a few more hours, and all will be over. I
reread your letter and try to take your words to
heart. No doubt I am a pea-goose, as you say, but
still I shake when Denby approaches me. I had my
last violin lesson this afternoon and was such a
bundle of nerves, I fear I did not play well. Señor
Valpondo was quite kind about it. The earl says he
may let me continue with the lessons if I prove all
he hopes for in a wife. What does he mean by that,
I wonder? I so wish you could come tomorrow,
but it is not to be. When next I write to you I shall
be the Countess of Denby! It is scarce to be believed!
　　　　　Your friend, Angela

/=/

Lady Evelina Mytton to the Countess of Denby
Curzon Street, April 21

My dear Angela,
　　How well I remember my own nerves before
my wedding, and how silly it all was. And I am
sure you will find the same thing, or perhaps are
discovering even now that the married state is not
so unpleasant, for I see by looking at that charming French clock on the mantle that Harry insisted
on giving me my last birthday–I told him it was
too dear, but of course I did not really mean it, for
it is really quite charming, and I am sure no one
else has one like it, no, not even the Queen, but I
digress again–at any rate, I see by looking at that
clock that the ceremony is over, the wedding
breakfast devoured, and that you in all likelihood,

are now ensconced at D's where, I am sure, he is about to devour you! And I do hope you will find much happiness in your marriage bed, my dear. As I have told you before, the whole experience can be quite enjoyable. You must simply not be missish, as your dear mama says. Think of your music, my dear, and imagine that D. is an instrument upon which you play. There, I think I put that quite nicely and poetically. Of course D. would, no doubt, prove to be a bass viol and not a violin, but I am sure some of the same techniques might apply.

In so far as what D. requires of a wife, why nothing much. Just to be pleasant, and charming, and solicitous, and concerned that he does not go hungry. For men do not like to be hungry–Harry gets quite cross when dinner is late, so do make sure meals are served promptly. If you can do that, and not complain when he comes in at all hours, and of course keep in looks, I am sure he will let your music lessons continue. In fact any wishes you have, such as for clothes–by the way, I saw the sweetest little bonnet at the milliner's, it would look quite darling on you–he will most probably grant. And you, my dear friend, possess a nature so innately charming that, I am sure, D. will find you the ideal spouse, so you need not worry on that count.

I must fly, and shall send this to D's–just think I am to address this to a countess!

Yours, E.

/=/

The Countess of Denby to Lady Evelina Mytton
Denby House, April 22

Dear Evelina,
I am writing to you as the Countess of Denby!

As he slid the heavy ring upon my finger, I shook so, it nearly fell off. He held my hand all the tighter and pushed the ring on–I have an ugly purple spot on my wrist which will not stay under my cuff, so you see, I cannot go out on a farewell call to you but must make do with this letter. And perhaps Denby does not wish me to go out on calls before we leave for Yorkshire, for he certainly seems to enjoy "the act" itself at any hour of the day, although I must confess to you that as yet I have found little pleasure in it.

I thank you for your advice in your last letter and pray all will be as you said, although, perhaps, I am not such a paragon as you seem to think. My thoughts today quite confuse me–I cry for no reason, and shake, and find it hard to smile pleasantly at my husband–I can scarcely write the word, did you see how the pen shook?

Dear Evelina, could you forward me your receipt for blemish lotion? I think I may need it, my complexion is not as flawless as it has been.

But I must fly, I hear Denby's voice; he is coming, and I must endeavor to charm him so that I may play the violin in Yorkshire.

Your friend, Angela

/=/

Lady Evelina Mytton to the Countess of Denby
Curzon Street, April 23

Dearest Angela–

I do hope by now things are more pleasant for you. Your last letter quite distressed me! But the first days of any new state can be quite trying–perhaps by now you are beginning to enjoy the bass viol a bit more! At least I sincerely hope so.

Here is the receipt for the complexion lotion–

take some elderflower water, a good quantity, along with lavender water–enough to give it a good scent–and some tincture of benzoin, and a little white arsenic. You can add tincture of wormwood if there is any discoloration, and from what you have said, it might be a wise addition. I have also added rosewater at times, for Harry likes the scent of roses. It is very helpful for skin eruptions, fleshworms, and any other discoloration you might experience. You can get all the ingredients quite easily at any apothecary's–they do have such things in Yorkshire, do they not?

Yours, E.

/=/

The Countess of Denby to Lady Evelina Mytton
Gretbridge Hall, May 15

Dear Evelina,

I am sorry not to have written for so long–it seems an age since I have been in London, although it has been only three weeks since my marriage. In truth, there is little news here. Gretbridge is an imposing pile, not of Palladian architecture but a gloomy, cold relic of grey stone, and the gardens have little to commend them. It is always cold inside, and the fireplaces smoke sadly.

Denby is busy with his horses, at least that is what he says, and I rarely see him, except at nights when, I must confess, I see all too much of him. I try to occupy myself but for some reason am seized with a dreadful *ennui* here and seem to spend most days staring out the window at this dreary landscape; already it is May, but it does not feel so outside. I fear I have let my music go sadly and seldom play now.

Thank you for the receipt. It is proving of great use, as my complexion is not what it was. The lavender gives it a pleasant smell, and the wormwood is proving of help as well.

I did beg a kitten from the dairy barn–Denby does not like pets, so I hide the sweet thing in my dressing room. It feels all too clandestine, but the little thing is dear–I wish you could see its little face, and I wish I could see yours.

Your friend, Angela, Countess of Denby

/=/

Lady Evelina Mytton to the Countess of Denby
Curzon Street, May 27

My dear, I am sorry not to have written before now, but, I confess, your last letter so depressed me that I did not quite know how to answer you. Do you suppose you could be expecting a happy addition to your household? I am told that condition quite frequently brings on such feelings of enervation.

At least I hope that is all that is the matter with you, and, of course, if that is the case I believe you would be within your rights to insist that D. leave you entirely alone, as it might upset things. It is something to consider, is it not?

But now I have news that just might set you up. Last night we dined at Lady S's, and she had musicians. You shall never guess who was there–no, do not even try to guess, for you know I shall tell you presently–of course Lady S. was looking quite lovely, despite the fact that she herself is looking forward to a happy event soon, but she has quite lost her figure, and her face is somewhat bloated. I confess I am not sorry that Harry and I have not been blessed in such a way–you may think me an unnatural woman, my dear Angela, but I must be honest with you if with no one else.

But I digress. Among the musicians was Señor Valpondo! He played quite charmingly, a little sonata of Mozart's, which quite moved me to tears as I remembered how much you loved your music, and the thought of you not playing upon your violin quite made me cry, although I did have to be careful not to muss my eyes or make them redden as we were surrounded by all the *haut ton*. I fancy, however, I cry quite prettily, and I know Harry cannot refuse me anything once I shed a few tears. But again I digress, and I certainly did not mean to, because after the performance was over I was most surprised to see Señor Valpondo approach us. He bowed so handsomely, despite his threadbare coat, and you will never believe it–the man had the temerity to ask after you! I told him you had gone to Yorkshire with your husband, and he asked for your direction–he said he wished to send you some music as a wedding gift. Well, what could I do but give it to him? Although I do think Gretbridge Hall, Yorkshire is probably not so difficult to find.

So you see, my dear, you must rouse yourself from these megrims of yours and dust off your fiddle, for you shall soon be receiving new music to play.

How is your kitten? At least, you may hope that it will get into your embroidery and spare you <u>that</u> trial!

Yours, E.

/=/

The Countess of Denby to Lady Evelina Mytton Gretbridge, June 10

Dear Evelina–

There is no chance that I am with child, and I am glad of that, at least. My kitten is back in the dairy barn–it was either that, or Denby threatened to drown it, or poison it with rat poison hidden in chicken meat. My blood ran cold to think of it, so I returned the kitten before he could do anything to the poor creature. And hid the rat poison, but he can get more, I know.

I have not received the music yet. I do hope he sends it; if you see Señor Valpondo again, will you give him my regards? Perhaps I shall endeavor to begin practicing again.

Your friend, the unhappy Countess of Denby

/=/

Lady Evelina Mytton to the Countess of Denby
Curzon Street, June 17

Dearest Angela,

I am sorry to hear that D. has been such a brute as to deny you a kitten. Still, they do say a man's home is his castle (in your case, my dear, that is altogether too true), and they do so like to have their whims obeyed. So I do think you were wise to remove the cat before D. could do anything to it, but I am sorry for your sake. I well remember as a girl when I kept a canary and it died; I was <u>desolate</u>–of course now Harry denies me nothing, and I am sure if I asked for a tyger from India he would attempt to find me one, let alone a kitten, but, of course, they make me sneeze, so that is an end to that. But you do not sneeze around cats, and so it is unfortunate that that comfort has been denied you as they do purr so sweetly, besides catching mice. But perhaps a bird? Surely D. cannot refuse you everything!

But now the news to divert you from your view of the moors. Lady S. has presented her husband with a girl, and Harry says that Lord S.

swore at White's he could not have been better pleased. Of course Harry lost money as he had wagered it would be a boy, and I believe Lord S. lost money as well, but they are rich as Croesus, so I do not think it will matter much to them. And I have not seen your papa and mama much around the *ton*. I do believe they have gone to Bath, but I am sure you must know better than I whether that is indeed true. Another person I have not seen is Señor Valpondo, so I do not know whether he sent your music or not.

I confess, the heat here seems to be making me dreadfully queasy these days, and Harry is talking about returning to the country soon, so my next letter to you may be from Oxfordshire.

> Yours, E.

/=/

The Countess of Denby to Lady Evelina Mytton Gretbridge, June 30

Evelina–

Well, it is of no matter now whether I get my music or not as Denby has broken my violin.

There are gypsies in the neighborhood and one of them played the fiddle so sweetly last night–I heard it drifting in my windows from where they were camped–it reminded me of some of the Spanish airs Señor Valpondo used to play. Denby swears he will shoot the gypsies, but perhaps he will not as he has not been feeling at all well. At least he does not bother me so much at night now.

But I worry over you, dear Evelina. How are you feeling now that you are in the country? Better, I pray.

> Your friend, Angela

/=/

Lady Evelina Mytton to the Countess of Denby
Long Crendonhall, July 3

Dearest Angela,

It appears there is a reason for my queasiness–
I am in an interesting condition, and Harry, pre-
dictably, is quite overjoyed. For myself, I am not
sure how I feel–most dreadfully sick, most of the
time. My mother has written and assures me this
will pass and proses on about <u>How Happy I Must
Be</u>–but I confess I am rather worried about losing
my figure and looking like a huge exotic elephant
of some sort and being forced to remain at home
next season while Harry amuses himself at that
beastly White's. I know I am an unnatural woman
and will probably prove an unnatural mother–and
there, Angela, is my greatest fear. I have never
thought babies particularly cute, and do not, as a
rule, coo over them the way some women do.
What if I hate my child? I must at least be honest
with you–I try to act as delighted as Harry pro-
fesses to be when we are together, but to you, my
dearest friend, I can reveal <u>all</u>.

And what of you? Can we expect similar news
from you? That, at least, would be something good
to come out of your match, for I must say, Angela,
I do not envy you your husband.

I must fly. Harry is here with a tisane, which I
doubt I shall keep down–
Yours, E.

/=/

The Countess of Denby to Lady Evelina Mytton
Gretbridge, July 7

Dear Evelina–

If I ever do become pregnant by my husband I

118

swear I shall kill my husband–and the child with him. But I am happy for *your* news and do not think you shall prove to be an unnatural mother at all. You will prove one of those doting mamas who spend all their days gushing over young Harry's (for he will be named after his papa, I do not doubt) skill at riding his pony or at childrens' card games (which is only to be expected, if he takes after his papa). If he takes after you, dearest Evelina, he will be full of observations and probably born with a quill in his hand–I do so appreciate your letters. I feel, sometimes, they are my sole link with my former life, my youth. I am no longer that young girl.

But there is society in Yorkshire, beyond that of the gypsies, who still reside in the neighborhood. We have had a visitor, rare at Gretbridge, an associate of Denby's, a Mr. Audley. He is quite young, perhaps only eighteen, wears too much powder and smells of breath pastilles and whisky. I was a bit surprised at never meeting him in London, but you must remember I was not out too long before wedding Denby. I find Audley nearly as odious as my husband; he leers at me and last night loitered in the hallway as I went to my chambers. I assumed he was lost and pointed him toward the library, where he and Denby stayed up late. I believe they argued over something, as I heard their voices later on, very loud, and then a crash. I did not go to look but discovered this morning they had broken a bust.

Your friend, Angela

/=/

Lady Evelina Mytton to the Countess of Denby
Long Crendonhall, July 15

119

Dearest Angela,

How do you manage to keep him ignorant of our correspondence? For I cannot imagine him sanctioning it, and yet I cannot imagine such a man not knowing of something under his own roof. But you were always so clever, I do not doubt you have contrived it somehow.

Harry is quite doting, which goes far to compensate for my lack of appetite. He has already picked out the pony and bought the commission for poor Harold IV. Well, I am only joking about the commission of course, but the pony already resides in the stables here. Please write soon, or better yet, flee your prison somehow and come and visit your queasy friend E.

/=/

The Countess of Denby to Lady Evelina Mytton
Gretbridge, July 25

Dear Evelina,

That terrible Audley remains here, and he and Denby spend vast quantities of time drinking together. Apparently they have some kind of business dealings; I know not what, nor do I care overmuch. I fear for the housemaids, however. I saw one with a torn dress and red eyes last night. She assured me it was nothing, but I misdoubt her.

It is the easiest thing to get my letters posted. I smuggle them out by my maid. She enjoys the romance of it all and has her own reasons to dislike Denby. Her sister was forcibly taken by him some five years ago and got with child; of course Denby would have none of her after that. He denied the infant was his and called the sister a whore. The sister died in childbed, and so poor Peggy's mother now has care of the child. Peggy escaped Denby's attentions, I believe, by being frightfully scarred with the smallpox as a child, but she has a romantic heart if not a pretty face and is happy to help me with my letters and other things. And she hates my husband, nearly as much as I do. There, I have said it at last. But I find the expression of my feelings gives scant comfort.

Your friend, Angela

/=/

Lady Evelina Mytton to the Countess of Denby
Long Crendonhall, July 31

Dear Angela,

Your last letter distressed me beyond words, and were I not so sick, and if <u>your</u> husband would permit it, I would fly to your side. However, Harry has already made inquiries and of course–you shall not be surprised here, I fear–D. quite firmly stated that he had not been well and thus visitors were unwelcome. Of course I knew this for a hum, as you told me of that unpleasant Audley's visit, and I suspected immediately that D. plans to keep you incarcerated at Gretbridge. How dreadfully Gothic the whole affair seems to me!

Yours, E.

/=/

The Countess of Denby to Lady Evelina Mytton
Gretbridge, August 15

Dear Evelina,

Please forgive me for not writing, but I have been quite busy here. It is surprising but Denby wrote Harry the truth; he has in fact been quite unwell, a gastric complaint of some sort, caused by a surfeit of rich dairy food and, perhaps, a careless cook who kept the food out too long in the summer's heat. The physician assures me it will improve, but so far it has not. In fact, Denby looks quite jaundiced.

Meanwhile, I have been quite busy with running Gretbridge. You would not guess, Evelina, how much is involved! What with the buttery, and the dairy, and of course the pasturage, and which fields are to be sown or left fallow–you would think me quite the farmer and laugh to see me out in the fields overseeing it all. But such is my daily activity, and I confess it gives me pleasure. I have had to avail myself of your complexion lotion however, as the sun has been quite strong here the past month–unusually so, the goodwives assure me.

The oddest thing happened yesterday. I was in the study–poor Denby is now confined to his room–and I found in one of the pigeonholes in his desk a packet of correspondence tied up with a ribbon, in color, remarkably like one which I had from Mme Bertrand–you do remember, the mantua maker who was murdered last spring? There was something familiar about the writing, so I looked, carefully slipping the letters out of the ribbon so I might not have to retie the bow–and they were from Mme Bertrand! So perhaps it was Denby, after all, whom you heard in her shop that day so many months ago! Just then the factor came in, so I was able to read only a little–she was quite intimate with my husband, poor thing. I pity her, but selfishly wish she were still alive to divert his attentions from me. Although he has been too ill lately to show quite the same ardor as he did; you can guess that I do not miss that!

At least that horrible Audley has left. He appeared quite concerned over Denby's health and left a tonic, which, he insists, Denby must take regularly. It smells like spirits, but Audley swears it will cure bilious humors. I have my doubts that it will work in this case but give it to my husband, along with other remedies.

And another piece of good news. I have resumed my musical lessons. There is a fiddler here who is not unlearned, surprising as it may be for you to believe that such a person could be found in the outer wastes of Yorkshire, and I was able to send for a passable violin from a shop in York, so perhaps all is not so bleak here as the moors appear.

Much as I appreciate your desire to come and visit, I think it best you remain in Oxfordshire, given your "interesting condition" and Denby's illness. It might prove catching, and that would never do!

> Your friend, Angela

/=/

Lady Evelina Mytton to the Countess of Denby
Long Crendonhall, August 25

Dearest Angela—

However did you find a violin teacher in Yorkshire? It must be one of the gypsies—I can just hear you now, playing Carpathian laments in lieu of your beloved Mozart!! I am jesting, but am pleased you have your music back as I know it gives you pleasure.

Oxfordshire is duller than a parson's sermon, so I have had sufficient leisure to be amazed by the news in your last letter. Mme Bertrand your husband's dollymop! It is not to be believed, but you say it is true, and so I must believe it. And perhaps it <u>was</u> his voice I heard in the shop that day—but no, you said D. was with your papa that morning. But dear, was he there <u>all</u> morning? It all seems a lifetime ago, and why you should remember it I cannot imagine, but it does titillate one's intellect, you must admit. And even <u>my</u> poor intellect is in need of a little exercise at times. But have you asked the *basso profundo* about this? What does he say? Of course he might beat you if he was irritated, so do not bother to ask him after all. I shall just wonder about it here in stultifying Oxfordshire while you busy yourself with corn rigs in the north.

Yours, E.

/=/

The Countess of Denby to Lady Evelina Mytton
Gretbridge, September 7

Dear Evelina,

Denby continues to feel poorly. Audley returned and left more of his "tonic"–although the physician says my husband should not drink spirits, his orders are mostly ignored. After Audley left, Denby seemed worse and could barely keep down the beef tea I spooned into his mouth.

Your friend, Angela

/=/

Lady Evelina Mytton to the Countess of Denby
Long Crendonhall, September 23

Dear Angela,

Now that I am not sick all the time, I find I quite like being in an interesting condition–well, perhaps I do not actually <u>like</u> it, but I find the state surprisingly more tolerable than I thought to find it at first. Harry caters to my every whim, and I do find that a pleasure, although his solicitude can be a bit overwhelming at times. Just yesterday he filled my boudoir with lilies, so hard to find this time of the year, but the scent made me nauseous. I thanked him, and he called me his angel, then went off to shoot. I had Patty take the lilies into the drawing room on the pretext that we would enjoy them better there.

I do hope that D. is somewhat improved.

Yours, E.

/=/

The Countess of Denby to Lady Evelina Mytton
Gretbridge Hall, October 10

Evelina–

Denby is very bad and it troubles me. I feel responsible, somehow. But the doctor again assures me it is a gastric complaint due to excessive eating of meats and dairy foods, and the bilious habits of many years. D. keeps little down, suffers burning pains in his extremities despite the cold weather, and is quite yellow. The doctor said his humors are deranged and has bled him, but it does no good.

I have spent most of the past days nursing him and gain some satisfaction from my duties. He calls me his angel (in between retching and puking)–alas I fear I am far from being an angel, but I do what I can to ease his torment.

I must fly, he is calling me–

/=/

Lady Evelina Mytton to the Countess of Denby
Curzon Street, October 17

Dearest Angela–

How terrible for you, and how exhausted you

must be with it all! I do hope you are bearing up under the strain and are not too fatigued with nursing the *basso profundo*.

Your letter chased me back to London–I suppose the total boredom of Oxfordshire made me a trifle peevish–at any rate Harry finally agreed to return to town and is now happily ensconced at White's whilst I am off to the dressmaker's. All my winter gowns will prove sadly tight this season–not that I would wear them two years in a row–and Harry will deny me nothing now. And now that my appetite has returned, it is Gunther's ices all day long. How I wish you were here and we could share an apricot one–that was your favorite as I recall!

We attended a musicale last night, and I searched for your Señor Valpondo, but he was nowhere to be found. I had thought he might like to know that you have found a violin teacher in the north after all. However, his friend the cellist (that funny Frenchman) said Señor Valpondo has not been in town for some time and he (the cellist, I mean) could not hazard a guess as to his whereabouts. Did you ever get that music he promised to send you?

I made discreet inquiries, and Mme Bertrand's murder remains unsolved. Bow Street has given up on it, I believe. I did not mention D's letters–you know me for the soul of discretion.

Well, I am off to fittings this afternoon, although how the mantua maker is supposed to accommodate something that can only be expected to aggrandize sadly during the next few months, I am at a loss to understand. If my figure is permanently lost, I swear I shall murder Harry!

Yours, E.

/=/

The Countess of Denby to Lady Evelina Mytton
Gretbridge, October 27

All is over at last. The house has that solemn
hush that one can almost palpate, the presence of
Denby's mortal husk still lies in his bedchamber,
and his spirit rests–who knows where?

His end was wretched. May God forgive me, I
wished him out of his misery at the last.

The burial is to be tomorrow, and the will shall
be read that afternoon. This estate is not entailed,
although most of his holdings are; my husband
hoped for an heir from this marriage. His hopes
brought him little joy, I fear.

I feel so odd; I cry and then laugh wildly by
turns. Peggy tells me I am fatigued and should
rest, but I find I cannot. I play my violin and ask
God to forgive me–I am <u>happy</u> he is dead, Evelina–and hope the dark clouds overhead will
bring the rain and let the tears run down my
cheeks.

    Angela

/=/

Lady Evelina Mytton to the Countess of Denby
Curzon Street, November 8

Dearest Angela–

How dreadful for you, my dear. And yet, perhaps now you will not rusticate in Yorkshire but
will rejoin us in London–after a suitable period of
mourning of course. You could be back in time for
a large portion of next season! I cannot but hope
that the delights of town might distract you in your
bereaved state.

You sounded desolate in your letter, Angela,
and must put it behind you. You did everything in

your power to ease D's suffering. Death comes to all of us, and though it is a disgusting thought to think of you or me being eaten by worms, still, there it is. My condition must be making me morbidly fanciful–I do not, as a rule, write such things! But you must cease berating yourself. There was nothing else you could have done for him.

As for asking God to forgive you–from all you have written of your husband, I find your feelings perfectly understandable. I am convinced you shall discover the benefits of widowhood as time goes by.

What did he leave you? I am all agog to know. Write quickly and tell me.

Yours, E.

/=/

The Countess of Denby to Lady Evelina Mytton
Gretbridge, November 15

Dear Evelina,

I am mistress of Gretbridge Hall, as well as having my own dowry back, and some additional settlement as well; I am sure I have Papa's marriage settlements to thank for that. Denby's heir is a third cousin, who is overwhelmed with his good fortune.

Audley showed up at the funeral services and looked quite done in over it all. He is Denby's bastard, Evelina! Which makes me even more thankful that I am not in your condition, as the thought of a son like Audley makes me shudder. Denby left him very little, however–I surmise Audley had hoped for more–and he stormed out of Gretbridge after the will was read.

I do not think the *ton* shows in my cards, as the gypsies say, at least not this year. I yearn for quiet and peace, but have troublesome dreams.

I trust you are in health and that Harold IV and you get on well together.

Your friend, Angela

/=/

Lady Evelina Mytton to the Countess of Denby
Curzon Street, November 30

Dearest Angela,

Well, at least you are well set up. I shall miss you excessively if you do not come back to town and, in fact, I cannot quite think what would keep you away from your friends and family at this time, especially with Christmas coming on and all. Although perhaps it is just my condition–I find myself quite horridly sentimental these days and cry for nothing. Harry thinks it vastly amusing, but I have developed a passion for fancywork and am currently working on a Christening gown for baby Harold–all I think of is his eminent arrival. In January, the *accoucheur* says. I do hope you will be here to greet him.

Yours, E.

/=/

The Countess of Denby to Lady Evelina Mytton
Villa Ulibarri, Isle of Capri, January 15, 1794

Dear Evelina,

I am sorry not to have written sooner, but the travel arrangements were quite consuming and the journey more fatiguing than I expected it to be. Peggy assures me it is only to be expected after all I have been through.

A curious thing has happened here. I was wearing the betrothal necklace poor Denby had given me, and an elderly Frenchwoman saw it and let out a torrent of words. It appears her daughter had a similar necklace–identical, she insisted. I explained this one had been in my husband's family, but the woman remained unconvinced. She lost her daughter in the Terror; they had somehow become separated, and she never found the girl. But I have yet to confide the most damning thing of all–this daughter's surname was Bertrand! The mother showed me a miniature of her daughter, and it is our Mme Bertrand indeed, although looking much younger and less careworn.

So I am now convinced that you did hear Denby talking with Mme Bertrand that day so long ago. And I feel certain he returned, killed her for the jewels that night, then gave them to me hours later. The thought makes my skin crawl, almost as though I felt his fingers on my flesh.

I have given the necklace–and the matching bracelet, as well–to the old woman. I want no more part of them, and this knowledge makes me happier with my decision. Perhaps now my tormenting dreams of Denby shall cease!

We saw the Marquess and Marchioness of Waterton a few days ago; as I believe they have returned to London by now, you have no doubt heard I am not here alone. Señor Valpondo is my companion, and I count myself lucky in his company. He ran me to ground in Yorkshire, and his support has kept me from madness.

Peggy stays with me also. After what we have been through together, I cannot let her leave me.

Señor Valpondo and I plan to marry next week. There is a small chapel here of the Romish faith, which is Miguel's, and I look forward to the day I shall style myself his wife in name as well as in spirit. We may return to London after the scandal dies down. Or perhaps not; I doubt that Papa would receive me if I do return. Although, as I am now once again wealthy, it might be that he would.

My thoughts are of you at this time and I hope Harold the Fourth's arrival goes smoothly.

Your friend, Angela

/=/

Lady Evelina Mytton to the Countess of Denby
Curzon Street, January 25

Dearest Angela–

I am safely delivered of Henrietta–imagine that, a girl!–and although I am sure Harry is disappointed, he bears up under the strain admirably, making cooing and gurgling noises at the little thing and acting absolutely besotted! But since Henrietta _is_ a girl, I suppose I shall have to do it all over again at some point–however, if my feelings for Henrietta are any guide, perhaps I shall not mind so very much. You would laugh to see her, her face is all red and scrunched up, and I think her quite the loveliest thing I have ever seen!

How odd that Señor Valpondo managed to find you in Yorkshire–and how _sly_ of you to keep it all to yourself for so long and not let me know of it! As a rich widow you may please yourself in these matters, so I suppose we must consider poor D's passing to have been providential! Still, I _do_ think you could have told me at least a _little_ about V. before now. I am sure it must all have been _excessively_ romantic–it certainly would have gone a long way toward diverting me whilst I languished at Long Crendonhall.

Speaking of D., just the other day I happened to mention you to Lady S. and she said that she had heard that Audley–she knew all about that sad young man and assured me he is every bit as odious as you described him–had poisoned D., thinking he would inherit more than he did. Of course I thought <u>immediately</u> of the "tonic" A. had left with D. Do you suppose he poisoned his own father and there is truth to what Lady S. related?

And what a tale you tell of Mme Bertrand's mother and your necklace! Of course, it <u>cannot</u> surprise me–I suspected D. from the first! Still, I <u>am</u> glad our little *affaire* is resolved, that Providence has punished her murderer, and that we had no need to involve Bow Street.

I must run. I hear my little Henrietta squalling and fear I do not entirely trust the nurse with her. She–the nurse that is–came with the highest recommendations, but I feel <u>I</u> know my daughter best.

Yours, E.

/=/

Señora Valpondo to Lady Evelina Mytton
Villa Ulibarri, Isle of Capri, February 23

Dearest Evelina,

All my congratulations on little Henrietta's safe arrival! I am sure she is an admirable little pet; how can she help it with you for her mama! I am sending a lace gown and blanket, which I hope you will receive before the sweet angel outgrows them.

I am distressed beyond measure to hear the gossip–and gossip it can only be, you may be sure of <u>that</u>–regarding the earl's death. The doctor stated unequivocally that Denby's death was from natural causes, and, for myself, I am <u>absolutely</u> certain that Audley did not poison him.

Of my new state I shall say little, except that I find playing upon the <u>violin</u> excessively more pleasant than playing the <u>bass viol</u> ever was. I can only wish my dreams were less troubled by disturbing nightmares, but the last year has marked me, like the Biblical Cain. Perhaps I shall never rest entirely well again.

Again, Evelina, I thank you for that receipt for face lotion. I doubt I shall need it in the future as the roses, Miguel assures me—how easy it is to call him by his given name, so unlike Denby!—have returned to my cheeks.

    Your friend, Angela

/=/

Susan McDuffie spent such vast amounts of time reading historical fiction as a child that she truly believed she had, through some cosmic mistake, been born in the wrong century. In the intervening years she has made a tentative peace with the twentieth century, just in time for the twenty-first!

An Unusual Correspondence is Susan's first mystery. She thoroughly enjoyed writing in the first person and getting to know Evelina and Angela through their letters. She has also completed two Regency romance novels and one historical romance, and is currently working on an historical mystery set in medieval Scotland.

When not writing, Susan works as a pediatric occupational therapist and previously worked as a potter. She shares her life with a Native American fetish carver and one extremely spoiled fifteen-year-old cat.

(Editor's Note: Susan's story was the highest scoring entry in the first Regency Press contest, which resulted in this book. Our second contest is currently underway, and the resulting book will be published in November, 2000. It will be titled A Regency Holiday Sampler.)

Mistaken identity, a plot device used by Shakespeare to excellent effect, also serves this story of a young miss about to make her come-out and a decidedly non-Continental dancing master. A fun story that could well be subtitled "Bella's Adventures at Almack's."

The Dancing Master
Anne Woodley

"But I can't!" The words came as if torn from the mouth of the fashionable young damsel standing stiffly in the centre of the sunny drawing room.

The other girl in the room, indeed the only other occupant, to whom this statement was directed, did not appear to put any weight either on the forceful selection of words, or on their dramatic delivery flung at her downcast head. She acknowledged the statement with the merest of shrugs and continued perusing the journal open in her lap.

A stranger wandering into that fashionable drawing room in Curzon Street might have viewed the scene as a sibling quarrel, not unexpected between two damsels so close in age, but those acquainted with the Welbecks would have been shocked. Miss Lucy Welbeck, the younger sister—demurely seated, eyes decorously downcast, quite at odds with her undoubtable vivacity—was even now reading, deafly oblivious to the arguments of

Miss Welbeck, the elder sister–well known for her malleable disposition–was expounding with considerable force.

Indeed, their mother, entering the room at this moment, was much struck, pausing on the threshold, her shocked gaze taking in the scene that would normally bring her a flush of pleasure, for her two daughters were, as she was somewhat sentimentally apt to refer to them, her "best and fairest gems." "So like me, in my youth," she would say, dabbing a wisp of lace handkerchief to the corner of her eye. Both young ladies had inherited their mother's dusky locks, celestial blue eyes and creamy complexion. Connoisseurs would hold that, while Miss Lucy had the more expressive eyes-alas, her nose was sadly upturned and her lips curled a little too sportively-it was Miss Welbeck, with her aquiline nose and moulded rosebud lips, who must be considered the beauty of the family.

"Darlings!" said their mother faintly. "Do not fight, I cannot bear it." She faltered slightly and only found her way successfully to the safety of the rose-upholstered sofa with the support of Miss Welbeck, who happily had recognised the onset of infirmity in her mother and had hurried to her parent's side to assist. Miss Lucy, who had also recognised these signs, acknowledged them with the roll of a knowing eye heavenward and resumed her reading.

"No, do not fuss," Mrs. Welbeck insisted, but accepted the cushion Miss Welbeck lodged comfortably at her back. "For you know how much I loathe having my weaknesses pandered to."

Correctly ignoring her mother's plaintive assertion, Miss Welbeck spread a soft rug across her lap, and said in urgent tones, "Mamma, tell Lucy I may not, *cannot!*"

Mrs. Welbeck, not inclined to do anything that sounded so taxing on her paltry resources of energy said faintly, "What, my dear?"

"Lucy insists that I must learn to waltz, but it is so improper, I do not know that I approve of it at all."

Lucy lifted her head and regarded her sister. "Piffle!" she remarked.

Mrs. Welbeck, now comfortably ensconced on the sofa, adjusted the rug with one trembling hand. "Don't use such vulgar expressions, my dear."

"Pooh," amended her daughter tractably, earning her a pointed look from her mother. Mrs. Welbeck, with much experience of her youngest daughter, felt it politic not to pursue a task which she knew to be impossible.

Seeing she had her esteemed parent's attention, Lucy shut the journal with a decisive snap. "You know you have vouchers for Almacks tonight, and Bella cannot waltz. She must learn, it is *imperative* for her success–for only think of the consequences, this may be everything, *everything*! You cannot wish for her to be referred to as a 'cheesemonger's daughter' merely because she cannot dance correctly, for very likely they will, you know, and you know how these reputations stick. She may arouse their censure, or perhaps worse," said Lucy with a widening of her eyes as she warmed to her topic. "She may prove a diversion for the *ton*, a laughing stock! And if she fails to take, then my come-out will be delayed and I may be on the shelf before we may ever expect Bella to receive even a halfway respectable offer. Well, I refuse to wait just because she has some fusty notion from papa about the respectability of the waltz."

It could not be said that the entire tragically asserted statement made much sense to everyone in the room, but the last part struck her sister greatly, feeling it in the nature of a personal attack. "It is not a fusty notion," Bella said hotly, "For how can one condone such a dance that requires one to be held in a gentleman's arms. Why, it sounds quite...quite..."

"Thrilling?" suggested her sister speciously.

"Improper!" Bella frowned.

Lucy, abandoning her prim pose, threw aside the journal and leapt up from the window seat to run to her mother's side. She cast herself down on a small footstool and clasped her mother's hand in a manner she felt conducive to arousing the dramatic admiration of her parent. "But it is danced *everywhere*," she cried pleadingly, and gazed up through her lashes at her mother's dazed expression. "Everywhere, and with the approval of all society! Why, if the patronesses of Almacks allow it, I do not see why we should be so superior."

"But your father..," faltered Mrs. Welbeck doubtfully.

"Is dead," said his youngest child ruthlessly. "And although it may not be filial to say it, for I loved him most devotedly, you know, yet he was a terrible old curmudgeon."

"Your want of delicacy..." uttered her mother.

Lucy pressed her advantage. "But it is true, for you know it also."

Mrs. Welbeck might have cause to admit it to herself, but never would she be found to have offered her daughters any cause to question the superiority or judgement of their late departed father. She began to say so, but her youngest daughter did not attend, clutching her mother's hand convulsively.

Miss Welbeck churlishly chose this moment to intervene on the touching scene unfolding before her. "I may not even be given permission to waltz you know. The patronesses may withhold..."

Lucy burst into laughter. "Because you are fast? I hardly think *that* likely. And should you refuse to waltz when asked, you will look like the greatest flat. But then you will look a greater flat if you assent to dance and cannot gracefully perform the steps." She appealed to her mother. "Only consider, Mama, it could blight her chances completely!"

The appeal had its desired effect on Mrs. Welbeck. "Oh dear!" She wrung her hands and gazed again on her eldest, her Bella. She held great hopes that Bella would contract a suitable match, for she was everything that was desirable in a gently bred daughter of the ton, her fragile beauty coupled with a charming and modest nature. "Perhaps Lucy is right, you know, if the patronesses do not object..." For a moment she looked undecided. "Jack must teach you!"

"Jack!" This was said simultaneously by both sisters, and they shared a look of intense understanding. Rendered speechless, since one should not speak ill of one's elder brother, Bella sat down on the plump cushions of the window seat so recently vacated by her sister.

Lucy was not restrained, as her sister was, by a refined sensibility.

"No, not Jack. That would never do!" she uttered scathingly. "Why, we would have to pinch at him merely to get him to agree and then he would do so only with the utmost reluctance. Worse, I do not think he knows a cotillion a from country dance."

Even Jack's devoted mother was forced to admit that her beloved firstborn had not the same natural grace on the dance floor that he displayed in his sporting interests, and his dedication to his sister's come-out had only been distinguished by his supreme indifference. "I expect he is far too busy," she remarked in vague accents.

"Which is *very* fortuitous for us," agreed Lucy genially.

"Well, it still leaves the problem of teaching Bella to waltz, for I do not know the steps." Mrs. Welbeck turned to her youngest daughter with widening eyes. "You do not..."

Lucy answered the unfinished question, "No, although I asked and asked Dustlow to teach me, for I felt sure *he* would know, I don't know if he does or not, for he wouldn't tell me. I was *most* put out."

Mrs. Welbeck after a gasp, and a moment's pause, attempted to render to her youngest daughter the impropriety of accosting the second footman for knowledge of intimate activities such as waltzing.

Lucy did not appear repentant, but merely laughed. "Yes, well...I have come to a much more satisfactory arrangement, I have engaged a dancing master to come this afternoon to teach Bella, for there can be no objection in that."

"You have done what!" asked Miss Welbeck in accents of horror.

Lucy was not attending, however, for at that moment she heard the harsh clatter of the knocker. "That will be him even now!" she cried, and in a swirl of sprigged muslin was gone.

Harlington was used to Miss Lucy's impetuous flights but could only admire the mien of the visitor whom he had just admitted through the front door. The gentleman's dark blond head had been bent, and he was patting his pockets distractedly, but at the slam of the upstairs door he looked up in some surprise and so was treated to the sight of Miss Lucy's hasty descent. He gave little sign of being either annoyed or entertained, but acknowledged it with the merest lift of one brow.

Miss Lucy came to a halt by Harlington and gave the visitor an engaging smile. "You are here!" she said, and then, leaning closer, she added in conspiritorial accents, "You must come immediately. It is imperative!"

The visitor protested weakly, but Miss Lucy would have none of it.

"You must come this instant, for if you do not, I may lose the advantage. All will be lost and I shall never marry!" she cried, discarding reason and unconsciously resorting to her mother's effective flair for the dramatic. "I know you do not like being rushed," she said, taking his arm and impelling him up the stairs, dismissing the butler in the same instant. "And my mother is forever telling me not to be so impetuous–well, she tells me that when she is not ailing, and she ails quite often, you know, usually when we have done something that may mean she has to exert herself. You are probably very put out, I know, for this is not the behaviour one expects of a young lady of breeding. Well, that is what I am told, although I don't imagine all young ladies of breeding wander around with books on their heads and such like, although I expect you are entirely proper and would expect that sort of conduct. Perhaps without the books on one's head, though," she said reflectively, then continued in rallying tones, "But collect I am not the one making her come out, my sister Bella is. And it is universally acknowledged that *she* is very well mannered, so there can be no objection to my behaviour."

The gentleman found himself irresistibly drawn on, even though he tried ineffectually to protest. "But really, your brother..."

Lucy interrupted him. "*He* cannot, for he will not learn himself. He says he doesn't have any use for this prancing about, although you would think he would show a little more dutiful interest, wouldn't you? However, we cannot repine but must move on." Having reached the drawing room door, she pushed it open, propelling him inexorably into the room.

"He is here, Bella! Mr. Giacomo-your dancing master."

There was a palpable silence as Mrs. Welbeck and Bella took in the visitor. He seemed a very well presented fellow, for he was above average height and had a figure that did not need to take advantage of a tailor's buckram wadding to bulk out his chest and shoulders.

Bella, who had risen from the window seat, protested gently at the rash treatment of the gentleman who seemed to be sporting a very hunted expression on his face. "I must apologise, for you must think that we are most odd, bringing you up so impulsively."

"Oh, I explained everything to Mr. Giacomo on the way up," said Lucy airily. "I said he shouldn't mind my manners, for yours are the ones which must be unexceptionable."

Mr. Giacomo spoke, but his voice sounded a little strained. "Ah, not actually Mr. Giacomo. The name is Hindley. Mr. George Hindley."

"Of course," remarked Lucy knowledgeably. "Mr. Giacomo is very busy, isn't he, and I sent the note around so very late. I expect he sent you in his place. You have no fiddle? Well, I am sure I can suitably accompany you." She had crossed to the pianoforte and was leafing intently through the music. "I do not doubt you are quite every bit as talented as Mr. Giacomo or he would not have sent you, would he?"

Lucy did not appear to need an answer to this question, which proved a happy situation, as Mr.

Hindley did not appear to have one. Mrs. Welbeck lay back with the faintest of moans, and so did not notice the very particular look that was shared by her elder daughter and the dancing master. For Miss Welbeck, in defiance of her gently-bred origins, was not demurely casting her eyes downward, but was returning Mr. Hindley's enraptured stare.

Lucy, supremely oblivious to the undercurrents in the room, continued speaking to her disinterested audience. "You are not all what I expected, you know, for you are quite well dressed." Her brother, more knowledgeable in such matters might have been able to point out to her, had she chosen to listen, that it was the hand of Scott that had fashioned the coat of such exquisite cut. In fact, there was a lot that Mr. Welbeck might have been able to tell his headstrong sister about Mr. Hindley, not the least being that men who wore coats fitted to perfection and undoubtedly eased on with the expert hand of a top valet, and who wore inexpressibles of such a perfect shade of biscuit, were unlikely to form the ranks of dancing masters. Nor were dancing masters likely to affect such admirably starched shirt points. Jack might also have pointed out that the spotlessly white neckcloth had been impeccably tied in the Mathematical, hardly a knot for the plebeian or the faint-hearted. Lucy did not, however, recognise such base details and continued her artless reflections. "I expected you to be much oilier, you know, for *all* dancing masters are."

"Vulgarity, darling," protested her mother.

"Unctuous," amended the damsel virtuously. She seated herself at the piano and ran an experimental hand over the keys. "Well?" she asked determinedly.

The demand made Miss Welbeck finally withdraw her gaze from the dancing master, and Mr. Hindley so forgot himself that he adjusted his cravat with one nervous hand.

"Do I play now, or do you teach the steps first?" asked Lucy insistently

"Ah, which dance are we practising?" inquired Mr. Hindley.

Lucy explained that it was the waltz and demonstrated her proficiency on the instrument by playing a few bars with only a dozen very trifling mistakes.

Mr. Hindley, becoming more mindful of his duty, suggested that they first establish the steps to the dance, and then they might push back some of the furniture and attempt the dance to accompaniment.

Never had two hours slipped by so quickly as when Mr. Hindley first felt that shy hand laid into his own. His arm slipped around her slender waist and it was as though Miss Welbeck melted into his arms, her angelic eyes gazing up at him as he gave her various disjointed directions. And even as he was shown out at the end of the lesson by Harlington, he left as though in a dream.

Mrs. Welbeck dabbed her eyes, "My darling Bella," she cried, "so graceful, so beautiful." The rest of her words were muffled beneath her handkerchief, although both her daughters understood them to be in a similar vein. Bella had collapsed back on the window seat. She leant her elbow on the window sill, cupping her small chin in her hand, and gazing out abstractedly.

Lucy frowned. "I did not know that dancing masters stumbled," she remarked suspiciously. "In fact, I should be surprised if he had been a dancing instructor for very long at all!"

"I thought him perfect," said Miss Welbeck, so faintly that no one else in the room heard it.

Mr. Hindley was deeply preoccupied as he walked down the street in his usual leisurely manner, but was roused by a voice hailing him.

"Jack!" he said, taking in the dark-haired young Corinthian addressing him in forceful tones.

"Dashed near had to shout in your ear, George. Brown study, is it?"

Mr. Hindley gave a startled cough. "No such thing, just had a bit to think about. Got a trifle distracted, that was all."

Jack Welbeck affectionately took his arm and fell into step beside him, "Didn't think to see you here yet, George. Thought you were staying in the country."

"I was," admitted Mr. Hindley. "Thought I'd give town a look in."

"Great bore here, you know, balls and such things, sister to bring out, too. Have to be quite firm else I'd be dragged round to a dashed sight more dull places than I already am. All the hostesses fish-faced, if you ask me, and Almack's-heard it's unspeakable!" Mr. Welbeck said amiably and continued, for Mr. Hindley's benefit, to describe it in detail. "...and no real entertainment unless you like a caper. Not for me, of course." As though realising that he had not been quite fair, he corrected his statement. "Cards of course, chicken stakes though. Oh, and orgeat!"

This final offence struck both of them forcibly, and there was silence between them for some moments.

"Well," said Mr. Welbeck, "must come and dine with us one evening. Invite you tonight, of course, but mother is taking Bella for her debut at Almack's. Bella's my sister. Making her come-out. Thought an intimate card party might be just the thing. Remember Lonsdale? Got a snug set of rooms over in Jermyn Street."

Mr. Hindley realised that it was incumbent on him to make a confession to his friend.

/=/

Mr. Welbeck incurred his mother's deepest gratitude when he walked into the drawing room an hour later with the airy assurance that he intended to accompany them to Almack's that evening. Wasn't too late, was it?

"Not at all, dearest boy," said his mother, affectionately holding out her hands and regarding him with an eye untroubled by the faults and flaws so clearly perceived by her daughters. He took her hands, kissing them and smiling down at her, impishly.

Lucy was not so easily deceived. "What are you up to? You never go to Almack's!"

Mr. Welbeck successfully avoided Lucy's suspicious look by the simple expedient of dusting an imaginary speck of dust from his jacket. "I am, tonight," he said blandly, and then, seeing Bella giving him a quizzical look, "Oh, keep a dance free, eh, Bella? Bumped into an old school friend of mine. Said you'd give him a turn on the floor. Don't mind, do you?"

Bella, who did not at all wish to prop up the wall, was pleased that she would have one guaranteed dance that night, and said fervently that she certainly would save a dance.

"Good girl," approved Mr. Welbeck. "And don't look so bracket-faced," he said indignantly to Lucy. "Can't a brother do right by his family?"

"Not when he is looking so particular about it, Jack. I believe you're kittle pitchering," replied his sceptical sister.

146

Mrs. Welbeck groped for her smelling salts.

/=/

There were some anxious moments before the Welbecks coud set out for Almack's, for Jack had not been able to find the knee breeches so strictly proscribed by the patronesses of the exclusive club. A search of the house had been undertaken, first by the valet, who resorted to tearing his hair at the vagaries of expensive laundresses who charged fortunes. Why this fact should be so relevant was lost on Harlington, who more quietly set the rest of the household staff to the search, and the breeches were located in the gentleman's wardrobe partially concealed beneath a large pile of neckcloths.

This set the party back, and more anxious moments were spent in the carriage on the way to the hallowed portals of Almack's, but the clock still wanted six minutes to eleven when the coach set them at the door.

Miss Welbeck, thought her mother, was in fine looks, for her cheeks were prettily flushed and her eyes sparkled with excitement and anticipation. She had chosen her dress well, a dark blue underskirt overlaid with lavender sarcenet. Her hair was simply dressed, the curls caught artlessly *à la sappho*. "My dear," Mrs. Welbeck breathed emotionally.

"Jig up, Bella," said her brother, vigorously taking her arm and propelling her forward. "Else you'll be late. Lock the doors on slugs, you know."

Once inside, the rapid descent on their small party by a number of young, fashionable gentlemen was enough to assure Miss Welbeck's doting mother of her daughter's success, and to arouse in Jack, fighting his way through the press on a mission to obtain a glass of orgeat for his mother and sister, the fervent hope that Bella would form an attachment. And soon.

/=/

Mr. Hindley found Jack some time later balefully regarding the dancing couples and was greeted by him with some relief. "Finally made it, did you George? Dashed dull evening. Only did this for you, you know."

Mr. Hindley, who had not been wasting his time that evening and ingratiated himself with his hostesses, had received the coveted permission he sought, and thus did not take exception to his friend's comments, but said, merely, "Bella, er, Miss Welbeck here?"

Jack nodded at a small knot of men. "She's got quite a court, it seems. Not sure she has a dance left, though I asked her to keep one back."

"Not an easy thing. Hope she took no offence at my pretence. Not deliberate, you know. Can't understand why I didn't explain at the time."

"Oh, I haven't told her," said Jack airily, ignoring George's startled look. "Thought it a great gig. Let you fuddle your way out of it yourself." He paused, watching his sister being escorted from the dance floor and grasped his friend's arm. "Come on."

Miss Welbeck was being delivered back to her complacently smiling mother as Jack dragged Mr. Hindley forward, and ruthlessly elbowed aside another hopeful young buck.

"Bella. Mother" Jack thrust George forward. "Think you know George Hindley? George—my mother, Mrs. Welbeck, and my sister, Bella. Ah, Miss Welbeck, I mean."

Mr. Hindley managed to murmur some polite

words...that he believed he had previously made their acquaintance and how delightful to see them again.

Jack grinned delightedly at his friend's discomfort, his mother's aghast expression and the high flush of colour that washed suddenly into his sister's cheeks. "Friend I was telling you about, Bella. School friend. Kept that dance for him, have you?" "Striking up for a waltz. Can dance the waltz, can you?" he added roguishly.

Mrs. Welbeck said weakly that Bella didn't have permission, but George intervened. "No, you do have permission, Miss Welbeck," he said and nodded at Lady Jersey, who was approaching them through the crowds.

Lady Jersey was wreathed in smiles. "Ah, my dear Miss Welbeck, may I make you known to Mr. Hindley, a most unexceptionable partner for a waltz."

Bella very properly cast a questioning look at her mother, who still had not regained her power of speech but was gasping helplessly. Lady Jersey linked the couple's hands together and politely hustled them away.

"Ah, what a pretty behaved daughter you have, Delia, quite charming manners and, of course, no one may say that modesty is not an admirable quality for a refined young lady. And she dances exquisitely, does she not?" Lady Jersey smiled benignly at the couple who were now slowly circling in time to the music.

Mrs. Welbeck felt able to provide only the briefest of answers to Lady Jersey's flood of comment and question. This was perfectly acceptable to Lady Jersey, who held forth in this genial way for some time, while Mrs. Welbeck watched her daughter in silent amazement. After all the protestations, Bella did not appear to be at all discommoded by making her first waltz at Almack's in the arms of a common dancing master.

Miss Welbeck could only gaze up into Mr. Hindley's eyes.

He gave an awkward cough. "I expect you wish to know why I, ah, um, what I was doing at...friend of Jack's, you see. All a mistake. No wish to offend," he stuttered.

Miss Welbeck gave his hand an encouraging squeeze. "You are not a dancing master, then?" she asked.

"No, not at all," he responded, heartened by her answer. "You might say I'm a farmer," he said, inaccurately categorising the large estate he had recently inherited.

"I am so glad," said Miss Welbeck, "for you were most ineligible, and I do not think my mother would have approved at all."

"Approved of what?" he asked with a frown.

Miss Welbeck dropped her eyes and, amazed by her own boldness, uttered "Of my forming a *tendre* for a dancing master."

Mr. Hindley missed his step, and there was a little confusion until they found the beat of the music again and resumed the dance.

"It was quite inappropriate to fall for the dancing master," he admonished.

Miss Welbeck gazed limpidly into his eyes. "I shall never do so again. I feel so comfortable dancing with you, I don't think I should ever be so comfortable with anyone else."

"I should hope so," agreed Mr. Hindley strongly, then proceeded to demonstrate the importance of his statement by gently murmuring a single word, "Bella."

Miss Welbeck, realising the powerful intelligence contained in that husky utterance, answered somewhere between a breath and a sigh, "George."

The sense of which would not have been apparent to anyone else, but appealed to the couple so much that this very conversation was then frequently repeated by them throughout the remainder of the dance.

Lady Jersey finally wafted away with an airy farewell and sly look, and saying that her dear Delia's daughter bid fair to make a promising attachment and that she would look in on them...in Curzon Street, was it? Yes, this week, tomorrow, maybe Thursday.

Mrs. Welbeck, who had been waiting in barely disguised agitation for the lady to depart, rounded furiously on her son. "Jack, what is the meaning of this?"

Idly, he twisted the stem of his glass in one hand and watched the couple. "Look good together, don't they? Dark and fair, quite pretty," he remarked indolently.

"But how did he get in here, how did...but you introduced them! Jack, how do you know him?" asked his mother, wringing her hands impotently.

"George? Harrow," he said uninformatively and sipped his orgeat with only the smallest grimace.

"He went to Harrow?" His mother asked faintly. "But he is a dancing master."

"Well," said Jack. "I expect he may wish to change his career now."

/=/

Anne Woodley is a New Zealander, who juggles her love of history with a passion for the outdoors. She worked as a public relation consultant, as a

151

journalist, and a sports feature writer for many years but has swapped that for the quieter life of bee-keeping. She writes Regency and historical stories in her spare time. (*Editor's Note: Shy, retiring [in her own words], Anne has a gorgeous web-site devoted to the Regency and also runs a Regency Ring on the web. Go to:*)

http://homepages.ihug.co.nz/~awoodley/Regency.html

The waltz was hotly-debated, hotly denounced, and enthusiastically danced in 1800s ballrooms all over Europe. The way this heroine's behavior changes after just one dance with a handsome devil—why, surely, it may well have been wicked!

The Wicked Waltz
Sheri Cobb South

From her chair against the wall, Miss Charity Cosgrove pursed her lips in disapproval at the sight of some two dozen couples whirling about Sir William Warrington's ballroom. Bonaparte might have been routed at last, but it appeared the tiny hamlet of Nettlefield was under attack from an enemy far more insidious than the Corsican Monster ever was. A waltz, was it? Miss Cosgrove could think of more fitting appellations! Such goings-on might be very well for those Londoners assembled in Vienna for the peace talks, but here in the English countryside, people had more moral fiber. Or had they? Miss Cosgrove's frown deepened as yet another couple swept by, laughing aloud as they twirled in time to the music.

Her brother the vicar had often denounced the waltz from the pulpit as the devil's dance, and events in Nettlefield had already proven him correct. Had not young Becky Rushton performed the wicked German dance with the squire's younger son at a local assembly, and had they not eloped to Gretna within a sennight?

Yes, the dance was depraved, and she intended to warn the local ladies of its dangers in an informative lecture she planned to present to the Nettlefield Auxiliary, a group of some half dozen likeminded gentlewomen, who met every fourth Tuesday in the Widow Latham's parlor to form plans for the moral edification of the village. Blotting out the offensive scene before her, she devoted her attention to planning her speech.

She had spent some ten minutes thus agreeably occupied when the entrance of a new-and quite late-arrival interrupted her thoughts. At the ballroom door, Sir William was pumping the hand of a gentleman Miss Cosgrove had never seen before-a gentleman whose elegant evening attire, immaculately tied cravat, and artfully arranged brown hair bespoke the London aristocrat. Miss Cosgrove gave a disdainful sniff and pushed her spectacles more firmly onto the bridge of her turned-up nose. No doubt this gentleman, whoever he was, was quite skilled at performing the waltz and would soon be filling the local girls' heads with romantical nonsense, as well as giving them ideas above their stations.

At that moment, the dashing stranger turned to survey the assembly through his quizzing glass, and to Miss Cosgrove it seemed as if he looked straight at her. She was struck with the fanciful notion that he had somehow read her thoughts from across the crowded room. Finding the room grown suddenly warm—due, no doubt, to Sir William's shockingly lavish use of candles—she snapped open her fan and began to ply it briskly back and forth. She had no doubt that the heat was having its inevitable effect upon her coiffure, and her hair was escaping from its severe chignon to form a halo of wispy chestnut curls about her head

Not, of course, that such a man would care how she looked, even if he deigned to notice. Thank goodness that, at the advanced age of five-and-twenty, she was considered on the shelf and need not fear being the object of unwanted attention from just such a one! She judged it a great advantage of spinsterhood to be spared the necessity of sacrificing one's principles in order to snare a man. No, she was quite content to keep house for her brother and to maintain a high standard of morality for the villagers to follow. Still, she could not resist the urge to trace the newcomer's progress as Sir William introduced him to each guest in turn, and she wondered which young lady would be the one to capture his interest for the next dance. Great, therefore, was her surprise when she found the gentleman bowing over her hand.

"Miss Cosgrove," said Sir William, "allow me to present my cousin Lord Billingsley."

Besides the advantages of birth and wealth, Lord Billingsley's forebears had conferred upon their descendant a pair of brilliant blue eyes and a countenance not unlike a piece of the Greek statuary currently in vogue. Miss Cosgrove, fully conscious of these attributes, could think of no more original reply than, "How do you do?"

"Charmed, Miss Cosgrove," he replied without releasing her hand. "Will you do me the honor of standing up with me for the next dance? It is a waltz, I believe."

"A–a waltz, my lord?"

Miss Cosgrove's principles warred with her pride at the thought that she, who usually languished against the wall, was the one with whom Lord Billingsley had chosen to dance. She smoothed the skirt of her best gown–the gray silk, which, Sir William's dashing wife often complained, gave Miss Cosgrove the air of being in perpetual half-mourning. She recalled the speech which she meant to make to the Nettlefield Auxiliary. Surely, she reasoned, it would be more effective if she could offer some personal experience of Terpsichore's tainted trap. In the interest of scientific accuracy, she could–no, she *must*–perform this dance as a sort of research, as it were.

"Yes, thank you, my lord," she replied, rising gracefully from her chair. She allowed him to lead her onto the floor, conscious of the astonished stares of the village matrons and the envious glances of their daughters, and aware of an unholy glee at having dashed so many hopes.

"Why, this is most–exhilarating," marveled Miss Cosgrove as she circled the floor in Lord Billingsley's arms.

"You sound surprised," he observed.

"I have never waltzed before," she confessed, still breathless from the movements of the dance. Or, perhaps, it was the partner rather than the performance which set her heart beating at a most alarming rate

"Never?" echoed Lord Billingsley in amazement. "I cannot imagine what all the gentlemen of Nettlefield have been about!"

"My inexperience is not due to a lack of partners, my lord, but a deliberate moral decision," Miss Cosgrove was quick to inform him. "As a general rule, I do not approve of the dance."

"Indeed?" Lord Billingsley regarded her with undisguised curiosity, as if she had just declared her disapproval of eating or breathing. "I must consider myself fortunate, indeed, to have prevailed upon you to ignore such scruples."

Miss Cosgrove's chin rose, and behind her spectacles, her gray eyes held a martial gleam. "It pleases you to mock me."

"Not at all," he assured her, although to her mind his blue eyes twinkled suspiciously. "I hope I am not such a narrow-minded fellow as to mock any opinion which does not concur with my own. I merely wondered why, disapproving of the waltz as you do, you consented to perform it."

"Like you, my lord, I try to keep an open mind," said Miss Cosgrove with, perhaps, less than perfect truth. "I am to address the ladies of the Nettlefield Auxiliary on the subject, and thought it might be beneficial to draw from personal experience." Still not entirely certain that he was not mocking her, she hurried to describe a number of the Auxiliary's charitable projects, from the school for village children to the collection and distribution of food for the needy.

"Most admirable, Miss Cosgrove," he said with a smile warmer than all of Sir William's many candles.

"I am glad you approve, my lord," she replied, permitting herself a smile which, had she but known it, erased at least five of her five-and-twenty years.

Alas, unbeknownst to Miss Cosgrove, her scientific experiment was being conducted under the censorious gaze of the Widow Latham, president of the Nettlefield Auxiliary. And so it was that on the following day, when the Auxiliary convened in her parlor, Mrs. Latham shocked the assemblage with the announcement that Miss Cosgrove's feet had slipped from the path of righteousness.

"For she, whose own brother has often cautioned us against it, danced the waltz last night with Sir William's cousin, Lord Billingsley," concluded the widow, pointing an accusing finger at Miss Cosgrove. "Do not attempt to deny it, Miss Cosgrove, for I saw you myself!"

"I hope I should never attempt to deny that

which is true," replied the accused with some asperity, rising to defend herself. "I did indeed waltz with Lord Billingsley."

Since this admission drew a startled gasp from the congregation, Miss Cosgrove felt compelled to offer an explanation.

"As I was preparing my speech on the subject, I was struck with the notion that it would be narrow-minded in the extreme to denounce the waltz strictly on hearsay. I decided to try it myself before passing final judgement."

Mrs. Latham looked unconvinced, but Miss Warrington, Sir William's spinster sister, nodded approvingly, and elderly Mrs. Biddle raised her ear trumpet and demanded loudly, "What's that you say?"

"Yes, Miss Cosgrove," agreed a new voice. "I, too, should like to hear your impressions of the waltz."

Miss Cosgrove could hardly have failed to recognize the voice, having passed much of the previous night in recalling from memory every word it had uttered. As she turned to confront the newcomer, she discovered to her chagrin that Lord Billingsley was every bit as handsome in a dark blue double-breasted coat, pale yellow pantaloons, and gleaming Hessian boots as he had been the previous night in elegant black and white evening dress.

"Lord Billingsley!" she cried, in some consternation. "What are you doing here?"

Looking about him, he blinked as if he had not, until that moment, been aware of half a dozen pairs of feminine eyes goggling at him. "Is the Auxiliary for ladies only, then? I do beg pardon."

"As no gentlemen have, as yet, honored our little group with their presence, the issue has never been addressed," conceded Mrs. Latham.

"Then I am honored, indeed, to be the first."

"I daresay gentlemen have more pressing concerns," Miss Cosgrove added hastily. "Pray do not let us keep you from yours."

"Oh, but if these good ladies have no objection, I should prefer to stay," said Lord Billingsley, taking a seat on the sofa beside his cousin, Miss Warrington. "Since you were broad-minded enough to waltz with me in spite of your scruples, Miss Cosgrove, it would seem only sporting for me to listen to your views on the subject."

Miss Cosgrove found herself trapped. What could she say? One could hardly blurt out to a gentleman that, while in his arms, she had not felt wicked at all, but alive in a way that the Nettlefield Auxiliary and all its worthy projects had never made her feel. Nor could she deny suffering any ill effects from her sojourn into sin, since to do so would make all her previous denunciations seem foolish in the extreme. As she looked from one expectant face to another, resentment flared in her breast. Surely she had been right about the waltz all along, if this was what came of dancing it! Distraught, she pressed her hands to her head and was distressed, though not surprised, to find that her chestnut curls had once again escaped confinement.

"I–I should not wish to set too much store by one dance," she stammered. "I daresay much depends upon the circumstances: the level of one's skill, for instance, or that of one's partner–"

"And what, Miss Cosgrove, was your impression of *your* partner?" Lord Billingsley inquired.

"I fear you would not find it flattering, my lord!" she retorted, goaded beyond endurance. "Nor do I believe you came merely to hear my views on the waltz. Pray state your business, sir!"

"My business, Miss Cosgrove? I confess, I had

hoped to discuss it privately with you at the conclusion of the meeting."

A collective gasp followed this announcement. Miss Warrington's eyes sparkled with anticipation, while Mrs. Latham's formidable bosom fairly heaved with indignation.

"What? What?" demanded Mrs. Biddle, aware only that she missed something of great importance.

Miss Cosgrove blushed rosily. "Just because I consented to waltz with you in a moment of weakness does not mean that I am so lost to propriety as to agree to a *tête-à-tête*!"

"Weakness, Miss Cosgrove?" echoed Lord Billingsley in some surprise. "But I was given to understand that your consent was something in the way of a scientific experiment."

"My lord, I beg you will say what you have to say, and go!" beseeched Miss Cosgrove, by this time quite crimson with embarrassment.

"I regret that I cannot," he replied, holding his ground. "What I have to say is for your ears alone."

"You can have nothing to say to me that cannot be said before witnesses!"

"As you wish." He shrugged. "Miss Cosgrove, will you do me the honor of becoming my wife?"

"*What*?"

"I just asked you to marry me," he explained helpfully.

"You cannot wish to marry me on the basis of one dance!" objected Miss Cosgrove.

"Oh, but it was no ordinary dance," he pointed out. "It was a waltz and, as you yourself have emphasized, that makes all the difference."

"Well!" cried Mrs. Latham. "I must say!"

"My lord, you cannot be serious!" protested Miss Cosgrove, all the while hoping against hope that he was.

"I assure you, I have never been more in earnest. I fear I lack your scientific objectivity, Miss Cosgrove. You see, I do set a great deal of store by one dance."

"But you–but I–that is to say, we–"

Lord Billingsley put a merciful end to this stammering speech by rising to his feet and clasping Miss Cosgrove's trembling hands in his steady ones.

"I realize you do not know me well, my dear," he said gently. "Take all the time you need before giving me an answer. Only tell me my suit is not hopeless, and with that I shall be content."

"Oh, no!" she stammered. "It is not–that is, I shall not need much time at all!"

"My dear Miss Cosgrove!" Lord Billingsley said huskily, then pulled her into his arms and kissed her soundly.

"Well!" repeated Mrs. Latham. "I really *must* say!"

"Then say it, Cordelia, and have done!" bellowed Mrs. Biddle, observing the embracing couple with interest.

Mrs. Latham rapped her gavel sharply on the table. "This meeting of the Nettlefield Auxiliary is now adjourned!"

/=/

Sheri Cobb South is a native of and lifelong resident of Alabama, and a graduate *summa cum laude* of the University of South Alabama, where she won the William R. Harvey Award for excellence in the study of English literature.

Sheri now writes full time and is the award-winning author of seven novels and numerous short stories in a variety of genres, including young adult, inspirational, and mystery.

Her first love, however, has always been the Regency, so she is delighted to announce the recent publication of her first Regency novel, The Weaver Takes a Wife, now available from PrinnyWorld Press. You may read the first chapter at **http://members.aol.com/PrinnyWrld/intro.html** or request a free brochure from the publisher by sending a self-addressed stamped envelope to PrinnyWorld Press, Dept. RS, P. O. Box 248, Saraland, AL 36571.

Two young Corinthians with too much time on their well-manicured hands find more activity than they bargained for in this hilarious tale of a wager gone wrong, a damsel in distress, and an outspoken parrot!

A Lady of Discretion
Janna Lewis

The Wager

"Preposterous!" sputtered Gregory Talbot, Earl of Chalmsley.

"Not in the least," countered Adrian Maxmillian Stoddart, Earl of Brexton. Slouched in a very worn, comfortable leather wing chair, long legs stretched toward the cheerful, crackling fire, Adrian stared at his life long friend over steepled fingers. His onyx eyes danced with mischief. It was late. He was bored. He was having a difficult time keeping his expression bland.

"Let me see if I have got the right of it." Gregory paused and sipped some brandy, firelight glinting off the cut crystal of his glass.

Had it not been for the subdued murmur of voices coming from the adjoining card room, one could almost imagine the earls of Chalmsley and Brexton lounging before the fire in the library of one of their London townhouses rather than a secluded corner of White's this rainy October evening.

"You are suggesting that any one of the *ton*, having been advised to do something they knew was not quite the thing, would nevertheless implement that advice, as long as they believed it came from someone they looked upon as an authority?"

"It is not a suggestion. It is a statement of fact." Adrian swirled the rich, fragrant amber brandy around the sides of his glass. "People do not like thinking for themselves. They prefer to be led and will follow any advice, whether it is good or bad. The 'authority' might not know any more than they do, but as long as an opinion is presented with the proper air, it is taken as gospel."

Gregory took another swallow of brandy and considered Adrian's pronouncement. He raised a blond eyebrow, then raked a careless hand through his neatly arranged hair. "That is utterly absurd. People have much more intelligence than that."

"I disagree. Members of the *ton* are so frightened of committing a *faux pas*, they would attend any advice which they believed would keep them in Society's good graces."

"Try as I might, I cannot picture anyone seeking your counsel."

"You think I would be unable to get people to follow my advice?" Adrian sniffed, feigning affront. "Dispensing advice is a matter neither of intelligence nor of common sense."

"Oh? Then what sort of matter is it?"

"I daresay the qualifications are not exacting. One need only be a busybody and evidence no squeamishness at prying into a stranger's life. And once one's reputation is established—" Adrian shrugged, a very Gallic gesture.

Gregory snorted.

"Do I detect a trace of skepticism?"

"The argument is academic, Adrian. You have no way of proving your theory. Unless–" Gregory's face lit with a wicked grin. He slanted Adrian an assessing look.

"Unless what?"

"You claim people are so desperate for guidance that they would listen to anyone presumed an authority."

"Yes." Adrian drawled. He knew Gregory was up to some rig but could not guess the direction.

"I believe I have just thought of a way in which we can put this theory of yours to the test." Gregory's countenance was positively diabolical.

"And what way is that?"

"If you are so set in this belief, then you should have no objection to posing as an 'authority' and dispensing absurd advice."

Adrian almost choked on his brandy. Gregory had adroitly pulled the rug from beneath him. He had been neatly netted. "Why, what a delightful idea." How exhilarating!

"I very much doubt that you could do it, Adrian," Gregory continued, his tone derisive. "And I am willing to wager 1,000 pounds that you will not succeed."

"Do stop your cackling, Gregory. You sound like a chicken." Adrian gave Gregory a grin that would have made the devil shiver with trepidation. "You are so willing to throw away such a sum?"

"Then you agree to the wager?"

"Yes." Adrian settled back into his chair and folded his arms across his chest. He could always depend on Gregory's quick wits to liven up a dull evening. "Would I be wrong in assuming that you have already thought up the terms for our wager?"

"Hmmm. Let me take a moment to think about that."

Gregory stared into the fire. After a short while, he sat back in his chair and crossed one knee over the other. "It would perhaps be best if you were to compose some sort of pamphlet. Then you could express your opinion on various issues. Let us say, matters of deportment, etiquette, and propriety?" He gave Adrian an impudent grin. "At the end of three months, we shall see what manner of following, if any, you have cultivated."

Adrian had kept a close eye on Gregory's face. A sixth sense told him that the esteemed Lord Chalmsley had not quite finished. "There has to be more to it than this. Out with it."

Gregory was ready with the *coup de grâce*. "You realize, of course, that doing this under your own name is absolutely out of the question. The scandal would be beyond all."

"You are suggesting that I adopt a suitable guise, a *nom de plume*?"

"Precisely. To maintain your anonymity, of course, but also to provide a dollop of spice, I should think."

"Whatever shall it be?" Adrian pondered, playing along, stroking his immaculately shaven chin.

"Ah, I have it!" Gregory bounded up from his chair. "A pseudonym that would suit admirably."

"And what would that be?"

"*A Lady of Discretion.*"

Adrian could not help himself. He laughed out loud. From the ridiculous to the sublime!

"Well?" prodded Gregory. "Do you agree to the terms? Do we have a wager?"

"Yes, Gregory." Adrian could barely get the words out, he was laughing so hard. "We have a wager."

The Outcome

Six Months Later
April

"There you are, Gregory."

Gregory Talbot sat in Adrian's study, comfortably ensconced behind his friend's Italian Renaissance mahogany desk, his chin propped on his fist. His elbows were buried in the mountain of letters covering the entirety of the desk's massive rosewood surface. He had been entertaining himself by flipping through the piles, finally selecting one of the more interesting looking letters. He was so deeply engrossed in reading it that he jumped at the sound of Adrian's voice.

With a slight lift of his chin, Adrian indicated the letter Gregory held in his hand.

"I see you have managed to find a way to pass the time. Tsk, tsk. Reading another's personal papers. Whatever would *the Lady* say?"

Gregory had the grace to blush. "It is about time, Adrian. I have been waiting for you this past half hour or more."

"I suppose you will read me the usual lecture about my success going to my head and making me too full of myself?" Adrian could not resist teasing. He smiled, remembering how easily he had won the wager they made that rainy night at White's. He had taken to dispensing advice as a duck takes to water. No one could have been more surprised than he to find that what had started as a lark had turned into a startlingly successful and unexpectedly satisfying enterprise. And so, with that in mind, Adrian had decided to continue his sham, posing as *A Lady of Discretion*. His second pamphlet and the resultant pile of letters on his desk evidenced his continued success.

167

But Adrian did not need his razor-sharp skill of reading between the lines to sense that his friend had something on his mind. He sighed. Best to open the way and let Gregory get it over with, whatever it was.

"Well, Gregory–"

"I am a trifle perturbed over you, Adrian."

Adrian groaned inwardly. Gregory looked unusually alert for this time of day. It was a bad indication. It meant that once Gregory started his beargarden jaw, he would run on for a quarter of an hour, at the very least.

Gregory picked up the second pamphlet that *A Lady* had ostensibly authored and issued just a week past. He selected a page at random and proceeded to read aloud.

"*Mama embarrasses the family with her fondness for sherry.*" He lifted his eyes from the page and pinned his stare on Adrian. "Your advice? '*Have her change over to port.*' Indeed!"

Adrian barely managed to keep his expression impassive and made do with a languid shrug.

Gregory, however, was nowhere near finished. He flipped to another page. "And this one–

> "*'I would like to purchase Lady A-'s hack, but after seeing Lady B-'s, I find I am unable to make a choice. I should very much like to have them both, but am sadly out of funds. How should I choose?'* Your response: *'Why should you settle for one or the other when you could have both by the simple expedient of bestowing your favor on a very wealthy suitor. Once you are shackled, you can have as many horses as you wish.'*"

"Oh, Adrian. For shame!" Gregory had barely gotten the words out before collapsing into peals of laughter. "And the populace is swallowing this stuff whole? No wonder your head is more than a bit swelled." He flung out an arm to emphasize his point and managed to knock some of the letters to the floor. He rose from his chair and went to pick them up, continuing his lecture. "You have turned Society on its ear. And not always in a good way, either, but we can save that for another time."

Adrian, in the meantime, not wishing to sit and wrinkle his flawless biscuit pantaloons, had perched a hip on his desk.

"Do you think you can get to the point by tea-time?"

"The point is that you are spending entirely too much time with this nonsense. I think you should get away from it for a while. You need a holiday."

Adrian brightened at that. Here was an unexpected turn.

"But while you are about it, you should think about the drivel you are dispensing. No matter what you might think, Adrian, you are not the Almighty. There is no telling what harm might come of it. You mark my words."

As Gregory bent to collect the fallen letters, the childish scrawl on one caught his eye.

"Well, well. And what do we have here?" He quickly perused the sheet. Dismay clouded his expression. "I would say you have landed in the suds with this one, my friend."

Adrian, who had absentmindedly been nodding his head to Gregory's admonitions, now gave him his full attention.

"Come now, Gregory. No need to be so dramatic."

"So say you. This proves my case. Haphazard advice can lead to all manner of ills. As we have here."

"And what sort of ills set this one apart from the rest?"

"It appears you have upset a young gentleman so very much, he had no recourse other than to write you himself." Gregory turned the sheet over and looked at the postmark. "I thought I recognized the name. I believe the lad is a country neighbor of yours."

"Indeed? Which neighbor might that be?" Adrian's curiosity was piqued.

"Lord Drummond."

Adrian tried to place the name. He finally called to mind the image of a very frail young lad, barely out of leading strings, the son of the Marquess of Adrenton, whose lands marched alongside his own in Sussex. Whatever could the lad have found to write him about?

Adrian had not been this entertained in ages. "Read it out, would you?"

Gregory cleared his throat. He rattled the paper, and began to read.

The Letter

> *At Woodlands*
> *9 April 1806*

> *To A Lady of Discretion:*
> *My cousin, Miss Zoë Langston, came to us almost a year ago, shortly after her parents died.*
> *She has not had a Season, and there is very little opportunity of her meeting an eligible parti here in the country. Oswald Galbraith, the squire's son, did recently express an interest in Cousin Zoë, but she has always said she would marry for love or not at all, and as she does not love Mr. Galbraith, she has not returned his favor.*

Cousin has assured us that she is happy here and has no wish to change her situation.

Several weeks ago, my Mama came across your pamphlet. You said a woman should make the best of what she had. It was with this advice in mind that Mama insisted Cousin Zoë make the best of it and accept Mr. Galbraith's offer.

Cousin Zoë said she would throw herself from a bridge before she follows your advice and accepts Mr. Galbraith's offer.

Mama is all up in the boughs and has threatened to put us both out of the house unless Cousin Zoë decides in Mr. Galbraith's favor. She must make her decision by the time Mama and Father return from Bath.

I like my cousin very much. She is a great gun. I support her decision in refusing Mr. Galbraith. If you knew him, I am sure you would agree also. I am very distressed at this turn of events, and I hold you to blame.

As this whole bumblebroth is your fault, I feel you should do something about it. I anxiously await your reply.

I remain,
Yr. Obedient Servant
Frederick Arthur Portnoy Langston
Viscount Drummond

At the end of Gregory's recitation, Adrian's eyebrows had risen so high they were hidden in the curls of his coal-black hair. He pursed his lips and let his breath out in a soft whistle.

"You cannot say I did not warn you."

"Here. Let me see that." Adrian took the letter from Gregory's hand and quickly read it through himself. He was aware that Gregory was watching him closely.

"This Miss Langston sounds a complete ninny with more hair than wit. Threatening to throw herself off a bridge? What a bacon-brained bit of reasoning that is."

In spite of his derisive remarks, the letter intrigued Adrian. Miss Zoë Langston was the first and only person Adrian had come across in the past six months who had refused to heed his "advice." Besides, he could not help but wonder at the kind of woman who had instilled such loyalty in a young man that he would pen so scathing a letter in her behalf.

"What do you intend to do?"

"I think it is time I visit my country seat."

"Conscience, Adrian?"

"No-were you not saying that I need a holiday? And if I just happen to catch a glimpse of this paragon so determined to become an ape-leader, well ..."

He watched in surprise as Gregory turned away and walked toward the door.

"Where are you going?"

"Home, to pack a bag."

"Whatever for?"

"I am going with you. I would not miss this for the world!"

The Rescue

Adrian set his team of perfectly matched greys into the deep bend at a spanking clip and, from the corner of his eye, saw Gregory holding his curly-brimmed beaver to his head with one hand and clinging to the side of the curricle with the other. As the vehicle dashed out of the turn, it missed the man and the boy standing in the middle of the roadway by a hair's breadth.

"Damme. Close one, that," commented Gregory in a lazy drawl. "I say, that was Drummond, was it not?"

Adrian slowed the horses to a walk, guided them to the side of the lane, and brought them to a halt. His tiger jumped down from his perch on the boot and went to the horses' heads.

It had been a while since he had seen young Lord Drummond, but even though the sickly, frail little gentleman of memory having grown into a sun-browned, lanky stripling, Adrian immediately recognized the younger and much better attired of the two men. It was without a doubt Freddie Langston, author of the letter that had brought him down to Sussex.

"Who—or should I ask *what* is that with him?" asked Gregory.

"I do not have the foggiest. Although I would venture to say he is awfully *round*..." Adrian lifted his quizzing glass and inspected the stranger from head to foot." And displays abysmal taste in coats."

"*I* should have climbed up." Freddie's distressed whisper wafted over to Adrian and Gregory.

"What the deuce?" Gregory stared at Freddie. "Odd neighbor you have, old man. Does he make a habit of talking to trees?"

Adrian had to admit that, from where they stood, it did appear that young Lord Drummond was, indeed, arguing with an oak tree. A rather large oak tree, at that.

"And have it forever on my head if you hurt yourself?"

Adrian's ears perked up at the sound of the soft, husky voice floating down from the profusion of leaves and branches.

"I believe he is talking to someone *in* the tree. A female, if I am not mistaken."

"Ah. It is all right, then."

Adrian shot Gregory a grin and began walking toward Freddie and his hitherto silent, albeit grim-faced companion under the tree.

Recognizing the earl, Freddie nodded a greeting and brought an index finger to his lips, cautioning him to silence. Then he pointed upward.

Adrian followed Freddie's pointing finger and sucked in his breath. Gregory, who had come up behind him, grabbed his arm.

"'Pon my word!" said Gregory.

And mine, thought Adrian.

A foot extended from the riot of greenery over their heads. Undeniably a female foot, judging by the white silk stocking and lavender leather slipper it wore. Small, dainty, exquisitely formed, the foot was attached to a beautifully shaped ankle, around which the apple-green satin ribbons of the slipper wound. Thick green leaves hid the rest of the limb and adjoining body.

"You have always had the damnedest luck with females, Adrian, but finding one in a tree—well, this has to top 'em all!" It was a moment before Gregory, craning his neck and twisting his torso in an effort to get a clear view through the vegetation, realized that Adrian was watching him. "I am hard pressed to see what she will look like," he stammered, color flooding his cheeks. "Are you not curious?"

Before Adrian could reply, he was even more startled to see a rather large, scarlet-feathered head pop out from beneath the leaves.

"Why, it is a parrot!" said Adrian.

"Yes, my lord. His name is Horatio," said Freddie. "This is his favorite game. He is forever setting himself free and escaping through the library window. He never goes far, and always ensures we see where he has gone off to, so that we may chase him and bring him safely home." Freddie paused and gave his round companion a sour look. "He is only in the tree now because Mr. Galbraith has upset him."

"You should leave the blasted creature to his fate," admonished Mr. Galbraith, leveling a withering glare at Freddie. "All this fretting and fussing over a silly bird."

"Allow me, my lords, to present Mr. Oswald Galbraith. The squire's son," said Freddie, his voice laced with venom.

"Ah. The infamous squire's son," Gregory said softly. "What an offensive whine the fellow has. And who would have thought him to be so round? Just look at him, Adrian. Round head. Round body. Why, even his spots are round!"

"Horatio does not like Mr. Galbraith," Freddie remarked abstractedly, keeping his attention fastened on Horatio's movement along the tree limb.

"Intelligent bird," muttered Adrian.

"There he is, Zoë, just there, a little before where you are. Do you see him?" Freddie was trying to contain his excitement but could not help hopping back and forth from foot to foot.

"Yes, Freddie, I see him," Zoë's voice hissed down at her young cousin. "Now would you *please* be still before you scare him off."

Adrian was intrigued. So, the intrepid female in the tree was Miss Langston. Zoë. The reason he had come all the way down to Sussex. Zoë, with the husky voice. Zoë with the beautiful foot connected to the most intriguing ankle he had ever seen. Zoë, who would rather drown than accept Mr. Galbraith's suit

"So that is Miss Langston," said Gregory, giving voice to Adrian's thoughts. "What a delightful creature. No lack of bottom there. 'Tis no wonder young Drummond holds her in such high regard."

"Steady on, old fellow. We have not as yet seen the daring creature."

Adrian stopped breathing as he watched the foot edge forward along the branch. It swayed gently under her weight. He prayed it would hold.

Horatio, swinging out from beneath a shelter of leaves, and using his great curved beak to lever himself onto one of the branch's offshoots, had apparently come within range. The foot disappeared into the greenery as Miss Langston lunged. All Adrian could see were two small hands closing around the feathered fugitive.

"Aaarrrwwwkkkkk! Unhand me!"

"There! You have gotten him, Zoë!" shouted Freddie as the branch groaned ominously, then gave way with a splintering crack. Miss Langston and her feathered prize plummeted toward the hard earth.

Adrian and Gregory reacted instinctively. They grasped each other's forearms to form a basket and managed to catch Miss Langston before she hit the ground. Gregory grinned and gave up his hold, leaving Adrian with his arms full of warm, sweet smelling female, sheer lavender muslin and lacy white petticoats frothing over the midnight blue cloth of his coat, collected from Weston the previous afternoon. Miss Langston's arms, in turn, were full of the largest scarlet macaw they had ever seen.

Miss Langston gasped. Adrian set her gently on her feet. Her ankle had not lied. She was a delicate, exquisitely formed creature, her head reaching to just about his shoulder. She turned and faced him. Adrian found himself looking into the clearest, the liveliest, the most intelligent, the most beautiful cloud-grey eyes he had ever seen. He was mesmerized. He was drowning in their depths.

She had no bonnet, no spencer, no gloves. Leaves and twigs stuck all about her honey-blond hair, and he could see where the rough bark had scratched the porcelain skin of one cheek. Otherwise, she and Horatio were remarkably unruffled, considering their close scrape with disaster.

She was a breath of fresh air in a stuffy, regimented Society. She was marvelous.

"*Squawk! Hello! Let go Naughty, naughty!*"

The grating, raucous cry yanked Adrian from his bemusement. "What in the world?"

Miss Langston laughed, a rich, warm sound that raised goosebumps along Adrian's spine.

"Permit me to properly introduce you to Horatio," said Miss Langston, allowing the bird to clamber onto her forearm. She gathered herself to her full height, then looked Adrian directly in the eye. "I must thank you for saving us."

"*Thank you, thank you,*" screeched Horatio in his surprisingly human-sounding voice.

"I second that, my lords," interrupted Freddie, "for had Zoë actually fallen to the ground, I would have had the devil of a time explaining to Mama how she had come to be broken." He turned to his cousin. "Dash it, Zoë, you gave me quite a turn!"

They had all forgotten about Mr. Galbraith until he came up and yanked Miss Langston by the arm and began shaking her. "Undisciplined hoyden! Bold as brass, up a tree, legs exposed for all the world and his wife to see!"

Horatio, clinging to Miss Langston's arm, hissed at Mr. Galbraith, much in the manner of an enraged cat.

Gregory, shocked almost speechless by the man's improper conduct, could only stammer, "Here, I say—I say!"

Adrian could not speak at all. Jaw clenched in

fury, he gripped Mr. Galbraith by the lapels of his coat and bodily set him aside, a good distance away from Miss Langston, who was looking a little pale, but seemed, in general, less concerned for herself than for the bird's ruffled feelings...and feathers.

Mr. Galbraith rounded on Adrian. "Better you should have let her shatter her bones on the ground. Teach her a lesson, y'know?"

"Here, now," said Gregory with a quick look at Adrian's tight face. "No cause for that, Mr. Galbraith. Least said, soonest mended, you know."

But Galbraith had not finished. He pointed an accusatory finger at Freddie. "And you! Behaving in your usual bacon-brained, slapdash way. You never should have allowed her to do it to begin with!"

Gregory caught Adrian's eye. *See what you have condemned the lady to?* was clearly written on his face.

"Do let us return to the house, Zoë. I am sure it is almost time for tea." Freddie turned to Adrian and Gregory. "You will join us, of course?"

The Squire's Son

The Gold Saloon was a beautiful room, spacious and open, and glowing in the mid-afternoon sun. It almost compensated for the effects of Mr. Galbraith's oppressive personality.

The squire's son was pompous, overbearing and crude, his air smug and patronizing. He had assumed the role of host in the absence of Freddie's parents, making it quite clear he thought himself on a par with Lords Brexton and Chalmsley.

Adrian had taken a strong dislike to the man immediately upon their first meeting, and Galbraith's actions so far had done nothing to alter this sentiment. He could feel Galbraith's eyes skittering over him, assessing him, weighing him.

Freddie, standing by the grate, Horatio looming huge on his shoulder, was saying, "We have no inkling as to where he came from, Lord Brexton. I went into the garden one day, and there he was." He glanced at his cousin, seated on a delicate Sheraton chair upholstered in lush-gold fabric. She was absorbed in conversation with Lord Chalmsley. "He does have a decided partiality to Cousin Zoë, I must say."

"Lord Chalmsley?" teased Adrian.

"Lawks, no! Horatio, of course," exclaimed Freddie, blushing a red so fiery as to rival Horatio's feathers.

Adrian also looked over at Miss Langston, whose somber face seemed better suited to a funeral, than an afternoon tea party. Adrian frowned, thinking how he had been unable to address a single remark to her without Mr. Galbraith finding some way in which to interrupt them. Galbraith's proprietary air enraged him, perhaps more than the man's earlier impropriety.

Poor Miss Langston. He sighed. Whatever had he done, consigning her fate to the likes of that boor, Galbraith. Gregory had been right to admonish him, but it was too late for recriminations now. The fat was in the fire, so to speak. But in all good conscience, he could not leave things as they were.

"Are you enjoying your stay in the country, Lord Brexton?" Mr. Galbraith's whine cut into Adrian's thoughts.

"You would have it that I am never at *The Briars*, Mr. Galbraith." Adrian was not about to explain himself to this rude upstart.

It was Gregory, softer in his dealings with people, who had overheard the exchange and spoke up. "I assure you, sir, we repair to the country on a frequent basis."

Galbraith sniggered. "Yes. A repairing lease, no doubt."

Adrian reached for the steaming cup of tea Miss Langston had poured out for him. He was tempted to toss the contents of the cup into the idiot's face.

Zoë.

Mr. Galbraith cleared his throat. "I must apologize for Miss Langston's unseemly behavior." He lowered his voice to a confidential level. "That will soon change, for I anticipate a favorable response to my offer of marriage. Once we are betrothed, I will lose no time teaching her a thing or two about propriety."

"Indeed," Adrian said coldly.

Galbraith puffed out his already full chest. He looked much like a pouter pigeon. "Miss Langston is a very fortunate young woman. She could do much worse than me, you know. I do her a great honor bestowing my attentions. A year on my Grand Tour, and a Season in London have not done me any harm." He gave Adrian a sly wink and nudged an elbow into the earl's side. "Nothing like a little town bronze to thrill and impress the fillies, eh?"

Adrian quickly looked over toward Miss Langston and Gregory. Thank goodness, they were still deep in conversation and had apparently not heard Galbraith's rude remarks. Adrian was astounded that this fool would speak so in front of Miss Langston, talking around her as if she was not even in the room.

Freddie, however, had heard Galbraith's pronouncement. "You are shading the truth, Ozzie." He turned to Adrian. "Mr. Galbraith would have you believe that his betrothal to my cousin is imminent. In truth, she has refused his suit, and I do not think she can be enjoined to change her mind."

Adrian, seeing Galbraith clench and unclench his hands, knew that his presence was the only reason Galbraith refrained from throttling Freddie.

"Adrian!" Gregory called out. "Miss Langston informs me there is to be a Spring Ball at the Assembly Room, Friday next, and has asked if we would honor them with our attendance."

Adrian knew then that Gregory, despite his conversation with Miss Langston, had been keeping one ear tuned to the other end of the room, and, sensing the animosity bubbling between the earl and the squire's son, had thrown in his question in an attempt to relieve the tension.

"I am sure their lordships will have returned to Town well before then," said Mr. Galbraith.

Adrian saw Gregory's eyebrow lift at Mr. Galbraith's presumption to answer for him and Adrian. This would never do. The encroaching toad had to be put in his place.

"Lord Chalmsley and I had planned on remaining at *The Briars* for no less than a fortnight." Adrian turned to Miss Langston and gave her a slight bow. "It would be our pleasure to attend."

The smile Miss Langston directed at him made the prospect of lingering in the country for an unexpected fortnight more than worthwhile.

The Discovery

Adrian set his travel desk on a small boxwood table, opened it, and removed the contents. It was fortunate he had had the foresight to bring his correspondence with him. In spite of the unexpected extension of his stay, he would be able to keep abreast of the flood of new letters his second pamphlet was sure to engender. He sorted through the stack until he found the particular letters he wanted, absent-mindedly dropping the others on the table. He did not bother to close the travel desk.

Before seating himself in his favorite chair, he succumbed to the unusually balmy weather and opened one of the glass-paned doors leading from his study directly onto the garden terrace. Staring out at the beautifully kept garden, Adrian caught himself thinking how he loved *The Briars*, and that he did not spend enough time here in the country. He smiled at that, wondering how much his acquaintance with Miss Langston had to do with this new-found fascination for his country house. His smile faded as his thoughts moved on to Mr. Galbraith. He must do something to extricate Miss Langston from the fix in which his offhand advice had placed her. Galbraith, puffed up with his own consequence, was quite tiresome. He did not deserve so fair a lady.

Adrian had no sooner settled comfortably in his favorite chair, than he heard the whirring of wings and, in a graceful swoop, long tail feathers flowing out behind him, Horatio glided in through the open door. Sending papers flying every which way, he landed on the table where Adrian had left his travel desk.

"Squawk! Hello! Stap me!"

A commotion in the hall immediately preceded the opening of the study door. Jimson, his butler, dashed into the room, young Lord Drummond and Miss Langston close on his heels.

"I cannot believe he made his way to *The Briars*!"

"There he is, Freddie, on the table! Oh, what a mess he has made of Lord Brexton's papers!"

They were well into the room before realizing that Adrian was there, as well.

"My lord! Please forgive the intrusion. I had no idea you were in here," apologized a red-faced Jimson.

Adrian rose." Good afternoon, Miss Langston."

"Lord Brexton—my apologies." Flustered, she joined Freddie at the table where Adrian had left his travel desk. Freddie had gotten Horatio to step up onto his arm and was trying to wrest from his beak a letter, one corner already reduced to shreds.

"Here, no need for you to do that," said Adrian, seeing Miss Langston attempting to gather the papers that Horatio's landing had scattered.

"But my lord, I have already—" She was looking down at the jumble of letters she held. Adrian reached for them, but it was too late. She had seen the salutations. Each and every one was addressed to *A Lady of Discretion*.

It was then that Adrian caught sight of the letter in Horatio's beak. As luck would have it, it was the letter Freddie had sent, the salutation and closing signature both bold and clear in the early afternoon sunlight.

Freddie also recognized the letter. He was not a stupid fellow. Adrian saw the light of comprehension dawn in his eyes.

"By Jove. Never say you are *A Lady of Discretion*? Famous!"

"What is going on here, Freddie?" asked Miss Langston.

Adrian, who had by now rescued the letter from Horatio's beak, said to Freddie, "She does not know you wrote this?"

Adrian and Freddie looked at each other,

finding themselves of a sudden unwitting allies in a complicity. Then they looked at Miss Langston.

Miss Langston was neither a slow-top nor feather-witted. She might not fully understand at present, but she was fast putting two with two and coming up with four. In but a moment their secrets would be out, and they would both be properly in the basket.

"You are looking quite splendid this morning, Miss Langston," said Gregory, choosing that moment to make his way into the study and join the party. Then, solely for Adrian's ears, he added, "I am sure Mr. Galbraith will be chomping at the bit when he sees her."

"Oh, do cut line, would you Greg?"

Gregory blithely ignored Adrian's tart remark, looked around, and asked, "Whatever is all the commotion about?"

"The cat is out of the bag, thanks to our feathered friend here," said Adrian wryly, pointing to the oblivious Horatio, who was now busy chewing at Freddie's collar.

"Gracious."

"I shall ask you again, Freddie," said Miss Langston, hands on hips, one little foot impatiently tapping the parquet floor. "Whatever are you about?"

"Perhaps I should try to explain," said Adrian, then did his best at explaining how *A Lady of Discretion* had come to exist.

"You? The Earl of Brexton? The author of this nonsense?" scorned Miss Langston, flapping the pamphlet Gregory had handed her.

Everyone started speaking at once, but it was Miss Langston's voice that rang clearest. "Of all the preposterous, mutton-headed starts! How could you do such a thing, Lord Brexton?"

Miss Langston did not wait for his reply. She

was furious, and paced the floor, raging. "Have you any idea of what you have done? And now you come down to Sussex to see the fruits of your mischief and laugh up your sleeve?" Again, she gave him no chance to answer. "It is because of you and your careless advice that I am embroiled in such a distasteful situation." She looked him up and down. "I have one suggestion, Lord Brexton."

"And what might that be, Miss Langston?"

"As you have gotten me into this tangle, my lord, you can very well get me out. If you do not agree to help me, then I shall expose your secret to the world."

Gregory, who to this point had kept his lips tightly folded, muttered something that sounded suspiciously like a muffled oath.

A slow grin curved Adrian's mouth, and he said, delightedly, "Some would call that Blackmail, Miss Langston!"

He saw Miss Langston's lips twitch. "That is precisely what it is, Lord Brexton. And you shall have until the Assembly to come up with a solution to this dilemma." She turned her nose up into the air. "Come, Freddie. Good afternoon, Lord Brexton. Lord Chalmsley." She turned on her heel and headed toward the door, giving neither gentleman a chance to reply.

"Good afternoon, Miss Langston, Freddie," Adrian called to their retreating backs.

Gregory gazed after her. "The lady is a feisty one, all right." He then took a close look at Adrian's face. "I say, old man, you are absolutely besotted with the chit."

"I believe I fell in love with her ankle in the tree. And I knew I wanted the rest of her the moment she tumbled into my arms."

"That is wonderful. What are you going to do about it?"

"I do not know. You have heard the lady claim she would marry for love or not at all. And now that she knows my secret, and that I was the cause of her dilemma with Galbraith, I am sure she must hate me for having put her in such a fix."

"She is right. You are to blame and honor bound to rescue her. Have you any ideas?"

"Not a one."

Gregory laughed.

"What are you laughing at?"

"You! The urbane, sophisticated earl afraid of being turned down by a simple country orphan." Gregory was in fits. "I have never seen you like this before."

"I have never been in love before."

"Perhaps there is a way you could win her over?"

There must be, thought Adrian.

The Announcement

"Why, you are looking even more splendid than usual!" exclaimed Gregory, running an admiring eye over Adrian's evening attire. "Superb coat. Weston? Or that new fellow in Clapham? Balleroy?"

Adrian knew the stark black superfine accentuated his dark eyes and hair. A whitework waistcoat and immaculate cravat, tied in a flawless *trône d'amour*, completed his attire. He wore no jewelry, save for a sapphire stickpin nestled in the snowy folds of his neckcloth, and a heavy gold signet ring. It would not do to have Miss Langston see him at anything less than his very best.

The past week had been an exercise in futility. She had taken a disgust of him and saw him in the worst possible light. She refused to listen to a word he said, returned his notes, and was bent on ignoring both his advice and counsel. He was truly in her black books. Perhaps his appearance tonight might distract her long enough for him to slip in under her guard and breach her defenses.

"You are quite the picture of cultivated decadence, a veritable hawk amongst pigeons," Gregory said, his eyes twinkling with mischief. "Not surprising, considering you nearly drove your man to distraction."

"Are you through with your embarrassing toadying?" Adrian's black eyes danced with laughter.

Rather than respond, Gregory lifted his quizzing glass with a languid gesture and studied the assembly room.

"Not a squeeze by any means, but an admirable turnout, nonetheless."

"Any sign of Galbraith?"

"I believe he is over there. And from the looks of things, he is up to no good. You can make book on that." Gregory tipped his quizzing glass toward the other side of the room, where the object of their interest formed the centerpoint of a knot of excitedly chattering locals.

Galbraith had elected to wear a burgundy-colored velvet coat, ruthlessly nipped in at the waist and weighed down by lavish gold brocade. His canary-yellow satin knee breeches ended in elaborately clocked stockings and mirror-polished evening slippers. He had at least a dozen fobs and seals dangling about his ample waist. The *pièce de résistance*, however, was his yellow-and-blue-striped waistcoat. Compared to Adrian's sophisticated black and Gregory's exquisitely tailored forest green, Mr. Galbraith's dress could only look garish.

Gregory said, "Are you *sure* the fellow is a

squire's son? I have seen the likes only among the Bond Street strollers."

"It appears our Mr. Galbraith fancies himself quite a cock of the walk." Adrian, grinned at his friend's offended sensibilities. "But make no mistake. He is a nasty article. Dangerous if cornered, unless I miss my guess."

"Speaking of cocks, I see our young Master Freddie. It appears he has left Horatio at home this evening. I am relieved to see he dresses much better than that Galbraith fellow."

Adrian and Gregory moved about the perimeter of the hall, deftly skirting the more energetic dancers, until they came to the small knot of people surrounding Miss Langston and Lord Drummond.

Miss Langston wore an apricot satin ballgown, the tulle overdress of which was studded with glittering stars. Tiny diamond pins were scattered throughout her simple coif. She herself could have been a shooting star, just fallen from heaven. She looked glorious. But the sparkle of her dress and gems could not match the glow of her eyes when she turned and saw their lordships approach. She took Adrian's breath away, and it was Gregory who greeted the lady first.

"Miss Langston, I must say, you are an absolute picture."

Indeed she was, thought Adrian, drinking in her beauty as he automatically went through the motions of acknowledging the introductions Freddie was making.

"You are looking especially fine this evening, Miss Langston," Adrian said at last.

She flashed him an impertinent grin. "I could say the same for you, my lord."

His heart began to soar. Not only were they the first words from her in a week, but *kind* words!

She kept her teasing smile when Freddie jumped in and unabashedly asked, "Have you figured a solution to our tangle yet, my lord?"

"Why thank you, Cousin Freddie, for sparing me having to ask that question." Her warm laughter was balm to Adrian's tormented soul.

The moment was spoiled by Mr. Galbraith, who, coming up behind Miss Langston, grabbed her by the arm. Mr. Galbraith paused only long enough to give Adrian and Gregory a smile of malicious glee, then dropped his leveler.

"My lords." His ugly grin was frightening. "You have come just in time. I have decided to announce our betrothal," he spat, and began to lead Miss Langston away.

Miss Langston's gaiety was doused. She had time only to throw Adrian an anguished look, her eyes begging him to do something, before Galbraith pulled her away.

Gregory hissed at Adrian, "I daresay, old man, if you are going to do something, now would be the time."

Adrian fought off the rage that clouded his mind and let him think only of planting Galbraith a facer. Galbraith's cavalier attitude and vicious handling of the lady–*my* lady, he corrected–was not to be tolerated. The man had finally gone his length. Gregory was right. The time had come to put period to this charade.

"Mr. Galbraith. Hold a moment."

Galbraith stopped and turned. He snapped, "Well? What is it?"

Adrian saw that they were attracting a great deal of attention, eyes slanting in their direction, waiting to see what would happen next.

"Might I suggest we find a more private spot for this conversation? One of the card rooms, perhaps?"

"Suit yerself."

The entire party–Adrian and Gregory, Miss Langston, Freddie and Galbraith, made their way to one of the smaller rooms set aside for cards or conversation. Once inside, Adrian firmly closed the door on the inquisitive crowd outside.

Adrian was quite angry but refused to allow the cur to provoke his temper any further. He drew a deep breath then remarked, as calmly as though he were commenting only on the fine weather. "You cannot announce your betrothal to Miss Langston."

"What?" exclaimed a startled Galbraith. Then, recovering from his surprise, said, "And why is that?"

"Miss Langston is already engaged."

Miss Langston's jaw dropped, as did Gregory's and Freddie's. Dumbfounded, they stared at Adrian.

"Impossible," said Mr. Galbraith.

"Not in the least," threw in Gregory, as much in the dark as everyone else, but standing by his friend nonetheless.

Hearing Adrian's claim supported by Gregory gave Galbraith pause, but only for a moment. He sneered. "And just whom does she claim to be engaged to?"

"She does not claim to be engaged," Adrian said coldly. "She is engaged."

"You still have not told me to whom."

"I do not see how it could be any business of yours, but very well. Miss Langston has done me the honor of accepting my proposal. We were betrothed Sunday last."

Adrian was as startled as anyone else when he realized what he had said. But looking at Miss Langston, he knew he had only spoken aloud what was in his heart. The thought of Galbraith putting

his hands on his lady had shaken him to the core
and made him face the truth about his feelings.

Adrian opened the door, pausing a moment to
listen to the music floating down the hall. He took
Miss Langston's arm and looped it through his
own. "I would very much like to dance the remainder of this waltz with my *fiancée*, Mr. Galbraith. If you will excuse us, I believe we have
said all there is to say."

The party exited into the hallway, leaving Mr.
Galbraith standing in the card room, his mouth
hanging open.

"My lord–please!" begged Miss Langston, trying to free herself from Adrian's clasp, but he held
her firm.

"We shall have this dance, Miss Langston, and
that is that." They took to the floor, all eyes on
them.

Adrian held her close and whispered in her ear.
"I shall call on you at *Woodlands* tomorrow, Miss
Langston. Please be so good as to expect me."

The music ended. The Earl of Brexton and
Miss Langston stood in the middle of the hall.
Miss Langston appeared stricken. She had been
pale before, but was now whiter than Adrian's cravat.

Freddie joined them, and Miss Langston said
to her cousin, "please call for the carriage. I wish
to leave."

Adrian bowed. "Until tomorrow, Miss Langston."

Horatio Saves The Day

"Oh, Horatio. Whatever am I to do?"
"*Aaarrrwwwwkkk*!"
Adrian stopped as the sounds of Miss Lang-

ston's voice and Horatio's answering screech came through the open door of the library. He had ridden over to *Woodlands* this morning, determined to talk some sense into Miss Langston. He loved her. He wanted the engagement to stand. He somehow had to find a way to convince her to accept his suit.

Quietly, he approached the doorway and looked in. He could see her standing near the terrace door, her back to Horatio's perch. She had not heard him, and he took full advantage; stayed where he was and blatantly eavesdropped.

"What am I to do? I cannot let him leave without speaking to him, but I do not know what to say."

"*Leave?*"

"Yes, my feathered friend. Lord Brexton is leaving. He is coming here this morning to tell me so." Adrian heard Miss Langston choke back a sob. "And I cannot bear the thought."

"*Cannot bear it...cannot bear it.*"

"No, I cannot bear it. I so wished that he would find he cares for me and wants me with him. I do not want to end the betrothal. I wish it could be real." Miss Langston was sobbing in earnest. "I do not know what to do."

Adrian was about to rush to Miss Langston and gather her in his arms when, to his stunned amazement, he distinctly heard the parrot say, "*If you love him, then you must tell him.*"

"What?" Miss Langston turned and stared at the parrot.

From his vantagepoint in the doorway, Adrian had no trouble seeing the gaudy bird bobbing up and down and scuttling back and forth from one end of the perch to the other.

"What did you say?"

" *If you love him, then you must tell him,*" repeated the bird, each word clear and distinct.

"I cannot believe this!"

"What is so hard to believe?" asked Adrian. "'If you love him, then you must wed him'."

Miss Langston spun and saw him standing in the doorway. Her lovely grey eyes widened, and a soft pink blush suffused her tear-stained cheeks.

"Lord Brexton!" she stammered. "How long have you been standing there? And Horatio said 'tell,' not 'wed.'" Her hand flew up to her mouth. "Oh dear!"

Adrian felt amazingly lighthearted of a sudden and had to struggle to keep his expression somber. Rather than answer Miss Langston's question, he posed one of his own.

"Why do you wish for the betrothal to continue?"

Miss Langston's cheeks grew even pinker, and she looked down at the floor, finding sudden fascination in the intricate patterns of the pastel carpeting.

Adrian could not find it in his heart to continue teasing her in such a manner. He crossed the room and stood before her, so close that her nose was almost pressed against his midnight-blue coat. Still she would not raise her head. Adrian put his hand beneath her chin and lifted it gently but firmly, forcing her to meet his eyes.

She obviously was mortified that he had heard her every word. He knew she had never been so embarrassed. He knew she wanted to run from the room. He took her small, trembling hands in his large ones.

"Be so good as to answer my question, Miss Langston. "Why do you wish for the betrothal to go on?"

Miss Langston pulled one of her hands free of Adrian's grasp and swiped at the tears sliding down her cheeks. He pulled his handkerchief from its pocket and handed it to her.

"Thank you, my lord," she sniffed, blotting the tears away.

"As you were saying, Miss Langston?"

"I do not wish to end the betrothal because–" She took a deep breath, drew herself up to her full height, swallowed, and pinned him with her direct gaze. "Because I have fallen in love with you."

"That is indeed an intriguing development."

Jarred by this nonchalant acknowledgement of her most intimate confession, she blurted, "Oh? How so?"

"I also have been thinking."

"Yes, my lord?"

"I, too, would prefer not to end the betrothal."

It took a moment for Adrian's words to sink in. She looked at him, afraid to ask the next question but unable to stop herself from doing so.

"Why would that be, my lord?"

"I think it is because I find that I have fallen in love with you."

"Truly?"

He pulled her into his arms. "Would you like my advice?"

"No, my lord. I have refused your advice to this point and mean to go on as I have started out. You must understand that I will never follow your advice." Despite the tears, her eyes had started to sparkle like stars.

"That is fair. But if you do not wish to heed my advice, then, perhaps, you would follow Horatio's?"

"How so, my lord?"

"You heard him suggest that you marry me."

"No, my lord. He did not say 'wed.' He distinctly said 'tell' you."

Adrian sighed in mock resignation. "As you

wish, Miss Langston. But you must admit that he is an unusually intelligent bird."

"Indeed I do, my lord."

"Then perhaps we should ask him his opinion. Do you not agree?"

"That is an excellent suggestion, my lord."

"Horatio, would you think Miss Langston wise to accept my offer?" Adrian tossed back over his shoulder.

"*Wed him! Wed him!*" rang out loud and clear, leaving no doubt as to what words he spoke.

"Horatio is unusually vehement in his sentiments," Miss Langston said, her great surprise evident in voice and expression.

She quickly regained her poise. "You are quite correct, Lord Brexton. Horatio is an unusually intelligent bird." She gave Adrian a smile that sent sunshine into the very depths of his soul. "And if Horatio feels that wedding you is the thing to do, then, I believe, I shall have to listen to Horatio."

And with this pronouncement, Miss Langston, gave herself over to Lord Brexton's kiss.

Neither Lord Brexton nor Miss Langston noticed when, a few moments later, Gregory and Freddie quit their hiding place behind the drapes by Horatio's perch and slipped out the open terrace door.

/=/

Janna Lewis, a native New Yorker, was born in the Bronx on Friday the 13th and lived most of her life on Long Island. Her primary passion is writing, but her other interests, which include a love for the English Regency period, antique clothing, costume, researching her family's history, and "playing pretend" have taken a unique turn, coming together in a very unusual manner-

participation in various Regency re-enactment events in the United States and England, in the guise of an alter-ego persona, the inimitable "Duchess of Penmore."

Janna's previous work includes a serial historical romance, a children's picture book, a number of re-enactment- and costume-related articles, and a motley assortment of short horror stories, the most recent of which have appeared in the on-line e-zine at www.peridotbooks.com.

She is a member of Romance Writers of America and its Regency Subchapter, *the Beau Monde*; the Society of London Ladies; and the Costume Society of America.

Yes, even the Regency had its share of shaggy-dog stories. This is one of them.

The Visit
Steven R. Abaroa

"*I want to know now!*" yelled the King, sending servants running for shelter as he began to throw his lunch in all directions.

The king, His Royal Highness, George the Fourth, was in the midst of planning his royal visit to Scotland. This was to be the first royal visit in 171 years. The writer, Sir Walter Scott, had worked so hard to get the king to come, and George wanted everything to be perfect, right down to the wearing of the Scottish kilt.

"But, Your Majesty," started his personal secretary, "Scots never tell anyone what they wear under their kilts."

"I don't care. There must be a Scotsman who is willing to tell, if for a bag of gold," said the King. "Search the grounds and find us a Scot!" he yelled as he stormed out of the dining room.

George Augustus Frederick of the House of Hanover, the Fourth King George of England and Scotland, was pompous, conceited, ill-mannered and just plain hard to get-along-with. Even his legal wife, the late Caroline of Brunswick, had found life to be much more pleasant away from George than near him.

However, not everyone felt the same way. The arts flourished under him and even the Scots gained a new identity with him on the throne. When the whole nation was in shock because he seriously hurt his leg, the Scots, on the other hand, were proud because he hurt it while dancing the Highland Fling.

Since it seemed to him that his Scottish subjects were about the only ones who cared for him, he wanted to please them by wearing a kilt. The kilt had long been outlawed by the English Government. Under George's rule the wearing of the kilt was gaining new life. And if the King wore a kilt, the old law would die a sure death. The truth of the matter was, the only fondness the Scots had for the King stemmed from the fact that he did change the kilt law.

/=/

Young Edward Forbes had been employed at the castle for five years. Being the fifth son, Edward felt that there was little for him in his village of Queensferry near Edinburgh. His dream was to buy a farm near Loch Katharine, close to the quaint village of Aberfoyle. He dreamed of the quiet valleys and the green hills, where his sheep would feed while he would play the pipes all day.

But, unless he had money, it would only be a dream. He had worked hard for his royal master, but he was no closer to his dreams.

He had just finished his task with the last of the evening meal dishes when Thomas Rowley, a half-Scot who liked to think that he created Scotland himself, was bragging how he turned down the offer to reveal what Scotsmen wore under their kilts. "That is one mystery Old George will never get from me," Rowley boasted.

By now the offer was two bags of gold and two fine work horses from the royal stables. Edward was caught up in his dreams again as he imagined the land he could buy with all that gold. But how could he betray his ancestors and reveal the greatest secret in Scotland?

Two nights later, Edward found himself filling in for a sick table servant. The King was still ranting on about the kilt. Edward knew that it was forbidden for a servant to speak to a king, but he so much wanted to leave service and live the life of a freeman that, with all the courage he could muster, he spoke up.

"With your permission, Sire," he started, as all eyes in the room fell on him. Feeling very uncomfortable, he went on. "I'll tell you, Sire."

The King eyed him at length. Edward thought that one way or another he would get his wish of leaving the King's service. The King turned to his Secretary and said, "We shall meet this young man in an hour."

Word spread quickly in the castle among every Scotsman that the secret of the kilt would be revealed. As Edward began his walk to the King's study, they all lined the hallway to stare at the man who would betray them. Edward felt guilty as he headed for the door, but he had thought about this and knew what he must do.

The King was reading papers of State when Edward arrived. George had ordered his secretary to leave them alone, but Edward stood by the door for a full fifteen minutes before he was acknowledged.

"Well, young man," the King started. "We

know what a risk you are taking, but we are pleased that you would share this great secret with us. To ease your mind, you will receive one thousand pounds for this information."

Edward almost fainted. One thousand pounds was more money than one could expect to make in a lifetime. His face was flushed, but he gathered all his wits and thanked the King.

"Very well, young man, what is the secret?" asked George .

"Nothing," answered Edward.

The King looked angry. "I have heard that many times, but I am asking as a king. I do not care what a poor Scotsman might wear. By God, man, there are Englishmen who wear the same under their finery. What would a king wear? *I want to know*!"

"Oh, I beg your pardon, Sire. I had no idea." Edward had to think quickly. "It is true that royalty must always dress in their finest, therefore, Sire, I will share a secret that was told me by my grandfather, who learned it from his grandfather."

Edward looked around; so did the King. He then bent low to the King's ear and began to whisper. At first, the King looked surprised, but then he smiled.

"You have done well, my son," said the King. "May you find happiness in your reward."

King George then placed a small case in Edward's hands and signaled for him to leave. Once Edward had gone, George called for his servants. "We have work to do!" he shouted. "I told you, Scotsmen will talk for money."

/=/

The summer of 1824 would be grand for Sir Walter Scott. He had longed for this visit by his king. It was August 14 when the royal yacht sailed into Edinburgh. A royal dinner was scheduled for that night. Sir Walter enjoyed himself immensely throughout the evening. He even slipped away with one of the King's drinking glasses so that he would have something to remember the evening. Sir Walter, however, forgot about the glass and sat on it, breaking it on the cab ride home that night. All would be forgotten the next day, when King George rode into the city as the first reigning king in 171 years to visit Scotland.

All morning the streets leading to the main square in the new part of the city of Edinburgh filled with people hoping to get a glimpse of the King. Word spread rapidly when the royal coach left the docks. The King was all smiles as the procession made its way up the hill to the sea of Scots waiting for him. Many had wondered what the King would be wearing. Rumor of a kilt had floated around the city for months. Even Sir Walter was unsure.

At last the carriage stopped at the main square. City and state officals waited to greet their King. As George stood up in his carriage, there was a low murmur from the crowd: The king was wearing a kilt. The plaid was the royal Stewart plaid. The people and the officials seemed pleased-until the door to the carriage was opened and the full figure of the King was seen. The crowd was shocked into silence, for, as the King stepped out, the people saw that he was also wearing very pink tights under his kilt. The crowd began to mutter, but the King was not worried. Edward had told him the people might act like this, because they would be surprised and pleased to see that their king knew the secret of the kilt.

/=/

Far away from the scene in Edinburgh, in a cottage not far from Loch Katharine, sat Edward Forbes. He was trying to play the pipes, but every time he thought about what must be happening in Edinburgh, he could only laugh uncontrollably.

/=/

Steven Ramon Abaroa was born and raised in San Diego, California. He attended Brigham Young University where he met and married DeeAnn Lewis. They are the parents of four boys.

In 1986, Steven and DeeAnn moved to Arizona, where he taught high school English and Journalism in the town of Gilbert. In 1997, Steven began writing editorials for the Arizona Republic.

Salome Riley, a consummate professional, knew better than to lose her heart. That was one of the first lessons Caroline had taught her. She just hadn't reckoned on handsome Marcus tumbling into her well-ordered life. An intelligent, compelling heroine and a well-crafted story. We predict big things for this talented writer!

A Singular Woman
Nina Caron Davis

"Oh, ma'am, did we have to come out in a storm like this?"

Salome Riley smiled with mild amusement at her maid, Sarah. Thursday evenings usually found both women in St. Giles checking on the needs of the tenants. Born to an unwed African housemaid, orphaned by consumption, Salome had been one of the fortunate few to escape this area of London. Now that she was able, little in this world would stop her from helping those trapped there. Certainly not a run of foul weather.

"Sarah, since when have you been afraid of a bit of thunder?"

A clap of thunder exploded, rattling their carriage. Sarah winced. "Since the Devil Himself decided to go to war above our heads."

"Never fear. We shall be safe at home short-ly..." Salome tumbled half into Sarah's lap as the carriage stopped abruptly. Struggling to tame her skirts and right herself, she called out over the horses' whinny, "John, if you have been pinching my good brandy again..."

"No, ma'am, I swear. Mad bloke stumbled and passed out in front of me horses. All I could do not to trample the sod into the cobbles."

"Oh, my goodness!" Salome threw on her cloak and was out the carriage door, in spite of Sarah's squeaked protests. Light from the carriage lamp shimmered off the large puddles as the rain continued to beat down on the road.

John, her coachman, and her footman Henry were already leaning over the prone victim. John suggested, "You may want to check an' see if he has pinched your good brandy."

Salome kneeled over the man to search for injuries. Even in the dim light of dusk she could tell he was a large man, broad shouldered, with dark hair pulled back in a queue. Reaching behind his head, she found a swelling lump at the base of his skull. "No brandy caused this. The bottle perhaps."

Salome looked around but saw no one able or willing to claim knowledge of the man. She could not leave him here to catch his death. "John, Henry, get him inside the carriage."

"Beggin' your Ma'amship's pardon," John sputtered, "but you cannot take stray strangers into your home. What if he does you harm? What if he steals your jewelry? What if he..."

"...Pinches the brandy?" Salome chuckled as John harrumphed in offense. "I have every confidence in your ability to protect me. Besides which, taking in a stray stranger is how I found myself a coachman."

To that there was no argument. John sighed in defeat as he and Henry hoisted the man up and headed for the carriage.

Marcus awoke to a dull headache and sore ribs, cradled in a softer bed than he had known in quite some time. All was not as it should be. That the bed linens held a faint scent of lavender confirmed his suspicions. Glancing about the room, he was met with blue-papered walls, a dark-stained dresser, and a blushing young chit in an apron and cap holding a pitcher.

He tried to sit up to speak, but could only groan.

She squealed, running out of the room, splashing a trail of water behind her. The shrill sound did little to improve his headache. As he buried his head in the pillow to block the noise, he heard a rustle of skirts. He peeked out of the downy cocoon to see a Black woman smiling kindly at him. Her air of confidence, as well as her straw-colored round gown, told him the maid had sought out her mistress.

"I am sorry, sir. Sarah is rather a timid sort. I hope she did not disturb you?"

He continued to stare at her, watched as, after several moments, her brow furrowed. Despite the haze in his mind, she looked familiar, but he could not place where he had seen her before. He could, however, appreciate the sight before him. She was all curves: fingers, shoulders, bosom, lips. Her chocolate skin, smooth and glowing.

"Sir?"

"Pretty lady."

Marcus watched her still eyes blink with deliberation, once, twice. Pretty eyes, too. Light brown with hints of green.

Pretty Lady sat down on the edge of the bed. Taking his hand, her voice came slow and soft, as his nanny's used to when she wanted him to pay close attention. "What is your name?"

"Nash. Marcus Alexander Nash."

The answer seemed to please her. He wanted to please her.

She continued. "Mr. Nash, I am Salome Riley. I found you in the road last evening, and brought you to my home. You came to for a moment, and I decided to give you a bit of laudanum for whatever discomfort you have. You were badly injured."

"I believe I still am."

Her laugh was even more beautiful than her smile. His sense of propriety dulled along with his pain, he reached up to touch her face but stopped short once his shirtsleeve came into view. He had not worn so fine a linen in months.

"Where are my clothes?"

Concern reappeared on her face. "Do you not recall?"

He shook his head.

She said. "We were in the middle of a rainstorm and got quite soaked through. Your clothes are drying in the kitchen. Your belongings are safe and sound."

"Please thank your father for the use of his shirt."

"I never knew my father."

"My apologies. I presumed."

She nodded her acceptance, then seemed to be wondering what she should say next. A look of decision crossed her face.

"It belonged to Richard. He preferred keeping a change of clothing and a few other personal items here. His eye for the ladies, wedded or not, finally placed him in the path of a jealous husband's sword." She hesitated briefly. "I thought of enquiring as to whether or not his widow would like his belongings returned but then decided it would not be quite the thing."

His instinct told him she was serious in her tale. "Richard was not your brother, was he."

Mirth crinkled the corner of her eyes. "No, not my brother."

He attempted again to remember where he had seen her. Patches of memory came to him. The King's Theatre a few years before it burned. His Grace, the Duke of Avondale, had entered his box, the dusky complexion of the woman on his arm noticeable even in the dimmed light. The eruption of whispers, both tantalized and scandalized, had been remarkable even for a place known for its rowdy attendees. He had overheard many referring to her as the next diamond of the demimonde.

The entire audience had pressed to get a closer look at her in the lobby afterward. He had been no exception. Those eyes. Salome.

Marcus heard himself utter one of her monikers. "The Black Venus."

She replied with a self-deprecating smile. "I thought it best you know whose hospitality you are receiving. If you are uncomfortable with the current arrangements, I am happy to send notice of your whereabouts."

"Thank you." A hint of sadness tinged his voice, "I no longer have much consequence to sully." He rallied. "Besides, most men would sell their stables to be in my place."

"Well then, sir, it is good you have a cheerful outlook on the matter, given you need to rest here several days. What, pray tell, did you do to earn such punishment?"

Marcus closed his eyes in thought for a moment. Odd, he could remember seeing her years ago, but he could not recall anything of the past few days. "I would not mind knowing myself. Alas, my memory is not forthcoming."

She tucked the bedclothes around him. "It is certain to return in time. But at the moment you need sleep."

Yes, he did feel rather exhausted. That was surely the reason he thought he saw lines of worry on his Pretty Lady's face before she turned to leave the room.

Once more, he closed his eyes. That he would be here for an extended stay did distress him, but not for the reason his hostess had suggested. An urgent matter awaited him. He was in no condition to pursue it, however, so it would have to keep.

/=/

"Bloody hell."

Salome then chastised herself for the slip of the tongue as she set the tray down on a table on the second-floor landing to steady herself. She allowed herself to use the cant of her youth now and then, but to slide back to cruder forms of street language? Unacceptable. She knew what the slip meant. All was not as calm and ordered in her world as she had pretended the past week. She resented the reminder. She resented the restlessness all the more.

After a few days' rest, Mr. Nash had begun talking about himself, in part as an attempt to bring back those memories still buried. He too had been orphaned early in life. He, however, had had family willing to take him in. A great-uncle and aunt and their son. He seemed to recall those times with great fondness. He had had a stable home. Part of Salome envied him.

His tales became sparser when he recounted his adult years. What stories he did relate were tinged by shadows that passed across his face. Perhaps here lay the foundation for the ties she now felt with him. She had always been drawn to those wounded, having once been one such herself, a little girl expendable and lost. She was but four when her mother died. One by one, neighbors who had known her mother had taken her in. But inevitably as the seventh, eighth, or ninth child was born, the extra mouth to feed meant a choice between the child by blood and the child by charity. Blood always won.

Then Caroline appeared, part mother, part angel. Caroline saved her from being caned by the victim of her first and last attempt to pickpocket. Salome had been sixteen, homeless, and starving. Caroline took her in, educated her and taught her the trade, as well as how to make the most of her attributes. Every written word raising a hue and cry that nobles were sullying themselves with a Black mistress served only to whet the appetite of the bucks in Town. They gladly courted scandal to seal their reputations as out-and-outers. She had been sought by these men, lords and commoners alike.

Caroline had also taught her that beauty faded and men's tastes became jaded, leaving many a demimondaine destitute in later life. Women of their ilk could ill afford to squander their earnings. Salome had learned her lesson well. Her coterie of gentlemen and their abundant generosity had allowed her the year before to purchase her own home. She had made wise investments. As a result, she no longer had to fear being turned out by anyone. This-she pressed her hand against the solid wall of her house-was the symbol of her long desired and hard earned security.

So why did she now feel so vulnerable? She sighed over the reason, who was lying in her blue bed chamber. There had to be an explanation. For one, she did not like the circumstances surrounding his injury. In his pockets had been a key, a full purse, and a miniature of a blonde lady. The purse should not have been there. That it was, meant something darker than a foiled frisker was at work. So, maybe, she suffered worry for his safety once he left her care. Or sympathy brought on by her anxiety.

She looked into the gilt-edged mirror above the table. *Oh no, my dear. You have always been honest with yourself. No retreat now.* Taking a deep breath, she let the truth sink in. Her household bustled with men who had struck her sympathy. She cared for them. In many ways they were more family than servants. But none of them stirred her body and soul. Thoughts of her patient, on the other hand, stirred feelings of an ever strengthening bond. And a deep attraction.

She was fast falling in love with Marcus Nash.

Damn.

Resuming her course to Mr. Nash's chamber-no, she must not think of anything in this house as his-she braced herself as if entering battle. Salome could hear her deceased mentor's voice uttering the mantra that kept a courtesan from losing herself to her trade: *Let few men win your body. Let no man win your heart.*

She shifted the tray onto her right arm, knocked a warning with her left hand, then entered. Mayhap the warning should have been for herself. He sat on the edge of the bed, bare legged, the hem of his lawn shirt resting midway up well-muscled thighs. The unfastened ruffled front lay open, revealing a broad chest dusted with dark hairs. Black disheveled curls fell upon his shoulders. A light beard now shadowed his face.

Pangs shot through her belly. Her mouth went dry as other parts felt moist. *Let few men win your body...* Salome sighed in desperation. Half the battle was already lost.

"Good to see you up, Mr. Nash." She sounded too bright to her own ears.

He glanced up in surprise while buttoning his shirt. "Have I offended you, ma'am? You did open the door before I could warn you I was disrobed." An impish grin spread across his face. "Though as quickly as you enter, sometimes I wonder if to catch me thus is your intention."

Steadying herself, she countered with a smile, "Indeed, you have offended me, sir. That growth upon your face is both unfashionable and abhorrent, and I intend to rid you of it immediately."

She placed the tray down on a table near the window and bade him sit in one of the low-back chairs. He still limped slightly. Whoever beat him did so to send a warning, of that she was now certain. She had to get him to remember what happened that night.

He interrupted her thoughts. "You certainly have the right tools." Upon the tray, razor, shaving soap, a bowl of hot water, and towels waited to attack his beard. He chuckled. "Since you are so prepared, far be it from me to deny a lady."

She noticed the wince that followed. His ribs must still be tender, but he had refused more laudanum. Pressing a hot towel to his face, she tried to think of what could, perhaps, take his mind back to that evening. She was still thinking as she removed the wet towel and draped him with a dry one.

He touched her hand. "You are skilled at this." It was more a question than a statement.

Salome reached for the shaving soap, gave it one last whisk with the brush, and slowly spread the lather along his jaw. If his presence was going to tease her so, she might as well give tit for tat.

"Miss Riley?"

211

She tested the razor once more for sharpness, making sure his black eyes followed the motion. She let her voice drop low, accompanied by a mischievous smile. "Very skilled."

He shot her a look. She could see his mind whirling, trying to decipher her meaning. Good.

As the blade made its first sweep across his jaw, she at last thought of a question that might work.

"Who is the lady in your miniature?"

She barely perceived the tightening of his jaw, so quickly had it come and gone. She rinsed off the blade with more care than necessary, waiting for his answer.

"My former *fiancée*."

Ignoring the skip in her heartbeat, Salome made another sweep with the blade in silence. The story was his to tell.

When next she cleaned the razor, he continued. "Your kindness and openness deserve the truth. It was a love match. At least on my part. I believe she was fond of me. She seemed remorseful when she broke off the engagement. Expressed sorrow at having to hurt me. But it had to be done. She could not very well marry a pauper without prospects."

"Yet she could become engaged to one?"

"I had a small estate near London. Comfortable income, though not wealthy. I had lost some in bad investments, but I managed to scrape by. Then Uncle Edmond passed away. He had promised me a modest inheritance. He was like a father to me. His passing..." His voice cracked; he cleared his throat. "I was nevertheless grateful to know I would receive needed funds. But, when Uncle's solicitor read the will, there was nothing for me." His jaw tightened again. "My cousin refused to help me, but then I had not believed he would. Our relationship became estranged as we grew older."

Marcus paused. Salome made no move to continue the shave, and after a moment, he continued. "I sold the estate, which covered the greater debts. Found work as a secretary, and lodgings on Green Street. Once I informed her family of my new financial situation, I was summoned to my future father-in-law's home, where I received my *congé*. From both daughter and father. At first her leaving hurt like the devil." He shrugged. "But I accepted fate. I could not blame them. Three months later, I read in *The Times* of her engagement to a viscount. Of course, he had no money either. With the prospect of his Cit daughter becoming a viscountess, however, her father did not mind opening his own purse strings to seal that bargain."

After a moment, Salome replied, "You profess not to carry a *tendre* for her. Yet you continue to carry her likeness?"

Bitterness crept into his voice. "A reminder of what caused me to lose her, lose everything."

He still mentioned nothing of the night of the attack. The only fruits of her efforts were resurrected memories of lost love. Salome felt ill.

He said nothing else, though she noticed he seemed preoccupied. As she finished shaving him, she wanted more and more to brush the strain from his brow, to kiss the sorrow from his eyes.

That tears welled up in her eyes startled her.

"Miss Riley?" Concern filled his voice.

She stepped back, hoping to hide her face, but he caught her. She felt the pad of his thumb brush a tear from her cheek. He pulled her down into his lap, cradling her, gently shushing her crying as her head rested against his shoulder. The scent of the shaving soap and of sandalwood in his hair wrapped around her. His breath skittered across her cheek, reviving faint scenes in her mind of her momma rocking her to sleep. She was safe then. Loved. Whole. But now there was no Momma. No Caroline. A hunger long buried burst forth in her soul. Instinctively, she reached out to fill it.

Her mouth sought his. Soft, warm, he tasted of his breakfast ale. Her soul hummed to each stroke his tongue played across her lips, drinking in with each gentle pull on his mouth the sense of sanctuary she felt in him.

Knocks at the door wrenched her from her haven. A knock once, then twice. Sarah's signal. Salome had till the count of ten to answer, at which point the girl would know not to disturb her. Her mind still reeling, she grabbed the chance to retreat.

Salome hurried to the door. "Yes, Sarah."

"*He* has come, ma'am. He is waiting in the drawing room."

From heaven to hell.

Salome knew her visitor's identity from the inflection in Sarah's voice. Her new client. Salome supposed she should not be prejudiced, but given the way she had become his mistress, she had ill feelings about his character. More than that, she had worked hard to reach the point in her life when she could be selective in her protectors. Having the choice taken from her still made her blood boil.

"I shall be there in a moment."

She turned back to Mr. Nash. "I-I am afraid I have to greet him." She swallowed. "I may not see you again till late, or perhaps the morning. I shall send Sarah for the tray."

She scurried from the room before he could respond. Guilt mingled with the anger and suspicion. She swore she could hear Caroline scolding: *I warned you.*

Salome ran a nervous hand down her white chemise frock as she stood in front of the drawing room doors. "Get control of yourself, girl," she whispered to herself. "Time to have all your wits about you."

She motioned her footman to open the door. Standing in the doorway, she met with the sight of a slender man, brown hair, well tailored in half mourning for his father. Rather overdressed for morning rounds, however. Lace ruffs indeed. *He feels the need to impress me.* In the normal mode of things, it was the other way around. She did not need the additional sight of his fidgeting hands to tell he was also nervous. He was obviously not the most confident of men, potentially dangerous to a woman in her position.

She swept into the room. "Welcome, Sir Jules. I trust you have not waited long. May I offer you port, sherry, or would you prefer to wait for tea?"

"Er, tea, thank you."

She knew Sir Jules tracked her as she crossed the pale-yellow-toned room to ring the bell, trying to measure her as she had him. Two pulls, pause, two pulls. She was becoming more and more thankful she had devised her little system of code. He fidgeted even more. If her greeting rattled him so, this would be a long meeting.

She sat on the cream-and-gold-printed settee and bade him take one of the pale-blue Hepplewhite armchairs. She waited while he cleared his throat, and through several false starts of speech whereby he opened and closed his mouth like a landed pike. Oh dear. She decided to relax him with the usual banalities about the weather, but suddenly he gathered his resolve.

"I say, fair place Tuninbury set you up in." His

voice came out high and skittish. He took a deep breath. "Shall we have plain speaking?"

She waited.

"Our agreement is for three months, but if you are wise and do well to please me, my dear–" Sir Jules raked his eyes down her figure, "I could do you much better. He may be a marquess, but I have him beat in the pockets, especially after that evening of *écarté* at Lord Westerley's." He sniggered at his joke.

Salome stiffened in indignation. Courtesans might not be daughters of Society, but there were means of courtship in procuring their services nonetheless.

"But as you say, sir, he is a marquess." Her voice rang with quiet dignity. "Furthermore, you are unfortunately misinformed. This 'fair place' is my own. There is no master here."

He flushed from her sting. Spite flashed through his eyes. Dangerous, as she suspected. Before he could regroup, Sarah arrived with the tea tray. Salome noted that she remembered to leave the door slightly ajar as she exited. Henry would be outside the door to hear any call for aid. As she poured tea, she glanced at the mantle clock and resolved to summon that aid in ten minutes.

She handed Sir Jules a cup, aware that she needed to diffuse the situation. She spoke with all the soft femininity she could muster. "Lovely weather, is it not?"

/=/

Marcus sat in his chamber staring at the door after it closed. His mind was a jumble. He had been about to tell Miss Riley that bits of his memory regarding the attack had returned. Two men waiting near his home. The first fist to his gut.

That was before he had seen her crying. Before

216

the kiss. He blew out his breath. She had been a sweet armful. He could not help but be jealous of the man below, no doubt her protector. Not that she had appeared happy at his arrival. He frowned. Indeed, he had caught sight of fear as she left. Not all men treated their mistresses well.

He threw on his breeches, stockings, and shoes, ignoring pain and the logical voice in his mind that said she had men-servants in the house to watch over her. He had grown attached to his Pretty Lady. What harm could there be in loitering about the stairs, just in case?

/=/

Ten minutes dragged on for what felt like hours. Finally the time had passed. These, plus the five before tea, made up the prerequisite fifteen minute call. Even in ridding oneself of an unwelcome guest, one need not be inhospitable.

Salome let her cup slip from her fingers. The delicate china piece crashed on the table.

"Gracious, how clumsy of me." Henry entered on cue. "Ah, Henry, look what a mess I have made. Mind you gather all the fragments."

She hurried to Sir Jules. "I trust no flying debris cut you, sir. I am sure it was a fright nonetheless. My humblest apologies." Arm in his, she strolled with him into the entrance hall. He sputtered contradictions, but she pressed on. "No sir, I insist you see your physician straight away." She looked up at him, pleading with a touch of coyness. "I shall not rest, Sir Jules, until I know the proper authority verifies your health is sound."

Sir Jules looked flattered. "If such a report will put you at ease, then it shall be done."

Her butler appeared as if by magic, bearing Sir Jules's hat, gloves and cane.

Sir Jules said."I did want to convey my apologies for not calling sooner. Rather urgent business surfaced. And though my father passed nigh six months ago, this inconvenient mourning prevents me from appearing with you as I would like at public events. Never fear, I now have the will, thanks to your beauty, to find a way to enjoy your company about Society. And I shall."

Display was more likely, thought Salome. "I anxiously await such an event, sir. Good day."

Relief washed over her when the butler closed the door. She remained in the hall for a few minutes to gather her wits, then sent up silent thanks to her little tea cup, so nobly sacrificed for her cause.

She ignored the muffled sound from upstairs. A servant, no doubt. Her maid's scream caught her attention.

"Sarah! Are you all right?" Salome called while running up to the second-floor landing.

Sarah was struggling to get up off the carpet. "He ran like a ghost was after him, ma'am. Plum knocked me over and still did not stop."

"Who?"

"Mr. Nash, ma'am. He headed for the back stairs."

Sarah followed as Salome took Mr. Nash's path. "I had just finished my polishing and was going to get the tray from his room. Did not even get my greeting out. Fully dressed he was, including his coat, half running, half hobbling on that bad leg of his."

"Think, Sarah, did he say anything?"

"No, ma'am. But you could almost smell the terror. I swear he had seen the Devil Himself."

Cook tried to flag her mistress down as Salome and Sarah made their way out the kitchen door. The gate in the railing at the top of the area steps rested open on the hinges.

Sarah ran up the steps, then looked up and down the street. "I do not see him. He cannot have gotten away on foot."

"No, he could not have, but there are plenty of hackney coaches, and he had money."

Thousands of questions swirled in Salome's mind as she watched Sarah latch the gate. The only man with the answers had disappeared. She intended to find him.

/=/

Madness, pure and simple.

Salome leaned back in her carriage seat, meditating to the vehicle's sway as it bowled through Soho toward Green Street. She disregarded what else explained her actions. Something had happened in her house, and whatever relationship they had, real or desired, was in dire straits. Given Marcus still needed to heal–she had stopped thinking of him as Mr. Nash while she stood on the area steps, her heart in the pit of her stomach–he could be in dire straits as well.

Within two hours of his abrupt departure, she had notices sent to her friends in St. Giles: five sovereigns to whoever found his lodgings and reported back first. People let rooms all along Green Street. She could have searched herself, but knew if Marcus spotted her or her servants scouring the street, he would run again.

For five days she had become a veritable harridan to live with. Barking orders to all, sending well-prepared meals back to the kitchen as pathetic drivel. Poor Sarah had gone into hiding. But news had come at last.

Now, feeling the carriage slow to a stop, Salome looked out the window, even though she knew she would see little in the dark of night.

Henry helped her down and accompanied her to the door. John knew to return in half an hour if they were allowed in.

Salome gave the knocker a sharp rap. The landlady poked her head out the door. She looked askance at Salome, but Salome knew the presence of Henry in livery tipped the scales in her favor. The door opened wider.

"Good evening, ma'am. Mr. Marcus Nash is expecting me."

Hesitancy still showed in the landlady's face, but she let the duo enter. The bluff had worked.

Salome smiled. "Mr. Nash told me which room is his, but I am turned 'round so easily."

"Third floor, first door to your left. Your man-servant can follow me to the kitchen."

Henry grinned his appreciation. He was a strapping, handsome man, and the landlady's cheeks glowed from that small gesture. Henry would have her thoroughly charmed within the quarter hour.

Salome's heartbeat pounded louder as she mounted the stairs. Not from physical exertion. She knocked. He opened the door and tried to slam it shut, but she was prepared and pushed her way in.

He glowered at her. "Get out. And if your master sent you, tell him I will consign his soul to hell even if I have to lose mine in the process."

"My master? What on earth do you mean?"

Realizing others could hear, he slammed the door shut.

He ignored her question. "I heard you fawning over that thatch-gallows cousin of mine. Your protector." He sneered the word. "And I heard him say he had my will back, thanks to you. The memories had started surfacing, but they came flooding back at that moment."

His words were rapid fire. "So tell me, was that dear John and Henry who beat me half to death? Or did Jules flex the power of his inheritance and hire two ding-boys? I should applaud you, my dear. Was taking me to your house, 'caring' for me, your stroke of genius? How perfect to have the troublemaker under watch. I assume he came there to congratulate you on a task well done."

Her mind raced, trying to keep up with his accusations even while deciphering them. She needed to level the field. "In truth, Mr. Nash, Sir Jules visited to inspect his winnings."

Marcus snorted, then looked at her more closely. "You never brought him up to my chamber."

"I am not referring to you, sir."

She watched her meaning sink in. She moved in. "After all the time we spent in each other's company, if in your heart of hearts you believe I duped you, you may show me the door. Otherwise, I shall be happy to explain and clear up this confusion."

He stood stock-still, staring at her as moment after moment ticked by. Then he sighed. "I cannot sit down, Miss Riley, until you do the same, and my leg hurts the very devil from my little sprint."

Salome turned to an armchair by the window, in part to surreptitiously wipe the tears that threatened to spill over. He had given her a chance. She would not squander it.

"My once and future protector, Lord Tuninbury, lost me at a game of *écarté* to Sir Jules. At a private party, I believe. Lord Tuninbury has yet to gather the courage to face me directly. He sent a letter that related the outcome only, so my knowledge of the details is sketchy at best. The term is for three months." She looked at Marcus. "Obviously, you overheard part of our conversation in the entrance hall. For now, I shall temper my curiosity as to how you managed that feat from your chamber."

Marcus shifted in his seat.

"What you missed was the rest of the statement, although, as you were apparently in a state of shock, that is understandable. Sir Jules said, if I may summarize, that he now had the will to find a way to parade me to his cronies."

Marcus scoffed. "Sounds like Jules."

"Nevertheless, his comment triggered a breakthrough for you. Now, tell me about this will."

Marcus did not reply.

She said, "After your opening tirade, I now know who was responsible for your beating and why. This same man now has access to my person. He has us both by the scruff. Alone, we cannot change our circumstances. Together, we may be able to."

His expression did not soften. "Understand, from my vantage point, this seems all too coincidental."

"Perhaps it is fate." She leaned forward. "You have to trust me. I know firsthand how difficult that can be. I had to trust Caroline on instinct, and it turned out to be the right decision."

Seeing his raised brow, she explained. "Yes, she taught me to be a courtesan. But let us examine her choices. I had tried to steal from her companion that day. She could have turned me over to the watch, and I could have become a career criminal or a resident in a compter. She could have sold me into slavery on the docks. I had a second to trust she would do me no harm. You had a sennight."

"You are a most singular woman Miss Riley."

Marcus cocked his head. "I could do worse than trust you, I believe."

"Indeed."

He sat up straight. "You know part of the story. You recall, I told you I did not receive expected money from my great-uncle upon his death. I swallowed my pride a second time and went to Jules about three weeks ago. I did not ask for the money, but Uncle had also promised me several keepsakes in his possession belonging to my late father. Those, I felt, I had a right to demand. I surprised Jules in his study. During our meeting, he was summoned from the room by some household crisis. I told him I would wait. His nervousness was tangible. I leaned on Uncle's old desk. I was not trying to read the papers, but your eyes cannot help tracking print. There it was, unfolded, the bottom half visible from beneath some other letter. 'I leave to my great-nephew, Marcus Alexander Nash, the sum of 15,000 pounds...'"

Recalling their earlier conversation, Salome could not help but interrupt. "You consider 15,000 pounds a modest inheritance?"

"Good heavens no, but apparently Uncle did. 'Modest' was the word he used."

"Pray continue."

"I snatched up the document, realizing Jules had either forged another will, or bribed the solicitor. Either way, I knew I could not let this will out of my grasp. I gave my excuses to the butler, then escaped as fast as I could. As Jules had not shown any interest in my well-being, I doubted he knew where I lived. I felt safe."

"But you were not," she said softly.

"I had forgotten he knew my employer, who naturally knew my address. And I underestimated his desperation. I went out a couple of days later, will in pocket, hoping to see my old solicitor, but he was not in his office. Jules's men waylaid me on my way back."

Marcus left his chair, clearly agitated. "You must understand. More than money is at stake here. After he turned me away the first time, Jules started dropping hints to his friends and Uncle's old circle that he had offered me a generous sum, feeling as it was only right that the cousin who had lived with him as a brother should have something." He barked out a laugh. "He said I had demanded twice as much or none at all, and was it not a pity how death brought out greed in people. It was not enough that he left me destitute. A good reputation is all a man has left when everything else is gone. Jules wants to sully that as well."

He leaned on the back of his chair. "Now he has the will back, probably destroyed by now. My last hope. I never knew the old boy was so jealous."

"Jealous?"

"Jules never lived up to Uncle's expectations of what his heir should be, a man who can hunt and play squire with the best of them. Jules was a quiet boy, more interested in books on geography than courses in estate management."

"But you were."

Marcus nodded. "Uncle took every opportunity to remind Jules of his disappointment, using me as the exemplary buck he should strive to be. I did not agree with his treatment of Jules but could do nothing about it. I suppose, had I been in Jules's shoes, I would hate me as well."

"Still, you did him no harm. His actions are unconscionable." Salome hesitated. "I have not known your cousin long, but I have known men like him. I doubt he has destroyed the will. It is a souvenir of his victory over you and his father, a treasure to bring out and gloat over. He does so like to preen. That works to our advantage."

"You have an idea in mind?"

"Oh yes. Her eyes narrowed. "And a certain marquess is about to have *his* marker called in, to help."

/=/

Two mornings later, Salome flipped through a copy of *The Lady's Magazine* while waiting in her drawing room for Simon Withers, Marquess of Tuninbury. That he had agreed to come spoke to the nature of their relationship, which had turned from that of lovers to that of friends. All the more reason why her summons had been imperious. Beyond camaraderie, they mutually benefited from the alliance. He, generous by nature, kept her monetarily so that she had no pressing need to accept any other offers. His ongoing relationship with her kept scandalized matchmaking mothers at bay.

She was rewarded by the sound of his footfall on the stairs. She rose to her full five feet, two inches, dressed to look imposing in a dark-blue greatcoat dress trimmed *à la marinière*, fichu tucked inside her bodice, her hair in a large unpowdered aureole of curls.

Simon entered, contrition on his face. His blond curls rested on the collar of his black frock coat, which was paired with buff-colored waistcoat and breeches. He looked every inch the Adonis cartoonists portrayed him to be. At the moment, his looks did not earn him reprieve.

Her voice was velvet-sheathed steel. "Pray tell me, Simon, how I managed to wind up as part of a wager, and even more to the point, how you managed to lose me to that odious man."

"I owe you a thousand apologies, I know. He needled me about my prowess at the tables. I let that mushroom goad me into a game. I was winning as I expected to. Then he made a wager for one hand, you as the winnings. I refused at first, but he called my manhood into question. You know full well I could not ignore that."

Salome rolled her eyes. "In other words, Simon, you were thinking with the wrong head and were royally fleeced like a little green pigeon."

He winced.

She began pacing with her hands on her hips. "The more I hear of Sir Jules, the less I like him. He has made you the latest *on dit*, but has hurt someone else much worse. He must be stopped. And, dearest Simon, you are going to help me."

"Your wish is my command, my lady."

She smiled. "There is intelligence left in that noggin of yours after all."

"What do you want me to do?" he asked, looking, perhaps, just a trifle wary.

"Sir Jules wants to show me off, but mourning won't allow him full access to Society rounds. We are going to give him his opportunity. Your assignment is to do some plucking yourself. Get Sir Jules to host a gaming party at his home. It will need to be small because of circumstance, but that will be fine. Hint that he can show himself off as a host, and that, naturally, you want the chance to win me back. Use that charm of yours to its fullest." She shot Simon a sidelong glance. "Pretend he's a female conquest."

Simon puckered his face. "Deuced ugly female."

She could not help giggling. "Nevertheless, it must be done. Your duty on the night of the game is to keep an eye on Sir Jules. I shall need to leave the room. When I do, if he leaves, follow him. I may need your brawn."

That sobered Simon. "What exactly are you getting into, Sal?"

They sat down side by side, and she explained about Marcus and the will she hoped to retrieve.

Simon whistled at the end of her tale. "Dangerous business, darling." He looked down at his shoes. "You have fallen for him that hard, eh?"

She felt a blush creep up her face.

"Well, that settles it. I have often fancied, if the circumstances of my birth were different, that I would have taken you as more than mistress."

"Simon-"

He held up his hand. "Lucky fellow, he is, and I hope he knows as much. We are still friends though, right, love?"

"Always, my lord." Her smile trembled.

"Then I give you leave." He clasped her hand. "Follow your heart, Sal, and make certain Mr. Nash knows he holds such a precious gem in his hands."

He rose. "Now to the business of Sir Jules Ashburn."

/=/

About thirty men mingled in the drawing room at Sir Jules's home in Hanover Square. Salome stood as the jewel in the crown, her hair lightly powdered, the emerald silk of her robe picking up the green in her eyes. Sir Jules's chest was swelled with pride. If all went as planned, she would burst that pride into tattered pieces.

She sat behind Sir Jules, watching as he won another 800 pounds from young Lord Montroy. Sir Jules was already shuffling the deck for the next game. The clock struck ten. At eleven would be the main attraction for this evening, the return game between Sir Jules and Lord Tuninbury for her favors. Now was her best opportunity to leave.

She made her excuses, then slipped out of the drawing room and down to the ground floor. She found the study near the back of the house. Thank heavens the footmen were busy with the guests upstairs. She closed the door gently behind her as she entered the room.

The only light came from a low burning fire. Marcus was already seated at the desk, carefully rifling through papers.

Salome crossed the room. "I see you made it through the back without difficulty."

"The Earl of Bedford allows his staff to host an annual servants ball today, the third Thursday in May. Uncle's servants have always been invited. Thus, I knew the servants' hall would be relatively deserted. I am impressed Lord Tuninbury was able to convince Jules to host his game the same evening."

Salome chuckled under her breath. "Mayhap Sir Jules is not such an ugly female after all."

"What?"

"Nothing." Enough fun. Time was of the essence. "The will was on his desk before?"

Marcus nodded as he attempted to pick the lock on the right-hand drawer.

"Never mind the desk, then. Your first theft scared him from placing the will there again." She glanced about the room. "Sir Jules thinks himself clever."

"Absolutely."

"Then where could he be clever with a will?"

"He likes word games."

She moved to the bookshelf. The spines of law books caught her eye. She stood on tip-toe, squinting in her attempt to read the titles. "Death...Marriage...Probate. Marcus, come get this down for me."

He obeyed and handed her the tome. She

rested the book on a side table, then flipped through the pages. A folded document slipped out. Salome opened the document, which was a will, and scanned for the verification that this was the one they needed. She found Marcus's bequest.

"We have it." Marcus returned the book. "One item of note I did find on his desk. A deck of cards."

"Why is that of interest?"

"Because, my dear Miss Riley, the cards are marked."

Salome's anger flared as the full ramification sunk in. "That little toad! I need to alert Lord Tuninbury. Give me the cards. And, Mr. Nash," she teased, "hold on to the will a bit better this time."

She heard the doorknob turn–too late even to look for a place to hide.

/=/

"What the devil!" Sir Jules stood frozen, then looked at the paper in Marcus's hand. He did not attempt pretense. "Could not steal from me in broad daylight, so you sneak back into my home like some night-crawling vermin."

He walked toward Salome. "But you, you have played me the fool all along. You little whore." He raised his hand to strike.

It stopped midair, gripped by Marcus's free hand. "That, dear cousin, would be your biggest mistake yet."

"I wholeheartedly agree." Simon appeared from behind Sir Jules.

"All of you together?" Sir Jules snatched his wrist out of Marcus's grasp. "All fools. This is my home, with my friends. Even if you told them about the will, Marcus, what is to stop me from claiming that yours is the forgery, a sad sign of how depraved you have become. Do you think they would believe you over a baronet?"

Salome called out, "Tuninbury, catch." She tossed the boxed deck to Simon.

Simon found the tell-tale marks on the cards and swore under his breath. He grabbed Sir Jules by the back of the neck. Salome felt a rush of delicious glee at the pasty color of Sir Jules's face, but signaled to Simon to do him no physical harm.

Salome approached Sir Jules. "Few things are more dishonorable than cheating at cards, though you managed to find them. You are correct, those men in your drawing room will not listen to Mr. Nash. But do you think they will believe you, a mere baronet, over the word of a marquess, whose title goes back to the Conquest? Are you familiar with the term *persona non grata*?"

Sir Jules started whining. "What do you want?"

"The easiest solution," Marcus replied," is to give me the inheritance promised me by your father. I can call on you tomorrow. Just think, Jules, you could boast of how generous you are, despite the grief I have caused you."

Sir Jules sniffled. "I never thought of it in that light. That would polish up my consequence."

Salome bit back her disgust. "And you will use a clean deck of cards in your game with Lord Tuninbury. Assuming a clean deck can be had in this house."

"His marking system is simple." Simon released Sir Jules. "I should have no problem circumventing it."

"Excellent. I have no doubt you will beat him soundly under fair odds."

"To ensure your compliance, Sir Jules, "Salome continued, "we will hold on to the will and the deck of cards. You will make the happy announcement of your change of heart toward your cousin to your assembled guests."

"Very well."

"Including your generous gift of an additional 5000 pounds."

"Absurd!"

"Rumors are amazing, are they not? They become truth in themselves. I wonder how fast the rumor that Sir Jules Ashburn had his own flesh and blood beaten in the streets would make the rounds, especially if Lord Tuninbury remarked that he had seen the bruises for himself."

"Surely it was not that severe. I instructed them to scare you, is all."

Marcus erupted. "Not severe! Let us take a look at 'not severe.'" He pulled up his coat, waistcoat, and shirt to reveal the glaring contusions along his ribs. Though fading, the bruising still showed the extent of the initial injury. "Tell me what wrong I did you to deserve such treatment."

"Dear God." Sir Jules almost fainted. "I had no intention..."

"I am touched, Cousin, by your concern. There may be hope for your soul yet."

Sir Jules sagged in remorseful defeat."The inheritance, plus the additional 5000 pounds, is yours. W-Why not go up and share the news together? Perhaps even a friendly game, like old times?"

Marcus shook his head. "One day, I may forgive you. However, I do not believe that day is in the foreseeable future. Until tomorrow." He bowed and took his leave.

Salome fought the urge to follow him. She instead offered a hand to each man. "Well, gentlemen, the night is still young, and your guests, Sir Jules, await."

Sarah bustled out to the little garden that bordered the area in back. "Mr. Nash is here to see you, ma'am."

Salome flushed hot and nervous. "Thank you, Sarah."

She had hoped for and dreaded this day. She debated with herself whether or not she should tell him her feelings. Could she risk telling him? She had already lost her livelihood. She could not go back to the trade, loving him as she did. She had searched all her life for a place to call home, only to find home in the soul of a man.

She had enough to live on for a while, but eventually she would have to devise a new means of employment. Money worries aside, she doubted she would survive losing her heart. It would surely leave with him, whether or not her body followed.

All too soon, she reached the drawing room. Marcus was pacing the floor.

Her defenses took control. "Sir, if you wear a hole in my Aubusson rug, I must ask you to replace it."

"That is no deterrent, ma'am. It would be my pleasure to buy you whatever your heart desires."

"Suppose what my heart desires does not hang in a shop window?"

His flirtatious mood faded. He closed the distance between them. "Then, where does your desire lie?"

There would be no other moment. She laid her palm against his chest. "Here."

He drew her into his arms, trailing feathery kisses on her brow. "I say again, I am willing to give you whatever you desire. Are you free to accept it?"

She knew what he alluded to. "Lord Tuninbury

released me before the gaming party." She raised her head. "He is my friend. I would give him up if you ask it of me–I would understand your reason– but I pray you do not."

"Never worry. I could not turn away a man who jeopardized himself for me, a stranger. He has even volunteered to help me search for another estate. He says you would fancy staying near London so you could continue your work in St. Giles."

Salome concentrated on Marcus's cravat. "About Simon. It does not bother you that he...knows me so well?"

Marcus grimaced. "I try not to think along those lines."

He cupped her face in his hands. "I adore you, Salome. Your past could only hurt me if it holds a man to whom you have given your heart."

"My heart belongs to you, Marcus. Only to you."

"Then will you do me the honor of bestowing the hand that goes with it?

She pulled his head to hers, kissing him in answer. Her mentor's old warning floated through her thoughts: *Let no man win your heart.*

For the first time in her life, she was happy to prove Caroline wrong.

/=/

Nina Caron Davis was born deep in the heart of Fort Worth, TX, and knew from birth she had one mission in life: to add as many gray hairs to her parents' heads as possible. She wasn't a bad girl, but being both a teacher's kid and a preacher's kid destined her to be a bit, well, different. Still, she earned her B.A. in English Arts from Hampton University and her M.L.I.S. from the University of Texas at Austin. She is currently a cataloging librarian for a large research university in the Midwest.

Her first taste of writing came through poetry. In 1994, Nina's poem, "Starry Night," was published in the anthology Dark Side of the Moon. In 1995, she combined her love of the English Regency with her research into the history of Blacks in Britain, winning the Virginia Romance Writers' 7th Annual Fool For Love First Chapter Contest in the Historical/Regency category. This is her first published work of fiction.

Wow! And Wow again! First-person narrative at its very best, a chilling tale of love and murder... and lifelong retribution. A classic tale you won't soon forget. Brrrrr!

Milady's Murderer
Sarah Starr

We Hodges are devoted to the Wrexwoods of Wrexwood. I had been milady's butler for six years when she died. Before that I butled for her father, the Earl Wrexwood, twenty years, coming to the position the same year milady was born, and even before that I was the house steward. My grandfather was the butler directly before me, and he groomed me to take the post upon his retirement, exactly as I am training my nephew now. Yes, we Hodges are devoted to the Wrexwoods of Wrexwood.

In 1814, the year of milady's murder, I was an imposing fifty-four. Like my grandfather before me, I could be described as portly. The gout had attacked my knees, but only slightly, not affecting my ability to do my work. I was the prototype of the trustworthy retainer, and I cared for nothing more than my mistress's welfare.

My main worry that year was milady's spinster status. Her beauty, which was unquestioned at her come-out, was starting to fade, and a permanent crease had appeared between her eyes.

When she made her debut eight years before, she had received exactly eleven offers for her hand-ten quite properly presented through her father, Lord Wrexwood, and one made to her directly, and passionately, in the south drawing room. She had refused the ten; Lord Wrexwood, entering at an inopportune moment, refused the eleventh for her. Butlers know of such things.

In her second season, though supplanted from her symbolic throne by fresh Incomparables, she was still sought after, and she still rebuffed all suitors. The following year, her father died and she retired quietly from the social scene.

Six years she sat apart from the exciting whirl of the Season. While she still maintained her Mayfair town house, the elegant address was no longer the site of balls or afternoon teas. Rather, it had the aura of a tomb. Milady daily perused the newspaper, and the only entertainment was the weekly political discussions she hosted. Even those were somber, dedicated to the war. Milady had become a bluestocking.

Do not misunderstand me-she was still generous to anyone who did her a favor. Her eyes were still the blue of a country sky, and her laugh, when it did sound, still brought a smile to my face. But she had adopted horn-rimmed spectacles and a cap in place of Olympian Dew and patches. Dismissing her lady's maid, she twisted her ringlets into a severe bun, and although a scattering of eligible men attended her Friday *soirées*, she made no attempt to secure the interests of any of them. There was the trouble. The Wrexwood line was in danger, and with it, the Hodges' secure future.

The situation was thus when, in the early days of June, 1814, just a week before milady's twenty-sixth birthday, I opened the door to a handsome stranger.

"Is Lady Emily at home?"

I hesitated. After fifty-four years I could recognize nobility across thirty feet of dark corridor, and there in the bright light of day, I had no question: this man was a baron at the least. Unfortunately, milady was never at home to visitors these days. However, she was still unwed, and I wished it to be otherwise. I dipped my chin in an austere nod. "One moment, my lord, and I will see."

The stranger didn't immediately offer his name, though I stood waiting, so I prompted him. "May I tell milady who desires her company?"

His eyes slid away for a moment, and his mouth twisted into a rueful smile. That should have been my first warning about the gentleman: why would anyone hesitate to give his name? But I was dazzled by the cut of his coat and the line of his jaw. As he hesitated, I made my own decision. This was no mincing popinjay or dry scholar. From his calfskin Wellington boots to the low-crowned beaver on his head, he exuded quality. Not only that, but his skintight pantaloons displayed muscular, well-shaped legs. Surely milady, if she was sensible to any feelings of the heart at all, would be attracted to this pattern card. I would let him in, no matter what his name.

At this point in my deliberations, he expelled a heavy breath and spoke.

"Fenton," he told me. "Tell her Charles Fenton is here."

Looking back, I remember gaping, but only for a moment. Then I bowed from the waist and said, "Follow me, my lord."

Charles Fenton! The passionate young suitor of eight years before! Once identified, I could see some resemblance in the face, but little in the

237

bearing or body. The straight, broad shoulders on the man I escorted inside had not yet been developed in the boy of eighteen, whose declarations were so ill-received. But if even a tenth of his ardent love remained-why, Lady Emily might yet provide an heir! As I sedately led him up the main stairs, my mind raced to sort such bits of gossip and history as it held. There was little enough there: I remembered something about the military, something more recent about an unexpected earldom, and, the important thing, nothing about marriage.

I opened the door to the same, fateful drawing room. "If you'll wait here, my lord."

He nodded and sat, and, slower, I made my way to milady's sitting room. The door stood open. I could see her at the heavy mahogany desk, unladylike as ever. I coughed gently. She looked up, her eyes showing surprise behind the spectacles.

"Yes, Hodges?"

I had decided how I would frame my announcement: I would make it dignified but incomplete. I would take no chance that she would refuse admission to this answer to my prayers.

"Milady, you have a visitor. I have installed him in the south drawing room."

And I left, reaching the bend in the hallway before she managed a surprised, "Hodges, who is it?" That far away, I could pretend I didn't hear. It was a blot on the Hodges name, that announcement was, but all for the family's good. From my position past the gallery, I soon heard milady leave her sitting room. She hesitated in the hall, undoubtedly looking for me, and then her quick steps turned south to the drawing room. After a moment, my own steps followed.

I would like to say, here, that instances of my

deliberate eavesdropping are few and far between. We butlers are often maligned as eavesdroppers, but the vast portion of our knowledge is gained honestly. It's one of the advantages of being lower class: the nobility often talks scandal before us, as unaware of our presence as if we were but another stick of furniture. Many's the time milady Emily's mother would call me for tea, tittering and chattering with a guest even as I poured. Not all servants enjoy furniture status, of course. Eager young maids and pages are shooed from the room at the first hint of indiscretion. But, as I've said, I have long been a trustworthy retainer. Long tenure plus a wooden face equals knowledge.

Nor did I resort to sordid, glass-against-door methods on this occasion. I knew milady would not rush to close herself in with an unidentified male visitor. As she entered the drawing room–leaving the door open, as I predicted–her clear voice came: "Good morning. I am Lady Emily. May I help you, sir?"

There was a second of silence, and then his voice. "Emily. My word, what are those spectacles? And your hair! What's happened to you?"

My romantic fancies wilted. These were not the words of a would-be lover. Certainly not the lover who had kissed each of Miss Wrexwood's fingers and vowed to buy a ring for every one. *That* Charles Fenton had sworn eternal love; this one was revolted by what eight years–scarcely an eternity–had wrought. I could not blame him, agreeing as I did, yet as their conversation continued, I began to grow angry.

"Charles!"

That one word summoned my protective instincts, the devotion of servant to master. For in that word I heard surprise, joy–and love–and I suddenly knew milady had a proper heart of flesh.

Why then the concern, you say? Here's the happy ending, Hodges old man, you say? No. There was to be no happy ending. My trained ears, those ears which heard the longed-for warmth in the single word from my mistress, had heard more than enough words from the object of her affection to know that the affection was not returned. And, in case I needed more, they came.

"Emily, I had to tell you in person. I've returned to England and–I'm getting married."

Milady's heart broke in the second before she answered. I cannot swear I heard it shatter–after all, it's been fifteen years–but the voice that followed tinkled like shards of glass. "Why, Charles, how wonderful for you! I'd have expected your marriage long since! I do hope you didn't think I was waiting for your return–I would feel so awful if our ridiculous pledges when we were–oh, just children–had troubled you in any way. Of course I did not think twice about it–haven't thought of you since my second season–well, how wonderful for you, really!"

Fickle Charles Fenton apparently heard the brittle tone as well. "Emily, I am sorry. You know I meant to marry you. I thought of you every night, out in the field. I treasured every letter you sent, and cursed your father for not permitting me to write back. But then I was transferred to the _nth, and Wellington was so close to victory–I couldn't just desert, you know–"

That explained milady's interest in the war, I thought.

"And then, in hospital, I met Caroline, and..."

"Perfect! A war story romance–you will be the sensation of the week!" Milady's voice was rising higher. "She must be very beautiful."

All my instincts told me to knock, to enter the room–somehow to release milady from the torment I'd unwittingly put her in—but I waited, hoping that the impossible would happen: that milady would regain the beauty drained by eight years of worry, and the earl would renew the vows I had helped to break. Or, at the least, that she would see the worthlessness of her ex-suitor. His callous speech certainly sickened me.

"Oh yes, Caroline is lovely. Not as beautiful as you once were—that is—"

The tight, awkward voice interrupted him again. "So she's a nurse, your Caroline?"

Fenton sounded confused. "No. Oh, I see. The hospital. No, she was visiting her brother. She's the youngest daughter of a baron in Hertfordshire. You'll meet her, Emily. With Jonathan's death I inherited the family holdings. That's part of why I wanted to tell you myself; we'll be living here in Mayfair."

I had long since taken a position behind the open door, but the crack offered a very restricted view, and I had seen little more than milady's back until, at this moment, she turned. A satinwood writing-table stood near the door. As I watched, she casually moved to the table and, her back toward the visitor and her skirts blocking his view, opened its single drawer. From it she slid the sharp dagger her father had used as a letter opener. My gasp was quiet; it did not disturb either of the room's occupants. I watched with a morbid fascination as, still facing the doorway, she moved a few steps closer to Charles Fenton.

"How nice. You will be living here in Mayfair. I shall see your lovely Caroline every day."

The earl swallowed. "Well, I don't suppose that will be necessary. I merely thought you would, well, meet at parties and such. Although they tell me you don't get out much nowadays, Emily."

Another few steps. I wondered if she would

really kill him; whether she *could* kill a grown man. She lacked the strength to best him in a fight, of course, but with the element of surprise, and a good swing... And if her first strike was true, it would be easy enough to finish the deed. But she'd be caught, arrested–hung as a murderer at Newgate Prison! I couldn't allow that, not when Fenton's presence in the house was solely my fault. In fact, all was my fault: I was the one who told Emily's father about the impoverished young suitor in the drawing room. If not for me, the two would have eloped, Lord Wrexwood surely would have bestowed his blessing–and estates–eventually, and milady would be happy now, rather than risking Newgate at twenty-six years of age. I shuddered. It all came to me. I would have to kill the earl. I had few years left, compared to her, and what years I had would mean little if the last of the Wrexwoods swung from the gallows.

These were the thoughts of but a few seconds, but milady was already in action. "I did love you, Charles," she said, then whirled with the gleaming dagger even as I rounded the door.

Horrified, Fenton and I watched together as, looking full into the earl's eyes, milady plunged the dagger into her own soft bosom. A shuddering gasp–she did not scream–and a spurt of blood, and she crumpled to her knees. "I did wait," she gasped. "I was faithful." And then, thankfully, her accusing eyes rolled back behind their lids and she lost consciousness.

Anger filled me; fury with the inconstant earl and with my own weak resolution, with the twist of fate that killed my mistress rather than her unfaithful lover.

She died quickly, the blood staining her gray bombazine a more fashionable crimson. We two stood silent, helpless, until her ragged breaths had stopped and her eyelids fluttered no more. Then we looked from her lifeless form to each other, measuring knowledge and intent. The heat of hatred filled me.

"Well, my lord," I said slowly, "your pledges are effectively broken now."

He wet his lips with a nervous tongue. "The scandal...Caroline...no one must know!" He pulled out his purse, and opened it eagerly. Bribing the trustworthy retainer. He did not know how close to death he was himself at that moment.

I studied his anguished face. I had been willing to murder him for her. Instead, my actions had caused her death. My actions, and his. We were bound together, Charles Fenton and I, by our mutual guilt. Each of us could truly be dubbed milady's murderer. It would avail me nothing to kill the earl. My guilt would still remain, the guilt of a pompous servant eight years before and the guilt heavy in this disobedient, deadly afternoon. No, if I was to live with my guilt, Fenton must live with his as well. That was to be his punishment. And so we dealt with the–incident–together. I calmly escorted the shattered man downstairs and summoned his carriage. He sent her flowers, with the accompanying note reading: "In remembrance of our reunion. I look forward to dinner Saturday." And I mentioned to several loose-tongued footmen that milady had seemed unusually distracted when I took in her morning tea. I even chanced a speculation that her upcoming birthday depressed her, being yet another testimony to her spinsterhood.

When the parlor maid found the body that evening, my words had done their work. Amid the screams and sobs, no one questioned the cause of the suicide. Those that did not blame her age, blamed her interests, and said that women should not become so engrossed in politics or war.

As I had often mourned, there were no Wrexwoods remaining to inherit milady's estate, but the house was not left masterless for long. A distant relative scurried to London within the month. He sold most of the estate's paintings and collectibles, sold the country estate but kept the Mayfair town house and its well-trained staff.

I chose not to stay. I could feel no family loyalty to one so obviously not a Wrexwood, and without loyalty to bind me, guilt forced me away. I found employment only seven houses down with a newly-married earl. It is unusual for a butler with my background to apply for a new position, but I was hired without question.

That was fifteen years ago. My gout is bothering me more now, and my silver hair is very thin. I expect to be pensioned off next fall, so I have been training my nephew to replace me. I have trained him in all aspects of the job, including an accusing, meaningful gaze. Other than that–and I have used it only when milord seemed too complacent–we Hodges are devoted to the Fentons.

/=/

Sarah Starr was born in Albany, Oregon. She spent twenty-three years there in the gorgeous, if gray-skied, Willamette Valley. She began working toward a degree in English and music education, but discovered, sadly, that panic attacks and music performances don't mix. She married her best friend from high school and quit college to support her husband through college by working as a bookkeeper. When Colin received a math teaching assistantship for graduate school, Sarah began writing full time. She has written Sunday School lessons, children's books, a young adult novel, and has sold more than 300 articles to various magazines and newspapers.

Milady's Murderer is Sarah's first published fiction piece. **Lady-Lessons**, her first Regency novel, will be published by Regency Press in April, 2000.

The Final Wager
Adam Naef

"I'm sore took, Miss. It's me head."

The coachman had pulled open the carriage
door, and his face twisted into a grimace that
would have made a banshee gape. But Miss Ariadne Clavering, seated inside, only emitted a
weary sigh and then searched quickly through her
brain for a resolution to this latest *contretemps*.

"Shall we turn the carriage around? Was there
not an inn a little way back?" Her steady voice
was designed to have a soothing effect.

"Turn around? No, Miss, that I could nivver
do! I'd not make it no more than two steps." He
put up both hands and clutched his head, as if it
might make a run for it if he did not hold on tight.

All this drama was not new to Miss Clavering.
She had long been privy to the ill-timed comings
and goings of Jeremy Rugg's headaches.

"John could take the reins," she suggested
calmly, referring to the young groom who had
been riding next to him on the box.

"By t'heart, Miss! That raggabash would lurch us inter a ditch afore I could close one eye."

Rugg's mention of taking a little nap inspired him. He pulled the door open wider and raised a foot to the step. She realized with dismay that he intended to climb in with her. Not that there was any room! The vehicle was only a light chariot with one forward-facing seat, and her bandbox and small valise occupied part of it.

"Wait!" she protested, rearranging the position of a portmanteau on the floor. "Help me down. Then you can rest on the seat."

"Thankee, Miss. Thankee." He took hold of her elbow, and his ginger manner implied that any such effort was way too much for him and perhaps quite beyond his duty under the circumstances. But once she was on the ground, a burst of energy possessed him. He clambered into the carriage without any attention to how he went and slammed the door behind him.

Miss Clavering found herself turning to address a closed window shade. "I see the rooftop of a house beyond some evergreens up the road," she called out loudly. "I shall inquire if we might stop there before it comes on to mizzle." She glanced at the forbidding sky. "It will not do to stay here."

She waited a moment for an acknowledgment, but none was forthcoming. Holding the collar of her lined pelisse higher around her neck, she paused to say a few words of encouragement to John, who was now at the horses' heads, and then she continued carefully along the rutted track that served in this part of Yorkshire as a road.

It was turning dark, and the autumn colours that dotted the hilly landscape were lost to duller hues. What a pretty pass things had come to! She knew she had asked for trouble by agreeing to such a long journey with Rugg, but Lady Blosset had insisted he drive her, saying that the notion of her dear Ariadne taking a hired chaise and being driven by a stranger into the wilds was too loathsome to contemplate. Lady Blosset, who was Maria Meath, her bosom-bow from school, had been very kind to her during the last eight years. She simply could not refuse the gracious offer. And now this bleak result!

Originally, Miss Clavering's future had promised to be bright. She was a pleasant creature–perhaps a bit tall and perhaps a bit too open and frank in expression–but attractive all the same, if one made allowances for the fact that her hair was dark brown instead of the more fashionable honey-yellow. Because she was the great-granddaughter of an earl, it was assumed that she had a respectable sum tacked to her. And she did. Or, rather, she had had such a sum until her father lost it in a foolish wager at White's. He was standing on the steps of that hallowed club one day with his crony, Lord Amory, when they suddenly spied two of their acquaintances crossing St. James's Street. Mr. Clavering bet that Bertie Houndlsow would reach the opposite side of the street first, and Lord Amory put his money on the other gentleman. This was not a wager of a few guineas. Mr. Clavering was so shot in the neck that he wagered virtually everything he owned, save his snuffboxes, a small collection he valued above all things. Praise Heaven, he refrained also from throwing in the hand of his daughter, as invited to do by Lord Amory, who was a widower with sixty years in his dish and three unmarried, platter-faced sisters at home.

The remorse he felt after losing the wager caused Mr. Clavering to sell his snuffboxes and purchase a commission in the cavalry with the intention of departing directly for the Peninsula to fight the French. He fell at Talavera in '09, and it was only then that his butler in Curzon Street remembered to post the note Mr. Clavering had hastily penned to his daughter before leaving England: "Going to fight Boney. Yr. Father." Lord Amory had magnanimously forborne to collect his winnings until he received news of his friend's demise. In fact, his Lordship had tried to prevent Mr. Clavering's departure by granting him a year of grace and suggesting he try to make some money for himself on 'Change so that he would not be completely rolled up when he paid what he owed. But Mr. Clavering was a mutton-head and did not make use of this opportunity.

The summer of Talavera, Miss Clavering was staying at the country seat of Sir Reginald Meath, Maria's father, a sojourn that had been arranged in the spring, and so she had been out of touch with her father for several months–a circumstance that was not unusual. She and Maria had just completed their studies at Miss Parkington's Academy for Young Ladies, and Maria was preparing for her wedding. She was not marrying for love. Her *parti*, Bertram Welby, Lord Blosset, had been selected by her father, against whom Maria could never assert herself. Blosset was not totally repellent, but he was a little extravagant in his manner, and his vanity drove him to wear bone stays in an attempt to hide his growing corpulence.

When she learned that her dear Ariadne was now penniless, Maria begged her to live with her at Blosset Park after the wedding. It would make life easier for them both to bear, she said. Miss Clavering was susceptible to her pleas but did not want to be in the position of a hanger-on, so she agreed to come as governess to Maria's future children. The idea of educating young minds appealed to her. She herself had done exceptionally well in school. Her French was fluent, and she was clever at drawing and painting. The only thing Maria was better at than she was music. Too shy to deal effectively with people, Maria had sought refuge with the pianoforte, and she played flawlessly.

Things did not work out precisely as planned. Maria bore Lord Blosset only one child. Happily for Miss Clavering, it was a girl, Cassandra by name, and the child was launched into an effervescent educational program as soon as she could focus on her governess. But Lord Blosset had other ideas. His deceased Mama was French, and he was so mesmerized by memories of her artful charm that he made plans for his daughter to be educated in a French school. Now, in October 1817, after little Cassandra celebrated her seventh birthday, he declared that, with Bonaparte in exile and things quieting in France, it was a propitious moment to send the child across the Channel. This prospect cast Maria into despair, but Miss Clavering succeeded in drawing her focus to the baby that was coming. Yes, Maria was finally increasing again.

Then a new disturbance arrived in the form of a letter from Sir Reginald, Maria's father. His older sister had turned more invalidish, and he requested that Miss Clavering come to serve as her companion until he found someone suitable for a more permanent stay. Maria did not know how to refuse him, and in order to prevent her from falling prey to the fidgets once more, Miss Clavering quickly assured her that nothing would afford her greater pleasure than to go at once.

And so here she was, stranded she knew not where in Yorkshire. As she walked away from the carriage and away from Rugg's megrim, she was startled by a distant rumble of thunder, and her steps quickened. Happily, the gates to the house she had seen stood open, and the approach drive, darkened by waving branches of sycamores, was short. The house was an impressive Georgian structure with large wings on either side, and the central portion of the building boasted rows of tall windows separated by Corinthian pilasters that rose three storeys to support an ornate pediment. She noticed none of these architectural delights, however, for she had lowered her head against the wind. She did not even prepare a speech for the inhabitants before climbing the steps and beating an urgent tattoo on the massive door.

The person who answered her knock seemed as surprised to see her as she was to see him. He was a man of some fifty years dressed in the fashion of an *Incroyable* who might have haunted the streets of Paris twenty years before. His long, shaggily cut hair, all disheveled, stood out from his head at alarming angles, and his face seemed to be sitting atop a pole because his neckcloth, which consisted of who knows how many yards of blue silk, was wound around and around from his shoulders up to his chin. His coat was surely the work of a tailor gone mad. Its wide lapels threw themselves stiffly out into space, well beyond his arms.

When Miss Clavering saw his eyes narrow in an unfriendly manner, she threw her thoughts together as best she could. "My carriage is stopped on the road, a few steps from the gates, and my coachman is feeling unwell," she said in a rush of words. "Might we take refuge inside?"

"*C'est impossible*, Mademoiselle. You muzz go!"

"Go?" Her voice echoed shrilly in the cavernous hall.

His eyebrows rose in disapproval, and he put his hands on his hips. He was fortified with the scent of a heavy *eau de cologne*.

She determined to brave the onslaught. "Pray tell me," she said, her voice raspy from the wafting fumes, "what house is this? To whom does it belong?" Had she succeeded in sounding authoritative?

He smirked in a way only a Frenchman could. "Everyone, they know this house," he proclaimed haughtily. "It is *la plus belle* of the whole region." He glanced to the side at his reflection in a gilt mirror and grew more impatient. "The dust, it is everywhere. *Nom de Dieu!*" He turned to her again. "You muzz go."

He made a move to shut the door, but she thwarted him by stepping inside. If he blenched, it was impossible to tell, since his face was heavily powdered and rouged. What did he mean by wearing face powder in this day and age, she wondered!

"And who, do you tell me, owns the house?" she inquired in pointed accents.

Her boldness so astonished him that he blurted automatically, "Lord Rayne." He managed, nonetheless, to give the "r" an ornamental trill.

"Be so good, then, as to inform *Lady* Rayne that Miss Ariadne Clavering craves a moment of her time in the direst emergency."

His laugh was swift and bore such a tinge of Gallic derision that she wished she could somehow vanish on the spot.

"Lady Rayne, she does not yet exist," he said smugly. "Eez Lordship is the unmarried man. *Très beau et maintenant très riche,* but without the wife."

"Oh!" She sought to make a recover, a thing that was not easily accomplished under his sardonic gaze. "In that case," she began rather haltingly, "Be so kind as to take my message to *Lord*

Rayne."

"Eez Lordship is not eere." His eyes were wickedly merry. He clearly took delight in tormenting her. "And more further," he went on with studied nonchalance, "he does not receive the young ladies in heez house. But I have no time for the quarrel, Mademoiselle. I make the preparation. Eez Lordship, he come from one minute to the next." This thought gave him pause, and his face began working in a way to bring on a tic. "He say to me, 'Baluze, we muzz go to Levenham Hall.' But he send with me the servants too few. *Allez*, Mademoiselle, *partez*!" He pulled the door open wide and motioned violently for her to leave.

Miss Clavering did his bidding. She saw no way to avoid it, and the whole scene had already taxed her every filament.

The door slapped shut while she was still on the top step. Another explosion of thunder, this one closer, encouraged her to return in all haste to the carriage. As she drew near, young John, still at the horses' heads, hailed her wildly.

"Miss, Miss!" he shouted. "Biggs was here! He come after us with a letter!"

"Dear me!" She ran the last distance. Thanking the boy for the news, she wrenched open the chariot's door. Jeremy Rugg was in the process of taking a sip from a little flask he carried on his person, and the abrupt sound caused him to flinch and spill a few drops on the front of his shirt.

"Lor', Miss! Ye'll bring back the curst throbbing!" He stuffed the flask into his coat pocket. "I was just coming to me wits."

"As I see, Rugg," she said dryly. "John tells me Biggs brought a letter."

"Just so, Miss. Just so." He wiped his hands on his breeches in an awkward and uncoordinated gesture, then reached for the single sheet that lay next to him. It was neatly folded into a square and sealed with red wax. "Her Ladyship sent him on our heels two hours after we took the road. He made good time, he did."

Miss Clavering considered his unsteady hand, as well as his flushed cheeks, and realized that he had been dipping deeper than she had at first supposed. And as for Biggs! She was amazed the groom had not reached them sooner, since Jeremy Rugg never drove above a snail's pace, but she suspected the young scapegrace had stopped at every alehouse he passed in order to fill himself with eatables and toss down a pint.

Rugg made no move to get out of the carriage, but she was thankful for that, given his condition. She took the missive he waved at her and then closed the door on him without ceremony. While standing in the road, she broke the seal and read a note scribbled by Lady Blosset:

> *My dearest Ariadne,*
> *I write this in desperate haste, for I must*
> *catch you before you have gone too far.*
> *An attorney arrived not two hours after*
> *your departure with news of the most*
> *pressing sort. He would not tell me any*
> *details, and I tremble in my bosom for*
> *fear his news might prove vexatious to*
> *you. But Bertram says we should not*
> *expect anything disagreeable because*
> *you have already lost everything and have*
> *no relatives to tease you further. I was*
> *very much horrified to hear him speak so*
> *and began to cry, but he told me to stop*
> *being a silly widgeon. He meant, he*
> *said, only that, given what has already*
> *happened, any attorney seeking you out*
> *at this present must be the bearer of*

*good tidings. I suppose there is some logic
to this. You know I do not possess a logical
mind, but you do, and thus I feel comforted
in the thought that you will not despair before
all is disclosed to you. The attorney's name
is Mr. Frye, and he desires you shall meet
him tomorrow morning at the <u>Green Man</u>
between Ingleford and Levenham. May you
be blessed with luck, dear one!*

Ever your friend,
Maria

"Good Heavens!" murmured Miss Clavering.
"What now?" She was momentarily distracted by
the opening of the carriage door. "No, no, Rugg.
Be so good as to stay within!"

"I'm returned more like meself, Miss. We had
ought to...oh! Ah! Oh!" He caught his foot on
Miss Clavering's portmanteau and fell back
against the seat cushions.

"John!" she called. "When I get up on the box,
leave the horses and climb inside with Rugg. He is
unable to drive. Take care he does not open the
door en route and tumble out." She lifted her skirt
and hoisted herself into position on the box.
"There! I am ready."

John ran by to get in with the coachman, and
as he passed, he looked at her with no small degree of shock. It must have been unnerving for
him to view Miss Clavering on the box, female
that she was. But he had known her for more than
half his life, and she was one of the most level-
headed people he had come across, female or not.

"Have we been through Ingleford yet?" she
threw out as he passed.

"Yes, Miss. I saw a sign by an inn a few miles
back."

"Good! That must be the Green Man I am

looking for."

She set the chariot in motion as soon as he shut himself inside. The road was wide enough in this spot to turn around, and she executed the maneuver without mishap. She had been accustomed only to driving a gig, drawn by a pony, around the grounds of Blosset Park and the nearby countryside, so holding the reins of a pair of carriage horses with plenty of bottom was a daunting prospect. She had no time for misgivings, however, since the task demanded all her attention. The fact that she knew they were in Levenham, thanks to Baluze, and did not have to flounder over which direction to pursue in order to reach her destination buoyed up her spirits and gave her a surge of confidence.

She drove conservatively until more rumblings of thunder incited her to speed up. The sky was growing darker by the moment, and she began to expect they would be caught in a downpour. Why had she not taken time to change her pelisse for the more hardy redingote that was packed in her portmanteau? She should have removed her bonnet, too! It ran the risk of being completely ruined, and she did like it most particularly.

She cracked the whip, and the horses began to cover ground with an almost reckless *élan*. Apparently they did not like the weather either. Miss Clavering was thankful that Rugg had insisted on changing horses in Eastwold. This pair still had their wind.

Lanterns glimmered ahead, and in a few minutes Miss Clavering distinguished a building in the distance. The Green Man! Suddenly there was a great crash of thunder, and the sky opened up. She urged the horses on to full speed. The gates to the inn's yard came into clearer view. The opening was wide, and she was convinced she could take the turn. Perhaps it would be wiser to slow down. She pulled on the reins, while the rain pelted her mercilessly, but the horses hardly slackened their pace. Heaven have pity! An open curricle was coming up the road toward her, and it was also heading for the gate. She ceased to breathe. What should she do? Her horses were no longer comfortably under her control. Should she try to veer away from the gate and continue on until she could pull up and turn around? That, at least, would avert a crash. No, her horses were moving left, bearing down on the gate. They knew where good, covered stalls were waiting!

Miss Clavering had no choice. She had to outstrip the other carriage. She cracked the whip and shouted frantically to the horses. Her chariot bounded ahead and swerved in front of the approaching vehicle, cutting it off. She would have ravaged a good deal of its bright blue paint, had the driver not pulled up with all his might and brought his spanking pair of greys to a dead halt. Sweeping by, her carriage did not stop until it was well at the end of the yard, almost in front of the stables. The ostler and two stableboys came running.

"Lawks, Miss!" cried one of the boys gleefully. "You pitched in fearsome good!"

The ostler regarded her grimly, and in order to stave off the lecture he looked ready to deliver, she mustered her breath and said in a pant, "My coachman is within–quite unwell. Would you please help him?"

She jumped down from the box without assistance and dashed to the door of the inn, which was a worn, half-timber affair with an overhanging storey. At the point of putting her foot to the doorstep, she saw, out of the corner of her eye, the curricle she had almost hit. With a pang of dread she noticed that the driver was not a coachman, but a fine gentleman. He was glaring at her with barely suppressed fury. She wondered if now was the time to apologize and offer him her sincerest regrets for the unpleasant incident. She wondered...A clap of thunder caused his horses to lurch forward. He had to struggle to bring them to order and did not need distraction now. Her opportunity was lost, and she rushed into the inn.

The taproom was filled with people conversing noisily amidst the smoke and loud clattering of plates and tankards. There was not a female in sight. Men of all ages were shedding their hats and coats in order to shake them out and dry them in front of the huge fireplace. A dozen vehicles must have arrived in the yard only minutes before. The air was thick and foul smelling, and Miss Clavering felt herself sinking into a faint. She spied an empty chair in a dark corner, behind some rough-looking brutes who were guffawing over a joke. She threw herself into it and squeezed her eyes shut to banish the offensive scene.

She remained thus, without moving, for a full five minutes.

"Miss! Miss! Can I bring you something?"

She looked up into the round, pink face of a young maidservant.

Miss!" the girl said again, sounding much pressed. With a loud scraping noise, she began to pull over a small table.

"Thank you," Miss Clavering mumbled faintly."I should be glad of a pot of tea. Very strong." She noticed a gluttonous oaf delving into a goose and turkey pie at the next table. "Where is the private parlour?" she asked quickly.

"Inside the door there, opposite," the maid replied, hurriedly removing some empty tankards from the table. "But it's bespoke. And there's no bedchambers to be had, neither." She darted off to the kitchen.

The man eating his pie belched and took a clumsy gulp of ale.

Miss Clavering stood up. She resolved to beg the indulgence of the person who had taken over the private parlour. If Fate was sympathetic, this person would be a lady of quality, one who would welcome her most graciously. She made her way to the door and knocked.

There was no response. With the din of the taproom, it was probably impossible to hear any civilized knock, so she ventured to open the door and peek inside.

"Is someone here?" Her voice was covered by the noise.

The parlour was dark, save for the light of the fire that was blazing in the hearth. The rush of warmth was comforting, and she could not resist. Drawing near the chimney, she stretched out her hands and sighed when waves of heat rose up to envelop her.

"So! After nearly running me into the gatepost, you think nothing of invading my parlour," boomed a rich, masculine voice from the shadows.

Miss Clavering winced, as if she had been struck.

"You do not stand on ceremony, I see," the voice continued mercilessly.

She peered into the dark recesses and discerned in the corner, stretched out on a chaise longue, a human form–a man shod in a well-polished pair of top boots. This was not the welcome she had anticipated, and words failed her.

"I do not wonder you have nothing to say for yourself. I never saw anyone display such an appalling lack of sense. And the impertinence of not even begging my pardon afterward and then barging in here like some brass-faced hoyden! It defies all..."

Miss Clavering burst into tears. She did not mean to, but a dam suddenly gave way. Her experience at the reins had left her emotions very raw, and now there was no stopping the torrents.

"Good Lord!" The man rose with an exasperated huff, and if she had looked up, she would have recognized him as the elegant driver of the curricle she had almost hit. He was like a Greek god who had set foot to earth, and if he showed few traces of having come in from a thunderstorm it was because he had been wearing a top hat and a driving coat with seven capes, both of which items were now occupying a chair near the fireplace. His thick black hair was slightly tousled and curled over his forehead in a nonchalant manner that accorded little with the severity of the scowl creasing his brow. His eyes, a tantalizing light blue, appeared icy as he approached. Any female would have felt weak when such a portrait of perfection bore down upon her, but the fact that he was a god in full fury made him terrifying, and when Miss Clavering raised her head and caught a glimpse of him, she was further undone.

He silently held out a handkerchief to her, but since she was now covering her eyes with her hands, she did not see it.

"Please take this," he said more awkwardly than one would have anticipated.

She did not hear.

He made a gesture toward her but stopped. Then he began again. He reached out and gently pulled her hands away from her face.

She stared at him like a cornered deer. This was not the intrepid Miss Ariadne Clavering known to her friend Lady Blosset.

"Please take this," he repeated.

She accepted the handkerchief with a silent nod of thanks and, after a few last tearful sniffs, dabbed at her eyes.

"I am sorry I made you cry." His irritation was gone, and he spoke with sincerity. "I am not in the habit of giving ladies a rakedown. It was a most regrettable lapse on my part, and I really do beg your pardon." The corners of his mouth rose in a conciliatory attempt to be cheerful, and at Almack's the effect would have been devastating. He was an exquisite specimen of some eight-and-thirty years and, no doubt, the object of many a heart's desire.

Miss Clavering listened gravely while finishing the restoration of her visage, and his unpretentious candor nudged her toward her more natural and self-possessed state. He was not at all like Lord Blosset, whose manner usually set her on edge. "Dear Sir," she began, still feeling a little ill at ease, "you need not apologize to *me*! It was all *my* fault, and it is *I* who must humbly beg *your* pardon. I am accustomed only to a pony and gig and would not have been driving that chariot at all, but for the sudden illness of my coachman." Her smile, at first tentative, widened under the influence of his friendly expression. "The sudden rain caused me to panic, I think."

"It is no wonder." He grinned devilishly. "You certainly did an amazing job of taking the turn. Next we shall behold you on the box of a coach and four!"

She let out an involuntary gurgle of laughter. "No, no. I hope not! I assure you I have no such aspirations."

"Are they doing what is necessary for your coachman? Is there some way I can help?"

"I thank you kindly." She relaxed further under his concern. "It is only Rugg's usual head pain...

261

and a trifle too much liquor."

"By gad, you should not have to endure such behaviour! Why do you keep him?"

This caused a sigh. "It is a long story," she said, "and you would be moped to death if I made a recital of it."

He smiled at the droll grimace with which she punctuated her words.

"Gracious Heavens! I am quite wet." She was only now aware that water dripped from her bonnet. "Oh, my pelisse!" She looked forlornly down her front.

"You must get it off immediately." He had the voice of a general ordering his troops. "Come. Let me help you."

She wriggled free. Thankfully, the fur lining of the pelisse had kept her traveling dress of light merino quite dry. He spread the outer garment over a ladder-back chair, which he moved closer to the fire, and then she took off her headgear and put it on one of the chair posts.

"I think I may be able to salvage my poor bonnet," she murmured thoughtfully, contemplating its bedraggled state.

"Now there's a piece of good news," he said encouragingly.

He was acting a bit wary, as if he expected her to dissolve into tears again, but he did not know Miss Clavering.

"You needn't treat me with kid gloves," she notified him promptly. "I am myself again. But I do wish I had the pot of tea I ordered before I disturbed you."

Just then there was a loud rap, and the maid-servant poked her head around the door. "Begging your pardon, your Lordship. Oh! Here she is. I thought Miss had disappeared."

"She will take her tea in here," he said. "And

would you add another plate when you bring in my dinner?"

The girl curtsied and shut the door.

"I have ordered veal cutlets with bacon, mushroom fritters, whatever vegetables they can offer, and sundry jellies and custards," he informed Miss Clavering. "Will that suit you?"

"It sounds perfect. I should not say it, but I am feeling half-starved!"

He laughed. "Good. We'll make a hearty meal of it, then." He pulled a table toward the fireplace and placed two chairs on either side.

She watched as he did this and felt his presence more keenly. He moved with the purposeful and lithe movements of a majestic animal from the wild. Some unfamiliar stirrings deep within took her by ambush and embarrassed her somewhat. She was unused to the society of elegant men, for Lord Blosset was wont to abandon his wife and child to the solitude of his country seat and entertain any elegant friends he had in London at his house in Grosvenor Square.

Miss Clavering attempted to divert herself from studying her host by gazing about the parlour, but it was a drab chamber with nothing to look at save the plain dark panels on the walls. Happily, the maidservant soon returned with her tea, but she only had time for a few sips before the appearance of a tray loaded with covered platters. One trip did not suffice for the dinner his Lordship had ordered, and the girl came back two more times.

"Surely you did not mean to eat all this yourself!" Miss Clavering exclaimed, quite without thinking, after the maid had gone. She looked up from the array of dishes to see her host smiling at her broadly. "Oh!" she went on in a rush. "That is not what I meant to say at all! I beg your pardon."

"No, pray say what you like. Don't stand on points with me. It is refreshing to sit down with a lady who does not hesitate to voice her thoughts."

She tapped her knife on the table. "I think I read a censure of my sex in your words, Sir," she said, pretending to take umbrage.

He laughed with good spirit but did appear to blush a little. "I see I am in a position where I must explain myself."

"No," she said quoting his former phrase. "Pray say what you like. It is refreshing."

This time he guffawed. "A flush hit, Miss...?" He looked all at once confused. "I do not know your name. We haven't yet introduced ourselves."

"I am Miss Clavering."

He nodded in acknowledgment. "I am Jasper Amory, Viscount Rayne."

"Amory!" She turned white. That was the name of her Papa's old friend! The man who had won the dreadfully absurd but ruinous wager. The man who had destroyed her life!

"Is something wrong? Are you not well?"

She shuddered involuntarily. "It is nothing." She latched on to her other thought. "You are Lord Rayne!" she said quickly. "I am just come from your house."

"Levenham Hall?"

"Yes." She took several breaths to buttress herself. "I would not be here at all, had your butler not turned me away." She forced a merry tone as she sought to cancel the name Amory and its every connotation from her mind.

He looked surprised but then launched himself into her game. "I don't have a butler," he remarked casually.

"But there was a man at the Hall who answered the door and was not in livery," she said in perplexity. "He was certainly an upper servant. He is French. I believe his name is Baluze."

Lord Rayne shot her a quizzical look. "If he heard you call him a butler, he would go off in an apoplexy. He styles himself my *maître d'hôtel*."

"Oh!" She laughed. "I must beg his pardon, then."

"That would only puff up his pretensions further. He eez, I make sure, heir to zee duc de Bourgogne."

She chortled at his perfect imitation of Baluze's accent.

"I shall have to scold him for turning you away," Lord Rayne went on more seriously.

"No, no! Pray do not! He seemed to believe I am some sort of designing female. We may surmise he was only protecting you from my schemes!"

His Lordship considered her thoughtfully. "Then he is a frippery fellow. Anyone can see you are the furthest thing from a designing female."

She feigned displeasure. "I wonder if I am to take that as a compliment. You appear to have been the victim of young ladies on the scramble for a gentleman of the first consequence. I suppose any number of matchmaking Mamas have attempted to run you to earth!"

"Please! You are spoiling my dinner."

She laughed brightly and returned her attention to her plate.

They were both so hungry that conversation was scarce during the rest of the meal, save for a few remarks on the sudden turn in the weather and how relieved they were to be able to enjoy the quiet and comfort of a private parlour. The maidservant came in several times to see if anything was wanted, and she told Miss Clavering that a merchant was planning to vacate one of the bedchambers as soon as the rain stopped. He was now having a little nap to prepare for his long journey, and the girl promised to inform her as soon as he was gone and the bed linen changed.

After the dishes were cleared, Lord Rayne suggested that they withdraw to the high-backed bench that faced the fireplace, for the temperature outside was dropping, and away from the hearth, the room was growing chilly. A stable boy eventually brought in more logs and mentioned that Rugg and John were fast asleep in the quarters above the stables and that Rugg would probably be fit as a fiddle in the morning. This was welcome news. Miss Clavering felt vastly relieved that everything was turning out so well. Soon the rhythmic crackling of the fire made her eyelids droop. Her day had been too taxing, and she was exhausted. Perhaps, she admitted to her fading faculties, she should not have accepted that glass of wine. But its effect was so deliciously warming!

In another moment her weary head gave way. She drifted into a silent doze and began to lean precariously forward. With care, Lord Rayne drew her back against him. Ordinarily he would not have been so free, but somehow it seemed like the most natural thing in the world to do.

The rain never stopped, and the wind swirled and howled savagely at the small leaded panes of the parlour windows. In her slumber, Miss Clavering snuggled against Lord Rayne's chest, and he put one arm protectively around her. He watched over her for a long time in a pensive mood, but then he, too, succumbed to the cozy warmth and closed his eyes.

They were in the same indiscreet pose when they awoke the next morning, an event which occurred to them both simultaneously, and their shock was so great that each one nearly tripped over the other while bolting up from the bench.

"Miss Clavering! I beg your pardon. I don't know what happened! I...we..."

"Say no more, I beg you." She felt her cheeks burning with mortification. "It was an accident. It was..."

"I am completely at fault." Lord Rayne's tone was grave. He hesitated. He seemed to be turning something over in his mind. "I shall do what is right to make amends to you," he said firmly, taking a few deliberate steps toward her. "Will you marry me, Miss Clavering?"

She shrank back. "Marry you, my lord? Amends! What are you saying!"

"I–"

"Stop!" she cried, moving further away. "Speak no more!"

"Miss!" The maidservant burst into the room in a flurry. "A gentleman is come to see you. Shall I show him in?"

Miss Clavering nodded mutely, and in another minute entered an ancient man, huffing and wheezing and poking his walking stick at the floor with every step. He had big tufts of white hair on either side of his bald pate and fly-away eyebrows.

"Heyday!" he cried, his sharp eyes fixed on Miss Clavering. He was a little bent over and looked at her with his head tilted up at an angle. "Lady Blosset's letter reached you in time in despite of the weather." He made an odd, sideways bow. "It's a pretty thing," he said, croaking his syllables, "to see a lady who can be dressed before nuncheon. That's what I like! Things running to schedule."

He seemed to be assessing her, and her first thought was that she must look a dreadful sight. She patted her hair, which had suffered remarkably little during the night, save for the fact that the braided coil on top of her head was slightly askew.

The curly tendrils that fell over her forehead and ears looked as if they had been arranged that way on purpose, and the general effect was quite fetching, even if she did not realize it.

"You are the attorney–Mr. Frye, I collect," she said in an effort to make him desist from scrutinizing her.

"The very same. The very same. Ho! You're here, too, my lord." He made a sideways bow to Lord Rayne. "Things proceed very well this day, I venture to suggest."

"Say you so!" Lord Rayne muttered, his voice tight. He remained near the fireplace, gripping the back of one of the chairs at the table.

"Yes, yes. So I say. So I say!" The attorney bobbed his head. "This business concerns you, as well, my lord. But you know that! No cause to waste time telling you what you already know. It's heartening to discover that the lunatic Mounseer you keep as a butler gave you my note. I thank you for coming so punctual. It makes things agreeable. That's what I like!"

"In point of fact," his Lordship rejoined dryly, "I never received your note and am here quite by chance."

This bulletin confounded Mr. Frye's vision of natural order, and the sudden agitation threw him into a fit of coughing. Dropping his walking stick, he tottered toward the pitcher of water on the table next to which Lord Rayne was standing, but anticipating him, his Lordship quickly filled a glass and held it out.

At first the sips the old man took made him choke, but finally he repossessed himself and was able to take back his stick, which the viscount had retrieved. "You are too good, my lord. Too good," he said, clearing his throat one last time. "Howsoever, time always wins if you don't beat it to the hour, so I move we commence instanter." He laid his leather case on the table and, after a brief struggle with the weathered clasps, opened it up. "Do you like to sit, Miss Clavering?" he asked, as he shuffled through a sheaf of papers.

She nodded and quietly took the chair opposite the one Lord Rayne was again gripping. As unobtrusively as possible, she darted a glance at Lord Rayne and noticed that his eyes wore a glazed and distant look. He seemed to have left his body.

"Hem!" Mr. Frye began, lifting his pince-nez. It hung from a chain attached to one of the buttons on his worsted vest, and he placed it gingerly on his nose. "I am come on the business of a certain document, the which his late Lordship, Lord Amory, bid me draw up."

Miss Clavering gasped, and Lord Rayne said "What?" in a resounding voice.

The attorney looked at them over his spectacles with a touch of choler. "I daresay I must revise my approach, or the matter won't conclude for another pair of Mondays."

"Do you tell me my uncle was involved in some way with Miss Clavering?" Lord Rayne inquired frostily.

"Your uncle!" Miss Clavering gasped again.

Mr. Frye put his handful of papers down on the table with a thud. "Involved? Involved? It ain't a word I would choose."

Lord Rayne glared at him.

"I porseeve you know nothing of your uncle's wager with Miss Clavering's father," the attorney grumbled in exasperation.

"Wager? What wager? I did not speak to my uncle once during the last ten years of his life. And anyone who is acquainted with me knows better than to mention his name in my presence."

Mr. Frye's scowl proclaimed his annoyance.

There would be no keeping to his schedule now! "I was not aware, my lord. Not aware. But we'll leave out the particulars and other such etceteras. Etceteras ain't what's needed!" He went on to say only that Mr. Clavering had lost everything he owned to Lord Amory in the year '09."

"Good God!" The viscount turned to address Miss Clavering, but her face was lowered and suffused with colour. "Miss Clavering!" His voice sounded harsh, and she did not look up. "I do not wonder that you recoiled when I introduced myself to you! The name Amory must give you little pleasure."

Mr. Frye made what he no doubt considered a discreet cough. "As to the matter at hand," he pressed on emphatically, "it concerns an offer his late lordship has made to you both. He desired you, Miss Clavering, to have a way to recover what your father lost to him. And he has extended to you, Lord Rayne,"–he nodded briefly to his Lordship–"the possibility to get back Levenham Hall, the which your late, lamented father lost to him in another wager."

"Levenham Hall!" spouted Lord Rayne, angrily. "My uncle was to leave that to me in his testament. He told me so in a letter he sent just before he died."

"Yes, but he lingered for more than a week after writing to you, and you did not come to him. He took it very ill."

"I was out of town," Lord Rayne informed him tersely. "I did not even see his letter until after he was dead." A light dawned. "Do you mean to tell me Levenham Hall is not mine? My servants are there now, putting the place in order!"

"You should have stepped round to my office first, my lord. His testament has not been made public yet, and everything depends upon how you and Miss Clavering accept his offer."

"Namely?" His Lordship was wary.

Miss Clavering looked up at last, but she was silent.

The attorney shuffled his papers needlessly. "Lord Amory's offer is..." He abruptly threw down the documents. "This ain't what I like! To see such a thing in writing makes my stomach lurch, and I told him so to his face. But he was fond of his notions, was his late Lordship!" He paused to take out his pocket watch and read the hour. "I shall be brief." He flicked shut the watch's cover and replaced the object in his vest. "Here is his offer: if you agree to marry each other, Miss Clavering will receive, as her wedding present, everything her father lost to Lord Amory. And your wedding gift, my lord, will be Levenham Hall and the sum of £100,000."

The muscles in Lord Rayne's face began to pulsate dangerously, and he looked ready to unleash a barrage of words, but Mr. Frye cut him off, holding up a hand and saying, "Tut, tut, my lord! You are too hasty. No one must speak until I have set out the offer entire."

His Lordship was silent but looked fully prepared to do a murder. His knuckles turned ominously white as he clenched the innocent back of the chair behind which he still stood.

"There is a contingency," the attorney continued, "to wit, I must ask you both for an immediate answer, and the person who first refuses the offer shall be the sole recipient of Lord Amory's entire estate, the which, I hasten to add, consists of everything mentioned in the offer plus another sum of £50,000." He paused to take out his pocket watch again. "There you have it. No need to waste more time." He put away his watch and removed his pince-nez. "I now ask formally for an answer." He regarded them expectantly.

Miss Clavering cleared her throat. Her mind was all chaos. What sort of freakish arrangement was this? Had she strayed into a madhouse?

"I refuse the offer," interposed Lord Rayne quickly.

Miss Clavering felt a sharp pain crush every breath out of her body.

"So be it," declared Mr. Frye. "You were the first to voice your refusal, you are thus the sole recipient of your uncle's estate." He gathered up his papers. "I have some documents for you to sign."

Lord Rayne nodded complacently.

With a stifled sob, Miss Clavering leapt to her feet. She snatched up her bonnet and pelisse and, clamping a hand over her mouth, ran from the room. She did not stop until she was out in the yard. There, to her immense relief, she saw Rugg and John driving Lady Blosset's chariot toward her.

She hurried to meet them. Rugg, who looked fit and in good spirits, tipped his hat to her, and John jumped down to open the door and help her inside. "Good morning, Miss," he said. "It wasn't so bad, after all, was it!"

Her senses were reeling, and she mumbled a completely disjointed reply. John gaped at her as if she were the chief exhibit in a raree-show.

"Drive on!" she cried. "Drive on! Why do you hesitate!"

"Hold!" The authoritative voice of Lord Rayne caused Rugg's whip to freeze in mid air over the horses' rumps.

Miss Clavering shrank back against the cushions. Before she could decide what to do, the viscount had pulled open the door.

He held out a paper folded several times into a

small square. "Take this, Miss Clavering," he said sternly.

Mechanically, she did his bidding, but she could not bear to look at him, and she did not speak.

Closing the door, he stepped back. "You may proceed," he told Rugg in his deep baritone.

The carriage rumbled sluggishly from the yard and turned north, in the direction of Levenham. Miss Clavering finally exhaled. It was over. She need never see Lord Rayne again. All he desired was money! He had looked so pleased with himself when he refused his uncle's offer. Clearly he preferred the entire estate to marriage with her. Yes, he had asked her to marry him. But for what reason? To make amends to her, he said. To follow some male code of honour more like! How unfeeling! How offensive! But did he truly believe he had compromised her reputation?

What an idiotish notion! No one knew they were in the parlour together all night except, perhaps, the maidservant, and she would hardly say anything. Who would ever discover what happened? She gave vent to a hollow laugh. Even if the facts became known, would it matter? She lived removed from society with Lady Blosset. There were no suitors to flee from her door after learning what had transpired. Without realizing it, she crumpled the note Lord Rayne had pressed upon her.

She became lost in dark thoughts and was gazing blankly out the window when she noticed with a start that they were passing Levenham Hall. "Good Lord!" she protested hotly. "Can I not be rid of that odious man!" For several minutes, as they jostled further along the road, she thought of any number of pointed things she might have said to him, had his offer of marriage not been interrupted by Mr. Frye. But she could not dispel the image of Lord Rayne's complacent smile. The greedy grab-all! If it was not greed, it was pure vindictiveness! Yes! *That* was what it was. Vindictiveness! When he saw she did not fall into his arms after he so magnanimously made her an offer, he claimed his uncle's entire inheritance to spite her. And then, to write a pretty *finis* for himself, he penned a note of apology! All at once, she became aware that she had not actually read the little billet she was crinkling in her hand. "I should not give him the satisfaction of reading it!" she snapped.

But when she looked at the folded paper, now almost torn, her curiosity got the better of her, and she opened it. The text caused her to shriek in astonishment, for it read: "I, Jasper Amory, Viscount Rayne, do hereby transfer to Miss Ariadne Clavering the entirety of what I have inherited from my late uncle, Lord Amory, free from all encumbrances." The short document, written in a hasty scrawl, was signed and dated by his Lordship and witnessed by Mr. Honorius Frye.

"How dare he!" Miss Clavering spluttered with rage. "I don't want his stupid inheritance!" She thrust her head dangerously out the window and called to Rugg. "Turn around! I must stop at Levenham Hall."

The carriage came to an abrupt halt, and she managed with difficulty to keep her balance on the seat, but her bandbox, which contained her best bonnet, was not so lucky. It fell to the floor, its lid bounced off, and the resourceful headgear rolled out with reckless abandon.

"There!" She clamored. "That's what I need! Another ruined bonnet." She took great pains to replace the truant in her bandbox without doing it further injury and thus missed out on the scenic delights of the short sycamore drive to the entrance of the Hall.

John helped her down from the carriage, and she took grim pleasure in seeing a liveried footman drive Lord Rayne's curricle around the side of the building. So! He had just arrived from the inn!

She marched to the door like a crazed Turk and beat a loud tattoo.

"*Encore vous*, Mademoiselle!" It was Baluze who opened to her, and his indignation was readily apparent. He waved her away with both hands. "I have told it to you before. Eez Lordship does not receive zee young ladies in heez house."

Miss Ariadne Clavering was, at this moment, in full possession of all her faculties and could have trounced any number of peevish Frenchmen. "That's as may be," she replied in clipped tones. "But I am not come to *his* house. This is *my* house." She brushed past him, holding up briefly the note that transferred ownership of Levenham Hall to her. "Now, where is he?"

"*Sacrebleu*! This, it is the top of everything. *Non*, Mademoiselle! You muzz not go in there. His mood, it is not good!"

He was looking furtively at a closed door toward the rear of the hall, and so she made her way to it without pause and burst into the room beyond.

Lord Rayne, who was inside lifting some heavy tomes from a shelf, was so taken aback that he dropped the books onto the floor. "What the Devil!" he roared.

"That is precisely what I might say in regard to this," she answered, hurling his note at him.

Baluze, who had followed her as far as the doorway, closed them inside the room and retreated with haste. "*Les Anglais*!" He clucked to himself in disapproval.

275

"How dare you!" Miss Clavering fumed, bright with fire.

Lord Rayne's raised eyebrows indicated that he had not anticipated a reaction of this sort on her part. "I did what I thought was right under the circumstances."

"Circumstances! What circumstances do you refer to, pray?"

"I think it is wrong for you to be obliged to suffer for what your father and my uncle did."

"But you transferred *everything* to me, not just what my father lost in the wager."

Lord Rayne smiled sheepishly. "I wanted you to have the rest as compensation for what you must have gone through these past eight years."

"Oh." She began to blush. He did not seem, precisely at this moment, the ogre she had fashioned in her mind. His intentions were rather... what? Charming? No! She was not ready to abandon all her wrath so easily. "I do not need compensation. And I don't need magnanimous offers of marriage, either!" She froze at her last words, for she had not intended to broach that subject.

There was an awkward silence as Lord Rayne crossed his arms and studied her in the most unnerving fashion. "Why do you call my offer of marriage magnanimous?" he asked in measured tones.

A muscle in his cheek betrayed an inner tension he was attempting to conquer, but she did not notice because she was racing through every crevice of her brain in search of a way to answer him.

She let out a long sigh. Her anger was slipping away, and she felt only the terrible hurt that had engulfed her when he offered for her hand at the inn. She made a helpless gesture. "Magnanimous was a barbed word," she said softly. "*You* have never received an offer of marriage made solely because a gentleman feared to have compromised you. You cannot *know* what it is like."

He grinned at her. "Indeed, I must own that no gentleman has ever offered for *me* at all."

Miss Ariadne Clavering then did something she had never done in her entire life. She stamped her foot. "You are making sport of me. What a low stratagem!"

He came to her and took her hand. She tried to snatch it away, but he held it firm. "Please forgive me," he said earnestly.

His tone was so warm and gentle that she left off her efforts to be free and stared into his eyes. Their arresting blue was like the caress of a cool, refreshing breeze. She had to struggle to focus on what he was telling her.

"I did not ask you to marry me because I thought I was obliged to do so," he explained simply.

"But that is what you said. You said, 'I shall do what is right to make amends to you.' Is that not so?"

He blushed. "Yes, I did say that."

"There!"

"But you were mortified at the realization that we had spent the night together, and…oh, plague take it! It just seemed the quickest way to get you to marry me."

"The quickest way? What are you talking about, my lord?"

"I am telling you that I am in love with you. The moment you slipped into a doze on the bench and I pulled you back to rest against me, I felt something I have never felt before. I felt that we belong together. But I knew I could not ask you at once to marry me for love. You would have refused, saying we are barely acquainted. You would have taken me for a half-baked moonling. I had to encourage you to believe our night together had compromised you."

This speech produced in Miss Clavering many pleasant sensations, yet she could not help but comment, "My lord, your plan may have seemed logical to *you*, however I must tell you it is not well designed to encourage anyone of *my* sex."

"Perhaps this would be more encouraging." He drew her close and kissed her with an intensity that made her shiver in his strong embrace.

"Yes, that *is* more encouraging," she whispered, when he let her catch a breath before recommencing his persuasion.

And persuade her he did.

"Ah! There you are! This is what I like. My time ain't wasted!" Mr. Frye threw the door open wider and began to pick out a route across the parquet with his walking stick. "You forgot to take a squint at these other papers, my lord. More signatures are required! You loped off before I could shout *Halloo*."

Miss Clavering had sprung away, but Lord Rayne still held her firmly by the hand.

"You may wish us happy, Mr. Frye," he said, smiling. "Miss Clavering is going to marry me... that is, I think she is."

She let out a trill of laughter. "Now that I have been discovered in a compromising situation by an attorney, I suppose I shall have to give my consent."

"It's too late," Mr. Frye told her roundly. "Lord Rayne refused his uncle's offer and received the estate in toto. The principal document has been signed."

"Good God, man!" his Lordship thundered. "I hope you don't think my refusal dictates any subsequent course of my life!"

"I ain't in my dotage yet! I didn't mean any such particular. I only meant you cannot win the wager by marrying Miss Clavering after the fact."

"What wager?" Lord Rayne and Miss Clavering cried in unison.

Mr. Frye regarded them as if they were schoolchildren who never paid attention. "His late Lordship's wager with you both. Did I not spell it out entire at the inn?"

They shook their heads.

"Well, it don't signify if I didn't, since nothing tangible is altered by it. Howsoever, he bet that one of you would refuse his offer. It was, he professed, his final and most stimulating wager."

Lord Rayne and Miss Clavering exchanged a droll, conspiratorial glance, and his Lordship asked, "If nothing *tangible* is altered, what did we stand to win?"

"His blessing, my Lord."

"And what did Lord Amory win from us?" inquired Miss Clavering, a twinkle in her eye.

"Why, the eternal satisfaction of having won his final wager!"

/=/

Adam Naef has lived in Milan, Paris, and New York and now makes his home in Providence, RI. He became interested in Regencies after reading *Charity Girl* by Georgette Heyer. "When traveling by train, I used to read Gothics," he says, "and I think I picked up *Charity Girl* at a station bookshop by mistake. When I began reading it, I couldn't put it down, and that was the beginning." His all-around favorite Regency author is Clare Darcy. Adam is the author of a Regency mystery: The *Barbury Hall Murders*.

Fabulous fantasy from the creative pen of a favorite of Regency readers! Neptune's court convenes at a remote, abandoned estate on the Severn River, all assembled to enjoy their annual festivities, when humans intrude and set everything topsy-turvey. Half-mermaid/half-human Sabrina, who loves to don human dress, falls for the very human Jake, who's on the run from his annoying ex-fiancée, in this very funny fantasy/farce.

Neptune's Quizzing Glass

Sandra Heath

Although it was an honor to be elected queen of Neptune's annual banquet, Sabrina's mermaid friend was in a great sulk. The English summer night was warm, the wide Severn river shone silver beneath a full moon, and everyone else was having a wonderful time on the wooded shore, but Anemone pouted and found fault with everything, including the god himself.

"How vain he is to use that stupid quizzing glass," she declared petulantly. "We all know he's so shortsighted he needs spectacles." She moved a coral candelabrum closer and raised her golden hand mirror to admire her long sea-green hair. It really wasn't the quizzing glass that was annoying her, but the fact that Neptune hadn't paid her as much attention as she wished. Tonight she had set her designing cap at him, sometimes flirting quite outrageously, but he hadn't given her a second glance.

Sabrina laughed. "How *you* have the audacity

to criticize someone for vanity, I really don't know."

"I cannot imagine what you mean." Anemone flushed, or at least became a deeper green. Then she tossed her mirror down, adjusted her shell-stitched robe, and lounged back on her mound of seaweed cushions to flex the new legs which all merfolk acquired for this one grand night of the year. She always found them very awkward indeed, and much preferred to be in the water with her lovely tail.

Sabrina smiled, smoothed her new seaweed robe, and glanced around the secluded clearing. She and Anemone were but two among hundreds of merfolk at the banquet, and everyone was either dancing or lounging around awaiting midnight, when the food would be served and Anemone's brief reign would begin. Sabrina would sing for them all then, too, and she was a little nervous, even though her skill with the lyre was acknowledged to be particularly fine, and her voice was reckoned more exquisite than those of the Lorelei, or even the Sirens. She hoped she wouldn't let her Uncle Nereus down. Nereus, who sat on a mound of cushions beside Neptune's throne, was host of the banquet and guardian of this stretch of the Severn. He was fiercely proud of the quality and lavishness of his hospitality, and this year–1814 by human reckoning–was already being spoken of as the best ever. The music was particularly exquisite, the food promised to be even more choice than previously, hundreds of extra candles cast a glow over everything, and the atmosphere was so delightfully convivial that no one could remember better.

Neptune and his entourage had arrived at sundown, the bearded, golden-skinned god riding in a pink mother-of-pearl chariot drawn by six of that rare steed, the white hippocampus. Now he was enthroned on a rock with his trident, his sandaled foot tapping to the music of the merman orchestra, and if something caught his myopic eye, he raised the quizzing glass that so irritated Anemone. Sabrina wasn't so sure he was ignoring her friend, rather that he was teasing her a little by *pretending* to. A case of playing hard to get, perchance?

The land chosen for the feast belonged to Winterleigh Court, a fine half-timbered Tudor mansion a quarter of a mile away on the densely wooded slope above the river. Isolated, tranquil, and always conveniently unoccupied, it nestled in a park carved out of the beautiful Royal Forest of Dean. A mile beyond it, on the turnpike from Gloucester to Chepstow, lay the small town of Blakenham, where even the advent of a temporary army camp made no difference to the house in its secret place. Winterleigh Court was closed because its owner, Sir Jake Cranwell, a dashing gentleman of the *ton*, had rarely left London since purchasing the property on the death of the last Winterleigh some ten years previously. His gamekeepers were supposed to patrol the estate and park regularly every night but had grown lazy, preferring to stay home in comfort, safe in the knowledge that absent Sir Jake was unlikely to discover their dereliction of duty.

The merfolk did not care that they were trespassing on private land, for the only laws they obeyed were those of Neptune, and so confident was Nereus that Winterleigh Court was unoccupied as usual, that this year he'd posted very few lookouts. However, the watery intruders were about to receive a great shock, because not only had Sir Jake's carriage just arrived unexpectedly, but at that very moment he was strolling onto the terrace at the back of the house. He'd left London to nurse his pride after the bitter ending of a particularly passionate affair, and all he sought now was peace and quiet. Behind him the house remained in apparent darkness, because the few rooms that were being opened up and lit by his coachman lay away from the Severn.

Jake went to the terrace balustrade, intending to admire the moonlit scene, but as he placed his top hat on a stone urn and lit a thin Spanish cigar, he noticed occasional pinpricks of light through the trees by the river. Suspecting salmon poachers, he crushed the cigar angrily beneath his heel, then walked swiftly down through the stepped gardens toward the rim of forest that stood between the house and the river. After all that had happened to him recently, the last thing he needed was poachers!

Meanwhile, the banquet remained carefree, except of course for Anemone, whose ill temper still centered on the unfortunate quizzing glass. "Oh, how I loathe that awful trinket!"

Sabrina became a little irritated. "For Atlantis' sake, *do* stop carping! The quizzing glass is hardly an 'awful trinket', it's studded with diamonds and must have belonged to someone very grand because it fell overboard from a royal yacht last summer."

Anemone resented being criticized again. "Sabrina, if you were perfect I wouldn't mind your comments, but you are not. You've never had a tail, and as Nereus's niece, you should long since have been queen of the banquet, but you haven't because you stubbornly insist on leaving your hair that disagreeable shade of red." She wrinkled her nose disparagingly.

"Russet," Sabrina corrected crossly. "And I do not want a tail, nor do I particularly wish to be queen of the banquet, I'm quite happy with my role of singing for Neptune. Besides, russet happens to be my natural color."

"As far as I'm concerned it is red, and it is unnatural. Merfolk should be green all over, but you have red hair, blue eyes, and white skin."

"That is because I'm part human."

"You look all human," Anemone said, glancing at the miniature of Sabrina's father that hung on a golden chain around her neck.

Sabrina's fingers closed protectively over it. "Maybe, but a true human cannot swim like a fish or live continuously underwater as I can."

Anemone looked at Sabrina's long, shapely legs. "Don't you ever wish you had a tail?"

"No."

"If you had one, you'd be able to swim much more gracefully than you do now."

"And if you had legs all the time you'd be able to walk with poise, instead of waddling as you do now," Sabrina retorted sharply.

Anemone flushed again, but then gave a rueful, disarming smile. "I'm being a pain in the fins, aren't I?"

"Yes."

"I'm sorry, it's just that I am dreading midnight."

Sabrina was taken aback by the admission. "Dreading it? But you have talked about nothing else for weeks, and all you have to do is serve Lord Neptune his food and drink."

"I know, but the way he has ignored me has upset me so much that I'm terrified of dropping something. Can you imagine how awful it would be if I deposited a clam chowder in his lap? Or a glass of barnacle brandy on his head?"

Sabrina gave a squeal of laughter. "Oh, Anemone!"

"It's not funny!"

"All right, all right, I'm sorry." Sabrina became serious again. "Look, I think you're quite wrong about him tonight. He's just teasing you, in fact, I vow he can play the coquet as well as you!"

Anemone's gaze flew hopefully toward the god. "Do you think so?"

"Yes. And apart from that, you can't possibly be more nervous than I. Why, I was all fingers and thumbs when I practised with my lyre this afternoon!"

Anemone smiled, and then shifted uncomfortably because of her new legs. "Oh, how do you manage with these things all the time? I must be the only mermaid who doesn't get on with them!"

"You aren't. I've seen some very peculiar walking and dancing. Anyway, I don't know how *I'd* manage with a tail," Sabrina replied, trying to sound lighthearted, but not succeeding very well. Talking about such things reminded her that she was neither mermaid nor human, just something odd in the middle that could live on land as well as under water. Her mother had been Nereus's favorite sister, and her handsome father had been human–a Winterleigh of Winterleigh Court–and they had met on this very night twenty-two years ago, when all the merfolk had again been human for a few hours. They had fallen in love at first sight, and so great had been their passion that before dawn broke they had not only found a merpreacher who had the courage to marry them, but she herself had been conceived. The merpreacher had risked much, because such a union was strictly forbidden by Neptune, but at the time the god had been exceedingly happy with a new love, and so had been disposed to be lenient. The marriage was cut cruelly short when her father died in a riding accident without even knowing his wife expected a baby. Then her mother had died in childbed, leaving only the miniature for her daughter to know her father by.

Anemone sensed the change in her friend. "You may be half and half, Sabrina, but we all love you very much," she said kindly, thus redeeming herself for being so difficult all evening.

Sabrina summoned a smile. "Everyone has always made me feel wanted, but I can't help how I feel. I only have to see my reflection in the water to know I'm only too different." She hesitated, and then made a confession. "Anemone, I'm so drawn to the land that sometimes I can hardly bear it."

Anemone gave her a sly look. "And you go ashore rather more than anyone knows, do you not?"

Sabrina could not help a guilty gasp, then having given herself away, saw no point in denying it. "How do you know?"

"I followed you one day. You came right here to this spot, climbed out of the river, and went toward those bushes over there. When you came out, you were dressed in human clothes, and you hurried away in the direction of Winterleigh Court. I watched you several more times after that, so I know it is quite a pastime."

Sabrina was dismayed. "I-I hope you have not told anyone else?"

"No, of course not." Anemone studied her. "What do you do? How did you get the clothes?"

Sabrina was embarrassed that her little excursions were known. "Well, I just like to see the world my father came from. At first I only went at night, because seaweed clothes would have looked very strange indeed to any human I met."

"They certainly would."

"One night while I was watching the comings and goings in the yard of the Red Dragon inn at Blakenham, a fine private carriage came in. The lady inside was in a terrible temper about having to stop at all, but one of the horses had cast a shoe. Anyway, when the carriage left, a valise fell from it. No one seemed to see, so when all was quiet, I took it and ran into the forest to see what it contained." Sabrina looked uncertainly at her friend. "Do you think that was wrong of me to take it?"

"No, of course not. Finders keepers is all right for Neptune and his quizzing glass, so it must be all right for you too."

Sabrina breathed out with relief "Thank goodness you think that, for I've been worrying a great deal about it. Now where was I?"

"In the forest with the valise."

"Oh, yes. Well, it contained a sprigged muslin morning gown, a leghorn bonnet, a brown velvet spencer, some shoes, and white silk stockings. The lady would have worn such clothes for walking in the countryside, and that was how I decided to wear them."

Anemone was taken aback by her friend's knowledge of such things. "How do you know when she would have worn them? I wouldn't know something like that even if I lived to be a thousand."

"Someone left a London journal behind in the forest after a picnic, and I could read it because humans in this country speak English just as we do. There were some pages about the latest fashions, for ladies and gentlemen."

"How does it feel to wear such clothes?"

"It feels right, Anemone," Sabrina admitted.

"I suppose that means you really are more human than mermaid."

Sabrina sighed. "It has to be faced, Anemone, the only mermaid thing about me is my ability to breathe underwater."

Anemone thought for a moment. "What is it

287

like in Winterleigh Court? Oh, come on, I don't believe you haven't been right inside."

"I have only looked through keyholes and some windows that were left unshuttered." Sabrina fingered the miniature around her neck, remembering what she had seen on peering at the great hall through the keyhole of the main door. The view had been restricted to just the beautifully carved wooden griffins guarding the foot of the staircase and the full length portrait of her father on the paneling where the staircase divided in two. She had no doubt it was her father, because the face on both the portrait and her miniature were identical.

"Have you ever seen Sir Jake Cranwell?" Anemone asked next.

"Oh, yes. It was about a year ago, on the same day I found the valise. I watched from the edge of the forest as he instructed his gardeners on the terrace above the ornamental pond. As you can imagine, from that distance I could not see much."

"Some of the other mermaids say he is very handsome. Is it true?"

"He is certainly tall and well made, and looked like an illustration out of the journal I found. Quite the, er, tippy, I think the phrase is."

A note was suddenly blown on a conch shell, and Anemone gave a dismayed gasp. "Midnight! Oh, Sabrina, how do I look? Is my hair all right? Have I pinned my robe to best advantage, do you think? Have I–"

"You look wonderful," Sabrina interrupted truthfully, for her friend always looked exquisite, no matter what.

Anemone handed Sabrina her golden lyre. "Do you feel in fine voice?"

"As fine as it's going to be when my heart is beating nineteen to the dozen."

The entire gathering fell expectantly silent as they both approached the throne.

The sound of the conch shell had carried to Jake as well, and he halted uncertainly. What in the name of Hades was that? he wondered. He could see more lights through the trees now, and he was sure there was movement. He listened, but there was only silence now, so he walked cautiously on down the slope.

Anemone took her position beside Neptune's throne and was at last smiling happily, for not only did the god greet her with exceptional warmth but he kissed her hand as well. Nereus, gray-haired and imposing, stepped out to proudly lead Sabrina forward, then returned to his place. Everyone held their breath, but before Sabrina plucked the first chord on her lyre, there came a loud crack as someone among the nearby trees stepped on a twig.

Everyone stirred uneasily, then one of Neptune's lookouts belatedly shouted a warning. There was instant pandemonium. All candles were extinguished, valuables were snatched up, and the whole gathering began to dash for the river. Numerous belongings and the telltale remains of the banquet were left on the grass, for there simply wasn't time to hide the evidence. As Neptune leapt into his shell chariot, taking Anemone with him, he realized the quizzing glass lay still on the throne. He shouted an order to a fleeing merman just in front of Sabrina, but the cowardly fellow pretended not to hear and dove into the water. Sabrina cried out that she would go back, and the god waved gratefully before urging the hippocampus team away from the bank.

But as Sabrina ran back to the rock throne, Jake strode into the clearing only about fifty feet from her. She froze, they stared at each other, then he shouted angrily, "Hey, there!"

Panic-stricken, she left the quizzing glass where it was and fled from him, but in the heat of the moment she made for the trees, not the river. She dashed through the fringe of ferns into the shadows, then flung herself beneath the bushes where she hid the human clothes from the valise, and lay as still as a mouse.

For a moment Jake was rooted to the spot, so shaken by seeing her that he did not even notice the debris of the banquet. Whatever he had expected to find, it had not been this. From the noise and number of lights, he had thought to come upon a considerable number of people; instead, there was only a solitary young woman in a robe that seemed to be composed of seaweed. Had he imagined her? No, he had not, for the ferns were still trembling where she had passed. Was that where her companions had made their escape as well? He ran to the place, but everything was now quite still. He paused, listening, but there wasn't a sound, except for the distant hooting of an owl.

Sabrina parted some leaves to peep out at him. The other mermaids were right, he was handsome; darkly so, with thick hair and long-lashed eyes that could only be the deepest brown. There was a fineness about his lips that hinted at a sensitive nature, she thought, and a quickness of expression that suggested a shrewd intelligence and willingness to smile, although he certainly was not smiling now. As for his clothes, they must be the work of London's very best tailor, she decided knowledgeably, for his wine-red coat and pale-gray breeches had been cut to fit like a second skin. His top boots had been polished until they shone, and the jeweled pin in the knot of his lace-trimmed neckcloth was very discreet and expensive looking. He was everything mermen were not—everything the redheaded Winterleighs were not either—and his very differentness drew her like a foolish little fish to a fisherman's flame, arousing sensations she had never experienced before; pleasing sensations that brought a bloom to her cheeks and a new light to her eyes. Was this how her mother had felt on first seeing her father? she wondered, unable to tear her gaze away.

Suddenly he seemed to sense the intense scrutiny, for he turned sharply to look directly at her. "Who are you? What are you doing on my land?" he demanded.

With a frightened cry, Sabrina scrambled from her hiding place, and fled once more, disappearing like a wood nymph into the dense forest. Jake stared after her, almost mesmerized by her haunting beauty, which lingered with him like a bewitching dream.

He drew himself up angrily. His pretty wood nymph was a trespasser and clearly up to no good, or she would not have made a run for it!

Turning on his heel, he strode back to the deserted clearing, and for the first time noticed the remains of the feast. What the dickens had been going on here? Certainly not salmon poaching! He moved bemusedly among the scattered seaweed cushions, fallen coral candelabra, and platters of some of the most *recherché* dishes he had seen in a long time. Prinny himself could not have tasted better fare, he thought, dipping a finger into a crab mousse which melted deliciously in his mouth. Someone very presumptuous had been holding a fine old junket on his land, and by the look of it he wished they'd had the courtesy to invite him! How much better to eat, drink, and be merry here in the moonlight than attend a grand over-formal function in London. But then anything was better than London at the moment.

He was reminded of the reason for leaving the capital. Nothing could have been more hurtful and sour than his parting from Lady Eveline Beaufort. He had thought her the most fascinating woman in England, and was so certain she loved him as much as he loved her, but then he had discovered her in the arms of his feckless friend, Harry Fenton! It was double betrayal, and after several weeks of trying to continue his life as usual, he had decided a sojourn in Gloucestershire would be just the thing.

Looking around at the scene in the clearing, Jake could not help a wry smile. Maybe Eveline wasn't after all the most fascinating creature in England, for, right now the mysterious wood nymph in a seaweed robe certainly had the edge on her! He noticed the golden lyre on the grass and picked it up to pluck a note. The pitch was perfect and seemed to echo gently through him like a lover's whisper. He smiled at such fanciful notions, replaced the lyre on the grass, and approached the rock throne, although he didn't realize it was a throne, of course.

He saw the quizzing glass immediately and turned it over so the diamonds flashed with cold fire in the moonlight. What on earth was such a costly item doing here? The most likely and rather uncomfortable explanation was that it was part of the proceeds of a robbery. Had his unexpected return caused a gang of thieves to abandon their celebratory feast? Yes, that had to be it, for empty Winterleigh Court was the perfect lair. And a convenient source of ill-gotten gains! Had the house been looted in his absence? All had seemed well when he arrived, but he had only briefly entered the great hall. A sense of premature outrage stung him but was followed very closely by a pang of disappointment, for if his guesses were right, then his wood nymph was certainly no innocent.

He continued to inspect the quizzing glass, and then his brows drew together as he realized he had seen it before somewhere. But where? Suddenly he remembered. It belonged to the Prince Regent, who had created a right royal fuss when he apparently lost it overboard from one of the royal yachts off the Isle of Wight. Well, it seemed Prinny's property hadn't been lost after all, but stolen! Although, how it had fetched up here on the banks of the Severn was a puzzle. Jake pocketed the quizzing glass and, after a final glance around, set off quickly back through the trees toward the house. The relevant authorities would have to be alerted immediately, for heaven alone knew what other stolen items might be scattered around. Then he'd be having a word with his gamekeepers, who should be patrolling the land with sufficient frequency to deter such goings on!

As he disappeared from view, a dismayed Sabrina emerged from the trees. What could she do now? Why, oh why had she not snatched the quizzing glass while she had the chance? Having given Neptune an undertaking, she did not dare return to the river empty-handed, which meant that somehow she had to get it back from Sir Jake. She hurried back to the bushes where she hid her human clothes.

Jake crossed the rustic bridge that gave access to the lowermost of the stepped gardens. Almost immediately his coachman hastened anxiously to greet him. "There you are at last, Sir Jake! You have a visitor!"

Jake was thunderstruck. "A visitor? At this time of night?"

The coachman, ruddy-faced and wiry, looked a little embarrassed. "It's a lady, sir. She, er, wouldn't give her name, but she's very London, very London indeed."

Could it possibly be...? "Is she blonde, and dressed entirely in blue?" Jake asked.

"Yes, sir."

Eveline! "Is she alone?"

"Yes, sir."

Eveline, but not Harry? Was the great affair over already? "Where is she now?"

"Waiting in the grand parlor, sir. I've lit candles and done what I can, but I'm no fancy footman, and she sent me away because I smelled too much of horses."

That sounded like Eveline, Jake thought, wondering why, after all that had happened, she should follow him from London. "I'll go to her directly. But first, tell me, have you found any evidence of someone having broken into the house?"

"None at all, sir."

"Good. Now, I want you to ride to the army camp we passed in Blakenham to inform the commanding officer that he and his men should come here immediately, as I have reason to believe a large gang of thieves is using my land."

The coachman's eyes widened, and he glanced at the woods as if a rabble of brigands might burst forth at any moment. "*Thieves*, sir?"

"That's what I believe. After that, I want you to go to my head gamekeeper at his cottage by the turnpike. Tell him that, unless he and his men get here without delay, they will be dismissed!"

"Y-yes, sir."

"Well, go on, man!"

Jolted into action, the coachman ran back through the gardens, but Jake remained where he was. Looking up at the western wing of the house, he saw that candlelight now illuminated the armorial glass window of the grand parlor. First thieves and an illicit outdoor banquet of some sort, now

Eveline. So much for peace and quiet, he thought wryly, wondering what could possibly be of such importance as to bring his former love here? She'd only graced this house with her presence once before, and had grumbled incessantly about how boring Gloucestershire was. Now she was here again, and under very unlikely circumstances, indeed. Whatever her reason, it was bound to be to her advantage; that much at least he had learned!

He ascended through the gardens, passing cascades, bowers, topiary, the large ornamental pond, deep and shining, where water lilies were in full bloom, and lastly the terrace. Going quickly around to the front of the house, where Eveline's dusty traveling carriage was drawn up at the porch, he entered the great hall. It was dimly lit by several candelabra placed on the dust-sheeted refectory table ranging down the center of the flagged floor, but no light reached up to the lofty hammerbeam ceiling. The coat-of-arms and griffin badge of the Winterleighs were painted on the stone fireplace, and suits of armor stood at even intervals all around the oak-paneled walls, as if living knights still guarded the house. Portraits hung everywhere, and one in particular suddenly arrested his attention as it never had before. It hung where the staircase divided, and was that of a handsome young man who was without mistake a Winterleigh. The light was very poor, but somehow the man seemed familiar, and not simply because the painting had always hung there.

For a moment Jake had to halt to look at it, but then he glanced more sharply around the great hall. *Had* anything been taken? No, all seemed exactly as it always had been; at least, he presumed it was, for he couldn't exactly claim to be that familiar with the place! He began to walk toward the grand parlor at the far end of the hall. The iron-studded door was ajar, and the room beyond was much better lit than the hall, but instead of feeling drawn toward it, to his surprise he knew he did not care whether Eveline was there or not. He was indifferent! The realization shook him; surely it wasn't possible to fall so completely out of love in such a short time?

The grand parlor was long and low, with an elaborate plasterwork ceiling that was yellow with age and candle smoke. Tudor furniture stood tall and angular in the warm light, the dust sheets tossed hastily aside by the coachman, but there was more comfortable, modern furniture too, like the crimson brocade sofa from which Eveline rose in a whisper of bluebell taffeta. She was as exquisite as a porcelain doll in her matching gown and pelisse, with golden ringlets tumbling from beneath her stylish tasseled hat, but she seemed oddly pale and nervous, he thought, trying to gauge his own feelings as well as hers.

"This is most unexpected, Eveline," he said, advancing a little into the room, and then halting. He felt detached, as if she were a stranger.

"I–I had to see you," she replied, gazing earnestly at him with imploring hazel eyes.

"How is Harry?" he inquired dryly.

She flushed. "Well enough, I believe."

"You only believe? Don't you know?" He grew more certain that she and his onetime friend had parted.

"He's gone to his estate near Dublin. Some boundary problems, I gather." She avoided his eyes.

Boundary problems? Fiddlesticks! Dear, unreliable Harry had bolted, just as Eveline had been warned he would. Now she had come here to save face, because a reunion with the lover she'd betrayed would enable her to claim that she gave

Harry his *congé*. Jake couldn't help a deep sense of satisfaction as he made a point of formality. "I'd, er, offer you some refreshment, but I fear there is neither food nor drink as yet."

She glanced around. "Why on earth did you not send word ahead to your servants?"

"Because I only decided to come here on the spur of the moment. Look, Eveline, let us get to the point. Why are you here?"

Tears suddenly filled her eyes, those lovely shimmering tears that she could always summon at will, then she turned agitatedly away. "Oh, Jake, I made a terrible mistake when I allowed Harry to seduce me." She paused, awaiting his glad response, but he remained silent, so she quickly faced him again. "You are the one I love, Jake," she whispered.

"I doubt that very much, Eveline. We parted because you made it patently clear that you preferred Harry,"

"I didn't realize what a fool I'd been until you had gone."

Until Harry had gone, you mean, he thought.

She came closer, and her lily-of-the-valley fragrance drifted seductively over him. "Forgive me, Jake. Take me back, and let us begin again."

If she had expected him to be carried away with joy, she was disappointed. He looked at her suspiciously. What was she up to? She had meant every cruel word in London, and now expected him to believe she'd suffered a complete change of heart? His days of foolishness where she was concerned were well and truly over. Well and truly. Oh, how good those three words were, even when only thought. "Eveline, you are the one who must forgive me, for, I fear, I'm taking this apparent change of heart with a very large pinch of salt."

"You–you don't believe me?" she whispered,

then, before he knew it, she'd flung her arms around his neck. "I *do* love you, Jake!" she sobbed. "I adore you with all my heart. And if I could turn the clock back, I would. You asked me to marry you once, but stupidly I turned you down. If you ask me again now, I will accept, for there is nothing on this earth I wish more than to spend the rest of my life with you! And if living here in the country is what you want, then I will gladly share your seclusion."

Live in the country? Was that what he wanted? Her words jolted Jake, and for the first time he realized how much he liked Winterleigh Court. He'd treated it shabbily until now, but that was going to end, if only to appease the great hall portraits, which, he was sure, disapproved of him! He smothered a smile. Yet another fanciful thought...

Eveline must have felt his hidden mirth, for she drew back sharply. "Please take me back, Jake! Please!"

"No, Eveline, for I no longer love you."

The possibility of rejection had not occurred to her, and for a stunned moment she could only stare at him. Then suspicion clouded her eyes. "Is there someone else?"

"If there was, it would be no more than you deserve."

"So there is!"

"No, Eveline, there isn't."

"Then why will you not give me a second chance?"

"Because your sin was too great. There will not be a reunion, Eveline, for if the truth be known, right now I find it rather difficult to even be civil toward you."

"I don't believe you!" she cried and stood on tiptoe to put her lips yearningly to his.

It was a kiss filled with passion, a skilled kiss;

a practiced kiss; too practiced by far... He unlinked her arms, and stepped away from her.

"You are no longer part of my life, Eveline," he said quietly, marveling at his own coolness. A few weeks ago he'd have been in the seventh heaven to have her return to him like this, but not now.

"Jake-"

"Have done with it, Eveline. I'm not fooled by your story of Harry's boundary problems. We both know he's cut and run, just as I told you he would. You have come here only to repair the damage to your vanity, and to your reputation as the lady every gentleman would give his entire fortune to possess. I'm right, am I not?"

Her face hardened. "How very shrewd, to be sure."

"You're a *chienne*, par excellence, Eveline, and Harry Fenton was just the cur you deserved," he murmured, taking off his coat and tossing it over a chair.

The quizzing glass fell to the floor, and Eveline recognized it immediately, for Prinny had admired her through it only the day before it was lost. "How do you have this?" she demanded, pouncing upon it and brandishing it before Jake.

"I found it tonight." How lame the truth sounded at times.

Her gaze, shrewd now, held his. "*Tonight*? Where?"

"Down by the river." Lame? It was a three-legged horse! He took the quizzing glass from her and put it on a table.

"By the river? How can that be, when it was lost at sea?" she replied in a tone that rang with disbelief.

"I don't know how it came to be there, except that I have reason to believe thieves are using my land." He glanced away as once again the elusive wood nymph flitted through his mind.

There was malice in Eveline's eyes. "I always wondered if Prinny really did lose it, or whether in fact it was...stolen."

She had made the implication so obvious that Jake's anger ignited. "Are you suggesting *I* took it?"

"Well, did you?"

"Please leave, Eveline, for I've had enough of you," he said curtly, feeling an almost irresistible desire to manhandle her to the main door, then apply his boot to her posterior.

"You will regret your decision tonight, Jake, I'll make sure of that!" she cried. "I can ruin you in society, all I have to do is whisper in certain ears about this royal bauble...

"Do as you damned well wish, madam, but for the moment just get out of this house!"

She raised a hand to strike him, but he caught her by the wrist and turned her toward the door. "If you do not leave this instant, so help me I'll throw you out!" he breathed, releasing her.

Knowing he meant it, she hurried from the room, but in the hall she halted with a sharp cry of fury. "So there is someone else after all!"

Jake strode out to see what on earth she meant, and was taken by surprise to see his wood nymph– albeit now modishly dressed in a leghorn bonnet, sprigged muslin gown, and brown spencer–at the foot of the staircase. If it weren't for the unruly red hair, which she had tried to twist up neatly beneath her bonnet, he might not have recognized her. Oh, but yes he would, for who could forget that sweet, beautiful face...?

He overcame the continuing fancifulness. Beautiful or not, she had clearly hoped to get into the house unseen, but her gown had caught on one of the carved wooden griffins that guarded the staircase, and Eveline had emerged from the grand parlor before she could free herself She was still struggling to pull the muslin away, but the griffin would not relinquish its hold.

Eveline turned to him, her lips thin, her eyes hooded. "No *wonder* you wish me gone, sirrah!"

"This is not what you think, Eveline. I don't even know who she is."

But Eveline could tell by his tone that he knew more than he was admitting. "I don't believe you, Jake, and I will make you pay dearly for spurning me in favor of this...this *demirep*!"

"She is not a *demirep*," he retorted coldly, feeling oddly honor bound to defend the fair intruder, who for all he knew might be a *demirep* of the lowest order!

Eveline's fury was almost tangible. "Your reputation won't be worth a jot by the time I've finished, Jake Cranwell, I will brand you a thief and libertine, and the whole of society will believe me! I–" Something dawned on her suddenly, and she broke off to whirl around once more to face Sabrina. "Those are my clothes! I recognize them!"

"Yours?" Jake stared at her, and then at Sabrina, who had given up the struggle with the griffin and now just stood there like a trapped fawn.

Eveline's nostrils flared. "I believed them mislaid last time I was here, but it seems they were purloined in the same way as Prinny's quizzing glass! You've been keeping this pretty little secret very well, Jake. Indeed, I almost admire your skill! I suppose she is the actual thief? She certainly looks the part."

Sabrina was stung out of silence. "I am not a thief, madam! My name is Sabrina Winterleigh, and that is my father." She pointed at the portrait

301

on the staircase.

In that moment Jake realized why the man in the painting had suddenly looked familiar. He and the wood nymph were very alike, so alike that there could be no doubt she was who she claimed to be. Sabrina. The name suited her. It was the old Roman name for the Severn. Dear lord, how she brought out the romantic in him...

Eveline was venomous. "Winterleigh? Well, you can only be from the wrong side of the blanket, my dear, but whatever you are, I want my property back, and I want it now."

"For heaven's sake, Eveline, can it not wait?" Jake asked.

"I want what is mine, sir."

Jake strode to Sabrina, freed her, then looked into her big blue eyes. "Go into the grand parlor and undress. You can wrap yourself in one of the dust sheets."

"Undress? Oh, but—"

"Do it," he said firmly.

Sabrina did as he commanded, and saw the quizzing glass the moment she entered. Instinctively she seized it, then ran to each window in turn, but to her dismay none of them would open. The only way out was through the great hall, and she would never be able to reach the main door without being seen.

Eveline called out impatiently, "Be quick, girl!"

Sabrina knew she could not escape and was almost in tears as she replaced the quizzing glass on the table, then hastily undressed. As she removed the bonnet, her mane of russet curls tumbled down once more, and she glimpsed the result in a wall mirror. How rustic and unsophisticated she looked compared to someone like the horrid woman called Eveline, she thought, feeling at a disadvantage in every way. She finished undressing, pulled a dust sheet around herself like a cloak, then took Eveline's clothes to the door and, in a gesture of defiance, tossed them out onto the floor.

Eveline was outraged. "Pick them up and bring them to me this instant!" she cried. Sabrina's chin rose mutinously.

Eveline looked to Jake for support, but he shook his head. "You want them, you pick them up," he said.

Nothing on heaven or earth would have moved Eveline to so demean herself, and she stalked from the house with fire and brimstone crackling from her heels. A moment later her carriage rattled away at high speed.

Jake came toward Sabrina, who shrank back into the grand parlor, and clutched the dust sheet as close as she could. He gathered the clothes, and pushed them under a shrouded chair so neither the coachman nor anyone else would see them, then stepped into the grand parlor and closed the door.

"I accept that you probably are called Sabrina Winterleigh, but who exactly are you? I know of no living Winterleighs. Indeed, if there had been such a person, this estate would never have come on the market. *Are* you from the wrong side of the blanket?"

"Certainly not!" Sabrina's eyes flashed indignantly. Her parents had been married according to merfolk rites and were as honestly and legally wed as any human bride and groom.

He was aware that he was drinking in every delicate feature of her face. She attracted him so strongly that it was like a shock running through his veins. The way her incredible red hair tumbled over her shoulders to her waist, the lustrous blue of her eyes, the flawless sheen of her skin, the way her lips trembled just a little... Oh, to kiss those lips. Once again he pulled himself sharply together. He mustn't lose sight of the fact that she was probably a thief, one of a gang that had the effrontery to use his land!

He went to pick up the quizzing glass. "What do you know of this?"

She did not reply.

"Surely you don't deny this is what you have come to the house for? I interrupted you just as you were about to get it from that damned rock."

"It–it belongs to someone I know."

"So you are acquainted with the Prince Regent, are you?" he inquired dryly. "Come on, Miss Winterleigh, you may as well tell the truth. Someone stole this from the prince, and you clearly know who that someone is."

She was stung into indiscretion. "It is against our law to steal! Lord Neptune found it on the seabed, and that is allowed!"

He stared at her, wondering if he could possibly have heard correctly. "I–beg your pardon?"

She bit her lip, and fell silent.

Jake stepped closer to her. "Who is this Lord Neptune?" he asked, deciding it must be the nickname of the head of the gang.

"Have you not heard of him?" she replied in amazement. Surely even humans knew of the god of water!

He waved an arm at the room. "As you can see, I haven't exactly been in residence recently, so I am not *au courant* with the villains of the neighborhood."

She was horrified. "*Villains*? You must not call the god of water a villain!"

Jake was dumbstruck, but then saw how earnest she was. "You really mean it, don't you?"

"Yes, of course I do." Oh, this was dreadful. She should not have come to the house, and certainly should not be saying the things she was.

"You said something earlier about 'our law.' What exactly did you mean? Whose law?"

"Merfolk law."

His lips parted incredulously. "Merfolk? Are-are you telling me you're a mermaid?" Involuntarily his glance moved toward the only too human toes peeping from beneath the dust sheet.

"I am only half mermaid, my other half is Winterleigh," she explained, withdrawing her toes a little self-consciously. "Please, you won't tell anyone about this, will you?"

Jake felt a perverse desire to laugh. So his wood nymph was more a water nymph! By all the saints, if he'd been drinking cognac all night he could understand all this, but he was stone cold sober!

She searched his face urgently. "You aren't going to tell, are you?"

He found his tongue. "My silence has a price. You must tell me all about yourself and the world you say you come from."

"Please don't ask me to do that."

"I want to know...Sabrina." He added her first name because he wanted to say it aloud; wanted to say it to her. He found her breathtakingly different, and more fascinating than Eveline could ever aspire to be. In short, he found her uncomfortably desirable. He replaced the quizzing glass on the table, then indicated a comfortable chair. "Sit down and tell me your story," he said gently.

"Only if I can trust you. Do you promise not to tell anyone what I tell you?"

"I promise." He placed his hand over his heart.

Reluctantly Sabrina gave in, and as he stood before the yawning fireplace, she told him everything. When she had finished, he gave her a rueful smile. "At least it's comforting to know my land isn't being used by an army of thieves." Army. Damn! The coachman would soon bring half the Blakenham garrison, to say nothing of the gamekeepers!

His smile had melted Sabrina's very soul, and she did not notice the perplexity that followed it. Oh, how she wished she didn't feel like this. Her heart seemed to tighten at every word he said, every gesture he made...

He searched her face. "If your parents had married in church, you'd have inherited this house, you know that, don't you?"

"But they did not, and now Winterleigh Court belongs to you." She paused. "I wish..."

"Yes?"

"I wish you'd look after it properly."

He smiled. "I've already resolved to do that."

She smiled too, and the atmosphere between them suddenly became charged with the desire they were both trying to conceal. He had known the emotion before, although never to such an unbearable degree, but she was torn, half wanting to stay close to him no matter what, half wanting to flee back to the security of the river.

Jake had to break the spell, and as a distraction he went to a covered cabinet in the corner of the room, where, if he remembered correctly, there was an old diary written by one of the Winterleighs. Perhaps she would like to see it. Behind him, Sabrina's need to return to what was familiar and safe got the better the better of her. In a flash, she grabbed the quizzing glass and fled to the door.

Jake spun around. "No! Sabrina, no!"

She dashed across the great hall with Jake giving chase. "Come back, Sabrina! Please don't go!"

Rushing out of the house, she headed for the

terrace at the back, with Jake gaining upon her all the time. As she ran down the stone steps toward the ornamental pond, she succumbed to the mermaid in her and letting the dust sheet fall, dove into the water. Jake did not stop to think but leapt in after her, and they both swam down into the depths. The moon gave just sufficient light for him to see her among the trailing strands of water lily, and he reached out to seize her wrist. She struggled, but he held her firmly, then pulled her close and kissed her. She ceased to struggle, and with their lips joined, they rose gently to the surface again. The quizzing glass slipped from her fingers, her arms moved tightly around him, and her whole being softened as she returned the kiss. As they reached the surface, he took a huge gulp of air, then cupped her face in his hands. This was perfection, heaven, ecstasy; *she* was heaven, perfection, ecstasy...

"Oh, Sabrina, Sabrina," he whispered.

She gazed adoringly into his eyes, but then the enchantment was shattered as lanterns bobbed on the terrace accompanied by the sound of voices and hooves. Her breath caught in fear, and Jake was dismayed to realize that the army and his gamekeepers had not only arrived, but must have seen him chasing her. How in the dickens could he explain it all away? Then his heart sank as he saw Eveline walking beside the commanding officer, who had gallantly dismounted in order to escort her from her carriage. Oh, with what joy she would have told him that either Sir Jake Cranwell or his strumpet had stolen the Prince Regent's quizzing glass! Now she was intent upon enjoying her triumph. Well, she would be denied her mean victory!

Quickly he took Sabrina by the shoulders. "Go down to the bottom of the pond and stay there until I beckon you."

"Oh, but–"

He stopped her protest with another kiss, then pushed her underwater. With a flick like a fish, she vanished. Jake promptly made much of splashing and laughing, as if very much the worse for drink. The commanding officer halted his men on the terrace, then maneuvered his charger to the balustrade to gaze down in astonishment at the scene in the pool. The gamekeepers crowded at the top of the steps and exchanged hopeful glances as Jake continued to make a drunken spectacle of himself If he was in his cups, maybe their laziness and inefficiency would be overlooked after all. Eveline watched Jake as well, her eyes quick and sharp. She'd seen Sabrina fleeing the house, but there was no sign of her now. The trollop must be hiding somewhere in the garden.

The commanding officer turned to her. "With all due respect, my lady, it would seem that at the moment Sir Jake is unlikely to provide us with any sensible information."

"His inebriation is an act! He was as sober as a judge when I left him, and he hasn't had time to get in this state. Besides, we all saw him chasing someone who most conveniently appears to have disappeared. Look, there is the dust sheet she had wrapped around her! Search the gardens and the house. Sabrina Winterleigh is here somewhere, and so is the Prince Regent's quizzing glass!"

Jake scrambled awkwardly out of the pond, making such a fuss about it that his rather confused coachman hurried down to assist him. "What's going on, Sir Jake?" he whispered.

"Just go along with anything I say," Jake instructed, and then began to sway from side to side, grinning foolishly at the others. "Where's me bloodhound?" he demanded, slurring his words most convincingly.

"Bloodhound, sir?" the commanding officer repeated.

"Name of Tattletail," Jake explained, meeting Eveline's gaze for a moment. "Damned thing ran off with me dust sheet," he went on, wending his unsteady way to the foot of the steps. "Why, Eveline, how nice you've come back," he declared, then wagged a finger at her. "You're very naughty, you shouldn't bolt when we're about to snuggle up together."

There were a few titters, and she rounded upon everyone. "How *dare* you laugh when I am dealt such a base insult!"

"No snuggly-wuggly for me now," Jake grumbled, and the titters became open chuckles.

Eveline felt her revenge slipping away. "Don't believe him! This is all pretense! There is no bloodhound!"

The coachman took his cue. "Oh, but there is, my lady. Tattletail is Sir Jake's favorite!"

Eveline almost choked. "You're lying too, you smelly little man!" She turned to the commanding officer again. "For heaven's sake, man, you have the evidence of your own eyes that *two* people ran from the house! Do you honestly believe the first figure was a dog?"

Jake wagged a finger again. "A bloodhound, Eveline, a bloodhound. Dog, indeed. Tattletail would be most offended."

She ignored him. "Please search the premises," she begged the commanding officer.

Jake hiccuped and swung an obliging arm to the world in general. "Search all you want, you won't find any glizzing-quasses," he declared.

The officer decided that a search was probably advisable, if only to silence the clearly vindictive Lady Eveline. He gave the necessary orders, and for the next hour the house and gardens were combed for any sign of the quizzing glass or, indeed, of Miss Sabrina Winterleigh. The discarded clothes were found hidden under the chair, but as Jake pointed out, still speaking slowly and slurring his words, they were Eveline's, who had come to Winterleigh Court for some snuggly-wuggly! Eveline's face was aflame, for it was only her word against his, and *she* was the one being made a fool of!

It was almost dawn when everyone departed, Eveline in the foulest temper imaginable, the army officer heartily sick of her, and the gamekeepers relieved not to have been dismissed on the spot. No estate in England would be better patrolled after this, not so much as a cockroach would venture forth unnoticed!

When all was quiet again, Jake returned to the pond, put a hand under the water and beckoned. Sabrina swam up to him with the quizzing glass, and he pulled her lovingly from the water, placing the dust sheet gently around her. "It's all right now, they've gone." Then he took her face tenderly in his hands. "Don't leave me, Sabrina," he implored. "Don't go back to the river. You belong here as much as you do under water, so why not enjoy the best of both worlds? Visit the river whenever you choose, but live with me. Become my wife, and mistress of your father's house."

She stared at him. "Your wife?" she whispered.

"I've known you for a few hours, but it is long enough to be sure how I feel. I love you, Sabrina Winterleigh, I adore you with all my heart, and I will do anything to keep you with me."

"Lord Neptune has forbidden merfolk to live with humans."

"But you're only half mermaid," he reminded her. "And what of your own parents? Neptune

310

didn't punish them, did he? And you told me he has always been kind to you. If you were to explain to him that history has repeated itself..?" He paused. "It has repeated itself, has it not? You haven't said you love me, yet I feel you do."

"I do, oh, I do," she whispered. He kissed her again, his fingers sliding sensuously into her wet hair. Then he looked adoringly into her eyes. "Please be mine," he begged, stroking her cheeks with his thumbs.

Her resistance melted away, and suddenly she knew that this was where she should be, where she was always meant to be. He saw the answer he sought in her eyes, and gave a glad laugh. "Oh, my darling, I vow I will adore you every minute of every day!" Then he took her hand. "Come, Neptune awaits his quizzing glass, and I will be at your side when you return it."

She smiled, and her fingers curled in his as together they walked down through the gardens toward the Severn.

Neptune was moved to be kind; indeed, as happened at the time of Sabrina's mother and father, the god was once again rather too distracted by pleasures of his own to deny the same to others. Over the past few hours he had successfully set about Anemone's seduction, and that young mermaid was sulky no more.

Sabrina and Jake were married twice, once according to merlaw, and once in church. And Winterleigh Court came to life again, soon to ring with the laughter of children who adored playing in the ornamental pond.

Where they swam like fishes, of course.

/=/

Sandra Heath was born in Cilfynydd, Pontypridd, South Wales. Her late father was an officer in the Royal Air Force, and at the age of eighteen, while living in Germany, she met her husband, Rob, whose father was also in the RAF. They have been married for thirty-two years and live near the cathedral city of Gloucester, England.

Sandra began writing in 1971 when her daughter, Sarah-Jane, was dangerously ill in hospital. Writing offered a form of escape from stress and anxiety, and when Sarah finally recovered, the completed novel, *Less Fortunate than Fair*, the story of Richard III's niece, Cicely Plantagenet, was accepted for publication. Sandra has been writing ever since, and loves every minute of it.

This is perhaps the most romantic story in the bunch, with an appealing, noble hero and a wronged and lovely heroine. A dreadful carriage accident at Christmas time brings Stephen, a wounded veteran of the Peninsular Wars, and Sarah, a single mother, together at the most magical time of the year, when all wounds are healed, and true love flowers.

The Viscount's Angel

Susannah Carleton

Chapter 1

December, 1815

The carriage slewed suddenly to the left. As the coachman cracked his whip and exhorted the horses, Stephen Lindley, Viscount Carrington, grabbed the strap, braced his feet and prayed the rig would slide into a nice, soft snowbank. Better yet if it remained on the road, but the way his luck was running lately, Stephen thought it far more likely that they would land upside-down in a rock pit.

After what seemed an eternity, the coach came to a shuddering halt. Apparently, there was a dearth of quarries in this part of Cumbria. They were not upside-down, merely listing sharply to the left. Glancing at the wall of white outside the window, Stephen realized that part of his prayer had been answered.

"Be ye all right, m'lord?"

"I believe so, Jem. How did you fare?"

The carriage tilted farther as the coachman climbed down from the box. "I be fine. Don't move aboot 'til I calm the horses and see what's what."

The viscount smiled slightly. Old Jem still ordered him about as if he was six instead of six-and-thirty. He listened to the coachman soothing the team, then unharnessing them. Patiently, Stephen waited for the grizzled man, who had been more of a parent to him than his own father, to assess the damages. Patience had been a hard lesson, but Stephen had learned it well: First in the Peninsula, then lying abed at Carrington Park whilst his leg healed, and he was waiting to see if his shattered knee would ever again support his weight.

It did, barely. Stephen was one of the few gentlemen in Society who sported a cane out of necessity, not as a fashionable accessory.

When Jem opened the carriage door, the vehicle tipped even more alarmingly. Jem's burly, heavily caped shape was briefly visible, then disappeared as the coach landed on its side with a soft thud, the open door gaping almost directly heavenward.

"M'lord?" called Jem. "Be ye all right?"

"Not as well as the last time you inquired." Stephen painfully righted himself, not an easy feat with a game leg, and when the left side of the coach had suddenly turned into a slanting bottom upon which he must stand.

"Can ye climb out, m'lord?"

"Do I have a choice?" Stephen swore comprehensively, thoroughly damning everyone who had contributed to his current situation: his father, his brother, the Frenchman who had all but destroyed his leg, and, for good measure, the coach builder. "Jem, if you can reach them, I shall hand up my greatcoat, cane, and hat. I will manage better without them."

"Aye, that you'll do."

After several thumps and bumps, Jem's weather-beaten face appeared, sideways, in the open-doorway. "Hand 'em up, m'lord."

That was the easy part. Pulling himself up, by his hands and sheer force of will, was an endeavor Stephen never wanted to have to repeat, and he was more than appreciative when Jem could finally grab him under the arms and help pull him through the aperture. Winded, his leg hurting like the dickens from banging against the doorjamb, Stephen lay sprawled on the upward-side of the coach.

"How be ye, lad?" asked Jem, concerned.

"I'll live." Slowly, Stephen sat up. He studied the surrounding landscape: snow-covered fields, an occasional fence, and the icy road. Not the most hospitable-looking area he had ever seen, but the mountains of the Peninsula had been worse. He turned his head to look at the land behind them, and pointed. "Jem, over there. Looks to be a house or farm cottage. Perhaps we can take shelter until the storm passes."

"I hope we kin. It'll take more than you 'n me to git this coach on the road again." Jem slid off the coach. "The sooner we git goin', the better. I'll help ye down."

Another feat that made Stephen grit his teeth. The moment his right leg touched the ground, it buckled, and if Jem had not been gripping him, he would have tumbled ignominiously into the snow. Despite the cold, sweat moistened Stephen's brow.

He donned his greatcoat and hat again and breathed a sigh of relief when Jem had helped him mount one of the carriage horses. The ordeal of dismount, later, he refused to contemplate.

Each leading a horse, they rode cautiously along the road. Stephen hoped there was a drive or path to the farmhouse. With his leg hanging straight as a poker, he would lose his seat if they had to jump a fence and traverse the fields.

The gods of bad luck must have been dozing. There was, indeed, a lane. Not a well-traveled one, but it led straight to the farmhouse door. Jem dismounted, handed Stephen the reins, and knocked on the door.

After a few moments, a plump, rosy-cheeked woman of about fifty answered the summons. Jem snatched off his hat. "Good afternoon, ma'am. Our carriage slid off the road aboot a mile back, and his lordship injured his leg. We wus hopin' ye might take us in 'til the storm passes."

The woman inspected the coachman from head to toe, then turned her gaze to Stephen. He doffed his hat and inclined his head in greeting.

"And who are you, my lord?" Her voice was rife with suspicion, but her accent was more cultured than he expected.

"Carrington."

After a careful scrutiny she turned and spoke, at some length, to someone behind her. When she turned back, she opened the door wider. "Her ladyship says you are welcome to shelter with us." The woman's tone conveyed her doubts about the wisdom of her mistress's decision. "We are a small household and cannot be fetching and carrying for you," she added in warning. "And you will have to take care of your horses yourself."

"I'll tend to the horses, soon as his lordship is inside," Jem replied, then walked back to the viscount. "How kin I help ye dismount?"

Stephen handed him the cane. "Try to keep me from landing face-down in the snow," he answered, his tone wry. He stretched out on the horse's broad back and slid his right leg over its rump. Then he wrapped his arms around its neck, angled both legs to the left, and lowered himself toward the ground.

The descent was quicker than he expected. Both feet hit the frozen path, hard. Just as his leg began to collapse, Jem grabbed him under the arms. With a sigh of relief, Stephen balanced his weight on his left leg and leaned his forehead against the horse's side.

"I gots your stick, but ye'd do better to lean on me."

"Very well." He draped an arm over the coachman's shoulders and walked slowly toward the open door, his bad leg buckling with every step.

By the time they reached the cottage, Mrs. Rosy Cheeks's look of suspicion had been replaced by one of concern. "What, besides compresses, do you need for that leg, Lord Carrington?"

"Compresses, cold alternated with hot, will do very well, Mrs...ah, ma'am. Thank you."

She bobbed a curtsey. "Mrs. Hodge, my lord." She closed the door, then directed them into a large parlor. "Sit by the fire. I will get hot water and a towel."

With single-minded purpose, Stephen headed for the wing chair by the hearth. He managed, with the help of Jem and the cane, to stand long enough to remove his greatcoat. Then, with a muffled groan, he plopped into the chair, closed his eyes, and leaned his head back.

A few moments later, a scraping sound jerked

him erect. A towheaded, curly-haired boy, six or seven years of age, was pushing an ottoman toward him. "Would you like to put your leg up on this, sir?"

"Why, thank you. That would help a great deal." When the footrest was positioned, he had to clasp his hands under his knee and lift his leg onto it. "I am Carrington. What is your name?"

"Matthew Bolton."

"Well, Matthew, I am very grateful for your assistance. And to your parents for offering my coachman and me shelter."

"I don't have parents, just Mama and Martha."

"Er, would Martha be Mrs. Hodge?"

The boy nodded vigorously. "Yes, but we just call her Martha."

Stephen mustered a smile. "You may do that, since you have known her a long time. As a stranger, I must call her Mrs. Hodge."

The lady in question bustled into the room, carrying a tray. She was followed by Jem, a steaming kettle in one hand and a bucket of snow in the other. "Matt, don't you be bothering his lordship."

"He wasn't bothering me in the least. On the contrary, he very helpfully provided a support for my leg." Stephen was charmed by the lad's bashful smile of gratitude.

The housekeeper set down the tray and tousled Matthew's curls. "Good boy. Go finish your lessons now. You can talk with Lord Carrington later, when he is feeling a bit more the thing." With dragging feet, and several looks back over his shoulder, the boy complied.

Mrs. Hodge turned her attention to the viscount. "Cold compress first or hot, my lord?"

"Cold."

"'Twould be better if you were out of those

breeches. I will bring a quilt you can use as covering."

"I prefer to retain my breeches..." *And my dignity.*

The housekeeper shook her head, as if chiding him for such foolishness. "If that knee swells much more, we'll have to cut you out of them."

"In truth, ma'am, the compresses will avert such a drastic step."

She packed snow around his knee, wrapping it in a towel. "I suggest a quarter of an hour with the cold, then changing to the hot." Placing the bucket underneath his leg, so the melting snow wouldn't drip on the carpet, she announced that she would prepare tea, then return to change the compress.

When Mrs. Hodge and Jem departed, Stephen settled back in the chair and glanced around the room. The furnishings were far superior to those in the home of his wealthiest tenant farmer. The carpet was an Axminster, of deep blue and maroon in a floral pattern; the draperies, a heavy blue velvet; and the sofa, chairs, and tables came from the workshops of Sheraton and Chippendale. The Boltons, whoever they were, were not farmers.

Perhaps when he met Mrs. Bolton, he would learn more. For a widow with a young child, she had shown remarkable hospitality–or foolishness– in offering him shelter. It was possible, he supposed, that she knew him. Or knew of him. He had held the title for only six months, however, so it was more likely that she knew his brother. If that was the case, her invitation had been extremely foolish. Henry had been a thorough reprobate, not to mention licentious as bedamned.

Perhaps, Stephen speculated, the Widow Bolton was looking for a second husband. In that case, she had chosen the wrong man. No woman with any claim to sense, character, or good looks would think him a likely candidate for matrimony. A scarred, battle-weary soldier who couldn't walk without the aid of cane, and whose father and brother had plunged the estate deeply into debt, was *not* a prime catch on the Marriage Mart.

He sighed and closed his eyes. His man of business had been urging him to trade his title for a fortune. Apparently, there were wealthy Cits who wanted their darling daughters to become Lady Somebody. He was determined to avoid such a drastic action, if at all possible. The viscountcy was an old and honorable one-or it had been before his father and brother held the title-and Stephen had vowed to do everything in his power to restore it to its former distinguished status. If he had to marry a Cit's daughter to preserve the estate, he would. But he hoped it would not come to that. He had discovered, much to his surprise, that he was a romantic: He wanted his wife to love *him*, not his title.

Some time later, the sound of footsteps roused him. Instinctively, as he opened his eyes, he reached for the sword that no longer hung from his side. The approaching figure wasn't a blood-thirsty Frenchman, however, but an angel. A beautiful, blue-eyed, blonde angel in a pink gown.

Chapter 2

Stephen blinked and swallowed hard. As he groped for his cane, the vision spoke, her voice soft and melodious. "Please do not get up, sir. Martha tells me you injured your leg in a carriage accident."

He bowed from his seat. "I am Carrington, ma'am. And very much in your debt for offering shelter to my coachman and me."

She dipped a graceful curtsey. "Lady Sarah Bolton. Were I lost in such a terrible storm, I would hope for someone to offer me sanctuary." She sat in the chair opposite his.

"Do unto others, eh? I, too, believe in the Golden Rule, but most people are not so charitable."

"Unfortunately not." There was a note of bitterness in her voice.

Mrs. Hodge bustled into the room carrying a tea tray. She set the tray on the table between his chair and Lady Sarah's. "I will change that compress in just a moment, my lord."

His hostess reached for the teapot. "I shall change the compress, Martha. I-"

Shocked, Stephen protested. "I am perfectly capable of changing it myself, ma'am."

The housekeeper gave him an admonitory glare. "Going to stroll over to the hearth for the kettle and to that table"–she pointed with her chin to one by the window–"for the towels, are you, my lord?"

"If need be." His tone dared her to contradict.

"There is no need for you to do so, Lord Carrington." Lady Sarah rose and collected kettle, basin, and towel. "I am accounted to be a healer, so you could do much worse than to have me examine your knee."

Stephen barely controlled the shudder that racked his frame at the thought of such a lovely young lady viewing his hideously scarred leg. To divert her attention, he addressed the other part of her comment. "What do you mean about being a healer?"

Mrs. Hodge snorted. "She means she cures people of what ails them." With that, she turned and left the room.

Smiling, Lady Sarah sat on the edge of the ottoman and removed the soggy compress. "I know a great deal about herbs and their curative properties and the local people come to me when they are injured or feeling poorly." She laid her long, slender fingers over his knee, then probed gently. "How did you shatter your knee? And how much damage was done to the bones in your leg?"

He started. *Was she a witch that she could tell all that merely by touching his leg?*

"What have I said to surprise you, Lord Carrington?" she asked, a hint of amusement in her voice. "'Tis obvious that the circular plate"–she tapped the bone in question on his other leg–"is missing. Unless you were born without it, you must have injured your knee at some time. I am merely curious as to what happened and if you damaged the other bones in your leg."

"I was shot in the knee by a Frenchman with remarkably poor aim. And yes," he conceded reluctantly, "there was some damage to the other bones."

"You were a soldier?" The inflection of her voice conveyed amazement.

"Have I said something to surprise you, Lady Sarah?" he inquired, returning the question she had asked him.

"It isn't often that peers, or the sons of peers, are soldiers. My father–" She stopped abruptly, her rosy lips compressed into a thin line.

"Your father would not allow his heir to do such a thing?"

His hostess gasped and paled. "You know my father?"

Angry at himself for having upset her, Stephen answered in what he hoped was a gentle, reassuring tone. "No, ma'am, I don't. Rather, I have no idea who your father is. As for my parent, I wasn't

322

his heir, merely the spare. I have been a soldier since I finished at Oxford. Sixteen years. Until I was invalided out after Waterloo."

Lady Sarah's tactile examination of his leg had progressed upward from his knee. He shifted in his seat, hoping she would not notice the effect her ministrations were having on him. Silently, he recited the multiplication tables. Backward. "The compress, please," he croaked.

"Hmm." She rubbed his thigh, over an old saber wound. "Did you suffer an injury here, as well?"

"That one is older." The words were terse, clipped.

"I have a salve that will ease the stiffness in your knee."

"I am sure that will be very helpful, later. For now, the compresses are best."

"Oh!" A delicate pink tinted her cheeks. "Of course." She poured hot water from the kettle into the basin, then dipped in the cloth, wrung it out, and wrapped it around his knee. As the heat seeped into his aching muscles, young Matthew burst into the room.

"Mama! Mama, look outside. See how hard it is snowing."

Lady Sarah smiled at her son, a smile of singular sweetness. "Just a moment, darling. First, you must make your bow to our guest, Lord Carrington."

The lad was fair dancing with impatience. Stephen, remembering that exuberance from his childhood, smiled at the boy and addressed his hostess. "Matthew and I have already introduced ourselves. It was he who provided the ottoman so I could stretch out my leg."

"That was very good of you, Matt." She kissed her son's cheek, then stood in response to his tug on her hand and walked to the window with him. Holding aside the draperies, she exclaimed, "My heavens!"

Stephen was too far from the window to see outside. "Is it a blizzard?"

She turned back to face him. "I believe it must be, although I have never seen one before."

The tremble in her voice was unexpected. He wondered if she was alarmed by the snow or by the prospect of unwanted guests–male guests. He couldn't do anything about the former, but he could rid her of the latter. "Matthew, please tell Mr. Thompson, my coachman, to ready the horses."

The boy headed for the door but halted at his mother's command. As Stephen stood, unsteadily, his hostess turned blazing eyes upon him. "Are we so far beneath you, Lord Carrington, that you would risk death rather than spend the night here?"

His angel had transformed into a fury, but she was still beautiful. Startled by her attack as well as by the bitterness in her tone, he wished, fleetingly, for the drawing room manners and social aplomb of a pink of the *ton*.

"Of course not, Lady Sarah," he replied, emphasizing her title and the superior social rank it indicated. "I have no particular desire to leave your cozy parlor and ride through the countryside in the snow. But neither do I wish to harm your reputation."

Judging by her chagrined expression, she had not considered that possibility. "I beg your pardon, sir." She raised her eyes to his and, realizing that he was still standing, waved him to a seat. "Please, sit down."

At the door, Matthew shifted from one foot to the other. "Mama? What should I tell Mr. Thompson?"

"*Ask* Mr. Thompson if he would be so kind as to feed the horses and settle them for the night. Charlie will not be able to come in this weather."

The boy nodded and skipped from the room.

Lady Sarah sank into a chair, allowing Stephen to do the same. "Please forgive me, Lord Carrington. I–"

"You need not apologize, Lady Sarah." He attempted to lighten the atmosphere and, perhaps, draw a smile from her. "No doubt you thought me demented when I spoke of leaving after you announced a blizzard."

"No," was the solemn reply. "I..." She shook her head. "No. 'Twas not your state of mind I questioned."

He wondered what she had been thinking, but she did not elaborate.

Cursing his lack of town bronze, he lifted his leg onto the ottoman, then reached for his teacup. *Would it be better to seek the reason behind her attack or to attempt to find a topic of conversation that would remove the bleakness from her beautiful blue eyes?* Stephen was a forthright man. He would feel better if they cleared the air, but he did not want to distress her further.

"Lord Carrington?"

"Lady Sarah?"

They spoke simultaneously, then paused, each deferring to the other. Before the silence grew awkward, Stephen took command. "Please, my lady. What did you wish to say?"

His hostess glanced quickly at him, then gazed into the fire. "I apologize for speaking so harshly to you. I was not thinking of my reputation. At least, not in the way you were." She bit her lip. "I shouldn't like to think of you, or anyone, riding through such a terrible snowstorm."

How many ways were there to think of a lady's

reputation? "My own manners are far too ragged for Polite Society, ma'am. Too many years away from the gentle influence of ladies, I daresay. And too many years of giving orders." He smiled ruefully. "If your neighbors and family consider Mrs. Hodge a proper chaperone, so that my presence will not harm your good name, then I would be pleased to wait out the storm here."

"You need not fear for my reputation, sir."

"I thank you, once again, for your kindness in offering Jem and me shelter. In truth," he added, "I would find it very painful to ride now."

"Oh! The compress." Lady Sarah rose. "It must be past time to change it."

Stephen glanced at the clock on the mantle. "Just about time, I believe. If you will slide that bucket of snow a bit closer to me, I will-"

"You, sir, will sit quietly whilst I change the compress." He opened his mouth to protest, but she gave him no opportunity. "I have no doubt that you are a very competent man, able to do that and a great deal more. But, surely, it must be better for your leg if you just sit still and relax."

"It is, yes, but I do not like to see you waiting on me."

She perched on the edge of the ottoman, the hint of a smile lighting her eyes. "Ah, but I am not waiting on you. I am doctoring you."

"Hmm. I do not see much difference between the two, but since you are far lovelier than the army surgeons, I shan't complain."

A delicate blush suffused her cheeks. "Thank you, Lord Carrington."

By evening, Stephen knew his luck had not changed a whit. Not only was he miles from his destination, but he was in the midst of a blizzard worse than any he had seen in the mountains of the Peninsula, in the home of an unmarried woman with minimal chaperonage, and his leg hurt more than it had since he had been carried off the field at Waterloo. As if that wasn't enough, he was far from well. He felt, alternately, as if he was sitting in the center of a blazing fire, or a hundred miles from the nearest ember. Lady Sarah would, no doubt, be delighted to use her healing skills on him, but he would much prefer that it wasn't necessary. She was too beautiful, and innocent, for his peace of mind.

Chapter 3

Sarah Bolton sighed, then pushed a wisp of hair off her brow as she gazed at the wonderful man sprawled in the middle of her bed. He wasn't handsome in the classical sense; his features were too rugged and his face too weathered for that. But with his curly black hair, dark-blue eyes, and tall, broad-shouldered, slim-hipped body, Viscount Carrington was the most handsome man she had seen in many a year. The fact that he was one of the few men she had seen in the past eight years had nothing at all to do with his appeal.

His best characteristic, in Sarah's opinion, was his kindness. In that category, she included his excellent manners. He had shown every courtesy to her, Martha, and Matthew, patiently answered her son's never-ending stream of questions, and helped the boy with the arithmetic problems Sarah herself dreaded. She had learned a great deal about Lord Carrington since he had arrived at her home in a midst of a snowstorm nearly a week ago, but she had learned most of it without his knowledge.

Nightmares and the delirium of a raging fever had revealed most of the viscount's history. As she

327

bathed his face and hands with a cloth dipped in cool water, Sarah contemplated all she had learned. He had lost countless friends during the war and grieved for every man under his command who had died. His father had fallen from his horse in a drunken stupor and broken his neck three years ago, after severe gambling losses that left the estate teetering on the brink of ruin. Then, his brother had dragged them even deeper into dun territory, had cheated at cards and was killed in a duel earlier this year. Finally, Lord Carrington–or Colonel Lindley as he had been then–was severely wounded at Waterloo and, according to his coachman, had spent four months in bed whilst his leg healed, worrying if he would ever walk again.

Despite these trials and tribulations, the viscount was not a bitter man. He was angry about his father's and brother's reckless squandering of their patrimony, but instead of ranting and railing about things that could not be changed, he worked to restore his estate.

Stephen Lindley was kind, courageous, loyal, honest, and honorable. Worthy of any woman's respect and admiration. Sarah was not at all surprised to realize that she had fallen in love with him.

It was a secret she would carry to her grave. He would never return her regard.

A low moan presaged the cries and thrashing that accompanied the viscount's nightmares. Setting the cloth aside, Sarah stroked the dark curls off his forehead and prayed that his fever would break. "Shhh. All is well," she murmured, attempting to soothe with words and touch. "Your battles are over and all is well."

/=/

Aching in every joint and muscle, Stephen awoke in a strange, and rather short, bed in an unfamiliar room. Gingerly, he moved his arms and legs, relieved to find that he wasn't as bruised and battered as he felt. There was a bandage on his knee, but a surreptitious examination revealed his leg and foot were still there.

"Thanks be to God."

"Lord Carrington?" The words came from the direction of the fireplace and were followed by the rustle of skirts and quiet footsteps.

Ah, his angel!

She was pale, with dark circles under her eyes, but she was still beautiful. "Lady Sarah? What are you doing in my room?"

She perched on the edge of his bed and placed her hand on his brow. "Actually, Lord Carrrington," she said, a hint of amusement in her voice, "'tis you who are in my room." As he gaped at her, she explained, "You have been ill and it was more convenient to nurse you here than upstairs."

"I am never sick." Uncomfortable about reclining in her presence, he sat up, then leaned back against the headboard, feeling weak as a newborn kitten.

She folded her hands in her lap. "I believe you must have caught a chill when your coach overturned. You became ill the first evening you were here and have been feverish for days."

"How many days?"

"Five. No, six now," she amended. "Your fever finally broke last night."

Six days? Good Lord! "Is that why I feel as if I have been trampled by a troop of inept cavalry recruits?"

"Undoubtedly." Her smile was gentle, and very sweet. "Are you hungry?"

"No," he replied quickly, looking away, determined not to be any more of a burden to her. She caught his gaze, as if she knew he had not spoken the truth. "Yes," he sighed. "Excessively."

"Good. The return of your appetite indicates you are on the mend." She rose and walked to the door. "I will return with your breakfast in a few minutes."

The moment the door closed behind her, Stephen threw back the blankets and swung his legs over the side of the bed. The resulting wave of dizziness nearly toppled him to the floor. Holding his aching head in one hand, he reached under the bed and groped for the chamber pot. Finished, he shoved the pot back and looked longingly at his dressing gown, draped over a chair across the room. Much as he wished for its concealment, he was no more able to retrieve it than to sprout wings and fly. Lady Sarah, or whoever brought his breakfast, would have to suffer the sight of him in a nightshirt.

Hearing her voice in the hallway, he scrambled back under the quilts. He would have liked to pull them up to his chin, but they reached only as far as his armpits. Tucking them firmly in place there, he propped the pillows against the headboard behind him and wondered how long it would be until he felt like himself again.

His lovely hostess entered with Jem, who carried a tray. "How be ye feelin', m'lord?"

"Not as well as I would like, but better than when I first arrived back in England."

The coachman snorted and placed the tray in Stephen's lap. "Plenty of difference between them two. Could ye be a bit more specific?"

"I will be fine, Jem," he assured his old friend.

The grizzled man looked at Lady Sarah, who nodded. "Lord Carrington will be right as a trivet in a few days."

Jem beamed a smile, obviously relieved. "I'd best go see to the horses. I'll be back to sit wi' ye later, m'lord."

After his servant left, Stephen glanced down at the breakfast tray, then quirked an eyebrow at his hostess.

"Soup, ma'am?"

"Broth. And tea and toast." As he opened his mouth to protest, she added, "I know you want eggs and whatever constitutes your normal breakfast, but your stomach is not ready for such fare yet. Eat this now and you can have a more hearty meal for luncheon."

His expression must have indicated disbelief. "Trust me in this, Lord Carrington. You would not like the aftereffects of a more substantial meal."

Stephen looked away, startled to realize that he did trust her. "Could I have coffee, at least?"

"Tomorrow."

Resigned, he reached for the teapot and noticed the second cup. "May I pour you a cup of tea, ma'am?"

"Yes, please." Accepting it, she retreated to a chair near the hearth.

He picked up his spoon and dipped it into the broth. As he ate, he contemplated his circumstances. And his hostess. Lady Sarah had invited him into her home during a snowstorm, then nursed him for five days and nights when he had fallen sick. She had given up her bed to him and, judging by her exhausted countenance, many hours of sleep. She truly was the angel he'd first believed her. Stephen could not recall any woman, other than his nanny, who had shown him such care and kindness.

What had he given her in return? Nothing. Not one blessed thing. Except, possibly...

"Has the snow melted yet, ma'am?"

"Hmm." It was a sleepy murmur. Then, more alertly, "What was that, my lord?"

"I merely asked if the snow had melted."

"It is still snowing." She rose, set her cup and saucer on the mantle, then crossed to the window and pushed back the draperies. "It is only flurries now, but Mr. Thompson says there is more than four feet of snow out there."

"Good Lord! Do you often get such heavy storms here?"

"This one is by far the worst I have seen, and I have lived here for nearly eight years."

"Did-"

A knock on the door, and the precipitous entrance of Matthew, interrupted their conversation. "Mama, Martha says you are to go to bed now. I am to sit with Lord Carrington until she comes." Belatedly, he remembered his manners. "Good morning, my lord."

Stephen smiled. "Good morning, Matthew. I would be pleased to have your company, but I must warn you that I am feeling a bit tired myself. I hope you won't hold it against me if I fall asleep."

The boy shook his head. "You are *supposed* to sleep a lot. That is how you get well."

Stephen bit the inside of his cheek to keep from grinning. "Are you a healer as well, Matt?"

A surprised expression crossed the lad's face before he ducked his head. "No, sir. I just know that from listening to Mama."

"Your mama is a very wise lady." Glancing at his hostess, he caught her hiding a yawn behind one elegant hand. "Lady Sarah, if I promise to be a model patient, and to entertain your son, will you go to bed?"

"Yes, my lord, if you promise to rest, too."

Stephen raised his right hand as if taking an

oath. "I promise." Turning to the boy, he requested, "Would you carry that tray to the kitchen? When you return, we can play a game."

When Matthew left the room, his eyes on his burden, Stephen addressed his hostess. "Please go, my lady. I feel horribly guilty for robbing you of your sleep."

As tired as she obviously was, she smiled at him. "There is no reason for you to feel that way." Before he could voice a protest, she added, "I will sleep as soon as I have changed the bandage on your knee."

"No!" It was an instinctive reaction, not a polite refusal. He did not want her to see his hideously scarred leg.

"Yes." Her voice was gentle but firm.

"It is no fit sight—"

"I have seen your scars, Lord Carrington, and they are nothing of which you should be ashamed. On the contrary, they are symbols of your courage."

Dumbfounded, he gaped at her as she drew aside the blankets and unwrapped the cloth binding his knee. She met his gaze for a moment, then lowered her eyes. "Any woman who thinks otherwise is not worthy of you."

By the time she had applied a salve and a new bandage, he found his voice. "You are the most amazing lady I have ever met. Your husband must have worshipped the ground you walk on."

Her expression strained, Lady Sarah rose from the bed and walked to the door. "I was not married to Matthew's father." With that startling pronouncement, she left the room.

Chapter 4

Stephen's thoughts, and his emotions, were in turmoil all day. He now understood Lady Sarah's remarks about her reputation, as well as her anger when he had announced his intention to leave just after the blizzard started. But, like most hard-learned lessons, the knowledge had come too late.

He was an excellent judge of character, infallibly correct, and he knew Lady Sarah was no light-skirt. If she had borne a child out of wedlock–which she obviously had–then she'd been tricked into what she believed was a marriage bed, or she'd been forced. For her sake, he hoped it was the former.

He enjoyed the time he spent with Matthew, playing chess and helping the boy with his lesson. It had been many years since the viscount read Latin, but he found the language much more interesting with a wiggly, inquisitive seven-year-old at his side than it had ever been before. From Matthew's chatter, Stephen learned that the household rarely had callers, and no relatives ever visited.

Mrs. Hodge, during her stint in the sickroom, revealed that the burden of nursing him through his fever had fallen mostly to Lady Sarah, although they all took turns. After an hour or so in her company, Stephen felt comfortable enough to broach a delicate subject.

"Is...will..." He gulped a breath and began anew. "Will Lady Sarah's reputation suffer because of my presence here?"

"With the roads impassable because of the snow, I think it unlikely that anyone knows you are here."

"You have not answered my question, ma'am."

The housekeeper skewered him with a look. "Perhaps not, Lord Carrington. But perhaps you are asking the wrong person."

Unperturbed by her ire, he replied calmly, "Possibly I am. More likely, there is no way to know the answer to that question yet."

"Probably not."

All day, he waited for Lady Sarah to return. Every time he awoke, someone was in the room with him, but it was never the person he most wanted to see. Finally, in the darkest hours of the night, he opened his eyes and saw her sitting in a chair by the hearth, sewing. Almost, he called her name. But, for tonight, it was enough to know she was there.

The next day was much the same: He spent time with Matthew, Mrs. Hodge, and Jem. The coachman helped him shave, and Stephen was amazed by how much better he felt afterward. A bath would, undoubtedly, make him feel like a new man, but his knee was too battered from exiting the coach to permit climbing in and out of a tub, so he settled for a thorough washing instead.

He resolved to be well enough, and strong enough, to get up and bathe and dress tomorrow. But there was something he wanted to do, needed to do, this evening.

Despite his determination to stay awake until Lady Sarah arrived, he fell asleep shortly after dinner. When he awoke, the room was dimly lit. His angel was sitting by the fireplace, her head bent over a tambour frame and her hair glistening silver as moonlight.

"Lady Sarah?"

She started at the sound of his voice. He sat up, resting against the headboard, as she rose and crossed toward the bed. Bending over, she placed her hand upon his forehead. "Is something wrong, Lord Carrington?"

He captured her hand in his own, then carried

it to his lips and bestowed a gentle kiss on her knuckles. "Please, sit down."

"I...ah..." She tried to withdraw her hand from his clasp, but he refused to relinquish it.

"Please. I wish to talk with you."

"It is late, my lord. You should be asleep."

"You are never here until late, my lady. And since I just woke up, a few minutes of conversation will not set back my recovery."

"Very well." She tried to free her hand. "Let me get a chair."

He patted the edge of the bed. "Sit here." She stilled, her eyes wary and fearful. "My intentions are not dishonorable," he assured her. "I wish only to speak with you."

Biting her lip, she perched on the very edge of the bed, smoothing her skirts with her free hand. He rubbed his thumb over her knuckles, hoping the bad luck that had plagued him for three years was now a thing of the past. Finally, she raised her eyes to his.

"Sarah, I admire and respect you more than any woman I have ever known. You are, to use a phrase of my dear grandmother's, a lady at heart."

When a frown creased her brow, he explained, "Some women are born to the title, by courtesy of their father's rank. Others attain it when they marry. Rarest of all are ladies at heart, those who deserve the title because of their kindness. You, my dear, are a lady at heart."

She ducked her head. "Thank you."

Patiently he waited until she looked at him again. "Yesterday morning, you made a rather startling announcement. I would like to hear the explanation that accompanies it."

"No." She shook her head wildly and tried to jerk her hand from his.

He twined his fingers with hers. "I do not ask

to torment you. I will tell you the reason for my request now, if you wish, but I would prefer to do so later."

"No." She turned her head, and the firelight limned her profile.

"Bear with my speculations, then. At the age of seventeen or so, you fell in love with a handsome scoundrel who promised marriage and persuaded you to elope. You–"

"No."

"Was love involved?"

She shuddered. "No."

Dear God! He watched her carefully as he spoke. "At the age of seventeen or so, you were, somehow, somewhere, accosted by a villainous dastard who forced his attentions on you. After enduring that horror, you found yourself with child. Your parents, whoever they are, exiled you here–"

When her tears spilled over, he leaned forward and put his arms around her in a loose embrace. Resting her head against his shoulder, she wept, her hands fisted in his nightshirt. He comforted her as he would a child, rubbing his cheek against her hair and stroking his hand up and down her spine.

Finally, the torrent slowed to a trickle, and her fingers relaxed. Grabbing his handkerchief from the nightstand, he pressed it into her hand. "I am sorry, sweetheart. I did not mean to make you cry."

"You did not. That is, I wasn't crying because of what you..." She huffed out a breath. "Your speculation is correct. I told my parents what happened, but they did not believe me. The man was a friend of my father's and..."

Her fingers knotted in the handkerchief. "They accused me of lying. When I realized I was with child, they banished me here. My father granted me a modest allowance, on the condition that I never contact any member of my family."

She raised tear-drenched eyes to his. "Martha was the only person who believed me. Until you."

He gathered her in his arms and brushed his lips against her forehead. "I believe you, Sarah. And I believe in you."

"Thank you."

"Can you endure a few more questions?"

"I...I don't know."

"Shall we try?" He tipped her face up to his. "If you don't want to answer, just say so."

When she nodded her acquiescence, he tucked her head under his chin and began with the most difficult question. "Who was the dastard who raped you?"

He felt her flinch. "Lord Calverton. He died last year."

"I hope it was a slow and painful death," he said, his voice grim. "Who are your parents?"

"The Earl and Countess of Lambourn."

He didn't know them—and had no wish to know them. "Do you think that, someday, you will be able to put that horrible experience behind you and welcome a husband's embrace?"

"I...it would depend on the man. If I knew him to be gentle and kind, and knew that he loved me, then I believe I could."

"What if I was the man?"

She placed her hands on his chest and pushed back so she could see his face. "Are you asking me to marry you?" The tone of her voice conveyed her astonishment.

He smiled at her. "Not yet, but I am working my way up to it."

"Why?"

"Why am I asking or why am I working my way up to it?"

"Both."

"The afternoon I arrived, I was dozing when you entered the` parlor. I looked up and saw you, and thought you were an angel. Now I know that you are. I–"

"I am no–"

"You are *my* angel, Sarah," he averred. "I fell in love with the angel in the parlor, but I love the lady in my arms even more."

She looked at him, as if searching for the truth behind his words. "Why are you working your way up to a proposal?"

"Because there is a great deal you don't know about me. I would not be considered a prime catch on the Marriage Mart. I–"

"You are kind, courageous, loyal, honest, and honorable. A beautiful man, despite the scars on your right leg and left shoulder. You inherited a mountain of debts but are working to restore your estate."

As he stared at her, she smiled and added, "You have nightmares about the war and ramble when delirious, but you do not snore. Any woman who thinks you less than extremely eligible is a fool."

His heart bursting with hope, he inquired, "Are you a fool, Lady Sarah?"

"I am not," she replied solemnly.

"Good." He brushed the backs of his fingers against her rosy cheek. "Will you consider your answer to the question I am going to ask you to-morrow night?"

"I need no time to contemplate my answer, Stephen."

"Yes, you do. There is very little money, sweetheart."

"I–"

"I want to propose when I am upright and dressed, after I have asked Matthew's permission."

339

"Shall you mind raising a son not your own?"

"I shall enjoy helping you raise Matthew. I...I would like to adopt him, if you have no objection. And if he does not."

She threw her arms around his neck and kissed his cheek. "Oh, Stephen!"

/=/

On Christmas Eve in the Year of Our Lord 1815, Stephen Lindley, Viscount Carrington proposed to his angel in a parlor bedecked with greenery he and the boy who would soon become the son of his heart had collected that morning. Lady Sarah accepted, and they were married at Carrington Park a month later.

Every Christmas Eve for the next fifty-two years, Stephen repeated his proposal, after telling his children–and, in time, his grandchildren–the story of the viscount's angel.

/=/

Susannah Carleton is a mechanical and bio-medical engineer, working in industry after fifteen years of college teaching. She discovered Regency romances at the ripe old age of thirty-three and promptly fell in love with the genre–since life among the *ton* in Regency England is a diverting change from that of an engineer. In the last twelve years, she has read several thousand Regencies, and the love affair is still going strong. A year or so ago, she took the plunge and began writing them as well. This is her second story. Susannah is married and has one son.

You *could be in our next anthology!*
Most of the authors featured in this book were
not previously published!

Our NEW short-story contest is currently underway. Simply have your story take place
between Advent and Twelfth Night - any year
between 1800 to 1820, and you're halfway
there! There are two lengths: up to 5000
words (entry fee - $25. US); 5-10,000 words
(entry fee- $50.US) and six categories: ad-
venture, fantasy, history, mystery, romance or
time-travel, or, any combination of the above.
Deadline is November 30, 1999. Best stories
will be part of

A Regency Holiday Sampler

to be issued in November, 2000. All authors
are eligible, whether previously published or
not. For required entry form and copy of rules,
send an SASE to us at:

Regency Press Contest;
P. O. Box 18908;
Cleveland Hts OH 44118-0908
or visit our web-site at:

http://www.regency-press.com/

Regency Press == Order Form

☐ **A Regency Sampler**
August, 1999   #1-929085-00-1 / $5.95

☐ **The Marplot Marriage by Beth Andrews**
October, 1999   #1-929085-01-X / $4.95

☐ **The Reluctant Guardian by Jo Manning**
December, 1999   #1-929085-06-0 / $4.95

===================================

Prices slightly higher outside the U.S. Payable in U.S.
funds only. No cash/COD accepted. Postage & handling: <u>U.S./CAN</u>. $2.50 for one book, $1.00 for each
additional book, total not to exceed $6.50. <u>International
orders</u>: $5.00 for first book, $1.25 for each additional.
We accept VISA or MasterCard ($10.00 minimum);
checks ($25.00 fee for returned checks) and money
orders, made payable to: **Regency Press.** Phone/fax
216-932-5319 or 1-87REGENCY9. [1-877-343-6299].
Or visit our web-site: **http://www.regency-press.com**
Please allow 4-6 weeks for delivery; foreign and Cana-
dian delivery 6-8 weeks.

Regency Press   Bill my: ☐ VISA   ☐ MasterCard
P. O. Box 18908   Card #_____
Cleveland Hts OH 44118-0908 Exp. Date _____

Signature: _____
SHIP TO:
Name: _____
Address: _____
City: _____
State/Zip: _____
Telephone: _____

Book (s) Total: _____
Sales Tax: _____ (7% in Ohio)
Postage : _____
Total Due/Enclosed: _____